RED DIRT

ROOTS MUSIC
BORN IN OKLAHOMA
RAISED IN TEXAS
AT HOME ANYWHERE

JOSH CRUTCHMER

*This book is dedicated
to all those Restless Spirits in the night.*

Contents

- Preface -

JOHN COOPER PUT me on the spot.

In April 2018, at Eskimo Joe's in Stillwater, Oklahoma, the Red Dirt Rangers co-founder and original tenant at The Farm spelled it out as clear as the sky over Payne County: "Man, if you don't write this now, it's gonna get lost to history."

I'd been talking about writing the Red Dirt music chronicles for at least 10 years, but Cooper was right. We crossed a threshold of urgency. We all, collectively, aren't getting any younger. Bluntly, the scene had lost Tom Skinner and Brandon Jenkins in the three years prior to that conversation and within a year would lose Steve Ripley. The need to act was, and is, clear.

But this book isn't wistful history-mongering. It's a celebration—a very detailed, story-heavy celebration of Red Dirt—that I hope takes you back to Bob Childers, Gene Williams and Skinner around Oklahoma campfires and keeps you with it right up to present day and how the scene engulfed Randy Rogers, Wade Bowen and a generation of Texans.

Along the way, we'll learn how far Cody Canada is willing to go for a practical joke. Garth Brooks will tell us just how much of an Okie Garth Brooks was at Willie's Saloon. We'll bring the Wormy Dog back from the ashes and transport you to Joe's on Weed St. in Chicago. We'll smile a lot more than we'll cry.

At the end of it, I hope, we'll all find our own ties to Red Dirt, to the spirit that binds it to its forefathers and to the land that lends it its moniker.

Ah. Right. Me. I am Josh Crutchmer. I am the print planning editor at *The New York Times*. I dive into our journalism and help craft it into the newspaper you pick up around the country every morning. I am a Poke—a 2001 graduate of Oklahoma State University who still obsesses over the Cowboys. (Well, and Manchester City soccer. Mid-2000s oil money and I have an understanding.) My parents are Steve and Julia and my sister is Callie. My partner in live music, once I learned what it was, was cousin Wes Crutchmer, now of the Twin Cities. Along with Wes's older brother, Matt, we grew up in the shadows of the athletic feats of our dads, Steve and Clyde, and their brother Larry, Okmulgee High School legends and college football players all. If you're into OSU wrestling or MMA and want to know if there's a relation with Kyle Crutchmer [and his brother Brian]: Also yes. Their dad, Kevin, is another cousin.

I am Red Dirt. I'll get into that in Chapter 4. For now, just know that this book is the culmination of a lifetime of Oklahoma music. I hope you enjoy it.

If you're quoted in here, I talked to you directly and am forever in your debt, moreso if you caught the uncomfortable questions.

This is the part where I toss out acknowledgements like guitar picks during an encore. Thank you, Andrea Zagata, for designing the logo on the cover, building a digital promotion for this and helping with dozens of interviews. Oh, also Andrea's full name is Andrea Zagata Crutchmer. We have been married since 2015.

I owe a thanks to Carlee Schepeler for editing this book and not forcing me to take a stand one way or the other on the Oxford comma.

The week this book went to press, we lost Abby, our 9-year-old doodle mix, without any warning, to cancer. Abby was not only a friend to everyone involved in creating this book, but she was a pal to several of the musicians in this book and a one-dog welcoming committee when they visited Manhattan. We'll miss her a lot.

Now, I get to thank some folks who went above and beyond to help make this happen: the Canadas, Kinzies, Platos and Hansens; Wade Bowen and Randy Rogers; The Turnpike Troubadours; Kyle Nix; Evan Felker; Stoney LaRue; Jason Boland; Ed Warm of Joe's on Weed St.; John Cooper and Brad Piccolo; the entire Braun family plus Jay Nazz; Nancy Seltzer and the team behind Garth Brooks, as well as Garth Brooks himself; Jamie Lin Wilson; Kaitlin Butts; Shawna Russell; Mike McClure and J.J. Lester; Kim Brian and Kyle Carter at Mile 0 Fest; BJ Barham; Robin Devin Schoepf; John Dickson; the Crutchmers and Zagatas; Jen Hakey for editing contributions; Chris Augerhole for the soccer watching and being the best merch pro in live music; my OSU classmate—and world's *premier* bourbon writer—Fred Minnick for the talks, connections and general inspiration; Sopan Deb for the advice; and Tom Jolly and my *New York Times* colleagues for their constant support.

Lastly, thank you, for reading this book, for rolling with a first-time [independent] author and for believing in the music that is shared between the covers.

I'll make it worth your while. That's what we do.

—Josh Crutchmer

Foreword

....

FOR REFERENCE, TODAY is what seems like the one-million-eight-hundred-and-seventy-thousand-millionth day of the coronavirus pandemic. It has been 4 months and 28 days since any of the bands I work for have played a full, live show. It has been 139 days since my husband, the tour manager, has tour managed. One by one, benchmark festivals like SXSW, Willie's Picnic, Braun Brothers Reunion, Hardly Strictly and countless others have cancelled or gone virtual. Dickson just announced MusicFest 2021 will not happen. Venues are shutting their doors for good. The night people are learning how to be day people again. The landscape of the entertainment industry has experienced a seismic shift to say the least.

Also for reference, it has been 319 days since Crutch asked me to write a few words explaining how this scene took over my life for the past 20 years. I've missed four deadlines and written roughly 100 different versions. In my defense, though, #globalpandemic. Life has changed a lot over the past five months. Ergo, my perspective has changed a lot over the past five months. But as of right now, at 6:33 a.m. on July 31, 2020, my response to how this scene took over my life for the past 20 years is this:

I let it.

In 1999, I was living in Amarillo, Texas, and working for American Quarter Horse Association. I traveled a lot for work but when I was home I was at the Golden Light Cantina. A lot. Countless, endless, boundless nights. Those pack-clothes-for-work-the-next-day kinds of nights. Eventually, that's where I would meet the Canadas and Cross Canadian Ragweed. Two shows, two nights in a row, every other weekend for a couple of months. My fellow Amarilloian music feeders and I were lucky. And gluttonous. We didn't miss a show. I met Shannon Canada the second or third time they played Golden Light. By the fifth time, we were BFFs. Around 2002 I quit my corporate job, sold my house and moved to New Braunfels with them to set up shop. 36D Management was born (thanks, Coco). We had a roster filled with Red Dirt artists like Jason Boland, Stoney LaRue and Mike McClure (post–Great Divide) and, of course, Ragweed. We traveled with the bands, helped load in, sold merch at their shows, settled at the end of the night, slept on hotel room floors, drove the vans to the next gig and then did it all over again. There was a period of time I felt like I was strapped down in a rocket ship aimed toward the sun—5, 4, 3, 2, 1. Tour managers, sound engineers and cotton slingers were hired. Vans became busses, bar gigs became shed gigs, record deals were signed and crowds multiplied times infinity. Over time we would also manage Wade Bowen, Bleu Edmondson, Randy Rogers Band, Charlie Robison and Seth James, among others. It was exhilarating to be part of. It was phenomenal to watch. It was miraculous in retrospect.

Amidst it all, I met and worked with the guy of my dreams, dated him, married him and made a genius human with him. I made ride-or-die friends. I got to hang out with Ben H. Dorcy III and play Smushball with Robert Earl Keen. I got to meet some of the most incredible people and also some of the shittiest, and I learned to trust my gut on who was which. I learned from them all. Good decisions, bad decisions, win or lose...I wouldn't trade a tree for any of it. Not even landing in the Hudson.

But here's the thing: For every story I could tell about this music and these people, there are 100 others out there who could tell a similar version. They all start the same: We all showed up for the music. We all stayed because of the people. We stuck around because these artists were inclusive and inspiring and because they made room for us in their circles. We were all witness to a generation of musical brothers and sisters who locked arms to support each other, lifted each other up, cheered each other on and, when needed, called each other out. But most importantly, they were honest, real people. We were privy to their stories: about where they came from, who came before them and what that history means to their music.

I liken it all to astronomy. There are 88 recognized constellations. Those constellations are typically identified by a handful of really bright stars that are visible to the naked eye. In reality, they are made up of giant clusters of thousands of stars in a multitude of layers. Deep within the layers are nebulae, crucial to the evolution of the galaxy and often the birthplace for new stars. You can find Orion by the three bright stars that make up Orion's Belt. You might be able to recognize Orion's sword. But there's also the Orion Nebula, Orion's Nebula Star Cluster and so on...

And so it is with the Red Dirt constellation: generational layers of musical artisans—identifiable by those we are closest to but in reality consisting of countless others who will forever be reflected in the music we listen to. And like constellations, we seek out music that guides us home when we feel lost, reminds us of the changing seasons of our lives and offers us some spiritual enlightenment on our journey. And if we want, we will find the same solace in all of the Red Dirt Nebula, Red Dirt Nebula Star Cluster...et cetera.

And like the stars, music is always there. Even enveloped in the clouds of this seemingly never-ending, heart-wrenching, crop burn of a global pandemic—it's always there.

I didn't ever really think twice about this scene taking over my life. I just let it.

—Robin Devin Schoepf

Introduction

I MOVED TO Raleigh in 2002 to attend NC State, and when I got here, Raleigh was recovering from its previous scene, the Ryan Adams scene. He was here in the late '90s and had a band called Whiskeytown. So with Whiskeytown, the Backsliders and Tift Merritt, it was an era. *Rolling Stone* named Raleigh "the next Seattle" because the alt-country scene was as big here as grunge was there.

Well, that scene died around 2002, and *then* I moved to Raleigh and wanted to start an alt-country band.

So, in American Aquarium's first few years in Raleigh, we weren't doing so well. And what we decided as a band was that the one way we were going to make it was to start touring heavily, and that's how we made it.

We were touring, touring, touring, and then based on the name we were building doing that, we got noticed by Jon Folk, the Red 11 Music booking agent. He had Jason Boland and the Turnpike Troubadours at that point, and he came to me and said, "OK. I'm going to start to put you in Texas and Oklahoma."

I said, "Man, I do not do well in Texas and Oklahoma."

You would go there, and there are these people who are royalty in this scene, and you've never heard of them. And they were playing these songs from their heart and they were songs you've never heard on the radio. And Folk said, "I'm gonna put you in it."

He sent us out, first, with Jason Boland for two or three weeks. Then he sent us out with Cody Canada for two or three weeks. And then, two years on the road with the Turnpike Troubadours.

And it was just exponential growth for us after that. People wanted us playing there every month. All of a sudden, we were this band from Raleigh, paying our bills in Texas.

For us, it had been like going to a frat party: When you go to the front door, they won't let you in. But if you try to walk in with one of the guys from the fraternity, then you're in. Well, we got in by going through that door with the fucking founders of the fraternity.

These guys were telling people, "We don't care where American Aquarium is from, they're fucking good."

And now, we're one of the very few bands that have a foothold in Texas and Oklahoma, but we still live in North Carolina. So, I still have a place to come home to. That's the anomaly. That's the feather in my cap that I think is pretty neat—that I was able to build a fan base there and stay in North Carolina. I get to keep a sense of my own identity.

The fan base lets me do that.

That's a big deal to me. There's a reason I have a Texas tattoo. I have two state tattoos, North Carolina and Texas, and it's because of that genre.

And that genre, Red Dirt/Texas country, itself is nationalistic almost. If someone comes up to me and says, "You're my favorite Red Dirt band," then I go, "Oh, you're from Oklahoma." And if they say "Americana," then you're from Brooklyn. "Texas," and you're from Texas.

The reason our music translates to all that is because, at the end of the day, we write honest songs that make people feel things. That's the only reason.

If you try to come into Oklahoma and Texas as a scene to make money and be famous, they see right through that bullshit. If you come in and you're true to yourself, which is what we did, well, they appreciate the honesty.

This scene is like a musical lie detector. If you come in with bullshit, they'll spit you right back out.

If your songs have legs and can stand up, they'll accept you, even if you're from Raleigh, North Carolina.

—BJ Barham
Artist, songwriter and American Aquarium front man

-1-

Essential Red Dirt:
Tom Skinner

"I'M REALLY NOT smart enough to have intentionally written something that would hold up for this long. To the degree that it does resonate is blind luck."

Tom Skinner delivered that line in 2011, in two sentences writing a more all-encompassing biography for himself than has been written before or since. Even after Tom died in 2015, the obituaries did not capture his essence the way he did with that quote. The bulk of Tom's 61 years were spent as a songwriting icon, as a stage maestro, as quite possibly the most influential artist to ever grace Red Dirt music, and all of that, to Tom, was baffling.

The Tom Skinner story, abridged, is as follows: A native of Bristow, Oklahoma, Tom joined the Air Force after high school, and after that, he found his way to Stillwater. The time frame was late 1970s, early 1980s. Ostensibly, he went to attend school. What happened instead was Tom found music, and the other way around. He and his brothers, Craig and Mike, formed a band, aptly named The Skinner Brothers, that played regularly across town. He befriended songwriters like Bob Childers and Greg Jacobs. He became a friend to musicians like John Cooper and Brad Piccolo of the Red Dirt Rangers.

And, notably as his story gets told, he was introduced to a musician looking to find a springboard from the clubs in Stillwater to the highest heights in country music. Tom was interested enough to form a band with the musician, and that's what he did—Tom joined Garth Brooks to create Santa Fe in 1986. His brother, Mike, eventually joined as well, and Santa Fe gave Nashville a shot a year later. It worked out well for Garth. Tom, with a wife (Jeri) and baby (Jeremy, his only child), did not last long in Music City, moving away with his family reasonably quickly—first to Baton Rouge, Louisiana, and then back to his hometown of Bristow.

After moving back, Tom cowrote a song, "Used to Be," with Bob Wiles about all the landmarks you can find traveling the old Route 66 highway in Oklahoma. The song was covered by Wiles' Red Dirt Rangers in 1995 and became the de facto anthem of Red Dirt music—eventually cut by The Great Divide with Jimmy LaFave contributing vocals, and remaining to this day one of the songs most often covered by bands in the scene.

Tom did not create Red Dirt, but he became the tie that bound its generations. Eventually, circa 2005, Tom joined the Mike McClure Band as a bass guitar player and occasional vocalist in the Oklahoma rock outfit. ("I decided that turning 50 was a good time to join a rock band," he often quipped.) And he moved to Tulsa, hosting a songwriters' night that he dubbed "Tom Skinner's Wednesday Night Science Project" that lasted until his death in 2015 and often continues to this day without him. Just about every artist with Red Dirt roots—from Childers, Jacobs and the Rangers to Cody Canada, Jason Boland and Stoney LaRue to John Fullbright and the Turnpike Troubadours—has been impacted and influenced, very directly, by Tom.

"Tom was the guy who, when he walked into a room, the place just goes, 'Tom!' and hangs on him," Greg Jacobs said. "Charismatic is what he was."

Most importantly, in his life, Tom defined Red Dirt—the music scene loosely based around Stillwater, dating back to the early 1970s, emphasizing songwriting and a tie to the earth that was nearly spiritual—with an accuracy that words have often failed.

Equally important, Skinner was both wildly funny and deeply fallible, occasionally at the same time, as one of the most told stories of his early musical career illustrates.

"One of my favorite stories is, Tom was at the Cain's Ballroom. I think it was maybe a Nitty Gritty Dirt Band show or something, just there as a fan," Brad Piccolo recalled. "And Tom got so into the music that he jumped up on stage, grabbed a guitar and started playing air guitar in front of everyone! The bouncers threw him on his face out behind the Cain's. So that was his intro to being on stage, and he laughed so hard forever when he'd tell that story."

Tom, always sporting a beard and always in sunglasses, went from a tall, lanky front man with The Skinner Brothers to an imposing, decidedly-not-skinny songwriter and bass player nicknamed "Tiny" by the end of his life. He became an inspiring figure to multiple generations of musicians across an entire music scene, and that he did so without ever quite understanding why anyone wanted to listen to him or his music ingrained humility in so many of the artists he influenced that the trait itself became a common thread throughout Red Dirt.

"Ah, Tom Skinner. His legacy seems to grow more and more as every day goes by," said John Cooper, friend of Tom and founding member of the Red Dirt Rangers. "Tom was the most giving musician I've ever been around. He would willingly give up a stage in a heartbeat...of course maybe that was so he could take a break and go smoke a cigarette...but anybody who wanted to get up on stage, he would get them up.

"I watched him do it, man. It was just, 'Here, come get this guitar! Ladies and gentlemen, Jason Boland!' and Boland was still wet behind the ears, man.

"He did it for us, too, man. I still remember him saying to me and Bob Wiles, 'Come over and jam.' We had only been together a short time, and he invites us over to his house to play. And I looked at Wiles like, 'No way. Tom Skinner just asked us to come jam.' It was like God himself said, 'Come over and let's jam.'"

Red Dirt is a collection of individuals more than it is a scene, and Skinner was possibly the lone artist who transcended them all.

"I can still remember the first time I saw The Skinner Brothers, and my jaw dropped," Cooper said. "Those harmonies were so tight. The musicianship was so good. And I knew right then: I'm gonna meet this guy. And I knew I wanted to do that. Watching Tom and his brothers do it made me want to do it.

"And then he's so open and giving on the other end of it. Tom was the biggest cheerleader for anything and anyone.

"It set the standard. It set that family feel. That we're-all-in-this-together thing. This is not a competition, this is about music. Tom and Bob [Childers] both laid that groundwork, but especially Tom. Bob wasn't really a performer, per se. Tom was truly a performer. Hell, Garth Brooks wanted to be in Tom Skinner's band, just like we all did."

His contemporaries respected him, and those who came after him looked up to him.

"Tom had left Nashville and moved to Baton Rouge," Jacobs said. "And he ran into Chris Maxwell, who ran a little record company called Binky Records. And Tom signed with Binky and was gonna record an album. So this is the first guy out of our little group who gets to record one.

"So, of course Bob Childers and I were both campaigning to get on the album, and we both wanted the title cut. And I had 'A Little Rain Will Do,' which I thought was a great name for an album...although I've never used it. And Bob had 'Times Have Changed,' one of Bob's best songs, a wonderful little song. And I don't know if Tom was onto this or not, but we were making a nuisance of ourselves. Tom may have worked out this compromise, and it may have just happened this way, but 'A Little Rain Will Do' ended up the first cut on the record, and Bob got the title cut with 'Times Have Changed.' Which was perfect."

• • •

Jim "Red" Wilhelm would know. Outside of the artists themselves, no single person spent more time with the musicians and songwriters who shaped Red Dirt in the 1990s and early 2000s than Jim. He was a regular at The Farm in its heyday and a tenant of the Yellow House at 57 University Circle in Stillwater when it succeeded The Farm as the mecca of the scene.

Jim will ask you, "What's the definitive Red Dirt album?"

You will answer, *The Red Dirt Sampler.* Because that 1997 compilation album featuring Skinner, Jacobs, Childers and McClure among a who's who of Red Dirt at the time is justifiably credited with spreading the word of the depth and versatility of the scene across the country.

Jim will tell you, "OK. That's an answer. It's not the *right* answer, but it is an answer."

"The right answer is *Times Have Changed.* If you took what Red Dirt music actually is, polished it and made it as aesthetically pleasing as you possibly can, the result is *Times Have Changed.*

"And as a result, for me, when you talk about the Mount Rushmore of Red Dirt, I don't really care who is Jefferson or Lincoln, but I care a great deal about who George Washington is. Tom Skinner is George Washington."

Scott Evans—himself a Red Dirt legend, longtime songwriter and part of the iconic Stillwater band Medicine Show in the mid-1990s—was friends with Tom and believes his essence as an artist reflected an introspective, deeply personal thinker who just happened to make music.

"For all of his charm, just his natural ability, it all came from some memory," Evans said. "His recall was unreal. He used to call other musicians 'unconscious musicians,' that's how he'd describe other great musicians. And I finally heard him say it so much that I went, 'Aha! Tom's telegraphing right there.'

"Tom *is* an unconscious player. Watch him play. Watch videos of him. He would play and he would just...look up and open his mouth. And the older he got, the more he did it, and it was just total surrender to the recall of it—the memory that music was bringing him.

"So because of that, it was like every song he had heard, he could play. All those years I was around him it was, 'Wow!' It was like watching a savant. How in the world? I'd go watch him every Wednesday, and every Wednesday he'd have two or three or four songs I'd never heard him play—or an entire set! So that was what was unique. Everybody you can listen to, they have basically the same set for 20 or 30 years. They'd add or take away songs here and there, but basically the same. Very rarely could you go see someone night after night after night and it was a completely different show. Tom was one of those."

Eric Hansen, who backed Tom on drums in the Mike McClure Band from the time Tom joined in 2005 until the end of 2014, and before that was part of a late 1990s side-band project of Tom's called Farmboy, recalls Tom in simpler terms.

"Skinner was the most musical. He loved songs more than any-fucking-body else I know," Hansen said. "He wasn't prolific, numbers-wise, as a songwriter, because he had ebbs and flows where he was in and out. But when he did find an idea that be-came a song, there's just so many of his that have kicked me in the gut."

Skinner felt most at home in the shadows. In a career that spanned more than 30 years, he released few albums. He put out *Times Have Changed* and *Acoustic Skinner* in the late 1990s on Binky Records, and *Farmboy* came out in 2003 on Binky as well.

Farmboy, incidentally, featured "Skyline Radio," a longtime Skinner tune about life and current events that evolved over time. Its refrain, "We'll be listening / on the Skyline Radio" is one of the most recognizable lyrics in Red Dirt history. And in 2011, Cody Canada & The Departed covered the song on their debut album, *This Is Indian Land*. It was during an interview about that cover that Tom Skinner gave the quote that kicked off this book. The one that chalked up his success to blind luck.

* * *

Mike McClure disagrees with Tom's assertion of luck. And Tom spent the last decade of his performing life with McClure in the Mike McClure Band as the bass guitar player and occasional vocalist. Much of that arc was spent as a trio—those two and Hansen on drums.

"It's weird when someone dies and was important to a bunch of people, and the following generation that hears about them can't ever meet them, because they're dead," McClure said. "That makes them immortal...or at least a level of legendary that everybody hopes they achieve someday."

McClure was instrumental in searing Tom's name in the minds of Red Dirt fans when, in the mid-1990s, with McClure as lead vocalist, The Great Divide cut "Used to Be" for the band's Atlantic Records debut album, *Break in the Storm*. At Divide shows from the mid-1990s through the band's initial breakup in 2003, McClure rarely failed to introduce that song as "a tune written by Tom Skinner and Bob Wiles." The band's popularity at the time ensured that even casual fans knew of Tom—and knew him for a song he wrote. Along with the Divide and the Red Dirt Rangers, the song was covered by just about any band with a tie to Stillwater. Cross Canadian Ragweed and Stoney LaRue covered the song regularly throughout the 2000s, and to this day the song is a mainstay in Mike McClure Band sets.

McClure has added a twist to the song's final refrain. Just before the line "There used to be a place to go dance in this town," he throws in a tag that references "Skyline Radio" by name and repeats "I miss you" over and over, with McClure looking up and opening his mouth a bit in the same manner Evans recalled Skinner performances.

But before he got to that point—McClure inserting unchecked emotion into what is otherwise a Red Dirt anthem—he first had to share a stage, and a few thousand Skinner jokes, with Tom.

It sprung from an altercation McClure had with a previous bass player in 2005.

"That bass player and I got into a fight on stage in Stephenville [Texas], and I had gigs the next weekend," McClure said. "So I called Tom and just said, 'Hey, can you cover a gig for me?' He goes, 'Yeah! Just give me some songs!' So he was just gonna cover some gigs, and then there we were 10 years later."

That part is notable because Tom had always been noncommittal as an artist. He rarely recorded solo albums. He was not much for sticking around in bands—Skinner Brothers 20 years before McClure came calling notwithstanding. He was open with his music but confident enough in himself that he did not feel the need to impose it on others. Others, of course, sought him out anyway.

"Tom was so noncommittal, yes," McClure said. "That was the thing about him that I think tickled all of us younger songwriters—just his lack of giving a fuck. But I learned he gave a fuck about the right stuff. Stuff that mattered, you know? That's why we lasted.

"God damn, I just miss him."

McClure produced *Tom Skinner*, which would end up being the final solo album of Tom's life, in 2012. He hadn't released any original material at all since the Farmboy project, and his last truly solo release had come in 1998. The album bookended Tom's career—and, it would turn out, life—with a collection of deeply personal original recordings and covers.

Tom was a baseball fan. Friends and family only half-joked after he died that Tom's first stop in heaven would not be old family members or Bob Childers, but rather Roger Maris, the former New York Yankee legend and onetime holder of baseball's single-season home run record. Tom's last album featured a Randy Pease song about a baseball player in the twilight of his career called "I Love This Game." Tom's delivery on his album was obviously both an expression of his love of the sport but also a projection—sub out the baseball player protagonist in the song and sub in a weathered songwriter, and you have Tom's views on his own life ("It's a hard thing to admit / that it might be time to quit / but God, I love this game").

The album also featured one of Tom's greatest assets—his sense of humor. The song "Nickel's Worth of Difference" is one that could have gone off the rails if sung without the proper mix of confidence and self-deprecating worldviews.

The opening verse: "There ain't a nickel's worth of difference between Kansas and Nebraska / a bunch of wide open spaces, and every now and then a tree. / I suppose if you were born there, you might beg to differ / but I'm from Oklahoma, they all look pretty much the same to me."

What follows is a near stream-of-consciousness brain dump from Tom that was as insightful into his mind as it was artistic. (When he sang it live, he'd often add in a verse that referenced the story of a NASA astronaut who drove across the country intent on kidnapping a romantic interest, and as the disputed story was told, wore adult diapers on the drive. Skinner closed the verse by singing, "It was an astro-nutty plan!")

But the final verse is where Tom married all of the above: "I try and try to write new songs, and I pray I come up with something / but as you can see lately I've got nothing intelligent to say. / Just yada, yada, blah, blah, blah, and so much jibber jabber / a little abracadabra, and some la de frickin' da. Yeah, la de frickin' da."

In the hands of a lesser artist, the whole thing can sound stupid pretty quickly. But Skinner's deadpan delivery is such that it's impossible to hear and not think, *Wow, he really did write a song about writer's block.*

Tom's son, Jeremy, was the one who inspired that particular song, due to Jeremy's love of Midwest folk rocker Dan Bern.

"Originally, that song was going to be called 'Just Like Dan Bern's Blues,' and Mike [McClure] made him change it, because nobody knows who Dan Bern is," Jeremy said. "He's somebody that I stumbled upon and became a big fan of. And I was like, 'You have to listen to this guy.' So, he wrote that song, not trying to imitate Dan Bern, but just being like, 'If Dan Bern can write a song about anything, I can do that, too.' So I always sort of felt proud that I gave him this thing that led to that song and it struck a chord with people."

That instance notwithstanding, Jeremy recalls Tom now as a parent first and a musician second.

"There's a little bit of a disconnect in my view, between him as a personality and a talent that people knew," Jeremy said. "At home, he was just Dad.

"He certainly fostered a love of music in me, but I have no technical skills. He tried to teach me to play bass a few times, and then he told me that I should own a record company."

By his 2012 solo album and the end of his career, Tom's performances and benefit concerts scheduled for any number of health issues that arose in his life featured the Tom Skinner logo: a silhouette of his facial hair and sunglasses that a great many artists and friends of Tom eventually turned into various tattoos after he passed on in July 2015.

Tom's story did not end with his death, following a series of heart issues, at St. John's hospital in Tulsa. It carries on to this day. An annual tribute festival—Tom Skinner's Skyline Music Festival—draws a mix of Red Dirt forefathers and contemporary artists to Tulsa for a celebration of his life and music that also partners with the nonprofit Red Dirt Relief Fund to support independent artists in and around Oklahoma. At the festival itself, performers can get such benefits as free dental exams and similar outreaches that musicians without insurance sorely need. If Tom's life and legacy could ever be distilled down into a single event, the Skyline festival did it.

Jeremy lays low at such festivals, but he is usually there. Despite forging his own way in life, Jeremy knows he also has a home in Red Dirt music.

"It's always been that way, even when I was a small child," Jeremy said. "I remember Greg Jacobs being over at the house a lot when I was a kid, and he would always show up with a chocolate bar for me. And I remember Bob Childers would come over and would always call me Little Hillbilly. And I am very much not a hillbilly, but that nickname stuck.

"And today, I feel nothing but welcome from that community. Dad always described Red Dirt as an umbrella. It's not one thing. It's not blues. It's not rock. It encompasses a lot of things. It's more of a spirit than a style. I feel like—and I think Dad felt the same way—there's probably a little pocket out there that has this vibe, but there's not too much else around like Red Dirt.

"When they do stuff like the Skyline fest, that's rough for me. I tend to hide back and not necessarily seek people out, at least in the beginning, when I'm uncomfortable. But then once I'm drunk, I'm very chatty. It can be a bit much for me, but that's my thing. It's not the community making me feel like I need to stay back and hide. If anything, the community is so warm to me that I feel I need to retreat a bit from it."

The final chapter in Tom's life was written in 2015, just over a month after he died, in rural Oklahoma—far enough outside the town of Kellyville that cell phone service did not reach. Quite literally, there was just never enough incentive for a company to put up a tower in a place that remote. There, on one of those Oklahoma summer nights when the air was hot enough to distort even the near horizon into a wavy landscape that could have easily been an image sent back from a robot exploring another planet, Tom Skinner was properly sent off.

The event itself was scripted by Tom. He knew his health was declining and planned his own memorial. As Jeffrey Lee Haynes relayed when he introduced the event, "He wanted to have a celebration instead of a funeral."

As such, Haynes read a farewell note from Tom that included poignant words for his son, Jeremy, and grandson, Flash, as well as a few dozen jokes for the road. ("A guy walks into a bar and there's a bowl of nuts on the bar. The bowl of nuts says, 'Hey, nice shirt.' So the guy asks the bartender, "What's the deal with the nuts?" and the bartender says, "They're complimentary.")

McClure was required to dress like Elvis Presley—cape included, per Tom's orders. Red Dirt originals like Gene Williams, Greg Jacobs, Randy Crouch, the Red Dirt Rangers, John Williams, Monica Taylor and his brother, Craig Skinner, led a tribute concert. Artists he inspired like Jacob Tovar, The Damn Quails and Bobby and Thomas Trapp contributed—possibly none more than Bryon White, whose renditions of Gram Parsons' "Grievous Angel" and Tom's own "Nickel's Worth of Difference" stood out as highlights—the latter in particular.

"That was the one that I always identified with the most, of Tom's stuff," White said. "Just because I think that song is genius in so many ways. If I would have started writing that song, and I got four or five verses into it and realized it wasn't about anything, I would have thrown it away. But, Tom wrote the last verse and it made everything genius. I've always appreciated that about that song in particular."

Eric Hansen backed anybody who wanted to play for Tom on drums one more time. Cody Canada performed "All Nighter," a song he had written initially about the death of a different musician but that felt right that evening. And as such, John Fullbright ended the night leading a powerful, reverent and inspiring cover of Leonard Cohen's "Hallelujah."

By the end of the nearly 17-minute song, Fullbright had left the stage, as had the musicians backing him, and he had wandered down into the crowd, surrounded by trees and darkness, the by then very-late-night air illuminated by lighters and smartphones.

But Fullbright did not stop leading "Hallelujah" until everybody who remained stood and sang along. Not loud. Not chanting. Truly singing, almost just above a whisper. They made the kind of music that becomes eerily haunting when recalled half a decade later.

They made the kind of music anybody who bore witness will never be able to forget.

They made the kind of music Tom Skinner made.

— — —

- 2 -

The Farm
and Red Dirt's Roots

WALK DUE WEST from the main campus of Oklahoma State University, and Stillwater gets hazy.

The lights and the noise from the college's main bar drag, "The Strip," a section of Washington Avenue immediately south of the mammoth student union building, fade. More accurately, they are replaced by the dirt kicked up in all four directions by the Payne County dirt roads. The dust is always red, owing to the iron-rich soil the Western Oklahoma farmers complain about after it rains and their tires kick it all over the rear of their trucks. The sun—rising or setting—won't hit the campus's monumental twin stadiums, Lewis Field for football and Gallagher-Iba Arena for basketball and wrestling. And wind. Always wind. Wind from the south in the summer. Wind from the west in the spring and again in the fall, right before the storm hits. Wind from the north in the winter portending the Arctic front—snow if you're lucky, ice and more ice if you aren't. And wind from the east once every four or five years when a tropical system meanders up Interstate 35 from the Gulf of Mexico before flaming out. Depending on the direction, the wind will prevent or promote the smells from the OSU veterinary farm even farther west from tickling the senses alongside Stillwater Creek, but always kicking up the dust from the red dirt.

At least, that's the way it was in 1979, when college sophomore John Cooper and his friend, Danny Pierce, went looking for a place to rent for the summer.

Today, the town of 50,000 sprawls out across all of that, ringing outward from the center of campus. First, Greek and athletic housing. Then, student apartments. Then, the city itself, most of its residents tied to the university. Beyond that, car dealerships, chain hotels, two Walmart stores and, thankfully, two Braum's Ice Cream and Dairy Stores. There's no break between the town and that veterinary farm anymore, and the part of Stillwater Creek that once seemed so distant is subdivision cul-de-sacs. Lewis Field is now the ultramodern Boone Pickens Stadium, owing to its late namesake and his oil millions, generously donated in the early 2000s. Gallagher-Iba Arena has doubled its physical size and imposes its will on the Stillwater skyline.

But for Cooper and Pierce, the land they found, walking distance—well, hiking distance—from campus, may as well have been the Sonoran Desert.

"In May of 1979, school was out. It was my sophomore year," Cooper said. "Somebody told us about a farmhouse outside of town a little bit. We rolled down the driveway—nice looking old farmhouse. We pulled in and there was a guy there, and we said, 'We understand the place is for rent.' He goes, 'Yeah, it is. It's not real nice, but it's yours. Five bedrooms, the water runs and the toilet works.'

"It was on 149 acres on the west edge of campus. But it was still out in the country. Dirt road. No neighbors. So we said, 'How much is rent?' and he said, 'A hundred bucks.'

"We said, 'Apiece?' and he said, 'No. For the whole place.' So I go, 'Oh, I think we can live here!'

"That was the beginning of The Farm."

Circa 2003, Cross Canadian Ragweed played Lone Star Park in Grand Prairie, Texas, and drew a crowd so large it caused traffic backups on nearby Interstate 30 from music fans parking on the shoulder. In 2019, the Turnpike Troubadours headlined an evening at the Houston Livestock Show and Rodeo for nearly 70,000 fans. A year later, Jason Boland and the Stragglers set off on a coast-to-coast tour celebrating the 20th anniversary of their album *Pearl Snaps*. The Great Divide landed an Atlantic Records deal in the mid-'90s. Somewhere in there, Randy Rogers met the management team that one day would land him in sold-out concerts at arenas and stadiums nationwide. Two bands of Braun Brothers found soul mates in Cody Canada. Jamie Lin Wilson, Bri Bagwell and Courtney Patton found a support group of fellow artists providing a boost to the top of Texas music—not always viewed as a gender-equal genre. And Greg Jacobs, Tom Skinner and Bob Childers became matches for the kerosene that was Garth Brooks, at the time looking to leap from Stillwater dance halls to Nashville's good graces.

All of that—to the letter—is what The Farm gave to music.

"It was mostly a party house, but musicians started discovering it," Cooper recalled of its earliest days.

"The first band we ever had play at The Farm was a reggae band called Local Hero. We threw a party. It went all night. We did the circle of love dance at dawn, all of it. From then on, we had the bug for getting music to The Farm. It was just too perfect not to do there."

For 20 years, The Farm provided the earth and the sky to a music scene that provided the light. Singers and songwriters found its campfires a proving ground. An adjoining shed became a concert venue that would get dubbed the Gypsy Cafe. Cooper would live there, as would Great Divide cofounder Mike McClure. Dozens of others would as well. Hundreds of others would claim to. Eventually, Childers, reeling from a largely failed venture into Nashville, would pull a trailer up to The Farm, living there until a fire destroyed it in the late 1990s.

"As it went on, The Farm got a reputation as a place where music was welcome," Cooper said. "Early Bob Childers, Tom Skinner, Greg Jacobs, the Red Valley Barnstormers, the Flat Mountain Boys...these were mostly acoustic, folk or bluegrass acts.

And that's what they wrote. Well, the Skinner Brothers were more country-rock. They were following Gram Parsons' way, even back then. Jimmy LaFave was a pretty big folkie at the time. But, really, The Farm was roots music.

"For me, that was the start of the Red Dirt music scene. It started as singer-songwriter folk music and roots style, sitting around campfires and trying out material."

Like every college town, a handful of buildings in Stillwater near campus change names and owners, but their purpose—entertain the kids and get them drunk—was unwavering.

In the early 1980s, Eskimo Joe's was a new bar, far from catching worldwide fame as "Stillwater's jumpin' little juke joint." Willie's Saloon was there, and it remains. Up Your Alley was a bar where Jimmy LaFave honed his skills. Pistol Patty's was on The Strip. The Lighthouse was in the building where modern-day J.R. Murphy's sat, right in the middle of the mayhem. These were the days that 18-year-olds could get inside the bars, so those places were full of live music. Stillwater was famous for "streaker nights," a byproduct of the proximity of students, alcohol and fun.

Right around the time Cooper and Pierce signed the first lease on The Farm, Gene Williams transferred from a junior college in Arkansas to Oklahoma State. The Muldrow, Oklahoma, native had played in bands since he was a teenager, and he found a gig with a local band—the West Street Band—that claimed the now-defunct Club 21 home.

"I was playing there," Williams said, "and Tom and Mike Skinner sat in with us. I was playing guitar, and I just thought they were great. So I made it a point to make friends with them. Come to find out, they were living just down the street from where I was living in Stillwater.

"The Skinner brothers had a house, maybe a half a block from Eskimo Joe's. I'd go up there and play with them. The Skinner Brothers, version one, was up and running, and they were playing a couple of my songs. They won a full day of recording at a studio in Tulsa. I went with them that day, and we recorded an album. Of course it never got released properly, but I still have a copy of it. At that time, Mark Lyon and Mike Shannon had been playing guitar. Well, they left the band, and I ended up playing lead guitar for the Skinner Brothers for about two years.

"It was all about having fun. We weren't too business-minded. We just traveled all over the state and played. It was the best band I was ever in—just naturally a great band."

Williams, in turn, mentored another aspiring musician who had moved to Stillwater.

Greg Jacobs, like Williams an Eastern Oklahoma native, moved to town in 1979 after a stint in the Navy and two years at the University of Oklahoma, 80 miles south of Stillwater in Norman.

"I started school there in the fall of '79," Jacobs said. "I had been trying to write songs. I was into the whole John Prine, Guy Clark, Townes Van Zandt, Bob Dylan thing. I had been trying to write, but I had not really played out. I was just getting to the point where I was thinking about it.

"I was working with a guy at the veteran's office, and he knew the guy who ran Stonewall Tavern," Jacobs said. "And he got me a gig there. So I'm playing my first gig ever, in my career, at an empty Stonewall Tavern, and Gene Williams comes in. And Gene is the first true, real-live musician I ever met that I worked with. Gene is the one who brought me in and introduced me to the Skinner boys. He was playing with them at the time. And they introduced me to Bob Childers, and Bob was playing with Jimmy LaFave. And that's how I got in. It's all Gene Williams' fault."

To this day, Stonewall is a Stillwater staple—a dive bar that sustains itself on live music every night it can manage and the throngs of football fans that stop in and party before Oklahoma State home games. And to this day, Greg Jacobs is a Red Dirt staple—an icon whose vivid tales of Oklahoma history are required listening for folks really interested in where the movement started ("A Little Rain Will Do," part of 1998's venerable *Red Dirt Sampler*, and "Farmer's Luck," which Jason Boland covered in 2012 on *Rancho Alto*, for anyone on an archeological search) and who would come to hold such sway by the early 1980s that a college-aged Garth Brooks saw him as a role model.

"It's a true college town," Jacobs said. "I know it's changed plenty. Stillwater's a metropolis now. But in the '70s and early '80s, Stillwater was a college town. It was disproportionately young. There was always a crowd. It was always hopping.

"One of the things that impressed me was the diversity of the music. Anything you wanted to hear, on a Friday or Saturday night, you could hear.

"There was a band in town called the Cimarron Swingsters, and they were fronted by Dub Cross, who was a big old, 6-foot-8, wide-brimmed-cowboy-hat Ray Bensen type, and that band would just blow you away with western swing. You could go two bars up the street, and Jimmy LaFave would be there with a rock-and-roll band just blowing the windows out. And on down the street, the Skinner boys would be doing all this Gram Parsons stuff. Anything you wanted to hear, you could hear in that town."

The names and faces changed plenty over the years, but it's worth noting that in 2000, you could walk that same stretch of Stillwater on a Tuesday night, and you could hear the All-American Rejects or the Flaming Lips playing at Mike's College Bar for no cover, then you could walk two blocks to the Wormy Dog Saloon and listen to Cody Canada, Jason Boland and Stoney LaRue for no cover. And if that wasn't doing it for you, Eskimo Joe's or Willie's Saloon were within walking distance, and you could catch Split Lip Rayfield—a string band with a single-string, gas-tank bass guitar.

From that early group, Williams, Jacobs, Childers and Tom Skinner would all trek to Nashville in hopes of landing songwriting deals in the early 1980s.

They would all fall flat.

"Songwriting was an evolution, and it cost me a marriage," Jacobs said. "You bring it all on yourself, all the problems, but then that turns into fodder to write songs. I have reached a point in my life now that I'm happy. I'm content. And writing a song is not as easy as it used to be.

"It all came out of that. We were all a bunch of emotional cripples and turmoils all the time.

"My dream—I wanted to be like Don Schlitz, who wrote 'The Gambler'—I wanted to write a country hit a year, and I could survive off my royalties, and then I could do whatever I wanted.

"We all went out to Nashville kind of chasing the same thing. We didn't go out together. Tom went out with Garth, and when Garth came back, Tom stayed for a while. Bob had already gone out. I went to Kentucky first. I married a girl there who wanted to work in the horse industry, so I would go down to Nashville occasionally and get with those guys.

"It ended up, Tom and I, Tom's wife and his brother, Mike, lived together for about a year. We tried, but we didn't know what we were doing. Nashville is a city of contacts, and I have one of the worst things a musician could have: I'm an introverted guy. I met with a few producers—at that time, you could call them up. So they would listen to my songs, and then they would tell me, 'You're a songwriter, but you're not a commercial songwriter. Go home, listen to your radio and bring me something like that.' And I tried. I couldn't do it.

"So, we all came back at different times. And when Tom and Bob came back to Oklahoma, they ended up in Stillwater. And that Red Dirt thing had exploded."

By the late 1980s, Red Dirt was a viable enough scene that Tom and Bob were all it needed. Skinner and Childers, now Nashville veterans, assumed roles of elder statesmen, and Red Dirt was no longer dependent on a small group of individuals. Artists began to come and go, and their influences were no longer tied directly to The Farm.

Steve Ripley, whom Cooper credits as owning the earliest use of "Red Dirt" when he chose the label name "Red Dirt Records" for a 1972 live album from his band, Moses, had predated The Farm. He attended Oklahoma State in the early 1970s. By the 1980s, Ripley was in California, creating guitars for the likes of J.J. Cale, John Hiatt, Jimmy Buffett and Eddie Van Halen. Ripley moved to Tulsa in 1987 and purchased Leon Russell's former recording studio, naming it the Church Studio. Ripley ultimately found mainstream success when he founded The Tractors in 1994 and cowrote their hit, "Baby Likes to Rock It." From Tulsa, Ripley and the Church Studio became their own source of Red Dirt, with bands including Cooper's Red Dirt Rangers regularly showing up to record.

Jimmy LaFave moved to Austin and became the de facto Red Dirt ambassador to the Texas Hill Country, giving a pipeline into the Austin scene for Childers and the Red Dirt Rangers, but more importantly becoming a one-man haven for Oklahoma musicians honing their chops in Texas. Students of music such as David Abeyta (lead guitarist for Reckless Kelly for 19 years) and Eric Hansen (drummer backing Skinner, Medicine Show, the Mike McClure Band and Cody Canada & The Departed over the course of 30 years) found their way into LaFave's inner circle first.

But Skinner and Childers settled back in Stillwater and assumed the roles of Red Dirt forefathers for a next generation of musicians making their ways to Stillwater. Childers, especially, was an instant icon.

"It all centered around Bob," Jacobs said. "The younger artists all wanted to make Bob king, and Bob thought he was king, so it was cool!"

The first of those younger artists was Scott Evans, who in 1988 was a burned-out, contemplative aspiring sketch artist who threw in the towel on a graphic-design trade school in Arizona and transferred to Oklahoma State.

"Somewhere on that drive from Arizona to Stillwater, my impulse to draw stopped," Evans said. "And music filled the void. It became the way I processed the world."

Evans, along with Brad James and Donnie Wood, would eventually form the Medicine Show, which took Red Dirt's folk overtures and added a heavy dose of the keyboard-heavy Tulsa Sound. Medicine Show expanded the possibilities for what Red Dirt could be.

After Medicine Show, a metalhead child of the 1980s named Mike McClure realized he could fit in with the same crowd. McClure and J.J. Lester started The Great Divide in the early 1990s, finding not only a major-label record deal but crossing bona fide borders. For a five-year stretch between 1997 and 2002, The Divide was as big in Texas, Oklahoma and the Midwest as Robert Earl Keen or Lyle Lovett. There was not a dance hall they could not fill nor a bar they could not run out of beer.

We'll get to The Divide—and the massive influence they carried on—later.

First, Medicine Show had a course to run.

"So I'm working with Mike Shannon at his music store [Daddy O's Music] in Stillwater," Evans said, "and he started introducing me to all his friends. So that's how I met Childers, Greg Jacobs and Tom Skinner. I had heard of Randy Pease, but it was years before I met him. And Brad James is one of the people who came into that store.

"Brad had gone to school in California and was influenced by a whole bunch of stuff out there. Well, some older Tulsa guys were part of that scene. That, through Stillwater and L.A., from Brad, was a connection to all those Tulsa greats. And that was our in for the Tulsa scene. Jimmy Karstein was the first one. He came to play with us early on in Medicine Show. He drove over to Tulsa, knocked on our door and walked in, and we just went, 'Wow.' So he became our drummer and then our percussionist.

"When we would play in Tulsa, all his friends would come out. The first one in Tulsa was Club One, on Riverside and Peoria. A little clubhouse in an apartment complex. That was the first one. Then we got into other places around town. Ended up at the Sunset Grill toward the mid-1990s. Then we played the Full Moon on Fifteenth, and here and there around town.

"And we met a lot of other players, Tulsa players. So suddenly, all those influences for me—when people say Red Dirt, if I'm a part of it, well it's all that."

More than anything else, Evans and his bandmates were responsible for what Red Dirt became and continues to be today, which is "whatever the hell you want it to be."

"When Red Dirt first came up, me and Mike Shannon used to joke, just sort of philosophically, critically, 'What is it?'" Evans said. "And Mike first observed to me: If you think of the other sounds, like Motown or Muscle Shoals, the reason they have the same sounds is because they have the same musicians. There was a continuity to it, at the fundamental level—it's a rhythm section, it's a utility player. Then you bring in different artists for the harmonies and solos. That's a real interesting mix, because the root is always the same.

"There's nothing like that in Red Dirt, because you have a whole bunch of different people. You had the Red Dirt Rangers doing psychedelic Tejano music at that time. But it had different themes all over. It had a western theme, that psychedelic theme, a rock theme, Tex-Mex. You name it, it's there. And we were, at that time, a Grateful Dead cover band that could also do Hank Williams and ZZ Top."

By the time Medicine Show folded in the late 1990s, the band had given Red Dirt enough staples to carry another generation. The Divide and Cross Canadian Ragweed would both eventually cut "Help Me (Get Over This Mountain)." Ragweed's cover of "Mexican Sky" was one of the band's most popular songs to play live. Stoney LaRue has covered "Hey Sarah" his entire career, along with Evans' heart-wrenching "Steel Heart."

And the band also came the closest anyone has to explaining what the scene has become.

"Karstein compared Red Dirt to the Tulsa Sound," Evans said. "And his point was, sounds don't become 'a sound' until there's at least *some* commercial success. It doesn't mean anything until there's some success by somebody, to associate with it as a social scene."

Red Dirt's resilience as a term can be romanticized as a type of music that broke free from Stillwater like water from a broken dam, spilling south to the coast of Texas before breaking back on itself.

But the reality is, it's a cultural artifact. The reason an entire generation of artists who never lived a day in Oklahoma can be embraced as Red Dirt has more to do with the success that Skinner and Jacobs found in Nashville, that LaFave found in Austin or that The Divide found from coast to coast than it does any laws of inertia.

Still, it's a hell of a lot more fun to imagine it the other way.

— — —

- 3 -

The Godfather:
Bob Childers

THE MOST CHALLENGING part of this book—and it is not really close—is the attempt to do justice to the life and legacy of Robert Wayne Childers.

He is certainly not the only important figure to Red Dirt music. Hell, he is not even the first forefather who has passed on to be extolled in this book.

Bob Childers was complex, but Tom Skinner was complex. It was very easy to convey Tom's complexities and very easy for others to do it too.

Bob Childers was a poet, but Brandon Jenkins was a poet. And bringing Jenkins' legacy to life requires little more prodding than "tell me a Brandon story."

Bob Childers was larger than life, but so was Jimmy LaFave. And describing La-Fave as an icon has been easy for anyone who has crossed his path, even if LaFave kept to himself a lot more than his forefather contemporaries.

Over and over again, people who knew Childers and were influenced by him try to describe who he was and invariably end up getting really spiritual, really quickly.

All of this, of course, is exactly who Bob Childers was. Bob knew that he was a mythical figure to both the artists with whom he helped forge Red Dirt and to the generations of artists he influenced. Bob saw very early that The Farm, and the Gypsy Cafe in particular, was a place for singers and songwriters to become inseparable from the music they made. And because he was incredibly self-aware, he was an incredibly disarming person. To Red Dirt, Bob Childers may as well have been Bob Dylan, but to Bob Childers, Red Dirt was a real, tangible playground that made him cool. The same Childers that helped launch Garth Brooks' career by putting him and his band up for a few weeks when they moved to Nashville in 1987 and offering him a crucial Nashville connection was elated in 2001 to join Jason Boland and Stoney LaRue—then in their early 20s—for all-night jam sessions at their home, The Yellow House, just off Oklahoma State University's campus in Stillwater. At that time, Childers was well over 50.

If Skinner was a deliberate artist, Childers was as free and easy as the land about which he wrote. "Restless Spirits" is both the essential Childers song and best two-word descriptor of his legacy that is possible.

Childers contained multitudes.

Before we get to that, here is Bob Childers 101: Born in 1946 in West Virginia, his family moved to Ponca City, Oklahoma, when Childers was 7. After high school, Childers spent a stint in Berkeley, California, studying music. He returned to Oklahoma, settling in Stillwater. In Stillwater, he either met everybody or became everybody. He released a debut album, *I Ain't No Jukebox*, getting help on the record from LaFave, in 1979. He performed for protesters in Washington, D.C., to an audience that included Arlo Guthrie and Pete Seeger, after the Three Mile Island disaster that also happened in 1979. Childers gave a go at becoming a Nashville songwriter in the mid-1980s. That's where the Brooks connection happened. From Nashville, he moved to Austin, releasing the album *Circles Toward the Sun* (which included "Restless Spirits") in 1990. A year later, he moved back to Stillwater. He settled at The Farm and welcomed musicians with open arms. He took seemingly any gig offered. He called himself the White Buffalo, and his band the White Buffalo Road Show, and he drove an old-model SUV he called the White Buffalo Truck.

He played The Blue Door in Oklahoma City with Terry Ware. He sat in with The Great Divide—who cut one of his songs ("Wile E. Coyote"). He sat in with Cross Canadian Ragweed—who cut one of his songs ("Headed South"). He sat in with Jason Boland & The Stragglers—who cut a ton of his songs (the earliest being "Tennessee Whiskey"). He ran with Randy Crouch, The Red Dirt Rangers, Scott Evans, Brad James and just about anybody else who wanted to run. He did this right up until his lungs had enough and he physically couldn't do it. He faced hardship with grace—including the time his house burned up and left him with nothing, and he responded with, "God said it's time to move," and the time his health became critical and the Red Dirt scene put out a 57-song, three-CD tribute album *Restless Spirit*. Finally, in 2008 at age 61, he died of the same lung complications that had been dogging him. Countless tribute concerts followed, and ultimately the benefits that had gone to him in his life spurred the Red Dirt Relief Fund, which continues to this day and aims to help Oklahoma musicians in need.

Childers lived the life of an icon. He also lived the life of a simple Oklahoman. In 2000, he worked part time at the old Pizza Shuttle restaurant in Stillwater to make ends meet. I witnessed this personally and was always taken aback to see someone whose songs had been covered by quite literally hundreds of artists needing that kind of a gig to pay the bills. But if he did mind, he kept it hidden and certainly was not embarrassed to do it. To him it was always part of a plan somebody had for him.

If Tom Skinner and Bob Wiles wrote the Red Dirt anthem when they wrote "Used to Be," then Bob Childers wrote the Red Dirt story when he wrote "Outlaw Band."

It is a song ultimately covered by both Travis Linville and Jason Boland and featuring lyrics that may as well follow the phrase "Red Dirt" when it eventually makes its way into the dictionary: "Out in the country, in the heart of the land / stood a restless kid, guitar in his hand. / He found him some others, who had the same dream. / All of them loaners, but somehow a team. / They were an Outlaw band from Oklahoma, rollin' through the night like a summer thunder / and the rain will wash us clean.

Yeah, the rain will wash us clean."

Childers loved the responsibility of carrying the torch for Red Dirt. He embraced his role as the grand old man as new generations of artists came to Stillwater. He was as eager to push others to write and play as he was ready to grab another song for himself out of the thick, humid Oklahoma air.

Some of the artists who encountered him through the years were more than willing to weigh in on Childers' legacy. A sampling follows, from Childers' longtime friend and fellow Red Dirt original Greg Jacobs, from Scott Evans, who wrote "Make Yourself Home" with Childers and who himself is one of the most influential and respected Red Dirt artists in history, from both Cooper and Piccolo of the Rangers, from Eric Hansen, who played drums on a pair of Childers albums and who has backed Medicine Show, Mike McClure, Jimmy LaFave and currently Cody Canada & The Departed, and from Stoney LaRue, who to this day has no problem waxing poetic about Childers in front of crowds of any size.

Jacobs: "Bob was a true spirit. He really was. He was just never in a bad mood. He just had that kind of attitude. He had this kind of spiritual thing he could do. Whenever I was down, you know, whatever life was dealing, Bob was a guy I could go to. Just, 'You know? I'm gonna go over to Bob's for a while and play guitars or something.' Bob was just that kind of guy. He could make you feel better. He was just a great guy. And I miss that guy. I miss Tom and I miss Bob. It's hard to believe.

"Bob was a showman. He understood his limitations. He wasn't much of a guitar player, and I'm not either. And he wasn't much of a singer, and I'm not either. But Bob knew how to make that work for him. I've seen him go up on stage at Willie's, with a rowdy crowd—you know how Willie's always was—and just get that room in the palm of his hand. It was fun to watch. When Bob was on, he was really good. And of course he's a great songwriter. I still do two or three of Bob's songs, and I kind of feel like I'm supposed to."

Evans: "Man. There's so many things about him that I like to just put it into something he used to say all the time to me. When I'd say, 'Hey Bob! How you doing?' He'd smile, he had this great big smile, and he'd say, 'Well, mostly I'm thankful for the pain.' And then he'd laugh just a little bit. He said that more than once. 'Mostly I'm thankful for the pain.' I don't know, as life has continued on, and there's pain that hits me, I think about that, and it just brings a smile. He was a real free spirit, that guy."

Cooper: "With Bob, I had met him in the early '80s. I had just started playing and writing songs, so I was hanging on to him as much as he would let me. Writing songs with him, constantly asking for critiques. He was always there for the pointers: 'You may want to think about phrasing that this way,' stuff like that. That's why every young songwriter that came to Stillwater, they knew really quick that they needed to meet Bob Childers.

"Bob—what a wordsmith. The guy could just turn a phrase and really get to the meat of the subject. One of his sayings was, 'Y'know, Coop? Our holy grail for songwriting is one chord and 25 words or less. You have to say what you've gotta say in 25 words or less with one chord. Of course, you never get there, but still, don't mince words. Get right in there. Tell people what you want them to hear. Repeat your hook often. That's just the way it is.'

"Bob is another guy who it can't be overstated how important he was to all of us. Especially since our scene is so songwriter-driven. It's all about the song. Without them you got nothing. And Bob had the songs. Now, of course he was so damn poor because songwriting is a vow of poverty, but he was truly a great songwriter. He wasn't a natural performer, that wasn't what he did, although he could perform. That just wasn't what he wanted or what he was after. I remember at the end, there was a song called 'Prisoner in the Promised Land,' which is a stunningly beautiful song. He was telling me about it, he goes, 'Man, I've got this song. I don't even want to write it, but it won't leave me the fuck alone.' That's just the way it was with Childers."

Piccolo: "Bob was the first guy that took me under his wing as an older, experienced musician. He was like my mentor early on. He was this the whole time I knew him, which was from the '70s all the way up until he died. We were like best friends. Me and him and the rest of our band were like brothers. He would take young musicians and just say, 'I love what you're doing.' He would encourage you to write your own songs. He was always open to cowriting, which is invaluable, to have an experienced person around the structure of songwriting and the philosophy behind it. He was really good about that."

Hansen: "From my perspective, I was just an instrumentalist, so I didn't look at Bob as an influence in a songwriter way. He was just kind of a social Don of that generation. I liked Bob, and Bob was responsible for helping me in a lot of ways [Childers connected Hansen with Jimmy LaFave, and Hansen played drums for LaFave for two-plus years], but trying to record a record with Bob Childers was like trying to stomp out a forest fire. He had no connection to the other musicians around him. The sense of time never developed in his brain, so it was like wrestling a grizzly bear to try to lay down a frickin' rhythm track for him. But because I was just experienced enough, which gave him a sense of comfort, which translated to him spreading the word. Because he was that social Don, more than music, more than even his peers were. It made an impact. His approach to writing songs was different, because he wasn't a musical person, but some of that translates. Bob was like Woody Guthrie. Woody didn't have a musical bone in his body, but he had a hell of a lot to say. And he was a poet and a social activist. That was what Bob was, too. He didn't have as much to say, so he didn't appear as activist as Woody, but he was just the social leader of that whole era."

LaRue: "I think of Woody Guthrie when I think of Bob. I think of music for the people, to aid them in times of need or celebrate with them in happier times. I think of honesty, simplicity, peaceful nature. I think of a hippie. He was a mentor who didn't seem to place me or others on any other level than friend and confidant. He was so cool, man."

Zach Childers (Bob's son): "I should say that it's hard for me to have any real perspective on Red Dirt music. The first music I heard on this planet was Red Dirt. Growing up, it was just the music my dad and his friends made. It's still a little difficult for me to think about it as anything other than that. A community rather than a genre.

"If I had to try to distinguish it, though, I would probably start with the centrality of the lyrics. Dad was always writing—scribbling in notebooks and on spare scraps of paper—and he encouraged people around him to do the same. Music was important to him, no doubt, but I think he saw it primarily as this incredibly powerful delivery mechanism for the language.

"He believed strongly in the healing power of all of this. I remember that he managed to get his hands on this branded aspirin hat that he would wear all the time. BC—Advanced Pain Relief.

"He taught me so much. I thought he would live forever."

My last encounter with Childers came in June 2004, when I was living in Oklahoma City. I was 25 and working at *The Oklahoman*. It was also common knowledge at the paper that I had ties to Red Dirt music. One night, I got a really disconcerting phone call from one of the music editors: "Hey, do you have a connection to the Red Dirt Rangers? There's been some sort of helicopter accident in Payne County and we hear they were involved."

It turned out, that's exactly what happened. John Cooper, Brad Piccolo and Ben Han had taken a helicopter ride before a gig near Cushing. The chopper crashed and landed upside down in the Cimarron River, killing the pilot and another passenger and injuring all three Rangers members. One of many moments of tragedy that have dotted the Red Dirt landscape over the years.

But at the time, neither I nor the colleagues asking for my help knew that. Moreover, I didn't know who I could call. I had Cooper's number. I had Piccolo's number. Neither of them picked up.

So I called Bob Childers.

At that time, that's just what you did if you were in Red Dirt and had a problem and didn't know what to do: You called Bob. I was no different.

"Hey Bob, it's Josh."

"Hey Josh, how are you doin'?" he shot back in his soft drawl.

"Bob. Have you heard anything about the Red Dirt Rangers?"

"Well, I just saw them a few hours ago, but I'm back at the house now."

"Bob, are you sitting down?"

I don't remember exactly what I told him after that, only that I'd heard that there was a helicopter crash and their names came up and I needed to know as both a friend of theirs and as a young journalist who was one of the few direct connections to this music scene my newspaper had.

I do remember Childers' response. Just a shaky-voiced "oh, no" over and over again.

"Oh no. Oh no. Oh no. ... Oh, man. I just saw them, and I heard someone talking about a helicopter, but I didn't see anything like that. Oh no. Oh no."

I apologized for breaking bad news to him. What can you really say, right? And I asked him to keep me in the loop. A few hours later, he called me and confirmed the rumors. He had also found their hospitals, spoken to their family members and learned they were seriously injured but were going to be OK. He was relieved for his friends and still baffled at the situation—two others did indeed die.

I don't really know where that story fits in with Childers' legacy. But I do think it's telling that, no matter who you were in Red Dirt, even as Childers approached 60, if you were worried about somebody, you called him. And I do think it's telling how completely shaken and scared Bob was upon hearing it. He was very much a guy who believed that bad things in life should happen to him so that they would not happen to others.

We call him The Godfather of Red Dirt now. And maybe he was. But in truth, he lacked the ruthlessness of a mob boss. He had spent too much of his life living out one of his most-remembered lyrics. He was the closest thing to Woody Guthrie that Red Dirt had:

Woody's road was rough and rocky.
Woody's road led everywhere.
I guess everywhere's where he felt most at home.
He was a ramblin' friend of man,
Reachin' out his hand.
Maybe that's why I went walkin' Woody's road.

— — —

- 4 -

Why I Wrote This Book

IN FEBRUARY 2000, I was experiencing something no 21-year-old college student had ever experienced before or since. Just completely unique.

I was restless.

You read that right: I was a college boy with no direction and lacking in motivation.

Oklahoma State and Stillwater were both great for me, but most of the rest of life was wildly uninspiring. I was writing for the college paper at OSU, *The Daily O'Collegian*. Me in a relationship at the time was like Oral Roberts in the NCAA basketball tournament—I was just happy to be there, and at that time, I most certainly was not there. On a full scholarship, my grades were fine, and at the end of that school year I would take the LSAT and apply to law schools.

Whatever.

Compounding that angst, the hot 1990s country I had grown up on and that had made Stillwater seem cool to me, well, was equally uninspiring. Dixie Chicks aside, Nashville was already headed down the golden-paved highway that led to a decade of songs about dirt roads.

But I had a lifelong friend in Stillwater, too—Jeff Humphrey, now a dentist in Massachusetts, but then a pot-smoking introvert who understood better than I did that anything considered mainstream was a money-making gambit.

Point is, college Jeff knew about Americana music. He had played a John Prine tape for me a few months before, and the nerve endings in my brain fried. When Okemah, Oklahoma, finally started honoring Woody Guthrie with his own festival the summer before, Jeff was the first person I knew to attend. Musically, Jeff knew his shit. While we were in Stillwater, he was married to my childhood soul mate (inasmuch as one can have a childhood soul mate), Hannah Holleman. She had introduced me to the concept of driving up to a mountain to watch the sun rise while playing folk music in high school, but it all didn't make sense until we were in college.

In February 2000, Jeff and I hung out at Mike's College Bar on Washington Street in Stillwater. That's The Strip, as this book will remind you over and over. The College Bar had more than 100 beers, and to someone whose first beer was a Natural Light four years prior, it was eye-opening. Did you know that in Belgium, they make beer that does *not* taste like the water wrung from a gym sock?

The College Bar was a musical mecca in its own right. That year alone, the Flaming Lips had a regular Tuesday night gig, and the All-American Rejects had a regular Wednesday night gig. But this night in question was a Monday night, and that was open-mic night at The College Bar.

Someone, I believe Drew Winn, got up and played a Gram Parsons song, and it sent Jeff and me down an Americana music wormhole. I don't remember the exact words, but I do know that I told Jeff that people told me if I liked Americana, I should check out the live music in Stillwater.

"OK, so we should go find this music then. Like, right now."

We tabbed out at The College Bar and walked into Willie's Saloon, a few blocks away. There was no live music that night. We had a beer and walked out. I know this much: Our plan was to walk to Eskimo Joe's, maybe 10 blocks away. We only made it one before we found ourselves standing on Washington Street.

I could hear an acoustic guitar and a raspy voice, and I could hear it coming from directly over my head. In front of me was Causley Productions, a T-shirt and memorabilia shop. The music was coming from the second floor of the building, above the shop.

"Does that sound Americana?" I asked Jeff.

"As fuck!" was his reply.

So we walked around the side of the building and saw the staircase leading up to this bar. At the top of the stairs, above the door, the sign was legible from the street: "Wormy Dog Saloon, Est. 1992."

"Let's go."

A flight of stairs. A small landing. A second flight of stairs. The door. Inside, a saddle-lined bar with a concrete-block front wall with a Levelland, Texas, sign screwed into it, fronting a 10-by-20-foot stage elevated maybe six inches off the rest of the concrete floor.

On the stage was a lanky blond guy about my age with a guitar, absolutely owning the crowd of 50 or so in the dive. A few feet to his right, on the wall was the sign "Tonight: Stoney LaRue."

And that's the story of how a college kid with no direction found his. That's the story of how I found Red Dirt.

* * *

Who the Hell Do I Think I Am?

Backing up a moment. You need to know where this is coming from.

Maybe you had a home. I did not.

In that I had a loving family and walls, food and toys all around me and generally felt a privileged, small-town middle class upbringing from infancy to adulthood, yes.

I had all that. I had it for 21 years in Okmulgee, Oklahoma, 30 miles south of Tulsa and 90 miles due east of "The City"—that's Okie for Oklahoma City—in a diverse town often derided as a mix of white trash, country bumpkins and street gangs. The town's nickname is Mug Town, and it's not for its abundance of coffee shops.

But it was also a bedroom community for Tulsa, and more than anything, filled with people who made the town work. That latter group was where my parents fell in. Dad, a diesel mechanic who left home at 7:30 a.m. and returned, covered in grease and cuts, at 7:30 p.m., and Mom, a fourth-grade teacher at the elementary school a block and a half from our house. Me, born in 1979, and my sister, three years younger, children of the 1980s in a six-decade-old, two-story brick house. Cars when we turned 16 and future valedictorian tassels. I remember having all that.

I just never remember being *home*.

What I did have was Charles A. Perry, my grandfather on my mom's side—by trade an assembly worker at the General Motors plant in Oklahoma City, but by birth an outlaw. His cousin was Loss Hart, who killed one of the last members of the Dool-in-Dalton Gang. He married into the lineage of both Jesse James and Belle Starr. He may have lived in The City, but he embodied country the way a native of Stratford, Oklahoma, would.

And what *he* had was a stereo system. Four Pioneer speakers bigger than toddler me, in four corners of his living room, a turntable and a 16-channel graphic equalizer. All he wanted out of that was country music. He liked it loud. He liked the treble turned up too high. He loved Willie Nelson and Waylon Jennings.

As that toddler, I had a thing for Christmas music, specifically "Rudolph the Red-Nosed Reindeer." So on one of my early visits to his house, he had a mixtape waiting for me. It was nothing but "Rudolph," over and over and over again, by name after name of Opry stars. Hank Locklin, Hank Snow, Mel Tillis and Nancy Sinatra. I had them all in my hand, and I spent ages 2 to 4 wearing out Fisher-Price tape recorders back at home playing them.

But one version of "Rudolph" stuck out to me. There's no way I can pretend to remember the conversations, but I very clearly wanted to know who this guy, who even sounded kind of like my grandfather, was. He played the song, well, better than anything I had ever heard. And when we'd play it on that stereo system at his house, the reverb from the steel guitar strings was crystal clear with that high treble. I didn't understand the concept of toe tapping, but I know that's how I responded, reflexively, to that sound. So I wanted to know who it was.

"That's Merle Haggard."

It probably wasn't my first love, as my mom made it clear she held that distinction, and to her credit she also forced music on me. She was a child of the 1950s and her genre was oldies, which I also took to. But the absolute second love of my entire life was this sound my grandfather called "Merle Haggard." Eventually, he handed over the *If We Make It Through December* cassette from which he had ripped "Rudolph," and from there I learned there were more songs than Christmas ones out there. Luckily for me, he had Haggard's entire catalog, and my childhood trips to Oklahoma City were spent exploring it.

I inherited those speakers when my grandfather died in 1997 and blew them all out in a year.

Before that, as soon as toddler me learned to retain information, I learned how radios worked and got one of my own. It even had speakers. The Merle Haggard fandom never left. It expanded to every big country artist of that era, in fact. But in Okmulgee, by around 1991, the radio was not bothered to play that anymore. Instead, country radio was all over this new guy from Oklahoma, and everything he was singing was turning gold and platinum.

By that, I mean, Garth Brooks led the soundtrack to my tweens.

Then, there was my dad. His musical contributions were limited to taking me to Walmart at 10 p.m. when I was in elementary school because I threw a fit randomly wanting to buy Don McLean's greatest hits album and letting me control the radio on car rides (of which there were hundreds). We lived in Okmulgee, but his shop sat on 40 acres on the edge of town, a mile from our house. Four farm ponds, cattle and a ranch house that, at various points in my life, housed my great-grandmother, dad's diesel mechanic office, a craft store and my high school parties. Dad was the son of an oilfield worker. He had two brothers, all tough as nails. As kids, if they acted up, the elders in their lives would instruct them to move piles of bricks from one random spot to another to keep them occupied. They all went on to play college football—Dad (you can call him Steve) at Southwestern Oklahoma State, where he met my mom, his younger brother Clyde at Colorado and his older brother Larry at Oklahoma.

That last part is important context: Larry made the rules. Our family was Sooner born and Sooner bred. Stillwater was taboo to Crutchmers, and Oklahoma State orange was a forbidden color.

I spent high school immersed in '90s country, even as my friends were into alt rock. I got into it enough to not feel left out and occasionally even liked it. I got into Pearl Jam, Nirvana and a band out of Phoenix called The Refreshments. Oh man, did I love The Refreshments. *Fizzy Fuzzy Big & Buzzy* became the soundtrack to my senior year of high school. An exception, sure, because I always returned to country.

Meanwhile, I played football until my knee stopped bending properly, got good enough at tennis to medal at state, earned an academic scholarship and generally bided my time until it all ended and I'd be off to Norman and OU. It was all laid out from the start for me: Four years at OU, I'd roll through the honors college, then I'd get a law degree, return to Okmulgee and work for the district attorney. It was damn near scripted.

I left for OU in summer 1997 to set this all into motion, and I left still dating my high school girlfriend, herself still in high school. Freshman year went according to plan. Long-distance dating worked. Garth released *Sevens* that year, and I lined up at midnight to buy it and subsequently developed an underage affinity for Captain Morgan rum, thanks to "Two Piña Coladas." And in summer 1998 I returned to Okmulgee, where a clerk job with the district attorney was waiting. Also waiting was the first week of July.

I remember the exact dates, because they were the two days leading up to July 4 and an annual fireworks-and-fishing bash at my family's land. Here is what went down:

July 2: A group of friends and my girlfriend piled into our trucks and headed out to the local rodeo ground (I left out a detail, by high school I was a cowboy) for a concert. Mark Wills and Rhett Akins co-headlined. Akins covered Matchbox 20, and that was cool.

At that show, literally between sets, my girlfriend dropped me like a bad habit. No pretense. Just "So, we should break up" and when I asked why, she said, "I just don't love you anymore."

For a teenage ball of emotion, I took it well. I told her OK and that I'd find my way home, and I caught the rest of the concert from across the crowd.

July 3: When you're 19, that stuff can mess you up, no matter how cool you play it at the time. My friends saw that in me and invited me out for an afternoon of golf at Lake Eufaula. It was there that we heard a radio ad for a rodeo that night at Bedrock Arena, south of Glenpool. I believe that the arena is a megachurch now, but it was also a furniture store sometime recently.

There would be a concert after the rodeo by a hot new country act called The Great Divide, according to the commercial.

I had heard The Divide on the radio before and liked them, but make no mistake, it was the rodeo part of the ad that excited me. I talked my friends into it, and we made a day of it.

After the rodeo, they rolled a flatbed stage out onto the arena dirt. My two friends asked if I wanted to stick around. Sure, what the hell? It's not like I have a girlfriend waiting on me. Let's do it.

The Great Divide took the stage that night and handed me the key to the first and only home I have ever known. Within a few songs, I realized I dug every word. By the time they fired off their biggest hit, "Pour Me a Vacation" (in hindsight, haha), I was hooked. I'd be buying every album this band put out forever. Plus, it felt a little cool to be into a band that wasn't topping the charts.

Then they came back for an encore. Skinny-ass, full-of-hair, shorts-and flip-flops wearing lead singer Mike McClure stepped up to the microphone, backed by three bona fide cowboys.

"This song is by Robert Earl Keen."

(Side note: The Divide used to absolutely kill this song and Joe Ely's "Me and Billy the Kid.")

A short electric guitar intro led directly into "Sherry was a waitress, at the only joint in town..."

That was the first time I clearly recall standing, jaw dropped, eyes as big as silver dollars, taking in a song.

We had a good time is what I'm trying to tell you. On the ride home and for pretty much the next year, though, one very specific thing sidetracked me.

"What the hell was that *song*?"

"The road" what? Robert who? I hadn't retained enough to look it up on the Internet, and even if I had, it was 1998 and probably was not online anyway.

But I did retain a Divide obsession. I never saw them play that song again live, but I did spend the rest of 1998 driving from Norman to Stillwater or Oklahoma City every time they played The Tumbleweed Dancehall or Incahoots. At one of those shows, they declared a song to be a Stillwater anthem, and then started playing it: "Them boys from Oklahoma roll their joints all wrong. They're too damn skinny or way too long." And again, I became obsessed with what it was and where it came from.

By the end of 1998, Norman was murky and blurry to me. What the hell was I doing with college, with my life? I didn't want out of Norman as much as I wanted some kind of direction. I hadn't made a ton of friends, and becoming a lawyer one day started to feel like a burden instead of a destiny. Then, late in that semester, an argument with my roommate led to the cops showing up, and I decided that "Sooner born and Sooner bred" made sense as a fight song but not a credo.

I had some friends who had gone to OSU. Garth made Stillwater seem cool, and The Great Divide called it home. Worth checking out, yeah? So I transferred at the end of the semester.

My big memory of my first months as a Cowboy was the local country station promoting a CD release party for The Divide at a place on Washington Street called the Wormy Dog Saloon. They were putting out *Revolutions*, and the Stillwater name-dropping song "College Days" was on it. Too young to get in and too dumb to get a fake ID, I settled for driving by. The line, in the middle of the afternoon, long before sundown and long before the concert, was down the stairs and spilling out onto the sidewalk.

"Well, that looks fucking cool," I vividly recall saying out loud to nobody else in my truck.

One other thing happened that spring. One of those longtime friends who helped make it easy to transfer to OSU went to a sorority party with his then-girlfriend. His name is Ott Holleman, and he returned from the party going on and on about this one particular song they were playing.

"Dude. Have you heard 'The Road Goes on Forever'?"

"Who sings it?"

"Robert Earl Keen."

The Divide had handed me a key at that rodeo concert. Almost a year later, my friend turned it.

Not long after, I found myself at Hastings in Stillwater, holding several Robert Earl Keen CDs and staring at a different one: *Live & Loud at the Wormy Dog Saloon*, by Cross Canadian Ragweed. On the track listing on the back: "Boys From Oklahoma."

I believe the technical term for such a breakthrough that eventually set my life on the proper course is: That shit was lit as fuck, man.

Within months, Ott and I were roping another of our lifelong friends, Brady Colombin, into driving us from Stillwater to Wichita Falls, Texas, and back in one day—five hours each way—to see Robert Earl Keen. I recall a gigantic fistfight that broke out during, and lasted the entirety of, the long instrumental jam at the end of "The Road Goes on Forever."

• • •

Home

I did not come by my flightiness honestly. My parents have had two houses in my four-plus decades. My sister lives in suburban Tulsa, 25 miles north of my parents.

They have homes.

Since Stillwater in 2001, I have lived in Oklahoma City, Phoenix, Omaha, Chicago, Minneapolis, Buffalo, Cleveland and New York. Those places? They came with the territory. I made it two semesters into those law school plans before I decided they were bad ones, too. My college journalism major had led to an internship at *The Daily Oklahoman* in Oklahoma City, and by the end of college, a job was waiting on me. Eventually I decided journalism made more sense for me than law school. Journalism is a reactionary career and I am wired to react.

It worked out for me. As I write this book, I am the print planning editor at *The New York Times*. My wife, Andrea, works two seats away as the sports art director.

When I leave work, I return to a place with walls, a roof and four cats—there was a dog too, Abby, who passed unexpectedly the week this book went to press. Pets are the limit for us because, in 2016, Andrea was diagnosed with breast cancer, and the best method of treating it was *poison everything in her body as soon as possible.* There's food and love and nagging each other to pay bills. There are patio parties for our friends (this is Manhattan, after all). It is, just like all the places I have lived, something that could easily be construed as a home. It's definitely home to her.

There is exactly enough of me that is aware of that to make me into someone vaguely normal. Like a guy who takes the trash out and buys replacement hand mixer parts online and usually does not show up to work hungover anymore.

The part of me who knows this is how I have to be is always in conflict. He is in conflict with the bigger, stronger, louder part of me who does nothing but hover over the normal me, 24/7, reminding me that I could be at a Red Dirt concert somewhere at that exact moment.

After I walked into the Wormy Dog that first time, Red Dirt took me in—a music family not limited to musicians. In Chapter 10, I get into how I met several of the figures. But all that matters here is that I did that. I became friends with them. I went on the road with them. I went to their houses, to their farmland, to their campfires, to their studios and, eventually, to their busses.

I knew how to write because journalism teaches you that. Red Dirt taught me when to add in honesty and when to make it personal.

More importantly, Red Dirt gave me something I could count on. No matter where I live, where I am at any given moment, there's a song out there that I can turn up louder than that reality. And I have.

In Red Dirt, I finally found what could settle my mind, no matter the situation. In my life, I've found soundtracks to weddings, funerals, starting jobs, leaving jobs, losing friends, making friends, divorce, pets, moving to a new city, traveling the world, marriage proposals and several hundred breaking news events that required me to focus intently.

The idea is always the same: Blast your brain to smaller and smaller pieces until you're holding it in your hand like a pile of dust. Drinking and therapy will do this too, but music is easier. Red Dirt made it OK to travel the world, farther and farther from anything I ever grew up thinking was normal.

It makes me feel at home.

Also, I mentioned marriage. About that...

I met Andrea in 2009 when she was a student at Michigan State University and I was working at the *Chicago Tribune*. We started up a friendship. In 2012, she was working at *The Detroit News* and I at the Minneapolis *Star Tribune*, and we started dating. It was long-distance, so a great many of our dates involved trips around the country, often to Cody Canada & The Departed concerts. Cody and I are family-level close, and his band and crew have treated me like one of them since 2000. I did not force Andrea to like them. But she did, and it made it easier for us to have a relationship. Andrea is an emo-punk girl who thankfully found she could also carve a niche in Red Dirt.

Long distance coupled with job success ultimately led us to the same place. She joined *The Buffalo News* in early 2012, and I followed suit in late 2013. By May 2014, we had both been hired at the Cleveland *Plain Dealer*. If there is one aspect of being a musician that absolutely overlaps with journalism, it's a requirement that you go where the work is, rather than wait for the work to come to you.

Over Memorial Day weekend of 2014, I did something pretty standard for me: I flew from Cleveland to Des Moines, Iowa, to meet up with Cody. The Departed had a show there that night, and the next night they'd play in Chicago at Joe's on Weed.

I have not missed one of Cody's shows at Joe's since 2008, when I lived in Chicago and he fronted Cross Canadian Ragweed, and the bar is absolutely a place I hold dear. At a guess, it's second only to the original Wormy Dog in Stillwater as far as number of shows I've seen in one venue. Ed Warm, the owner, told me on my first visit that any friend of Ragweed's was a friend of his, and I took him up on it. We shared obsessions in barbecue and original music, and let me tell you, that's more than enough to create a lifelong friendship.

All this to say, the plan in motion was: I flew to Des Moines. I would ride the bus to Chicago the next day, and Andrea would meet me there. We'd catch the gig at Joe's that night. We'd have a good time, and frankly, none of this was out of the ordinary. This time, though, I carried a diamond ring in my pocket.

I had tipped Cody off that I planned on proposing at Joe's, and he said I could do it during the show. "Pick a song, man. I'll learn it."

When I got to Des Moines the day before, he asked me which one. I asked him if he'd play "All My Life," by Todd Snider. It was a favorite of his anyway. He said he would.

Then the Des Moines show happened, and it was just an all-encompassing great night. One of those times you say things like "music heals" and you didn't even realize you needed to be healed. After the show, I made a beeline for Cody. One of my favorite songs of all time was one he'd written for his wife, Shannon, called "Flowers." Its tagline, "We're the best thing / we've ever had" is an incredible turn of a phrase.

"Uh, so you know how I asked you to play 'All My Life' tomorrow? Am I an asshole if I ask you to forget about that and play 'Flowers' instead?"

Cody was relieved at not needing to learn a new song. "Man, I'm really, really glad you just said that."

The next night, it went off just like we planned. Cody called Andrea and me up on stage, and he played the song. During the final bridge, he yielded the mic to me, and I said, "This place has always felt like home to me and treated me like family, and there are some things you really want to do at home in front of your family."

The crowd lost its shit and Andrea was wide-eyed, stunned. This is easily findable on YouTube.

She said yes.

We danced to "All My Life" at our wedding a year later. We posted the video of that dance online. When we check it out now, there is a solitary comment on it: "Todd Snider was very moved to see this."

. . .

The Expectation Setter

This book is a conflict of interest.

In college in 2000 and 2001, I wrote about Red Dirt like I was auditioning for *Rolling Stone*. Sometimes, I'd write three or four articles or columns in a week about it, all from my position as sports editor of the campus paper. In 2002, a little more than a year out of OSU, I wrote a long takeout piece for *The Daily Oklahoman* about the rise of Red Dirt and specifically Ragweed. After that was published, I declared my retirement from covering the scene. The reason is simple: Writing stories about a scene I claim as my own and about people I am as close with as family crosses every ethical line for a journalist.

In the 18 years since that article came out, I have limited my writing about Red Dirt to opinion-heavy columns, and I have always disclosed, usually in the text of the column itself, that I consider myself a part of the scene and that readers should not expect objectivity. That seems fair.

Occasionally, I stepped out of Red Dirt writing, usually for heavy events. I wrote George Jones' obituary for the *Nashville City Paper*, and I wrote an appreciation for Merle Haggard for the Cleveland *Plain Dealer* when he passed. I also did that for the *Plain Dealer* in 2015 when Tom Skinner died. But even in writing those, my point of reference was Red Dirt.

Moreover, these friendships, which make writing objectively a conflict for me, have grown rather than faded. When I left Oklahoma in 2005, I thought I'd be relegated to everyone's memories as a guy—one of thousands—who played a little part in Red Dirt's biggest rise. Instead, every time I returned, the artists, friends, bartenders and crew members remembered me and demanded we catch up.

I even tried putting Ragweed in my past when they were in the heyday of a Universal South record deal. I'd show up at shows and not tell them and leave without seeing them. They had become too big for me anyway, right?

Finally, in 2008, I lived in Omaha, and Cody Canada caught on to this. He set me straight: "You are welcome with me anytime, anywhere, so stop laying low and stop hiding out, you got it?"

A decade later, that friendship spawned ones with Wade Bowen and his band and family, the entirety of the Braun Brothers and a great deal of the artists who have toured with Cody on any of the hundreds of times I have tagged along in the bus.

All of that is why I say this is a conflict, and that has always been important for me to disclose. So please read this book knowing that the author has a bias: I like Red Dirt, and I want you to like it.

But this book is bigger than me. It's for the musicians and songwriters. It's for their stories. They deserve to be told, and you deserve to hear them. And in telling those stories, I wanted to act like a journalist. Even though a conflict of interest existed, I could still be fair to the stories.

The result is a book that sometimes acts like journalism, sometimes acts like a history lesson and sometimes acts like a memoir.

When it came time to tell stories, I went to the artists themselves. If someone is quoted in this book, unless I explicitly write otherwise, it came from an interview I personally conducted. In cases of content conflict or controversy, I made an effort to reach out to people who could give another side. There will be plenty of artists and stories that I miss, too, so I hope you see this book as a representative sample and a taste of Red Dirt.

When I tell my stories, they're told as I recall them. I will use my past reporting as a guide. And there will even be some never-before-published quotes from prior interviews that will make this book. When they do, I'll be clear about them for you.

There are questions I cannot answer as well. I do not know for sure whether this rumor from social media or that rumor about who was sleeping with whom from a message board is true, and this was never intended to be that kind of book.

My hope is that every chapter in this book can stand alone, like a collection of essays, but that each also builds upon the next.

The original plan was gonzo journalism. I intended to write the final chapter at Medicine Stone—the pinnacle of the Red Dirt calendar from 2013 to 2019, held every September at Diamondhead Resort along the Illinois River in Tahlequah, Oklahoma—and I wrote about the festival as it happened. The plan was to write about getting drunk and stoned and taking it in. I did not know where that may lead, but I knew it's where this book would stop.

That was in September 2018.

Well, things happened.

Barely a month after that festival, the Turnpike Troubadours abruptly canceled a weekend of shows in Louisiana and Texas, and then announced a month's hiatus. By the following May, they were on indefinite hiatus.

I paused finishing this book as well, hoping partly for a clear-cut happy ending for Turnpike, but also to do things like pitch the book to agents who never quite understood who might buy it or publishers who did understand but were a little busy right then and would get back to me.

On the last possible day before this book went to print in August 2020, I got the clarity from Turnpike that I had been waiting for. You'll find it in here.

Speaking of 2020, I am sitting in isolation, along with most of the world, in an apartment on Manhattan's Upper East Side, refocused on this writing by the same coronavirus pandemic that has me at least nominally worried about whether I'll be around when you read it. Ideally, when this book is in your hands, you'll read this paragraph and wonder why it never got changed to the past tense. An oversight, you'll say.

With the nation at a standstill, live music is on hold. I knew it would take two years to tell the story of Red Dirt, but now it's most important to me that you have this in your hands when that music starts again. Some of the proceeds will go to the Red Dirt Relief Fund, directly helping artists and crew members whose lives were upended in this crisis. The urgency, here and now, for me to tell this story of this music scene has never been greater, and I'm acting on it.

So, for now, enough about me.

- 5 -

The Legacy of Jimmy LaFave

JIMMY LAFAVE IS the reason Red Dirt is Red Dirt.

He was not the first to use the phrase. Steve Ripley picked the name Red Dirt Records to release a 1972 album from his band Moses. But LaFave did pay tribute to Payne County's iron-rich soil with the song "Red Dirt Roads at Night," and the Red Dirt Rangers found their name in the lyrics.

Other artists have been far more bold in their trumpeting of the name, none more so than the Rangers, but there have been others. Stoney LaRue's first solo studio album was called *The Red Dirt Album*. Hell, Brandon Jenkins flat-out became known as the Red Dirt Legend.

What LaFave did for Red Dirt, most simply, was spread it. He sprang up in Stillwater and then traveled the world referencing this scene from his hometown called Red Dirt, so much so that the name stopped being an inner-circle nickname in Oklahoma and started being the mainstream method of referencing the music.

LaFave, born in Wills Point, Texas, spent the most formidable years of his youth in Stillwater, and by the time he graduated high school, he was accomplished enough on the guitar to find night gigs around town. He also released the albums *Down Under* and *Broken Line* in 1979 and 1981, respectively, while living in Stillwater.

That time frame is important, because it overlapped with Red Dirt pioneers like John Cooper, Bob Childers, Greg Jacobs and a dozen other songwriters finding their way to Stillwater. LaFave was a contemporary, heavily influenced by Woody Guthrie and hell-bent on imparting a blues sound on his own music. He took all that with him in the early 1980s when he left Stillwater, bouncing around to a few interim stops before settling in Austin in 1986.

Had he stayed in Stillwater, he would certainly be thought of to this day alongside

Red Dirt's other forefathers.

Where LaFave set himself apart, even among the iconic founders he ran with in Stillwater, was in his career after he left. He put out a cassette in 1988, *Highway Angels...Full Moon Rain*, independently, but it received the Readers Poll Tape of the Year award from the *Austin Chronicle*. From that point until his death from a rare brain cancer in May 2017, LaFave was applauded, revered, studied and followed as one of Austin's premier songwriters, combining folk lyrics with blues melodies. He played across the U.S. and Europe, cofounded Music Road Records with Fred Remmart and Kelcy Warren and kept a rotating cast of world-class talent in his band.

But while he became an Austin superstar, he did not back away from his Red Dirt roots. He returned to Stillwater annually to host a songwriter's night at Willie's. He frequented the Blue Door in Oklahoma City and became a mainstay at the Woody Guthrie Folk Festival in Okemah. He produced a wildly successful Guthrie tribute show, *Ribbon of Highway, Endless Skyway*, in 2003. He received the first Restless Spirit award at the Bob Childers Gypsy Cafe, a one-day singer-songwriter festival in Stillwater, in 2017.

In many ways, LaFave's greatest contribution to Red Dirt came after he bolted the scene. His Austin success was the first known Red Dirt–to–Austin blueprint, followed for the 30-plus years since by artists looking to expand their footprint. He also provided Red Dirt with a crucial connection in the Texas capital.

It is safe to say that Red Dirt would have thrived in Stillwater with or without Jimmy LaFave. It may have had a little less soul, but it would have thrived. It is equally safe to say that the path out of Stillwater—the inroads followed by artists to this day into Texas, the ones that eventually allowed Red Dirt to first infiltrate and then become one with Texas music—would never have been possible without the doors he opened.

His legacy looms large in Oklahoma. It looms large in Texas. What follows is a collection of songwriters and musicians who knew and played with him sharing their insights, memories and feelings on the impact he left.

Brad Piccolo of the Red Dirt Rangers:

"In the late '80s, the seeds of Red Dirt had blossomed in Stillwater. And in Austin, you could already see some elements represented by people like Butch Hancock, all the Flatlanders and Joe Ely, those guys were all doing what we were doing. It was relatable. That's the scene I tapped into. Through Jimmy, I met so many great musicians. One time, my girlfriend of many years had just broken up with me. I was so brokenhearted. It was my birthday. And Jimmy goes, 'Hey, man. My friend's recording today. Do you want to go to the studio with me in San Marcos?' I went 'Yeah, sure, I need to get my mind off this shit.' So he took me down there. I spent all day in a recording session with Townes Van Zandt, on my birthday, '89. Just me, Jimmy, Townes and an engineer or two. He was one of my heroes, and Jimmy introduced me to him and all these musicians. Hell, he introduced me to Bob Childers. We even took our name off one of his songs, 'Red Dirt Roads.'"

John Cooper of the Red Dirt Rangers:

"Any Okie band from Stillwater or really anywhere else who went to Austin, Texas, owes a huge debt to Jimmy LaFave. He was the first guy down. He planted the flag for every Okie who came after him. For that alone, he is to be exalted and held up high. He plowed the ground for all of us to go there and made it cool for Okies to come down. Every band or solo act that goes down there owes him a debt, whether they know it or not.

"Jimmy is out of the old school Red Dirt songwriter scene. Jimmy has written some of the finest songs from our scene, ever, as far as I'm concerned. 'Buffalo Return to the Plains'...hell, 'Red Dirt Roads,' which we covered for years. He may have been the first guy who actually did a Red Dirt song. He really pushed Red Dirt. He was the biggest proponent in the early days of the term and of what Oklahoma music sounded like.

"He always talked about Oklahoma having a certain thing about it as far as music that's different than Texas or Kansas or anywhere. We have a certain feel and a certain rhyme and reason for what we produce in music that's different from anywhere else on the planet, and LaFave really held that up. He was a huge Woody Guthrie follower. Woody was his idol, and Dylan also—nobody I know covered Dylan as much as Jimmy LaFave, and he did great with those covers. The Ribbon of Highway tour that he brought Childers on, he wrote the script for that, and it was just simply Woody's life through song."

Eric Hansen, drummer for Cody Canada & The Departed and former drummer for LaFave:

"LaFave had a gift. LaFave was gifted with this weird-ass, alternative tonality to his voice, and the ability to control that voice and do things with it that were not normal, everyday stuff. A LaFave track came on the radio in any circuit, and you knew it was Jimmy because there was only one LaFave voice. He didn't necessarily want to accept that his voice was what made him capable of being a successful songwriter and musician. He didn't accept that it was just a God-given accident. He could squawk and squeal and do all that other stuff like nobody else, and that's what made Jimmy, well, Jimmy.

"Later, even after my years, Jimmy finally let go of the reins and let somebody else produce his records and come in with song ideas. And the last records that Jimmy did were his best records, by a long way, because he gave up control and let somebody else give direction to that voice of his and know how to come across with the product he did possess."

Greg Jacobs, Red Dirt forefather and songwriter:

"Jimmy was a really nice guy that I never really felt like I got close to. Jimmy was talented. I was jealous as hell of how good Jimmy could sing. Man, he could just grab a room and just hold it in his hand with his voice."

David Abeyta, former lead guitar player for Reckless Kelly and Bartlesville, Oklahoma, native, who played with LaFave in Austin:

"The great interpreter of Dylan songs and one of our best interpreters of Woody Guthrie material. When we're in Oklahoma, sometimes I'll sing 'Oklahoma Hills,' and I learned that from Jimmy. I do basically Jimmy's version as best I can—I have to do it lower, because I don't have the same great voice. One of my favorite tracks is, Jody Denberg at KGSR [Austin radio station], they did a thing. And it was Jimmy and Eliza Gilkyson. I don't remember who else was there, but I remember Jimmy and Eliza. It was a recording on the record *Trail* of Jimmy's, and it was just taken from that live on-the-air recording, and it's my very favorite 'Oklahoma Hills.' Last time we played

Cain's, I went down to the Woody Guthrie Center, and I told someone, 'I'm playing up the hill at Cain's, and I'm going to do 'Oklahoma Hills.' And they told me, 'You know, there's no actual recorded version of that. There's even some dispute over the words.'

"Well, I just do Jimmy's version.

"Jimmy, to me, is a hero. Great heart. Always generous with me before he had any need to be nice to me. He would always come up to me and say, 'Ah, there's that other Okie.' And I remember that to this day. It's the Okie connection, you know?"

— — —

- 6 -

The Red Dirt Rangers' Thirty-Year Success Story

SOMEONE HAD TO see it all.

To be sure, Red Dirt has fallen on countless eyes and ears since its inception. Steve Ripley, of Red Dirt Records fame, makes his home in Tulsa, barely an hour-long drive east of Stillwater, to this day. Gene Williams and Greg Jacobs found their ways into the scene before it was a scene, and they're still active to this day. Same for Scott Evans, Brad James, Monica Taylor, Chuck Dunlap, Gene Collier—I'm going to stop with the list if only because the point is clear that plenty of Red Dirt originals are still making music and playing their hearts out somewhere in Tornado Alley tonight.

But someone had to be the mainstay. Someone had to be the band that got in on the ground floor, grew up, musically, under the influences of Bob Childers, Tom Skinner and Jimmy LaFave and stuck around not just long enough to be seen as forefathers themselves but to have personally witnessed every artist, venue, next big thing and flameout that came since. Part by design and part by luck of the draw (Skinner and Childers both fit this description themselves right up until the end of their lives), someone had to be the Red Dirt mainstay. Without one, the scene would have been lost to history, and whatever came next would have been distinctly and unabashedly not Red Dirt.

Enter the Red Dirt Rangers.

The Rangers were a band before The Great Divide was a band. They watched Cross Canadian Ragweed, Jason Boland & The Stragglers and Stoney LaRue take their own baby steps in the scene before collectively lifting its ceiling. They can tell you about John Fullbright before he was John Fullbright and the Turnpike Troubadours before they were the Turnpike Troubadours. Hell, they were *the* band that got to name themselves after Red Dirt.

And they were difficult to pin down for this book because they had gigs to play.

The Rangers have rotated through plenty of members, but John Cooper, Brad Piccolo and Ben Han have been Rangers as long as there were Rangers. Cooper and Piccolo, both of whom opened their minds and hearts to get their stories on the record, were there for the entire art of The Farm. Cooper even helped found it.

"Stillwater was just far enough away from Tulsa and Oklahoma City that we couldn't just jump in the car and go," Cooper said of his earliest days in the scene. "And the roads were really shitty back then. There was a two-lane highway from Stillwater to I-35. There was no Highway 412 from us to Tulsa. So we were kind of isolated, and by God, we created our own fun."

Cooper and Piccolo both grew up with heavy musical influences, but along different paths. Cooper sang in church choirs in his early youth but did not pick up an instrument until he arrived in Stillwater in the early 1980s.

"I grew up in Oklahoma City—went to Putnam City High School—and my first real musical experience started in church, like a lot of people," Cooper said. "That's still one of my favorites. Singing chorally with 20, 30, 40 or even 50 people sometimes, there's nothing that matches that sound. That's unique. It can take you places that you've never been, even without the religious aspect. Just the sound of 40 human voices together, I loved it. That's what got me started in music. I was 6 years old when the Beatles hit, so I was a little young to understand what was going on, but I knew it was something big."

While the harmonies were hooking Cooper, the melodies did the same for Piccolo—also native to Oklahoma City.

"My first love of music and playing music came when I was about 14 years old," Piccolo said. "My parents had, in the living room, one of those old console, all-in-one type stereos. And one day, I was there by myself, and I went, 'Better check this out.' Well, in their record collection, there was Buck Owens and the Beatles. I didn't know much about music except what was on top 40 radio. So the first song I played on it was 'Can't Buy Me Love,' and 'You Can't Do That' was the B side on this 45. I heard that, and that just blew me away. The second that first note, that first chord rang out, I said, 'This is what I want to do.'"

That was followed by a realization that Buck Owens sometimes covered the Beatles and that there were no rules saying that music had to be held back by genres or labels. And for Piccolo, that was followed by the need to get a guitar in his hand as fast as possible.

"Right after that, my 15th birthday was coming up, and I started hinting to my parents that I wanted a guitar," he said. "So, turns out, I got to go pick out a 1976, brand-new at the time, Fender Mustang, banana yellow, and a little Peavey amp from this place called Bill's Guitar Shop. I got that and just started listening to records. Instead of 45, I'd put it on 33—slow it down so I could hear the licks. And almost immediately, I started writing my own songs. I thought, If they could do it, I could do it.

"That got me through high school. Then, when I went to OSU from Oklahoma City, I loaded up my '72 Chevelle. This was 1979. I had one bag of clothes and my guitar. I brought it with me. At that time, I had also just gotten an acoustic guitar—I painted some guy's house and he paid me with an acoustic guitar. When I got to Stillwater, that's what I played most. People were playing around campfires, picking on porches. So I started doing that—and drinking beer and going out to watch the people who were there at the time, like Jimmy LaFave and Bob Childers."

Cooper, whose Stillwater pilgrimage you may recall involved showing up with a friend on the tract of land that became The Farm, just west of campus where the roads turned back to dirt, and signing a lease for $100 a month—for everybody—to live there in a farmhouse, did the same thing: He immersed himself in the music around him.

"It was '82, '83 [ish]. I met Piccolo. I had some other friends who came out to The Farm some," Cooper said. "But I didn't really play in the early days. I would just get up and sing. I just knew a lot of songs in those days, it was weird. 'Old Muddy Waters' or old blues or country standards. Then, Piccolo brought me a mandolin."

That little instance—one guy deciding the other one needed to learn an instrument—was the moment that became fate for the Rangers. Cooper plays mandolin in the band to this day.

"I lived with a guy in college named Bob Wiles, the original bass player," Piccolo said. "We bonded over a love of music, and that's when I started bringing back out my electric guitar. Another friend had loaned us some drums. And one night, we were sitting there jamming, and we decided to do a talent show. It was at OSU—Aunt Molly's Rent-Free Music House. It was an open mic, on campus in the student union. So Bob and I signed up for it, and we had become friends with Coop.

"He didn't play anything at the time. But he started tagging along to some of our gigs and we started getting him up to sing, like 'Mannish Boy' by Muddy Waters. So at that talent show, it was me and Wiles and we got Cooper up to sing. And that was the crux. About '82 or so.

"After that, Coop was such a rabid music fan that I had brought to town an old mandolin, a cheap mandolin that my grandmother gave me one year. And I said, 'Man, you're always coming around, you need to learn to play something.' So I showed him three chords on it, and I said, 'Now you know a million songs.'

"He took me up on that. He practices, and almost right after that, we started writing original songs. It didn't take a long time for something to be there with us."

It was another decade before the Rangers began releasing albums—debuting with the now-out-of-print *Cimarron Soul* in 1990—but the groundwork for the band was laid when Red Dirt was more of an unspoken feeling than an understood musical scene.

"Things were building to a head," Cooper said. "There was so much music in Stillwater. The Farm was really going on, and the bars were really going on. Something was bound to come out of it. We came up with our name—it predates the Red Dirt scene, it just sounded good. One of those, 'Let's just call it Red Dirt Rangers.' It just happened.

"People would always ask me, after we got going pretty good, what kind of music did we play, and we'd say, 'We play country-blues-bluegrass-jazz-funk-cajun-Tex-Mex swing.' We just got tired of saying that! So it just became, 'We play Red Dirt music.'"

For the better part of the '90s, there was no music the Rangers wouldn't touch. Wiles, along with Skinner, wrote "Used to Be" about the landmarks along Route 66 in Oklahoma. The Rangers cut it with a heavy twang and treated it like swing. At about that time, they also released "Idabel Blues," with such a heavy blues tempo that it belonged in a Cajun soul dive.

So much so that in 2011, when Cody Canada was picking a Rangers song for *This Is Indian Land*, the debut album for Cody Canada & The Departed, which was filled with Red Dirt covers, he tried and failed to cover "Idabel."

"I really, really wanted to do 'Idabel Blues,'" Canada said in a 2011 interview. "I called Cooper and he was on board. Then I started really listening to it, and I had to call him back and say, 'Man. Uh, we can't do this song because we don't have the soul to pull this off.'"

That is one of the most versatile artists to ever come out of Red Dirt saying he did not have the musical range to pull off one particular Rangers song. (Canada instead covered the Rangers' "Staring Down the Sun," a piano-heavy, gospel-and-jazz-in-fused song about the singer's back being perpetually against the wall with lyrics that paint a decidedly Payne County picture.)

"We really loved Tex-Mex and Cajun music," Cooper said. "At that time, the early 1990s, Doug Sahm was our hero. He was a huge influence on the Red Dirt Rangers. We loved the Texas Tornadoes and that whole Tex-Mex bit. That's why we had two accordion players, rhythm and lead. But we're also doing Woody Guthrie, we're doing Bob Wills' 'Take Me Back to Tulsa.' We're doing Leon Russell and a lot of the Outlaws. Willie and Waylon were also our heroes. But we also loved rock and roll.

"We were just being the mixed bag that the Rangers have always been. I think when it comes to our taste and the music that comes out that we write, nobody else is like us, for better or for worse. We love what we love, and our music reflects that. We never tried to be anything other than what we are. There was no talk of being a Nashville. For us, it was just about making music and being a part of the Red Dirt scene. That's what we wanted to be. We were completely happy and content to be right where we are. I love the place we occupy in our scene."

In that time frame—since officially becoming a band in 1987—the Rangers took that last line to heart, becoming more than mainstays. They turned a post-Thanksgiving party at the Oklahoma City dive bar VZDs into an annual festival that eventually moved to the Will Rogers Theater before morphing into Leftover Turkey, a Jason Boland-led festival at Cain's Ballroom in Tulsa. They founded a similar Christmas show, Red Dirt Christmas, which lasted two-plus decades. They played coast to coast. They played in Europe. They once pulled off a 30-shows-in-30-days tour.

"In June of 1994, the Rangers decide that we're going to do an Oklahoma World Tour: 30 shows in 30 days in the state of Oklahoma," Cooper said. "We had an old-school bus we renovated. We put giant bunks in it. Of course, no air conditioning, but nobody cared. We load this thing up, and off we go, man. We hit little towns and big towns. We go from Kenton in the panhandle—the only town on Mountain Time in Oklahoma—all the way down to Wilburton. Miami down to Hollis. It's the greatest publicity stunt we've ever pulled. We got more press off it than anything we've ever done."

The Kenton gig—actually it took place at Black Mesa, the highest point in Oklahoma—fostered not a fun or particularly grand story by any means, but one that certainly paints a vivid picture of what the band went through at the time.

"We played in Black Mesa," Cooper said. "Some of these shows, we didn't actually have gigs, so we called them campfire shows. We'd go to a campground and play for whoever was there. Usually, there were a few people there, but we go to Black Mesa and there is nobody there. It's just us in the bus, and up comes this ranger. He walks up with a big burly voice and goes, 'Hey. What are you guys doing? What's this school bus?'

"So we go, 'We're just here to camp and play a little music.' And he goes, 'Oh, I don't know about that!' and gives us a really hard time. He doesn't make us leave, but he's really shitty to us.

"Well, we had a friend who worked in tourism in Oklahoma, and we tell him about it. 'Hey, we went out to Black Mesa and this game ranger gave us a really hard time.' My friend asked who it was. I don't recall his name now. Ranger Ed is all I can remember. He says, 'Man, that guy's had a lot of complaints on him. I'm going to look into this.'

"They ended up firing the guy! Our friend told us our performance was the last straw. We felt very vindicated by that."

The tour brought about the press, but it was a specific venue that legitimized the band, and not one in Stillwater.

"VZDs was the first time, and I can remember it vividly, that we all made a hundred dollars apiece," Cooper said. "And I knew I was never gonna work again.

"That was our home. Our rehearsal room was about a mile away from VZDs, so that and Willie's in Stillwater became our home base."

The same asset—versatility—that made the Rangers unique has also helped keep them fresh while contributing to the band's staying power.

"I don't know what our status is as far as a career," Piccolo said. "Once you've played in the same band for 31 years, everything's normal all the time. So I think it's like anything else—clothes, art, fashion, whatever—it's cyclical. It came back around. When it started out, we were real popular because we were the new kids on the block. We had good energy. We weren't that good musically, but come to find out, what's more important musically was heart and soul. And here we are now."

Getting there has entailed both the solid foundation that Cooper, Han and Piccolo bring and the talent of a three-decade rotating cast of Rangers. A very incomplete list of former members or contributors would include Wiles, Randy Crouch, Dave Clark, Charlie Peaden and K.C. Moon (the aforementioned lead and rhythm accordion players), Scot Buxton, Alan Crider, Dale Pierce, Jimmy Karstein and Don Morris.

In 2018, the band recorded a live album, *Blue Door Nights*, at Greg Johnson's venerable listening room in Oklahoma City and featured John Fullbright, Terry "Buffalo" Ware and Rick Gomez—along with Morris and Crouch—sitting in with the band.

These days, the Rangers are seeing a crest in popularity. After the recession of 2008, a lot of longtime venues in Oklahoma closed. VZDs is still around, as is the Colony in Tulsa, but many other places the Rangers played for two decades have shut down, usually replaced on musician calendars with casino gigs that never really suited the band. So they tried to wind down between 2016 and 2018. Cooper, Piccolo and Han all got day jobs and tried to take the band part-time. No sooner than they decided to do that did the phone start ringing again.

"Red Dirt Rangers have been busier and are having better gigs than ever," Cooper said. "It's crazy to wait 30 years and think you're getting out of the music business because we've all got jobs, and all of a sudden here come all these great offers. We're an overnight success story, 30 years in the making."

Part of their current surge stems from the same devil-may-care attitude that led them to get day jobs in the first place. Red Dirt has always been about honesty, and the Rangers always embraced that. But in the current polarized, political climate, the Rangers have become outspoken, almost activist-level in their embrace of Woody Guthrie's spirit. Cooper was nearly banned from hosting a radio show, Red Dirt Radio Hour, on KOSU in Stillwater, after making on-air comments viewed as anti-Trump.

The band outwardly pushes social equality and similar causes that skew progressive, in person and on social media. That has cost them fans but, as it turns out, won over even more.

"Within the last few years, I personally have been hearing this phrase a lot: 'Shut up and sing,'" Piccolo said. "In other words, 'We don't want to hear a musician talk about politics.' Well, for me, the response is, 'Fuck you.'

"I'm going to do what I want, and I'm going to say what I believe. If you don't like it, don't come see us. That's what's great about the Rangers. We've been doing it so long that we're not scared of losing a gig because of free speech. We're keeping it real now. We're fine to say that Donald Trump is an asshole, and if people want to never come see us again, who gives a shit? We're being ourselves now.

"The freedom that comes with doing something for a long time—you're entrenched. Little things don't bother us anymore. We know there'll be another gig. We know that our fans love us, and we love them. We know that if we say something politically, it's gonna piss people off, but in the long run, more people are going to love us because we're keeping it real and saying what's in our hearts."

They also have a heavy respect for what Red Dirt has become, which is much bigger than Stillwater. And they are aware that they played a heavy role in influencing the bands that carried Red Dirt far from Stillwater, all the way to the corners of the earth, where it doubled back on itself. That is all fine and necessary for the scene. But they are also very clear that Oklahoma farmland will always be the ancestral home for the scene and the band that shares its name.

"To me, if you look at it in generations, I would call people like Steve Ripley first generation," Piccolo said. "Then after that, up come LaFave and Childers. That's the second generation. We're the third. And after us, it's guys like Boland and Cross Canadian Ragweed. That's the fourth. Then those guys went and spawned six or seven generations, and now it's Turnpike and what's next. But you can draw the lines, and we're right there in the middle of it."

- 7 -

Garth Brooks and Red Dirt

THERE IS SO much to his story—enough to fill a five-part anthology series he is writing himself and releasing annually—so let's play this straight and to the point.

Garth Brooks, the best-selling solo artist in U.S. history and long-revered as the prodigal son of Stillwater, launched his career into the musical orbit and used Red Dirt as the fuel.

His story is too unique and layered with too much support to credit the scene alone with his rise, and those close to him describe an artist so driven to reach country music's summit that it's almost certain that Garth would have become Garth no matter where his roots lay. But these are the facts, and this is how it played out.

Garth Brooks, his mother a former Capitol Records artist, grew up in Yukon, Oklahoma (the son of Colleen and Raymond Brooks), moved to Stillwater to attend Oklahoma State, and, in the process, picked up a guitar and started playing for anyone who would listen. He developed connections across the community and friendships with fellow students like Ty England, Dale Pierce and the late Jim Kelley—all of whom were integral during his formative years. Early gigs at Shotgun Sam's, a pizza joint in Oklahoma City, and Willie's Saloon on The Strip in Stillwater helped craft a stage persona to reflect his drive. Eventually, that gave Garth the confidence to travel to Nashville in 1985 and give proper country music a try. That trip lasted 23 hours and included a record executive's suggestion he go back to Oklahoma. That's what he did, hiding out in Yukon for a bit before returning to Stillwater for a second stint in the town's music scene.

This time, he formed a band and called it Santa Fe. When it hit its stride, the band consisted of Mike Skinner on fiddle, his brother Tom on bass and vocals, Matt O'Meilia on drums (later replaced by Troy Jones), Jed Lindsay on guitar and Garth on guitar and vocals.

The band became Stillwater heroes, packing old venues like Bink's and the Cimarron Ballroom and later, The Tumbleweed, and in 1987 the entire band moved to Nashville. They had an ally waiting this time around. Bob Childers had moved to Music City to try his own hand as a songwriter. Childers gave Garth and the band a place to crash when they arrived and introduced him to a songwriter named Stephanie Brown. Later, Brown would introduce Garth to Bob Doyle, and Doyle created a publishing company with Garth as his first client.

Santa Fe did not last—Tom Skinner left Nashville for Louisiana and later returned to his hometown of Bristow, Oklahoma, with Mike returning home a short time later—but it had served a purpose, providing the foundation from which Garth went on to become, well, Garth. When an artist can go by his or her first name and have nobody question who's being referenced, that's one indication of how big they are and the style this chapter will use. His world tours being ranked among the highest-grossing in the world in the 1990s and again from 2014 to 2017 (along with his wife, Trisha Yearwood) is another indication, as was his always-sold-out solo acoustic residency at the Wynn Casino in Las Vegas from 2009 to 2014.

His time in Stillwater yielded stories that have themselves almost become cliches. He had a regular gig at Willie's Saloon, met his first wife, Sandy Mahl, while he was a bouncer at the Tumbleweed and famously returned to play both Gallagher-Iba Arena at OSU and the Tumbleweed after he hit his stride. When Tom Skinner died in 2016, most of his obituaries quickly referenced him as a former Garth Brooks bandmate from Santa Fe.

These stories, while easy to tell and easier to turn into myth, do little to explain what it was like for Garth as he was cutting his teeth and even littler to explain the role Red Dirt played. Reducing his time in Stillwater and that of those around him to folklore on the path to stardom overshadows both the influence and fun that was had.

O'Meilia wrote extensively about life in Santa Fe in a 1997 memoir, *Garth Brooks: The Road Out of Santa Fe*, and some of the above context came directly from there. But Garth's story in that book was very much third-person, as he was not able to participate in it.

Garth's ongoing anthology series is also heavily focused on his roots and the people and places from which he learned his trade. But again, his story is much greater than Red Dirt.

At the same time, the years he dabbled in the scene were awfully important to both artist and genre. The story of Red Dirt is not complete without Garth, and his story is missing a major link in the chain without Red Dirt.

So, in September 2018, Garth agreed to reflect on it all—as much as one can in a 20-minute telephone interview—and in doing so he reconciled his time as a Stillwater stage icon with his still-solid perch atop the entire music world.

"The crazy thing is, we came out of retirement to do a deal with Steve Wynn out in Vegas," Garth said. "And my two hours a night, when I'd have buddies come out from home, they'd look at me after those two hours and go, 'This is the same show you did at Willie's.'

"It never changes. It never does. You're built and born with the music that's in you. You might explore new avenues, you might stretch out. But what I did at Shotgun Sam's, what I did at Willie's, what I did at Wynn, what I do every night on stage when it's back to me and a guitar—it's all from Willie's."

That alone is both a heavy and enlightening way to view someone whose stage presence is one of his points of biggest pride. The same presence that landed Entertainer of the Year awards spanning nearly three decades from the Academy of Country Music and Country Music Association is the presence he cultivated on the tiny stage in the middle of The Strip.

"First of all, there have been way too many things in my life that I never planned, so I know that I have higher powers looking over me," he said. "Because, truth is, I played music for girls to start. That's what everybody does—that's why they play music, why they play sports, it's for girls. But doing that, you find the stuff you love. I was lucky enough to be the last of six kids, so my hunger for music and my knowledge of all kinds of music was a huge plus for me.

"And, people may not understand this if they're not from there, but to me, Oklahoma is the land of common sense. You're standing in front of all these people who, you know exactly what they've done all day. You live it, you're there, so you already know what they want to hear. You know what they believe, what they like. And it was easy to play music for them in these dives, when it's just you and a guitar.

"No matter the amount of alcohol that someone might have consumed, for some reason music just disarms people."

That last part is important, because Garth heavily emphasized that same disarming feeling to connect with fans at even his largest concerts.

"One hundred percent. I know what our gig is," he said. "And, our gig is to make everybody in that building just disappear for two hours. Get them away from what's bothering them and let them just sing. Let them have no worries for two hours."

The stage presence is one asset that he carried out of Stillwater. So, too, was the influence of Childers, the Skinners and longtime Red Dirt songwriter Greg Jacobs.

"I am so glad you brought up Jacobs, man. I was going to make sure we didn't get off the phone until we did," Garth said. "Please tell him that I love him and that I have sang Greg Jacobs songs for as long as I can remember. His originals were just fantastic."

"Greg Jacobs was who you wanted to be. He was like Tom Skinner. He was real confident. He wasn't cocky. He was one of the guys who taught you, 'Have a conversation with me. Don't sing to me, don't try to impress me. Just talk to me.' Jacobs was great at that."

Garth described himself as a straight-laced cowboy singer while Red Dirt was full of soul and jazz and blues, and that was infectious. He couldn't help but be influenced by it.

"Let's start with Childers. Childers was more like the guru to all of us because of the age difference [Bob was 10 years older than Garth]. But also because Childers had this Bob Dylan kind of vibe about him," Garth said.

"And one of the greatest lines ever in music history comes from a Childers song—'You're up to your ass in broken glass, and you're still slingin' stones.' It was phenomenal.

"So that's what he had. He was the old guy guru to all of us young kids who went, This is what we want to be."

At that time, Childers was known as the White Buffalo and would play concerts as the White Buffalo Road Show. It ultimately didn't lead to Nashville success, but it made him a Red Dirt legend, and the dabbling in Music City led to that extended hand when Garth made his second move, with Santa Fe.

"He decides to move to Nashville right before we do," Garth said. "So when we get to Nashville, we have a buddy. He lets us sleep at his place while we're looking for a house.

"If Childers is not in Nashville then, Garth Brooks would not be in Nashville today."

But of all the artists who went on to become Red Dirt forefathers, none is more closely associated with Garth than Tom Skinner, the bearded bass player who, along with his brother Mike, brought Rodney Crowell and Guy Clark influences to Santa Fe.

"It's hard to say Tom Skinner without the Skinner Brothers," Garth said, "because I think they as brothers were even bigger than Tom, but Tom was the leader.

"Gosh, talk about talented and witty and quick on stage, and he could play any instrument. And Tom is another reason why—I wouldn't be in Nashville if it weren't for him."

There was also a time in Stillwater, strange as it seems today, when Garth was the one who wanted to play the Skinner Brothers.

"Dale Pierce, a buddy of mine who was a banjo player, got me and Tom together. He said, 'You and the Skinner Brothers need to get together and see what you can do,' and I said, 'Whoa. The Skinner Brothers are huge.' I'm just a guy with a guitar in Stillwater at this point.

"So we sit at a table, and Tom Skinner, the first thing he says to me is, 'Let's put a band together.' Instead of interviewing me, instead of asking me questions. And I was just like, 'Oh shit, really?' and it just made me feel so good and so welcome. And we really jumped on it."

That's how Santa Fe began. Tom Skinner, Lindsay and O'Meilia—who joined a country band for the first time in his life after his punk metal band, Tons and Tons of Hair, broke up—joined Garth initially, later joined by Pierce and Mike Skinner. Ultimately, Pierce did not move to Nashville with Santa Fe, and neither did O'Meilia, who was replaced by Jones.

"Jed, Mike, Tom, myself and Troy, that's the group that moved to Nashville," Garth said. "That's the reason I'm standing here today."

That support system showed off the same backbone of Red Dirt that allowed it to take off like wildfire across the country in the 2000s. Artists helped artists and backed them up. And for Garth, between his first and second trips to Nashville, Red Dirt did the same for him.

"This is a great thing, and you're going to get this one hundred percent—everything that is a blessing is a curse, and everything that is a curse is a blessing," Garth said. "So Stillwater never changes. And that can be a blessing or a curse, however you look at it. For me, it was a blessing. How they treated me was exactly how Stillwater treated Mike McClure, how they treated Jacobs. They're always there—always there for you.

"They scrambled together some money to send me the first time to Nashville. I stayed here for 23 hours, moved back home and hid out at my folks' house for a couple of weeks, because I was just too embarrassed to face them.

"And the first person I faced in Stillwater when I told them, 'I just got scared and came home,' the first words out of that person's mouth were, 'You're goin' back, aren't you?'

"This is the kind of people that they are. They're just always pushing you and always pulling for you. And I think that's why Stillwater has to be the manufacturer of a lot of great 'product' that they send out to the world in all areas of life. The who's who at Oklahoma State is pretty cool."

The aftermath is a story that can be told in several ways. Childers and Tom Skinner ultimately returned to Oklahoma and mentored an entire next generation of artists, including McClure and The Great Divide, Cody Canada, Jason Boland and Stoney LaRue. Truthfully, they both deserved more fame, money or esteem than they lived their lives with. But on the other hand, they both died—Childers in 2008 and Skinner eight years later—having molded Red Dirt into a way of life that carries on far beyond Stillwater today.

At the same time, Garth did not abandon the scene after he shot up country music's ladder. He was instrumental in bringing McClure and The Divide to Nashville in the early 1990s, where they eventually landed an Atlantic Records deal. He later put McClure's "Rather Have Nothin'" on a box set he released in 2005. And tangentially, he introduced mainstream country music to the late Chris LeDoux, who went on to headline the Tumbleweed's Calf Fry along with The Divide, right up until his health declined in the early 2000s. It was the highlight of the Red Dirt calendar for several years.

So how does he view his relationship to Red Dirt in a career that is objectively historic in music terms?

"Red Dirt was too cool for me. When you're seriously white, you can't be soulful. So Red Dirt was cool, and I wasn't. This isn't a statement of humbleness. It's honesty: I've never been cool," Garth said.

"But I gotta tell you, at the very heart of Garth Brooks' music—take the first single, 'Much Too Young (to Feel This Damn Old).' That grew from Red Dirt music.

"For me, the most important thing is, I don't care if people remember the artist. If they remember the music, that's the important thing. And if you strip that music all the way down to the very seed of it, it's Red Dirt music.

"But I didn't know that. It's just what I called growing up in Oklahoma. But that is Red Dirt music. It's just a common-sense, raw kind of dirt-tasting, soil-tasting truth or honesty that you feel as somebody growing up in Oklahoma."

— — —

- 8 -

The Divide

FEW CHAPTERS IN Red Dirt history are as important as The Great Divide's.

For nearly a decade, few chapters in Red Dirt history were as unfair as The Great Divide's.

Important because the band blazed the path out of Stillwater that artists still follow to this day, and unfair because already multiple generations have come and gone without realizing the significance of the four-piece Red Dirt ensemble. There are musicians playing tonight in some town like San Angelo who are marketing their show as Red Dirt—a label that can instantly multiply attendance by factors of two, three or ten—without realizing that the rock they're leaning on was placed there with the blood and sweat of The Great Divide. Important because they did it all their way, and unfair because they are not selling out 200 amphitheaters a year today.

The Divide was as popular as Cross Canadian Ragweed. From the time the band put out its Atlantic Records debut in 1998—*Break in the Storm*—until 2002, the band toured sold-out dance halls from Lincoln, Nebraska, to Corpus Christi, Texas. The Divide headlined its own Independence Day bash at City Limits in Stephenville, Texas, the first Red Dirt music festival to gain a foothold in the Lone Star State, with crowds that rivaled Pat Green's and Robert Earl Keen's. They matched it in Stillwater at the Tumbleweed Dance Hall with an outdoor, back-to-school festival called College Days.

The Divide was as musically tight as the Turnpike Troubadours. At heart, they were a four-piece—Mike McClure on lead vocals and lead guitar, Kelley Green on bass, and brothers Scotte and J.J. Lester on rhythm guitar and drums, respectively—but they had no problem adding keyboards, slide guitars or fiddle to their live shows, and they often did. They had no problem giving a young Cody Canada a trial run before sending him off to form Ragweed. They could give covers of Joe Ely or Van

Morrison a one-off feel that differed from the songs' creators and they could change their originals on the fly so their live music provided completely different experiences than their album cuts.

The Divide was as influential as Tom Skinner, Bob Childers and the Red Dirt Rangers. It is not hard to argue that, were it not for the band giving prime opening spots to Ragweed, Jason Boland and the Stragglers and Stoney LaRue, those careers would not have launched with the pace they did in the late 1990s and early 2000s. The band's Stillwater anthem, "College Days," remains an icon in the college town the way the Rangers' "Used to Be" remains an icon along Route 66. The Divide also laid bare the bridge between Red Dirt and gospel music—both with original songs like "Mr. Devil" and "Outlaw's Prayer" and with an entire album, the 1999 Red Dirt compilation *Dirt and Spirit*.

The Divide, really, ended up being the closest thing to a Red Dirt nutshell that ever existed. The clever lyrics of the Stragglers and the range of LaRue were both matched by The Divide. For a band that fell decidedly on the country side of the Red Dirt spectrum, it was nothing to see them sing blues like Jimmy LaFave or folk like Bob Childers.

In truth, it was not until Ragweed and Turnpike smashed the ceiling that The Divide had only cracked and made Oklahoma music cool from coast to coast circa 2011 that a band came out of the Red Dirt scene without drawing a constant comparison to The Divide. Even then, Turnpike itself happily draws them unprompted.

"At some point, I think everybody in our band had either a punk rock band or a heavy metal band or something in between as a background," said Turnpike bass player and cofounder R.C. Edwards. "The Great Divide, and Ragweed and Jason Boland, made it cool to play country music when you were young. You know, when you're a teenager, there's a whole deal where country music isn't cool sometimes. They made it cool.

"And that made me want to learn about their influences. That's how I learned about Robert Earl Keen, about Todd Snider, about Guy Clark and Townes Van Zandt and John Prine. They sent us down that rabbit hole."

They did it all, almost by accident.

● ● ●

Simple Origins

The Lester brothers and Green started the band long before they met McClure in Stillwater.

J.J. and his two brothers (Scotte, the oldest, and Dean, the middle brother, who never pursued music) grew up in a trailer house, in the front yard of his grandparents' farm in Payne County, near Stillwater and Perkins, and learned music from them starting just about at the time he could walk.

"My grandparents would play rodeo dances and stuff, and it was all 'Oklahoma Hills' and Roy Rogers and Gene Autry," J.J. Lester said. "Cowboy stuff. So when we were little kids, of course they had a TV, but it was one channel if you were lucky. From the time I was about 4, so that's what they did.

"I thought that's what everybody did. I thought, on Friday or Saturday night, everyone's neighbors came over and they sat around and played music."

J.J. played drums in some classic rock cover bands after high school but gave it up, found a "real" job and got married in 1991. By 1992, he had settled in Stillwater and had a job with Causley Productions—a local sporting goods shop with an owner, James Causley, who was a fan of the era's Red Dirt artists.

"Beginning of the summer of '92, I was having lunch with Scotte," J.J. said. "At a New York Bagel Co., down the street from Causley's. And Scotte was at the fire department and had been for about 10 years. As we were walking to the bagel shop, we ran into Scotte's friend. And as we were catching up, Scotte asked him what he's doing.

"He says, 'I'm putting a band together, and I'm looking for a rhythm guitar player and drummer.' And immediately, Scotte goes, 'I can play guitar and my brother's a drummer,' and looks right at me.

"So I get home that night, and I tell my wife, 'I'm going to go out and play some drums with Scotte and this friend of his,' and she looks right at me and says, 'What are you talking about? You don't know how to play drums!'"

Lester's wife, Tommie Lee, quickly got up to speed on his talents.

"Well, it was terrible," J.J. said. "We were in this guy's garage and I was rusty. But my old roommate had come out to drink beer—that's just what you do. And after we played, he said, 'This guy just moved in next door to me, and he plays guitar and he has written some pretty good songs. Maybe you should check him out.'

"That was Mike McClure."

McClure, at the time a college-aged kid who had also grown up rural—in Tecumseh, Oklahoma, and heavily influenced by the rock bands of the 1980s—picks the story up from there.

"When I first moved to Stillwater, I was trying to find a house," McClure said. "And I stopped at this apartment, and the manager goes, 'Do you like Pink Floyd?' and I said, 'Yeah, why?' And he goes, 'Well, there's a mural on one of the walls in there of Pink Floyd. I'll leave it up if you want it.' So that's the reason I rented the apartment. And that day, someone painted over the mural. And then the wind shifted, and the smell from a swine barn blew right in my bedroom window. I was probably a thousand yards from a swine barn.

"So I was sitting on my balcony one day. I had a balcony! Nice! And this guy lived next door to me and heard me playing—Donnie Pitchford. And he says, 'I got these buddies, and they need a guitar player.' It was the same Great Divide guys, and they had a singer already. So I took my PA over, and we jammed a bit. And after the first few songs, ol' Scotte Lester looks over with his cowboy eyes and goes, 'You're too loud.'

"So I went, 'Alright. See ya.'

"But after that, I was into writing. So I wrote some songs, and I wanted to record them. So I called J.J. [Lester]. And he and I went to Oklahoma City and made a cassette. That was the start of it. That cassette kind of got kicked around among my friends and their friends, and we decided that I'd try to do those songs with their band. That's how it got started."

The original plan was never to become a performing band. J.J. Lester fell in love with McClure's songwriting and decided they would start a publishing company and demo and sell those songs.

"Yeah, in our infinite wisdom, we decide that," J.J. said. "We're going to start Riverbend Publishing. We even had cards made. And Mike and I are gonna go record these demos.

"At that time, Scotte and Kelley Green are playing in a band called Brush Creek. So we ask them to play with us. With two more guys, we can record more for less money. Smart business, right? We can do all four at once. So we all had this meeting, and I remember specifically saying, 'We're not doing gigs. We're going to write songs. We're going to get them published. George Strait's going to record us, and we're going to save country music.'

"Well, I had a cousin in Perry, Oklahoma. He used to have this Labor Day team-roping event that was huge. It would get more than 100 entries. And he said, 'You guys should come over and play my rodeo.'

"We get there, with our one monitor and our one microphone, and we play our 12 songs to a bunch of drunk cowboys. And after every song, this one guy would yell for 'Sweet Home Alabama.' Well, Mike blew him off and blew him off. But after the last song, he asks, for the 12th time, 'Sweet Home Alabama'!

"Mike gets halfway through 'We don't kno-' and the guy says, 'I got 20 bucks!'

"Well, yeah now we're gonna play 'Sweet Home Alabama.'

"Afterward, we loaded up our stuff, and my cousin came over and said, 'We passed the hat, and you guys made 81 bucks tonight.' And I'll never forget all of us looking at each other, like, we can do this? It never occurred to us that you could actually get paid for playing gigs. And from that point on, we were gonna play gigs."

• • •

Red Dirt's First Superstars

From that formation in 1993, The Divide cultivated a catalog of originals and Red Dirt covers. They put Bob Childers' "Wile E. Coyote" and Tom Skinner's cowrite with Bob Wiles, "Used to Be," on major-label albums. They used support from established Okie artists ranging from Garth Brooks to Gary P. Nunn as a springboard into the state's music conscience.

Their debut album, 1994's *Goin' for Broke*, featured a road trip song called "Alive and Well" that liberally referenced Austin and landed on jukeboxes across Texas.

A following emerged in Stillwater, and the band found an early home in the Wormy Dog Saloon, which had opened on Washington Street the same year The Divide was formed. Word spread, and soon, Amarillo, Lubbock and Stephenville, Texas, all had pockets of Divide diehards. The size of the sudden bases was matched only by the speed at which they formed.

J.J. Lester's favorite example of winning over an entire city instantly is Lincoln, Nebraska, after the band released "Never Could," the first single from a sophomore album called *Break in the Storm*.

"We finally got booked up there," J.J. said. "We hadn't put out the second record yet, and we played this little boot-scooterie, so to speak. And they hated us. I think there were 100 people there, and they were all asking for Brooks & Dunn. Just, 'We want something we can line dance to!' all night. Well, no. Go away. We're not playing that. And we left saying we'd never be back.

"That year, we started playing Calf Fry [the annual music festival at the end of the school year at Stillwater's Tumbleweed Dance Hall] with Chris LeDoux, and we got really close with his band. After Calf Fry, LeDoux's band and merch guy were at a gig in Kansas City, listening to our record on the bus. And this radio deejay from Lincoln had come down to watch their show. He's on the bus while they're playing us, and he goes, 'Who *is* this?' Clay LeDoux tells him who we are and gives him a copy of our CD. And he goes back to Lincoln and starts spinning 'Never Could.'

"Within a month, we were the top-selling album, in all genres of music, in Lincoln, Nebraska. I remember record stores calling us, and we're thinking, 'Lincoln? They hate us in Lincoln! We suck!' and they're asking us to send them every record we possibly can. Almost a year to the day after the first gig, we went back up there to a sold-out show. It was crazy."

Latching on to its popularity, Atlantic Records picked up The Divide. Two albums came of it: a label release of *Break in the Storm* followed by *Revolutions*. The first album included "Pour Me a Vacation," a tropical hit that hit 59 on the U.S. country charts, a big deal at the time. But it also shifted the definition of success.

"We fell so hard, like a cult, in the belief that what we were doing was right," J.J. said. "We never questioned it. We would have conversations like this: 'Do you think, in 30 years, people will still listen to our records?' That was more important to us than radio play or sales.

"We wanted to make great art."

According to Lester, the last hump—building enough of a fan base to give the band members time away from the road, to spend at home or with family—was the one that never came.

"When we signed with Atlantic, what we wanted was to get big enough to where we could play festivals, we could play arenas and then we could take six months off. And that's what never happened. We figured it out, between 1997 and 2000, we were playing 300 shows a year, not including going into the studio. Just doing gigs.

"You want the answer to: What is Red Dirt? I played with a broken foot. My brother played with a broken hand. We did the gig. Doesn't matter. Mike can't sing, he's got laryngitis? Who cares, we're doing the gig. The wheat has to be cut, the harvest has to be made. We're playing tonight."

The dedication to concerts eventually led to the most important inroads Red Dirt ever made into the then-separate notion of Texas music.

• • •

Texas Barnstormers

Mattson Rainer is the general manager of KNBT-FM in New Braunfels, nationally known for its Americana format and one of the most important stations in Texas music. Rainer's previous stops had been in Boulder, Colorado, and Connecticut, before arriving at the station in 1993. At the time, Rainer's musical tastes were shaped by New York City and Boulder. Rainer refers to his tastes as hippie and is a Grateful Dead diehard. His tastes were not in step with KNBT's top 40 country format, and within five years, Rainer would switch the style, focusing KNBT on Texas-based artists and original music.

"I just felt like Garth Brooks was getting enough radio airplay and didn't really need us," Rainer explained. "I was an old Deadhead, so I understood the concept of bands connecting with their fans. I saw that with Robert Earl Keen, and it was a similar feel to how I used to feel when I'd go to a Dead show. I just thought, *This guy. This is the kind of thing that I want to be doing.*

"These fans are loyal. They follow them around. They know all the words. That's what I want to do."

In October 1998, New Braunfels and the surrounding Hill Country was hit by a major flood. Damage estimates came in at $500 million, and 25 people died. In the wake, Rainer and KNBT organized a series of flood benefit concerts at Saengerhalle, a now-defunct dance hall that at the time rivaled Gruene Hall in size and stature among bands looking for big weekend gigs between Austin and San Antonio. Shortly before those benefits, Rainer had befriended Great Divide members at an Americana conference in Lake Tahoe. So he called up J.J. Lester.

"I said, 'What are you doing in early December?'" Rainer said. "He said they were working on a new album at Cedar Creek Studio in Austin with Lloyd Maines. It would have been *Revolutions*. So he says, 'We can come down on a Sunday and do a little show for you.'

"The Great Divide came down, and the bar owner at Saengerhalle fell in love with them. So he asks them, 'Why don't you guys come back and do an actual real show?' They did, and when they booked them the second time, The Great Divide brought Ragweed with them to be openers.

"From that point, Ragweed went from opening for The Great Divide to headlining at Saengerhalle. And Cody and Shannon [Canada] kind of fell in love with New Braunfels. And then, eventually, Randy Rogers, Wade Bowen, Stoney LaRue and Jason Boland all follow suit.

"But that's the way it started—The Great Divide did a show for us in '98. They came back with Ragweed as their opener. The rest is history."

The Divide was an early headliner at the KNBT Americana Jam, an annual May festival the station has put on since 1997, and their popularity at Saengerhalle helped spark a rush on music venues in the city. Today, New Braunfels is the thriving hub of Texas music, with venues as small as coffee shops and as large as Whitewater Amphitheater, which holds upwards of 5,000 fans. Rainer says, without The Divide (and its paving the way for Ragweed), that musical movement in New Braunfels may never have happened, certainly not in the manner it has played out.

● ● ●

Independence and Unraveling

After the second Atlantic album, McClure took the view that the music was a success, in no need of repair. The rest of the band saw a chance to get over that last hump, and their accompanying time off. Reaching that level would require cleaning up the sound to fit what radio and record companies wanted.

That impasse and an indulgence in the party scene eventually wore on the band.

"It was a little bit hypocritical," J.J. said. "Because we felt very responsible to our audience. We wanted to give them what we thought was the best. But at the same time, that did not hinder any of us from drinking too much or smoking too much or sniffing too much. Whatever *it* was, we did too much.

"There's no 'probably' about it. That was part of the downfall of The Great Divide."

The downfall could also be chalked up to pure, dumb, bad luck. Atlantic's country music label—booming for most of the 1980s and 1990s as country music expanded its footprint—was in the process of going under, just as The Divide hit its highest stride. Atlantic would close its Nashville offices for good in 2001 in a wave of label closings and consolidations.

This contributed to strange friction for the band in summer 1999 at the annual Country Radio Seminar in Nashville, just after *Revolutions* had been released.

"There was a thing during CRS called CMA New Faces." J.J. Lester said. "It was very elite. You were chosen to be put in front of the top 200 program directors. And you were expected to be the future of country radio. We got selected.

"It was us, the Dixie Chicks and Allison Moorer. And, we killed it. We only played two songs, and we *killed* it! We walk off stage, and the Atlantic Records national airplay representative comes backstage and tells us, 'Home run. We're going to have a number one song in two months. It's done. You just got over the hump.' High fives all around. We're awesome. This is great."

The next morning, that tone changed 180 degrees. J.J. Lester got a call from the band's manager—who had fielded a call from the same Atlantic representative saying, essentially, *never mind.* The representative had been told that McClure went to an afterparty and verbally trashed country music and Nashville—which McClure asserts did not happen. No other stories or evidence ever surfaced to corroborate or even lend credence to the initial accusation, but it was still made. Moreover, in the heat of the moment, when the band first heard about it, McClure was not present to weigh in at all.

"By then, that same representative of Atlantic's national radio promotion had been informed of this party, and he had called our manager and said, 'It's over. You just killed what you accomplished last night.' That was my first realization that we're not getting over the hump."

The incident was more strange than it was a crisis, but it coincided with the larger turmoils at the label and the industry, and the band did not get the support for its second album that Atlantic put into its first.

Revolutions was a regional hit, with or without a boost from CRS. "College Days," an album cut, became a cult favorite in every college town The Divide played. It was filled with references to Stillwater (*I wonder who's playing down on The Strip tonight,* for one) but its refrain of *If you're goin' downtown to the liquor store, bring me a bottle of wine* radiated from tailgates and backyard barbecues across college campuses in Oklahoma and Texas throughout the early 2000s.

The group, however, saw no point in going forward with the label.

"We exercised a right in our contract to leave Atlantic if they had been inactive on our behalf," J.J. said.

When they left that contract, they found an independent Nashville label, Broken Bow Records, and released *Afterglow*—recorded at Oklahoma City's Will Rogers Theater and including a video with the first single, "Out of Here Tonight"—in 2001.

The band was still playing sold-out shows across the Midwest. It headlined two major festivals: The Great Divide's Independence Day Jam at City Limits in Stephenville and College Days at Tumbleweed in Stillwater.

The latter, conceived after LeDoux's liver cancer ended a long stretch of The Divide and LeDoux closing out the Tumbleweed's Calf Fry, was a multiday, outdoor event in August that had the distinction of being the first large-scale Red Dirt festival, as the Tumbleweed's outdoor arena had a capacity upward of 5,000.

Losing Atlantic had not ended the band, thanks to a Plan B built around its core fan base in Texas and Oklahoma. But, its aftermath and a return to an independent label opened enough personality and philosophical differences that McClure became pitted against his mates, and at least one—J.J. Lester—dug his heels in.

"I panicked," J.J. said. "And when I did, instead of going, 'Let's have a talk. If we actually accomplished this, how are we going to get to Plan C?'

"Instead, when things got really bad, I called Scotte and Kelley, and I called our manager, and I said, 'I'm done,'" J.J. said. "This was coming off the end of *Afterglow.*

And I just said, 'I'm not doing this.'"

Lester did not leave, though. In 2002, the band released the truly independent *Remain*, with no label backing. It also brought McClure's concurrent solo debut album, *12 Pieces*.

What McClure had seen as a jumping-off point to share a different style of music from The Divide—more rock and blues and less country—succeeded at showing him an exit door.

"When we decided to call it quits, we had a case of another producer trying to 'polish up' our stuff," McClure said. "And I get polish, and it's necessary sometimes, but sometimes it's not. And I think the magic thing about our records was the fluctuation. You know, we weren't that great, but we'd go out and play bars, and it would just work."

In late 2002, that magic dried up. McClure announced he was leaving.

He gave six months' notice.

"I was a dick," McClure said.

The time frame was long enough for the normal stress of the road and band expectations to boil over into bad blood as the curtain came down.

"Six months of riding around on a tour bus with people that were pissed off at me," he said. "I'll never do that again, and I wouldn't advise it. We put in 10 years, and I didn't want to leave them high and dry.

"But it got ugly."

The band's farewell show was in 2003 inside the Tumbleweed in Stillwater. They ripped the soundboard audio to a pair of CDs: *Absolutely Live at Tumbleweed, Vols. 1 and 2*, marking the only live albums the band ever released.

The concert was sold out and possibly well above capacity. Usually, when a venue is sold out, you can still elbow and move through the crowd, maybe to the bathroom or to get beer. And you can usually elbow and move your way back. On the night of the final Divide show, such movement was impossible. After that: nothing.

The Great Divide and McClure split—abruptly, even by breakup standards.

"People were pissed off," McClure said. "But I remember whining to Ray Wylie Hubbard, and he goes, 'Hey man...The Beatles broke up.' That kind of *reeeally* fucking cleared some air for me. That was pretty sage advice."

In the heat of the breakup, the plan was for everybody to go their own way—McClure would keep on jamming as a solo artist and the other three would sell their instruments and start new chapters in life.

Instead, the rest of The Great Divide kept playing. For four more years, they picked up a new lead singer—an Ohioan named Micah Aills—and toured the Midwest relentlessly. They packed the Oklahoma City incarnation of the Wormy Dog Saloon regularly. They drew fans in Stephenville. They carried on. The band's website boasted that Aills was "no prima donna."

"We all had a lot invested in The Divide when we split up," J.J. Lester said. "I lost the house I had built. I had to move to a duplex. To this day, I'm still digging out.

"We kept it up with Micah, God love him, until we had paid back enough of what we had invested in the last Divide album that we could be done. Then, we were done."

McClure's first album that was completely free from the band, 2004's *Everything Upside Down*, was a 19-song musical divorce. The most biting number, "Just Not Good Enough," flat-out features the line "I gave you nothing but my best" before launching into a chorus of *Was it just not good enough for you?* repeated in a near rage.

• • •

Redemption

Pretending things ended well for The Great Divide at that moment is pointless. But after the breakup, months turned to years. Time did its thing.

McClure's writing remained deeply personal but by his follow-up, *Camelot Falling* in 2005, the undertones of contempt were gone. By *Did7* in 2008, McClure was bent toward love songs. The Divide played with Aills until 2007. J.J. Lester continued producing—notably for the Eli Young Band and No Justice—and became a pastor. Scotte Lester ended up being a company owner and a rancher, and Kelley Green became an AutoCAD technician. Finally, The Great Divide had its sunset.

The difference for this band, though, was that the sun rose again. It didn't rise as high, but from some certain angles, it shined brighter.

Backing up for a moment. The Divide's members were always driven by faith, regardless of how they lived. They routinely played gospel songs at shows and on albums, including the popular "Mr. Devil," which made it onto *Revolutions*.

They also funded and produced a Red Dirt gospel compilation album, *Dirt and Spirit*—viewed in the scene as a sequel to *The Red Dirt Sampler*—in 1999 and featured Childers and Skinner as well as Cross Canadian Ragweed and a very young Jason Boland and Stoney LaRue. More than 20 years later, LaRue still plays his contribution to the album, Skinner's *Blind Man*, regularly during his shows. All of this is to say, sour ending or not, being men of faith means being willing to forgive.

"It really hurt. It hurt more than anything," J.J. said. "But I'm a big boy. I can take some punches, and after about four or five years after Mike left, Scotte asked me if I'd be interested in a reunion show. I said no way.

"I wasn't ready. I had been made to be the villain in the breakup, and all my old friends who had supported me were all Mike's friends. They say Red Dirt is a family, I know you're going to say it in this book. But that's bullshit. It's not a family. It's just like any other thing, when bands break up, people pick sides."

But, in 2010, Scotte tried again.

"Scotte calls me and asks if I'd do a reunion show," J.J. said. "And this time, he says, 'Before you say no, I want you to know that Mike has made some changes.' And I'm like, 'Look man, if Mike wants to call me and come face to face, I'll consider it.'"

This time, J.J. heard him out. He wasn't thinking only of himself but of his wife, their daughter, Halle Jae, and their son, Jevyn Thomas.

"After that phone call, I thought about what I said, and this is what I did: I took a sheet of paper, I drew a line down the middle and on one side, I wrote all the ways I felt like Mike had wronged me. And on the other side, I wrote down all the ways that I sin against God every day.

"Mike's list wasn't very long. *My* list was really long.

"How can I not forgive him and reconcile with him when God forgives me daily? How can I not do it? What does that say about me, when I'm saying what I believe and then I refuse to do it because I'm angry?"

They laid it all on the table in 2010 when all four met up at a coffee shop in Stillwater—actually sat down for the first time since the initial breakup—and as McClure put it on social media at the time, "All it took was one gut laugh to cut through eight years of tension."

J.J. recalls the meeting directly: "Mike said, 'I'm sorry. I didn't handle some things well,' and I said, 'I'd love to reconcile.' Will we ever play a note of music again? I didn't know, but let's reconcile. Let's not hate."

McClure recalls it the same way: "That was getting back to why we were in it in the first place. Not trying to figure out how the machine works, just gettin' in it and *being* the machine."

Wounds healed some more a year later when the band played a true reunion concert at Tumbleweed. It was 2011, and during that Tumbleweed show, McClure kicked off *Pour Me a Vacation* by announcing, "This is gonna suck!" and was met with a thunderous ovation.

Scars faded in 2018, when the band played a summer full of 25th anniversary gigs, capped by an outdoor concert at Eskimo Joe's in Stillwater to a crowd that, save the grayer hair and earlier bedtimes, could have been mistaken for one celebrating the *Revolutions* release back in '99.

The Great Divide never got over that hump. But it did get its breakthrough.

For the band, one day, on the other side of itself—through its own looking glass, the band found peace. They toured only sporadically, while its members all worked day jobs.

"It goes back to what we wanted to do in the first place," J.J. said. "Well, here we are, 25 years later, and people are still singing along.

"Maybe we did do it right. Maybe we did deservedly achieve what we wanted to do in the first place, which was to make great art."

Individually, they all are some distance from the unbroken spirits who wasted away in Stephenville two decades prior. And that's true to enough of a segment of the band's heyday fans to relegate them to relics of Red Dirt's past.

But in Oklahoma, poetry always surrounds. It's why the scene existed in the first place. In the cracked sidewalks and potholed highways, in the overhunted bottomlands where deer always return and the overfished lakes where largemouth bass still spawn, in the cotton fields converted into Indian casinos and in the college-town strip malls converted into Indian casinos, there is always evidence of the past and hope for renewal.

The final song The Divide sang back at the Tumbleweed in 2003 was "Floods"—more than anything a song about fear and doubt pushing a person, or an entire band, to their breaking point. They inundate a mind and soul the way floodwaters can, and occasionally have, reclaimed Oklahoma from the ancestors of its settlers. But "Floods" actually concerns a narrator carried by faith. The refrain, "Let the water take me higher," is a statement of faith—a prayer for triumph.

Time's own floodwaters have carried The Great Divide far from its roots, but they also found a way to replant them.

Since reuniting, the band has done exactly that—gone longer through the looking glass than it held together in its first incarnation. Today, The Great Divide shows up at gigs and shares its art. Attendance, merch sales, paychecks and music charts play out in the background.

"It's easy to lose that scope of why you're there in the first place," McClure said, "which is what I really enjoy about playing with The Great Divide now: It doesn't fucking matter. That's not our sole source of income. It's us getting together and playing our songs, which is the way it was in the beginning.

"That's the magic, the impetus and the spark of all of it."

- 9 -

Cody Canada
and Cross Canadian Ragweed

"IT WAS LIKE a drug," Cody Canada said.

"It made me want to just do more and more."

Ah, yes. That classic rock-and-roll cliche. The thing is, someone would need a pretty compelling reason to kick off the story of Cody Canada and Cross Canadian Ragweed with it.

Sure, a good crowd fits the metaphor (Ragweed had those).

So does a veritable catalog of music that defines a genre for a generation (Ragweed had it). Hell, actual drugs do that too (Ragweed? Again, yes). Generally, everything about being the gold standard for Red Dirt music and for Texas music, back when those two were not considered the same thing, is like a drug, almost by definition, if not by practice. The phrase could fit so much.

But that's never been how Canada thinks.

Artists are complex creatures—driven by fame, spite, sex, demons, love, money, fear, passion and permanent residence atop a pedestal.

Canada may be complex, too, but part of it is chalked up to his simplicity.

Through the arc of Cross Canadian Ragweed, fronted by Canada and flanked by Jeremy Plato on bass guitar, Randy Ragsdale on drums and Grady Cross on rhythm guitar, Canada got an up-close look at all those driving forces. Some got a closer look than others, but none of them stuck to him.

From riding the wave of The Great Divide to breaking through at Larry Joe Taylor's annual festival to crowds that could drink any venue up to and including Billy Bob's Texas completely out of beer to the most outwardly stunning band breakup in Red Dirt history, Canada took it all in.

"It was like a drug."

Here is the kicker, though. Canada was reflecting on the first time he looked down at a setlist made up of nothing but Ragweed songs.

This is the story of a garage band that caught fire.

• • •

Beginnings

It is really easy and really inaccurate to cast Yukon as some kind of prodigal Red Dirt town when in reality, Garth Brooks happened to live there, and later, Cross Canadian Ragweed happened to live there. Yukon is the suburb that keeps the wheat fields to the west from enveloping Oklahoma City. The state's sprawling capital and largest city sits immediately to the east of Yukon, permanently instilling an identity crisis in its 22,000 residents. It's as much a bedroom suburb as it is a gateway to waving wheat and oil fields—too close to The City to be its own small town while fiercely fighting that notion at all times. Yukon is designed to keep people in, and it's a wonder that anybody who turned to music saw a path out.

For a 15-year-old Cody Canada, a relic theater in Oklahoma City's Capitol Hill district less than 10 miles from Yukon was the first glance at a life away from the burb. Originally from Pampa, Texas, and raised in a broken home, it's fairest to say he had simply been planted in Yukon during his teenage years.

"I was 15 and a half, playing the Oklahoma Opry. I really don't even know how I got there. It was basically *America's Got Talent* in Oklahoma City. They wouldn't let me play during school hours. They made me wait until evenings. My grades were so bad, I don't even know why it mattered. I met Dave Dodson, a DJ, there one night. He asked me what I was doing and why I was playing cover songs. He said, 'This doesn't really seem like you,' and I told him that I didn't really know what 'me' is. And he said, 'Well, if you need any help, I'm here.'

"Fast-forward a year. I got a fake ID, and I saw him at Incahoots [Oklahoma City's best-known country dance hall]. He told me not to tell anybody that I saw him there, because he wasn't supposed to be partying. I wasn't going to say anything because I wasn't even 17 years old yet. He said, 'I'd like to take you to Stillwater to introduce you to this band called The Great Divide.'

"I had never heard of them."

Turned out, The Great Divide, itself just a fledgling band, yet to make its 1996 breakthrough album, *Break in the Storm*, was in the market for a guitar player. Canada got and nailed an audition. He joined up with Mike McClure, J.J. and Scotte Lester and Kelley Green.

"So I played with them for a few months, working at a western-wear store on the side, with McClure telling me the whole time that this whole cowboy thing wasn't my gig," Canada said. "They took me on the road with them. We went to Larry Joe's sixth annual festival in Possum Kingdom. That was my introduction. I met Rusty Weir, Gary P. Nunn and Larry Joe Taylor—all these people who I had only slightly heard of."

That introduction ended up being the primary benefit of Canada's nailing his audition. After a roughly three-month stint, The Divide voted 3 to 1 to boot Canada, with McClure the one.

"They said, 'We're not kicking you out because we don't like you. We're kicking you out because you need to do your own thing.' Mike didn't like it, but he was outvoted.

"So I said, 'Well, I'm gonna go home. I know this guy that's been bugging the crap out of me to start a band.'"

So circa 1994, Canada and Randy Ragsdale started a band.

Teenagers to a man, they nabbed Cross, along with bass player Matt Weidemann—all friends since elementary school—mashed up their last names and called themselves Cross Canadian Ragweed.

"We practiced for seven months, seven days a week, busting our asses," Canada said. "We were all working, too. This was all after work."

Ragsdale came from a musical family, and his father, Johnny C. Ragsdale, proved to be the enabler, allowing the band to practice in the family room, up to and including in front of the TV during the Super Bowl.

There were also several trips to Stillwater. They didn't make the drive to play, though. Rather, they would drive up to watch The Divide practice. They were young, and Canada wanted to take it in.

"I wasn't a very patient person. I wanted a gig," Canada said. "They invited us up to The Underdog [the Wormy Dog Saloon's downstairs 18-and-over outpost] to watch them practice. Well, Mike showed us something then: When the band's jamming and it's loud, you come down from that and you play softer and sing. That's dynamics! I didn't know that, man. It was an eye-opener. So we went back and started practicing really, really hard.

"About then is when McClure handed me *Songs for the Daily Planet* by Todd Snider. He said, 'You won't like this, but I dig it.' Mike got busy and trailed off with Todd, and now the person who follows him like crazy today is me."

Stillwater infected Canada, and crossing paths with Tom Skinner gave him the push he needed to relocate.

"Skinner was playing the Bullpen. Mike was in and out of town, but he loaned me his bicycle a lot," Canada said. "So I biked over to the Bullpen. I walked up, 17 years old, and Skinner was walking in. He said, 'Hey, Cody!'

"And I said, 'Hey, Tom. Can I come watch you tonight?'

"He goes, 'Why couldn't you?'

"I said, 'Because I'm 17 years old.'

"He goes, '*Ohhh.*'

"And the next thing he says is, 'Well, tonight, you're my nephew. Take my guitar. Come in, don't drink or anything.' I really didn't anyway. It wasn't my thing. I was clear-headed.

"I sat there all night long, listening to him. And then he invited me out to The Farm.

"Weeks later, we're at The Farm, and he sang in the Gypsy Cafe, and I sat in the front row in a lawn chair watching him. And he goes, 'I wanna get my friend Cody up.'

"I don't think I've ever been as terrified in my life.

"It was Bob [Childers] and [Eric] Hansen. Medicine Show lived there. Brad James was there.

"Tom knew I played the 'Ben McCulloch' song by Steve Earle, and he loved my version. So I got up and played that, and it was seriously just, like, a blackout. It was so incredibly adrenaline-filled that my mind erased most of it because I was so excited. That's my Farm story.

"And then I just kind of holed up on their dirty-ass couch. Nobody said anything, and gradually I started bringing the band into town."

Canada had been kicked out of high school during his stint with The Divide and had no problem moving to Stillwater, but Ragsdale and Weidemann were seniors.

Ragweed's first gig came at the now-defunct Fifty Yard Line sports bar in Yukon, and three years of steady gigs in Stillwater followed. Meanwhile, Canada sat in on songwriting sessions with McClure, Skinner and Childers, as well as more locally known songwriters like Mike Shannon (Daddy O).

But in the band, an early turnover changed the entire life course of Ragweed—and Canada. Weidemann got married, and the band played the wedding, but they needed a bass player to stand in for the groom. They found it in Canada's 19-year-old truck-driving friend named Plato.

"I called for him from the get-go," Canada said. "The others did not. But I won, eventually."

Plato stepped in at the wedding and within weeks replaced Weidemann as Ragweed's bassist.

"I was a truck driver at the time, and I looked like a fucking lumberjack," Plato said. "We had a practice the night before, and I had never played with dudes who would just keep playing, no matter what. I was not used to that. We kept playing, and I got a feel for these songs. So we went to play the gig the next night, and it went off without a hitch.

"So I go home, and the next thing I know, it was two weeks later and, 'Hey man, do you wanna play bass for us, dude?'"

Canada made the call from a pay phone.

"We had a chance to open up for David Allan Coe, and I go, 'Are you in?' and Plato barely whispers back, 'Yeah man, I'm in.'

"And I'm like, 'It's David Allan Coe, man, aren't you fuckin' excited about this?' and he goes, 'I'm asleep, man, I gotta drive a truck in the morning.'

"Oh, OK."

Plato nailed the gig, and from that point, Ragweed moved ahead barrels blazing.

"Ragweed was not Ragweed until Plato came on," Canada said.

∎ ∎ ∎

"Carney Man"

Canada went from dabbling in songwriting to observing masters of the craft, at least in Red Dirt circles, like Skinner, Bob Childers and Scott Evans.

Somehow, that was also when Canada and McClure wrote "Carney Man."

The song was allegedly not meant to be the Red Dirt "Margaritaville" that it became—a song so associated with Ragweed and Canada as to become a burden, Canada's own personal answer to Guy Clark's wry line: "Be careful what you write, because you might have to play it for the rest of your life." But surely on some level, it was.

It began as a tropical ballad.

McClure, in particular, was writing several tropic-themed songs at the time. He cowrote "Pour Me a Vacation" with Randy Taylor, and that song became The Great Divide's own albatross. He also wrote "Alive and Well" and "Rather Have Nothin'"—both vacation-themed early Divide tunes.

"If he had run with that, he'd have been 10 years ahead of Kenny Chesney," Canada said. "Can you see McClure in the water, singing without his shirt on? In his Taiwanese fishing pants?"

The original lyrics to "Carney Man" were: *I watch the sun go down / on this sleepy town / I'm feelin' my motor runnin' / I've gotta go / Down where those warm winds blow ["Warm winds! Warm winds" if you know the Carney cadence] I wanna lose myself out on some hidden beach / Out where the world I know is / Temporarily out of reach.*

Canada picks up the songwriting story from there.

"I had smoked weed, at that point, maybe a dozen times. And, McClure and I had some beer.

"He always says that the original idea was mine and that he's the one that came up with 'Carney Man,' the parody part. The song had a verse, and then we smoked some weed and drank some beers, and I don't think either one of us needs to claim it, because we wrote it together, but I know it was his, because he was the one in the Buffett phase.

"So I just started saying something, and the weed was good, and we were giggling about it and we just kept on and on and forgot about the real song. And then 'Carney Man' happened, and we just rolled and laughed.

"I said, 'Well, you're gonna play this for your band, yeah?'

"He goes, 'Shit, no. They ain't going for that. What kind of shit dumb song is this?'"

Ragweed debuted the song at a wedding gig in Guthrie.

"We played it, and nobody had ever heard it, and that wedding party lost their mind," Canada said. "It was like a light bulb.

"At the time, I wasn't thinking about how dumb the song was. I was thinking about how much *fun* those people had and how they liked us. It was really the only other goal I had other than playing my music. I just wanted people to like me.

"Our next gig with the band is at the Wormy Dog, and someone says, 'We should do that 'Carney Man' song.' And then, seriously, it was like dropping a match in dry grass. Everybody started singing it and singing along. Because it was dumb and it was fun.

"I realized at a young age that this one song will rope 'em in. Then they'll listen to 'Jenny' or 'Leave Your Leaving' or 'Alright.' As dumb as it is, I owe a lot to it. It's not like people were writing anything like that, and it came from smoking a joint and giggling with a buddy."

In a present-day footnote, the song would eventually drive Canada's decisions, musically, after the breakup of Ragweed in 2010 and the formation of The Departed (we'll get to that). He avoided it in most shows despite near constant requests for it. It has only been since roughly 2017 that Canada has made enough peace with it to semi-regularly play it again.

"I used to get so mad, and then I saw myself one time—I *caught* myself with a fan. It was in Dallas. I pissed her off so bad that she ran to the front, flipped over the merch table and ran out.

"And I was like, 'OK, although *that* was hilarious, I need to grow up.' Because people dig this song, and if you play it, what is it, three minutes? You do it and you're done.

"I saw Todd Snider answer someone who asked him if he was sick as shit of playing 'Beer Run.' And he said, 'You mean, I drove 800 miles to play in front of a sold-out crowd to hear people sing my words back to me? Absolutely not. I'll play that song at every show forever.' And that was just another thing Todd taught me.

"'Carney' has its place. It has its purpose. And when people are 42 years old, driving to pick up their kids from school, it makes them feel like they're 20 years old again."

I want a big red nose / I want some floppy shoes. I want a squirtin' flower / Squirt it on you. Like all the bad clowns do. ("Bad clowns! Bad clowns!")

• • •

Shannon

Back in Stillwater, Canada had found his footing. He had found a place to showcase his band, and he had smoked his way into the strangest signature song in Red Dirt history. But he found something else in Stillwater.

Shannon O'Neal was a bartender at the Wormy Dog when Canada was an underage performer there.

"He was young. I was always working there when he was there, even when the cops would give him a hard time for being underage. But he was 17 or 18 and I was 23 or 24, so there wasn't a huge spark there," Shannon said. "Then, one night, I went in on my night off, and we sat down and had a conversation."

"I had tried to talk to her before," Cody said. "But someone I thought was her boyfriend kind of threatened me, so I backed off. You know? You don't rub another man's rhubarb.

"But that night in February 1998, we got to talking, and I was venting to her about some of my family woes first. Then I brought up her boyfriend, that he had told me to back off—I don't know if I was a sparkle in her eye, but I was on fire—and she said, 'Oh, wait. No, we have been broken up for months!' And I just went, '*Ohhhh.*'

"I said, 'Well, tomorrow's Valentine's Day. What you got going?' And she said nothing. Well, my truck was broken down, so to take her to the movie *The Wedding Singer*, I had to borrow Jason Boland's old shitty Trans Am. And he polished it up for me all nice, but it rained that day, and it ended up with two inches of water on the floorboard. She took one look at it and said, 'I'll drive.'"

A budding romance—Shannon is now Cody's wife of 20-plus years, and they have two children, Dierks and Willy—happened right as Ragweed was about to release its debut album, *Carney*.

Before Plato joined, Ragweed had cut an album that it has kept hidden since, mostly full of Bob Wills covers and early originals. But they acknowledge that album only in the context of "the one that doesn't count" ahead of *Carney*.

"First date went good, so we went on a second date," Cody said. "To Eischen's Chicken [in Okarche]. Kissed for the first time. And right after, she said, 'Aren't you making a record?'

"Well, we were, but we didn't know how we were going to fund it."

Problem solved: Shannon loaned the band $1,800. There were others. Family and friends pitched in too, but Shannon's early investment in *Carney* made her a partner of sorts. At the time, the band kept its money in a lockbox, and Shannon suggested to them all that maybe she should carry around the lockbox while they just make music.

Shannon has managed or co-managed Cody ever since. The two married in Las Vegas in 1998.

• • •

Live and Loud

The album that set Ragweed on a path toward not just Red Dirt stardom but the actual worldwide fame that followed was 1999's *Live & Loud at the Wormy Dog Saloon.*

The record, recorded on a shoestring budget with help from Jeff Parker, Shannon and a host of other Stillwater and Yukon friends, wound up on bar jukeboxes in nearly every college town in Oklahoma and Texas. It featured the two songs that became Ragweed's show stoppers: a hilarious two-take version of "Carney Man" with Jason Boland, and Gene Collier's ode to marijuana, "Boys from Oklahoma." When they put out the album, Cody already knew the door he wanted it to open for Ragweed.

"*Live and Loud* was recorded right when The Great Divide debuted a video for 'Never Could,' and it had people just *crying* in the front row and losing their mind," Cody said. "I knew I wanted that, and I knew after *Live and Loud* that it was very attainable. We just had to hunker down and do it right, really just following their lead."

The album was Ragweed's signal that they were serious in their dreams, and it was a signal to both Canadas that Cody had both the musical chops and songwriting skills to lift up Ragweed.

"My wife was so enthralled by what I was doing, and the passion that I had for music was crazy to her," Cody said. "And watching her being passionate about me being passionate—it's like the songs wouldn't stop. I just wrote song after song after song. I was so motivated by love and wanting to move up to the next level.

"One of my ultimate goals was to play the Zoo Amphitheater in Oklahoma City, you know?"

• • •

The Crew

Live and Loud came out in 1999, followed quickly by *Highway 377* in January 2001. By the end of that year, Ragweed would be invited to record a live album at Billy Bob's Texas, trademarked as the World's Largest Honky Tonk.

Almost concurrently, Tim DuBois, the songwriter and music executive most famous for signing Brooks & Dunn, Alan Jackson and Brad Paisley to the Arista Nashville label in less than a two-year span, was looking for artists to fill out the roster at the Nashville-based Universal South offshoot of Universal Records. The label had already landed Pat Green, and Green's endorsement of Ragweed, along with a handful of other friends of DuBois, caught his attention. He met with Ragweed at a concert when the band was on a co-headlining tour with Reckless Kelly and offered the band a label deal on the spot.

"I remember being really happy for Ragweed and also like, 'What the hell? We're right here, man!' when we found out they got offered at that gig," recalled Reckless lead singer Willy Braun.

We will pick up that narrative again soon enough.

Between *Live and Loud* and the 2002 release of *Cross Canadian Ragweed*, the band's Universal South debut, Ragweed assembled one of the most important and popular road crews in all of Texas, members of which continue to carry a heavy influence on the state's music and its biggest acts. Their role in Ragweed and Red Dirt needs to be acknowledged. Canada weighed in on all of them for this book.

Chris McCoy (front of house sound engineer)

"I got drunk one night and passed out, out of my mind, outside the AGR house in Stillwater. And I was ramming my head against a fence because I thought it was funny. And I hit my head really hard and fell backward. I opened my eyes and I heard, 'Hey, bro!

Why you gotta do stupid shit? Let me walk you home.' And I asked who he was. He goes, 'I'm Chris McCoy. I'm about to start running sound at the Wormy Dog.' And that was when he asked if he could put our music on Napster. He said, 'You're not gonna get paid, but it's gonna go out to a lot of people.' And that began our friendship. So not long after that, we weren't happy with our sound man. We were having five-hour sound checks, missing showers, missing dinner. But I still had my Tuesday night Wormy Dog gigs. So I asked McCoy if he would go on the road full time. Chuck [Thomson, bar owner] didn't like that, but Chuck didn't like anything so we just had to deal with it."

Nathan Coit (merchandise)
"We were at Czech Day in Yukon, and I saw Coit. I knew him through friends, but not personally. I remember that night because we painted his toenails and he passed out. Then he woke up pissed off at us. So I stepped in with, 'Hey, we need a merch guy.' And Shannon goes, 'Can you start tomorrow?' And Coit is in. Now we have a crew. Four band members, Shannon and two crew members, and we're in our second van."

Brian Kinzie (monitor sound engineer)
"The small success of *377* got the attention of Billy Bob's. That got the attention of the record label. And then came *Purple* [*Cross Canadian Ragweed* is better known as *The Purple Album*] and that's when it blew up. Now we're coast-to-coast. And McCoy said, 'I need help, man. These crowds are getting too big. I can't do monitors and front of house and set everything up. I need some help.' He said he had a friend in Stillwater he wanted to hire. I said, 'Do you trust him?' and McCoy goes, 'Fuck yeah, I trust him.' So I just said, 'Alright. Get him. Throw him in and we'll hit the road.' And it was Kinzie.

"I remember saying, 'Here's the deal. We like to smoke weed. We like to drink. But I don't like it when somebody gets too drunk and can't do their job, and hard-core drugs are absolutely off-limits.' I said, 'What are your addictions?' and Kinzie said, 'Sleeping.' So I said, 'You got the job.'

"He's sweet, kind, soft-spoken. Meeting his parents after that, I realized he was just salt of the earth. Well, now we got a good crew. We got a good team."

Bert DeBruin (tour manager)
"Shelby, Shannon's sister, was living with us for a while, and she was going through a rough time. Just had dated a run of bad dudes and was really kind of unhappy, to the point I started writing a bunch of songs about her, about how sad she was, just so I could process everything. And at one point, she wanted to drive back and forth to California to meet up with this guy she knew from high school named Berta. *Berta*. That's weird. So she'd get in the car, make it to about Amarillo, then turn around and come back. Then she'd do it again.

"Fast-forward, we went out to California. We were playing in L.A. and were in trouble. We had actually dropped our axle—it fell out of the bus. The bus company sent us another bus, and we're terrified, and we finally get to L.A. So we're tense when we get there, and we meet this guy that was Shelby's friend. Immediately, he and I bowed up. He was lanky, tattoos everywhere, bald and wearing a wifebeater shirt. I judged him. He was from Fresno, and that's got a pretty hard reputation. So I shook his hand and went back on the bus. Middle of the night, I get up on the bus, and in the front lounge, there is this guy, passed out, with rap on, and he has a cigarette burnt to his fingers. And I go, 'This guy's gotta go. I am not taking this guy back to Texas with us.' And Shannon says, 'Don't do that. Don't judge him. Get to know him.'

"Two days later, I swear, we were the best friends on the planet. We were doing shots, smoking weed, partying like we have known each other forever. The other guys in the band saw this.

"At this point, in Texas, we're selling out big places. This is right before we played a 24,000 gig in Grand Prairie [breaking the attendance record at Lone Star park] and a 50,000 gig in Houston [at the Houston Livestock Show and Rodeo]. And I remember we played a stupid-ass dove hunt for a bunch of drunk doctors. And I told the guys, 'I think we're going to take Berta with us. We need help. We need security. Look at the size of this guy. We need this guy.'

"I'm going to be honest. I knew it was a good decision, but I also needed a buddy. It was tough to get through the crowd and get our job done.

"But I told him I wasn't going to call him Berta. That was stupid. So that's Bert. Him, McCoy, Coit and Brian. That was us. That was Ragweed for a long time.

Joel Schoepf (guitar tech)
"Bert lost his fiancée a couple of years in, and he needed a vacation. That's when Joel came in. He had been managing, several years before. I had gotten drunk with Joel plenty of times. He had been with Roger Creager before, and we liked him already. So he's with us for three months tour managing.

"I hadn't seen Bert in three months, and we're playing in Stillwater. Before the show, Shannon says, 'I gotta go. I'll be right back,' and she shows right back up with Bert. He was happy and healthy, and you could just tell he was back. What a night. We got the whole crew back together.

"And Joel was kind of like, 'Well, this is it for me. I helped cover for Bert.'

"Shannon goes, 'You can't let him go, can you?' and I go, 'Nope. He is just a kick-ass hand.' And she says, 'OK. Invent a job. Find something for him to do. He's still on.' So I told Joel, 'We can't lose you, man. If you want to stay on, we want you to stay on. Can you guitar tech?' and he goes, 'Yep. And if I can't, I'll learn it.'

"I thought we had the best damn crew in the scene. We *did* have the best damn crew in the scene. I thought we had the best damn crew, at least until Turnpike. They have a kick-ass crew too, and their crew all has tattoos that say W.W.B.K.D. for 'What Would Brian Kinzie Do?'"

That crew of five, plus the band, plus Willard Kendall, who toured with the band for four years as the lighting technician, made up the "ten out of ten" that went free in the song "51 Pieces."

After Ragweed, DeBruin stayed on and managed Cody Canada & The Departed for its first year. Schoepf stayed on with The Departed, first as guitar tech and then as tour manager after DeBruin. Schoepf left the band to help manage Floore's Country Store in Helotes, Texas, before signing up as Reckless Kelly's tour manager in early 2020. Coit left the music business after Ragweed. McCoy went immediately from Ragweed to the Randy Rogers Band, where he runs sound to this day.

And Kinzie? Kinzie is the tour manager and sound engineer for The Departed.

• • •

The Purple Album

"September 11th had just happened that week," Canada said. "Boland, Shannon and I went out and got hammered one night for no reason, just to do it. And the next morning was 9/11. Everybody knows what that did to everyone. It changed everything. Later that week, we played a Pat Green show at Wolf Pen Creek in College Station—Aggie Kickoff, I think they call it.

"We had all this patriotic stuff we were planning on doing. We did 'Pink Houses.' Pat did 'Only in America,' I think. But we did it. We *had* the crowd. It was Pat's show, but we nailed it too. We just felt everything building up.

"We were getting ready to go to The Tap to have beers after the show. I sent Shannon, Jennifer Plato, Ashley [Ragsdale] and Robin [Cross], all the wives. I told them to go to The Tap, and we'd load out and meet up.

"This female officer comes up and goes, 'Is Randy Ragsdale here?'

"We go, 'Yeah. What's up?' and she said, 'His mother and family have been in an accident.'

"I said, 'Well, how bad is it?' and she said, 'I cannot tell you that, sir.'

"They told us at the hospital. We all got there. We were drunk, but we made it. We thought it was his mom. And Randy goes, 'Mandi didn't make it.'"

Mandi Ragsdale, Randy's 9-year-old sister, died in a head-on collision three miles east of Kurten, Texas, just after 11 p.m. on September 15, 2001, after Ragweed's set at Ag Kickoff. Her mother, Ruth Ann Ragsdale, had been driving. Ruth Ann survived with serious injuries.

Roger Creager, who lived in College Station, let the band stay at his house while Ruth Ann was hospitalized.

Pat Green gave Ragweed full use of his tour bus to get the band and its family members to and from Mandi's funeral in Oklahoma.

"There are lines in the sand in Texas and Red Dirt music," said Mattson Rainer of KNBT-FM in New Braunfels, "before Pat did that for Ragweed and after. Before, there was a lot of shit talk from Texas about Oklahoma and vice versa. After that, not a word. Everyone was a family then."

Mandi's favorite color was purple.

The cover of *Cross Canadian Ragweed* was a deep purple, crossed by a ray of light for Mandi.

That is why the album is more commonly called *The Purple Album*.

"I'd never seen anybody pull together like that," Cody Canada recalled. "There was all this going on, with September 11th, and it was so distant. We all lost our baby sister.

"It just brought out the good in people. We got to see who our friends were in Texas."

In 2002, Cody and Shannon Canada moved from Yukon to New Braunfels. They have been Texans ever since.

• • •

Taking Over Everything

The Purple Album cracked the Billboard Top 100 country albums chart: good enough for the band to have made it, but not the flash that DuBois and Tony Brown may have hoped for when they signed Ragweed to Universal South. However, the album has held up well in Red Dirt lore, featuring cuts that Canada regularly performs with The Departed now, like "Suicide Blues," "Anywhere but Here" and "Constantly." But it was another single and its accompanying video that turned the most heads.

Canada and Jason Boland had a late night in Yukon in late 2001, and they ran out of beer. It was on the trip to the store to get more beer that Boland noticed Canada white-knuckle driving and ducking, aware of the Yukon police patrolling the city. Boland remarked, "Isn't it funny how you're always 17 in your hometown?" And Canada fired right back, "If you don't write it, I will."

He wrote "17" within days. The last time I rode along with Ragweed in their van was to Odessa and Del Rio immediately afterward, where Canada debuted the song to crowds to immediate ovations. Hazily, I recall Canada and Ragsdale workshopping the end of the song, and I recall shouting my thoughts on it from the third row back in the van—still the closest I have come to being part of the songwriting process.

The song was a quick hit when it was released, and its accompanying video gained steady play on Country Music Television.

In its wake, Canada struck up a friendship with a pair of artists who shaped the second half of Ragweed's existence as a band. The first is Lee Ann Womack, best known for her harmony cameo on "Sick and Tired" from 2004's *Soul Gravy*.

"She came to a couple of shows, and I was really intimidated," Cody said. "Then we opened for her in front of 50,000 people or whatever the capacity is at the Houston Rodeo. We met her backstage, and she was sweet as could be. She hates it when I say that, but she is.

"And I say, 'You wanna sing a song with us?' And she goes, 'I would love to. Let's sing a Willie Nelson song.' Well, I go, 'You name it,' and she says, 'Why don't *you* name it?'

"So I pick 'Angel Flying Too Close to the Ground,' and she says that's her favorite.

"They brought her out on a golf cart. Paul Rogers brought her out. And there we are—wallet chains, sleeveless shirts, bandanas, tattoos. And she walks on stage, just elegant.

"She got up and sang that song with us. She didn't even practice! She didn't need practice. And after that, we're backstage and she's just beaming. And we're looking at each other like, *We just had a superstar sing with us.*

"So I said, 'Will you sing with us, like, on our record?' And she said, 'Of course. You name it.'

"I go, 'I want you to like the song first.' And she goes, 'Well, I don't know you guys very well, but I'm pretty sure you're not gonna record something I don't like.' It was such a good night. I can remember everything I was wearing, it was such a good night.

"Anyway, we were experienced with female background vocals because of Monica Taylor [a longtime Red Dirt artist], but we thought it was going to be one of those recordings where we mail the tracks. And she asked where we were recording it, and I told her the studio. She goes, 'That's not too far from my parents. I'll meet you there.'

"She rolls in by herself. No entourage, nothing. And she walks in with a six-pack of Budweiser and a Whataburger. And she didn't touch either of them until she was done.

"She listens to the song and goes, 'Oh my God. I love it. Can I just run free with it?'

"'You do whatever you want.'

"The whole thing took three, maybe four takes. We had it."

The song was, naturally, the first single from *Soul Gravy*. The accompanying video made it to No. 3 on CMT's charts, and the album charted at No. 5 on Billboard's country albums chart. The barbed-wire-and-roses pairing of Ragweed with Womack had given the band a breakthrough. Right at the same time, an up-and-coming artist named Dierks Bentley had been lined up to open for Ragweed on a series of shows in Texas and Oklahoma.

"We were at the Exit/In in Nashville," Canada said. "And we had Enzo Divicenzo working for us, another guy who just got it. Enzo had worked for George Strait and Lee Ann. He'd worked for MCA and one or two other big places. And Dierks had come out to that show, and he was leaning up against the wall all by himself. And Enzo says to me, 'This is Dierks Bentley. He's a big fan.' And Dierks goes, 'I really am, bro.'

"I asked what his story was, and he goes, 'I'm a musician in town. Just got a record deal.' Well, that's cool.

"He left, and Enzo goes, 'He's the next big thing.' And that was it."

After that, Divicenzo brokered Bentley as an opener for Gary Allan and Ragweed. It went well enough that Ragweed took Bentley on a run through Texas as an opener. The crowds dug Bentley and his debut single, "What Was I Thinkin.'"

On that run, Bentley told Canada, "Thanks for making us look cool."

Texas, even for a young Dierks Bentley, could be daunting. Bentley played three tours with Ragweed dubbed High Times and Hangovers, and even when it became clear that Bentley's star was brighter than Ragweed's, Bentley insisted that Ragweed headline at Texas venues. He never forgot Canada's early gestures.

That's not to say things were sappy and morose between the two. Canada, known for pranks, pulled one at a concert in Las Vegas by purchasing a cheap knockoff of Bentley's guitar, switching it out with his real one and smashing it on stage in front of him.

"He lunged at me," Canada said. "I'll never forget the look on his face when he saw me smash that thing. After the show, he went straight for my guitars and said, 'You smash one of mine, I'm smashing one of yours,' and I had to give up the gag."

Bentley's 2007 No. 1 single "Free and Easy (Down the Road I Go)" features the lyric, *Ragweed's rockin' on the radio / free and easy down the road I go.* Two years prior, when Cody and Shannon were expecting their first child, not knowing the gender before the birth, they settled on "Dierks Cobain" for a boy and "Mandi Lynn" for a girl. The child was born on the weekend that Hurricane Katrina hit the U.S. mainland.

"So we're in the delivery room, and the doctor asks us what we're naming it," Cody said. "And I said, Dierks Cobain or Mandi Lynn, and she says, 'Well, here's Hurricane Dierks!'

"He's a good guy who means a ton to us, and we wouldn't name our kid after someone we didn't love like we do him."

▪ ▪ ▪

Life at the Top

What worked for Ragweed was the support of Universal South. DuBois and Brown are most often name-dropped in association with the band's time at the label, but there was actually a team backing the band from the top of the label.

"I remember watching them get excited for us, saying how cool this could be," Canada said. "In the beginning, when we were with the label, and it was Tim and Tony and Susan Levy, with all those people, that was a *team*. And it was a *good* team. It wasn't a bullshit thing. Yes, they were answering to a higher power, they were out to make money, but they were actually involved and loved our music. They got it.

They understood it."

The band's catalog turned over like clockwork. *Soul Gravy* was followed by *Garage*, which featured a new recording of "Alabama," a song that battled with "Boys" and "Carney" for the title of Ragweed fan favorites. *Garage* was followed by *Back to Tulsa: Live and Loud at Cain's Ballroom*, recorded over two nights so hot and humid in Tulsa that the venue power blew for more than an hour before the second show. Then came *Mission California*, in 2007, and their final album, the rage-filled *Happiness and All the Other Things*, in 2009.

They toured the country, headlining their own festivals at Oklahoma City's Zoo Amphitheater, the Fort Worth Stockyards, Oklahoma's Lake Eufaula and Cain's Ballroom in Tulsa. They played Bonnaroo and they played the Country Rendez-Vous Festival in France. Along with John Dickson, they held an annual music cruise through the Gulf of Mexico, the CCRuise, even bringing along Bentley in 2005.

Remember how Canada's goal at the outset was to play that zoo? The Cross Canadian Ragweed Family Jam, benefitting Mandi's Ministries, the charity created after the death of Mandi Ragsdale, was the band's pride and joy. One year, Canada created a lineup that had Lee Ann Womack playing immediately before Buckcherry, right at the time the Los Angeles hard rock band had their first chart hit, "Crazy Bitch."

"That was my idea," Canada said. "I was a fan, but I didn't listen to them on a regular basis, so I didn't know *that* would be their song of the moment. And I remember Keith [Nelson], their guitar player, telling me that Josh Todd, the lead singer, woke up, looked at the day list and said, 'Lee Ann Womack is playing before us? Do these people even know who we are?'

"Keith tells him, 'Yeah. I think this festival is kind of just like this guy's playlist of people he really likes. Is that OK?' And Todd says, 'Yeah. Lee Ann Womack! I love her!'"

Perhaps most importantly, Ragweed became embroiled in a prank war with Reckless Kelly.

"We put a catfish in a towel, put it in their van and ruined their van," Canada said. "Sorry, guys."

"They got on stage during one of our shows dressed as a two-person donkey and dropped 25 pounds of horseshit on the stage.

"We dressed up as clowns, killed their power and pumped 'Carney Man' through the speakers, then did cartwheels and sprayed Silly String on their stage.

"They dressed up as bunnies on Easter, came on stage and tried to steal our mascot, Henri [a chainsaw carving of the clown from the *Carney* album cover done by Doug Moreland].

"They put me as a big, buff guy in a pink Speedo in one of the pamphlets for the cruise and had it say, 'Manly massages, men only.' I kind of wish I still had that.

"I can't remember what I did next. I was going to steal their van and have it painted like the Texas flag, but they upgraded to a bus.

"Willy Braun put stink bait inside the screen of my microphone. We played Larry Joe Taylor's festival, and he told me that everyone in the band was sick and had the shits, and they played right before us. And I smelled it, and I went, 'If somebody wiped their ass on my microphone, this friendship is done.'

"Someone tipped me off to what it was, and I took it and ran back to my bus, and Willy's in the front lounge telling these two girls what he did and how I reacted. I was mad. It almost made me vomit. And I get on there and I hear him say, 'You should have seen his face!' and I immediately go, 'Was it anything like this?' and I hit him with it, in his mouth and up his nose.

"There's no showers, and he had to hop a flight right after that to go play with Ray Benson, and he was pretty mad.

"Anyway, that's how we learned how to do jokes."

There is an old George Strait song that Canada still performs on occasion called "Lonesome Rodeo Cowboy," featuring the lyric: *When you're on top, you've got a million friends / but when you're down, buddy, you're all alone.*

Canada lived that out during Ragweed's heyday, but a handful of those friends hung around. One of them was Dean Stiffler.

Stiffler lives to this day in Rancho Cucamonga, California, on the edge of greater Los Angeles, where the desert starts to fight the urban sprawl. Stiffler is a Rodney Crowell fan, and in 2005, he picked up a music magazine because Crowell was on the cover. Inside, there was a list of up-and-coming bands, and Ragweed was listed. It stuck out to Stiffler. He was in a personal funk, having just lost his brother. He was and still is married to Merylee, but the strain of his brother was wearing on him, and he was in the mood for something different. He filed away the name "Cross Canadian Ragweed."

"I picked up *Purple*, and I played the shit out of it, just over and over and over," Stiffler said. "And rather quickly after that, I see that these guys are going to play the Coach House down in San Juan Capistrano, not far from me. One of my favorite little hangs. We had really good seats. And before the show, I remember Cody came down, and Merylee recognized him, and she goes, 'I'm gonna go get his autograph.' And she did, and he was so cool to sign that just before he went on stage.

"Next time they're out here, they played the Belly Up in Solana Beach, and *Garage* had come out. And I heard 'Breakdown,' and that's what I did. Just bawled my eyes out. I came home, put it on the home theater and told Merylee, 'You gotta hear this song.'

"I lost my brother in late 2004, and *Garage* came out in 2005, but I never had time to grieve. I was too busy keeping the family's shit together. But that song made me realize I need my five minutes too, people."

At the Belly Up show, Merylee insisted that the two meet Cody after the show and find out about the song. Cody recognized them from the previous show, and the two hit it off. They struck up a friendship, and the Stifflers started traveling around California to Ragweed shows. Eventually, they were invited onto the bus for some late night jams and weed smoking.

Within a year, the Stifflers were close enough to the Canadas to be a guest at their home for Thanksgiving. Dean would routinely join them at festivals like The MusicFest at Steamboat when the Canadas' first child was very young, and they noticed he took to Dean and, if they needed to hand off a young Dierks and know he wouldn't cry, they could trust Dean. Things snowballed.

Today, Dean and Cody are as close as brothers.

"I know he's a talented person and he has this career," Stiffler said. "But the beginning of every conversation is, 'How are you?' He's grown to my extended family now. At first, was I in awe because he's a rock star? Sure. But now, it's just, how can I help my brother when he's going through some rough times? During the Ragweed breakup, I was just his sounding board. The fact that he's willing to reach out and just listen like a friend and a brother would—what I get out of that relationship is, I have more family now. I have Texas family now."

. . . .

Putting All That in the Past

"You want to know what I miss about Ragweed? It was fun. We just had a lot of fun. There. It's your book, I'm not going to lie in it," Canada said.

Ragweed grew apart.

That's what happened. There was no moment. No onstage fight. The four of them just got tired of one another's company.

It did not help that Randy Ragsdale's first child, J.C., had autism, and the demands of the road were taking him away from parenthood. And it did not help that the leadership of Universal South that had signed Ragweed all left the label by 2009, and the label merged with Toby Keith's Show Dog Music label. Those were factors, but not the driving force, behind the end of Ragweed.

"I started to lose control of myself and of my band," Canada said. "Shannon and I weren't doing so hot. We were trying, but it was really just so hard. She went from being on the road with me for seven and a half years—we did everything together—and then all of a sudden she is pregnant and can't be there. And I lost focus."

With that as the backdrop, the band suggested that Shannon step aside as manager. Canada put his foot down, and suddenly, hard lines were drawn in a group that had largely avoided any type of internal drama for 15 years. The argument over Shannon as manager spiraled into debates about whom the band should be opening for, which venues they should be playing and the money they should be commanding. The disagreements came fast and furious, leading to internal threats of legal action by 2010.

"Here's the thing," Brian Kinzie said. "I had no idea how things worked for a long time. I came on as a sound guy who just thought this was the normal route. You join a band, they get popular, you ride the wave, you go across the world. You see everything. And then you go back home. I thought that was the normal thing. It just seemed like it was a ride that was going to last forever. And then, suddenly it wasn't. It happened that fast."

Those lines landed all the members on a conference call in May of that year. Mild disagreements over half a year snowballed into an avalanche that buried Ragweed as fast as it had risen.

The background to that call *was* an onstage moment. In early May, Ragweed headlined at the Tumbleweed's annual Calf Fry in Stillwater. This was a regular gig by then, and one of Canada's running gags during Calf Fry was to stand on stage with a baseball bat while fans threw empty, plastic beer pitchers at him, and he'd bat them back into the crowd. A harmless, if messy, running joke in Stillwater.

That night, someone threw a liquor bottle from the crowd. They couldn't have thrown it more directly at Canada's head if they had been a pitching machine at batting practice.

When you're on stage, the lights are blinding. You cannot see more than a few feet in front of you if you're up there. It has to be that way.

So when that bottle is thrown, from Canada's perspective, it really does appear out of nowhere. You can't dodge it from that position.

It smashed directly on his head. Concussion. Stitches. Canceled headlining gig the next night in Kansas City. Could have been worse. Did not need to happen at all.

Canada's bad mood boiled over.

"I felt betrayed," Canada said. "Like, man, I've given everything I can to Stillwater, and talked up this town, and some asshole has to throw a fucking bottle at me? And now you put a scar on my face and this town?"

The timing was almost worse than the incident itself.

"The beginning of the end was when Cody got hit by that bottle," Kinzie said. "That was when Grady and Randy were really fed up with our direction, and so were a few of the crew guys. There was frustration with where we were going, and now Cody is pissed about this bottle, and the atmosphere on the bus just went haywire."

Is it possible that if that one-in-a-million incident had not have happened that Canada would not have jumped on a conference call with his bandmates ready to call the whole thing off? According to Canada, probably not.

"I don't want to paint myself as innocent," he said. "I said no a lot. I'm not the easiest to deal with when it's my music. It's *my* music. I liked the last record [*Happiness and All the Other Things*] for a bit, because I was mad, but I was changing. I was tired of playing 'Carney Man.' I wanted to sing about love, about my kids, about loss and about real shit. Well, some others wanted the beer drinking songs and the party songs, and they wanted the money that came with them.

"And we got on that call, and nobody budged. We weren't firing Shannon, it was a nonstarter.

"At one point, I said, 'You know what this means, right? This is stupid. Let's cut for a bit. Let's take a break. Let's just do 50 or 100 shows. Let's cool down. This is a heated decision.'

"It didn't fly. That was it. The end of Ragweed.

"All I said was, 'Well, I'm gonna keep doing it.'"

The band canceled every gig it could cancel, including the 2010 Family Jam, but honored the ones it had to honor, including its commitment to Bonnaroo the same summer.

After their penultimate concert, a casino gig in Dubuque, Iowa, Jeremy Plato, Randy Ragsdale, Grady Cross and Cody Canada locked arms and bowed during the curtain call.

Cross Canadian Ragweed's final show was one night later, October 24, 2010, at Joe's on Weed St. in Chicago.

Wade Bowen and Stoney LaRue opened with an acoustic song swap.

Lee Ann Womack joined to sing harmony on "Sick and Tired" and stepped in for Cody when he missed some lyrics.

Canada introduced every crew member and every spouse and shared their stories.

The last song Cross Canadian Ragweed performed was Neil Young's "Rockin' in the Free World."

After the three-hour set, there was no curtain call. The band did not lock arms and bow. The four members scattered across the bar and then across the city without even a handshake or backstage hug.

Ragweed was done.

"The end was one of those things where I had been trying to throw buckets of water out of a boat that was done," Canada said. "And then, when it sank, I realized, Oh, that *needed* to happen."

. . .

The Postscript

Canada and Plato stayed on the road, regrouping as The Departed and playing their first show with the new band at Gruene Hall at the end of December 2010, barely three months after Ragweed broke up.

Ragsdale and Cross went home to Yukon, where Cross bought the old 50 Yard Line bar, where Ragweed had played their first-ever show, and remade it as Grady's 66 Pub, named after its address on historic Route 66. The venue regularly hosts live music, often seven nights a week. Ragsdale spent the 2010s working outside of music—mostly. He also spent time on the road playing drums for Stoney LaRue and joined Canada and Plato for a quasi-reunion set at The MusicFest at Steamboat in the early part of the decade. However, in late 2019, Cross and Ragsdale formed a new band alongside Oklahoma-based country artist Jason Young. Cross, Ragsdale and Young played their debut concert at Grady's 66 Pub that fall.

The Departed underwent several incarnations in its first six years. The original makeup was a five-piece and included longtime Red Dirt keyboardist Steve Littleton along with Seth James and Dave Bowen, plus Canada and Plato. That group recorded *This is Indian Land*, a tribute to Oklahoma songwriters and an echo of the original *Red Dirt Sampler* from 14 years earlier. Ultimately, The Departed settled into a three-piece, with Eric Hansen—a Red Dirt veteran who had played drums for 12 years with the Mike McClure Band—falling in alongside Canada and Plato. By 2020, The Departed had released three albums of original music and Canada had released two live acoustic albums recorded at the Third Coast Theater in Port Aransas, Texas. One was a solo, and the other, *Chip and Ray, Together Again for the First Time*, was a duet album with McClure. The Departed also released an album of old country songs, with Jeremy Plato as lead singer, called *In Retrospect*, in 2016.

Canada wrote enough new material that The Departed could play entire shows and never touch a Ragweed song. He was stubborn about it, too. Ragweed, he said, was in the past, and The Departed was who he had become.

That was the case until Hansen set him straight.

On The Departed's bus in fall 2018, the topic of Ragweed material came up in small talk. Songs like "Alabama," "17," "Number" and "Hammer Down" had fallen off the setlists altogether. And then there was "Fightin' For," which Canada had written after an actual fight with Shannon, and which cracked Billboard's Top 40 country singles chart—the only time that ever happened for him. Canada lamented that he never won over fans who came to shows hoping to hear those songs.

Hansen asked, matter-of-factly, "So what's wrong with making people happy all the time?"

Canada's response? "Well, fuck. Ain't nothing wrong with it."

• • •

The Legacy

At MusicFest in Steamboat Springs, Colorado, founder and operator John Dickson annually stages a tribute to an artist of his choosing, viewed as influences to the artists of the day. The musicians at the festival take turns playing one of the tribute artist's songs and sharing stories, and it generally goes down the way you imagine a tribute to go down. Occasionally, as was the case in 2009 with *Undone: A MusicFest Tribute to Robert Earl Keen*, the whole thing gets recorded and released as a live album.

Around 2016—when enough time had passed for the worlds of Texas and Red Dirt to accept that Ragweed truly would never reunite—Dickson decided MusicFest needed to honor Canada in the same way.

"For one thing, I know how much influence Ragweed had on everyone, and I mean of all ages," Dickson said. "Young, old, whatever. They had such a style and image. It wasn't only Cody's writing and it wasn't only the instrumental parts. It was their presence. It was being such great guys. And it was a wonderful group of people behind the scenes. There is no doubt that they were *the* influence for a long time."

The wire tripped in Dickson's mind when he asked people in their 20s who he came across or worked with what they remembered about Ragweed, and the response was "I was too young." It was apparent that there was already a generation of artists and fans alike who never experienced Ragweed, and Dickson wanted MusicFest to serve as the reminder.

Canada shot down his suggestion in 2016, and then again in 2017 and 2018.

"Here's how I knew we would eventually get him," Dickson said. "He's pretty straightforward with me, and whenever I brought it up, he never told me to fuck off. Cody has a way of letting you know that something never had a chance, and he never told me that. He'd say no, but with Cody, that was never a dead end.

"I called up Wade [Bowen], wanting to get him on board. Wade said, 'You know how Cody is, he's as stubborn as you and me.' Well, yes, I know that, and that's why I wanted Wade's help. And it was at his charity event in Waco [the 2018 Bowen MusicFest], when Cody actually listened to me when I asked him to be the tribute artist. When I saw him listening, having a little dialogue, I realized that something was happening here. He still told me no, but it was the first time he heard me out.

"And then, at the 2019 MusicFest, he started playing a bunch of Ragweed songs. He hadn't done that in nine years. And I looked over at Shannon, with just a big question mark over my head, and she mouthed, 'He's back.'

"I was just like, holy shit, what is happening here? And when he came off the stage, I asked him if he was playing Ragweed music again, and he goes, 'I wrote this. This is my music.' And that's when I knew. I said, 'Can we do the tribute?' and Cody said, 'You can do the tribute.'"

The event itself was a wild ride—electric and acoustic concerts spread over two days, kicked off by an elaborate roast of Canada in a video featuring all the artists ("Cody Canada? Somebody get me Dickson on the phone," from Bowen was one). And after that, even by the standards of a tribute that had previously gone to Lee Ann Womack, Bruce Robison and Keen, this one overshadowed them all.

"I've never been that emotional at a tribute," Dickson said. "I'm pretty sure I never will again."

The electric show on the first day featured Koe Wetzel leading off with a (censored for an all-ages show) version of Ragweed's "Leavin' Tennessee." Reckless Kelly played "Fightin' For." Micky and the Motorcars did "51 Pieces." Wade Bowen was joined by Jamie Lin Wilson for "Sick and Tired"—a song they would reprise a day later at the acoustic set and not leave a dry eye in the room. There was Jonathan Tyler playing "Wanna Rock and Roll" and Parker McCollum doing "Constantly." In the two-hour set, all of Ragweed's staples were covered, before Canada and The Departed took the stage for a seven-song set that ended with "Boys From Oklahoma" and "Alabama" with full participation from the crowd at the festival's main stage.

As fun as the electric set was, it did not prepare anybody, least of all the Canadas, for the ride of the acoustic set the next day. Set on a smaller stage, in a ballroom with tables set in the front for Canada and his family and friends, the show became an outlet for artists to say, to Cody's face, the impact he had on their music.

In song-swap style, rotations of artists took the stage, told a story and interpreted Canada's music via their voices for three straight hours. There was McClure doing "Carney Man" as a ballad and Bri Bagwell performing "Run to Me" so commandingly that audience members would not even breathe loudly, lest they break a sound wave's path across the room.

Doug Moreland had played fiddle on the original *Purple Album* version of "On a Cloud." He told a story of how he had gotten the fiddle on his way to record that song and, on the same drive to the studio, learned that his grandmother had passed away. And then he went ahead and played the song as if he were ensuring that his grandmother, wherever she was now, were in the front row listening. Tears fell around the room like the snowflakes on the mountain outside.

Bruce Robison, himself the tribute artist a year before, did a rendition of "Breakdown" that was nearly as emotional.

"I found out that Cody was the tribute artist, and I thought it was wonderful," Robison said. "So I said I'd love to be a part of it if they needed another artist, and they sent me back two songs, probably late in the process where everyone else had picked songs.

"I didn't know that song, and I heard it, and I loved it. There is so much music out there, you can't hear it all. And for me, it was really wonderful, all these years after he recorded it, to discover that song, get inside of it and sing it.

"I like songs where there are a lot of different layers to it. The more you peel back, the more it moves you. It's a special song to me in that way."

Robison's career as an artist and songwriter predates Ragweed, and his music has been covered by the Dixie Chicks, George Strait and Gary Allan. His older brother is Charlie Robison, who took his baritone, Hill Country drawl to heights in music that paralleled Ragweed's. And their sister, Robyn Ludwick, is a songwriter with music at least as deep as that of her siblings, if not more. The point is, Bruce Robison would know. And he understands how to navigate the waters of Texas music.

"This whole thing is just the definition of grassroots," Robison said. "There is no media that is dictating any of it. It's not dependent on any mass media. It's only grassroots. I've always been on the edge of it, and my brother was way more in it. But I've never seen anything like it, anywhere else in the world that exists—that there are this many people going to clubs to find music that's not necessarily heard on the radio and seeking it out every night of the year. It's amazing to me."

Back at the acoustic set, nearly every song could have been the highlight of the festival on its own. After some pointed words for Cody, William Clark Green walked the audience through "Johnny's Song," the tribute to Randy Ragsdale's father, Johnny C., from *Highway 377*. Kaitlin Butts played "Lonely Girl."

"Cody Canada, before I even knew that *he* knew what my name was, he had pulled me up on stage to sing a song," Butts said. "He and Wade Bowen were playing a show at MusicFest, and they called me up on stage, and I didn't even know he knew my name. But that's just what people do in this scene."

Courtney Patton did a stripped-down version of "Alabama." Dalton Domino brought Dierks Canada on stage to play guitar on "Bluebonnets" and he stayed on stage to join Jamie Lin Wilson's rendition of "17."

Randy Rogers played "This Time Around," a cowrite with Canada that both Ragweed and the Randy Rogers Band were well-known to play. Canada insisted that Willy and Cody Braun play "Fightin' For" again and that Bowen and Wilson redo "Sick and Tired." But it was BJ Barham who got to play Canada's autobiographical "The Years," after telling a story about Canada hearing his band, American Aquarium, on KNBT radio and calling the station demanding to know who was playing it and subsequently organizing a Texas tour with American Aquarium opening for The Departed, which introduced Red Dirt to Aquarium.

"I didn't grow up in this scene, I saw it from afar, so let me be clear: Cody Canada is a fucking celebrity," Barham said. "In the state of Oklahoma, he might as well run for governor. I totally believe that. He is a statesman for Oklahoma.

"I told him straight up, 'I didn't grow up with your music. It didn't change my life like it did so many of these musicians.' And initially, when I heard of the tribute, I wasn't going to do it. Because I want to be honest with people, and I don't want to get up there and talk about how it changed my life, because I wasn't familiar with it until Cody and I became friends. And I sure didn't want to get up there and just play one of the hits, just posing.

"So I called Cody, and I said, 'I want to do this, because I love you and your family. But I want to do a song that, one, nobody really knows. I want to do a deep cut. And I want to do the songwriter's song. I want the one that you are most proud of as a writer.' And he goes, 'Oh, man, easy. That's 'Years.' If you feel like pulling it off, do it.'

"He sent it to me, and it's just, like, a professional song. It's talking about family, and it's letting people in. It's what I do on a daily basis making music. It's being too honest. It's shining a light on the darkest corners of your life.

"I told him, 'This is perfect for me. This is right in my wheelhouse. It's something artistic that you did, and I would love to do it.'"

Canada ended, like he had the electric set the day before, by taking the stage and powering through a half hour of his music, too. Fans got another chance to sing along with "Boys From Oklahoma" and another round of tearful embraces between Canada and artists and Canada and his family. And they got another round of shoutouts and thank-yous, including a curtain call for Kinzie, the last of the ten out of ten who went free in "51 Pieces" still in Canada's crew. Since joining that crew in May 2002 and meeting his wife, Melanie, at Cowboy's in San Antonio two years later, Kinzie's family has been Melanie, their daughters, Caroline and Rosemary, and whoever has been making music alongside Cody Canada and Jeremy Plato. He knows he could name his price to work for any band, venue or sound company in Texas, but that doesn't move him much.

"It's a love for Cody and for Shannon," Kinzie said. "They've taken my wife and me around the world, man. They've treated me like family for so long. I don't know if there's anything else I even *want* to do."

— — —

- 10 -

January 27, 2001

A COLLEGE DIVE bar, designed from top to bottom as a home for college music, sat shy of capacity—two hours before its "one in, one out" fate for the night was sealed. But all the seats were taken.

In a party town like Stillwater, Oklahoma, 7 p.m. on a Saturday night in January is early. And this dive bar, longer than it was wide, with wooden booths lining the left side, wooden picnic tables on the concrete floor in the middle and a saddle-lined, beer-only bar on the right side, had its earlies—the people for whom six hours of beer drinking in the same bar meant a guaranteed seat. Miss a seat at 7:00 and the punishment when Cross Canadian Ragweed started at 10:00 was standing so close to the next person there was barely room to lift a beer to drink it. The earlies had to be hard-core, sure, but they knew what they were doing.

Or they did, on this night, until the news alert scrolled across the television above the bar.

"Report: Plane carrying Oklahoma State basketball team missing."

A gasp or two. Fingers pointing. A second wave of gasps. A wave of "What?"

Silence.

Stares.

The Wormy Dog Saloon perched one story above The Strip—the stretch of bars along Washington Street in Stillwater running south from campus where the fraternity and sorority houses fade into apartments and off-campus living. The Strip is far enough from Eskimo Joe's so as not to step on its toes, but close enough that a long barhop is possible. Moreover, The Strip is the closest off-campus entertainment district to the residence halls.

In 2001, the Wormy Dog was the northernmost bar on The Strip and closest to campus, the gateway to a three-block stretch of facades with names like Willie's, the Copper Penny, J.R. Murphy's and Mike's College Bar. Each had its own vibe. It just happened that the Dog was the Red Dirt venue. On Saturday nights during the school year, every bar on The Strip dabbled with its 200-ish capacity, with clientele varying with the vibe.

They were all doing just that when the sun went down on January 27, 2001. By the end of the night, they were all backdrops to the same heartbreak.

By the end of the night, a Beechcraft King Air charter plane had crashed in rural Colorado.

By the end of the night, Nate Fleming, Daniel Lawson, Bill Teegins, Will Hancock, Jared Weiberg, Pat Noyes, Kendall Durfey, Brian Luinstra, Bjorn Fahlstrom and Denver Mills were confirmed dead. Two Oklahoma State basketball players, the Oklahoma State radio play-by-play voice, the lead media relations director, four members of the basketball program and two crew members, all dead. They were returning on one of three planes bringing the basketball team back from a defeat at Colorado that afternoon. They were on the one that did not make it.

A few blocks away, at a friend's house within walking distance of the bar, Cross Canadian Ragweed got the news while getting ready to headline the Dog a few hours later.

Fronting the band, Cody Canada and his bandmates, Jeremy Plato, Randy Ragsdale and Grady Cross, had rolled into town from the previous night's gig in Tulsa that afternoon to load in, joined by Canada's wife, Shannon, sound man Chris McCoy and merch slinger Nathan Coit.

"I remember everybody being super excited about the gig," Cody Canada said. "And I remember getting out of the shower and coming downstairs, and all the girls sitting in front of the TV just crying. I remember not saying anything to them but just looking at the TV and saying, 'Holy shit, man.'"

The news reports swept across Stillwater in waves. From 7 to 8 p.m., sketchy news of a plane that did not return. From 8 to 9 p.m., unconfirmed reports of a crash in Colorado.

From about 10 p.m. on, the pieces all fit, in the worst way imaginable.

From about 10 p.m. on, the Wormy Dog's capacity hit, with 200 (give or take) people inside and barely room to move and another 10 to 15 lined up on the stairs outside, hoping to get in.

From about 10 p.m. on, Ragweed had a gig to play.

"We were kids, man," Cody said. "We were 21 but not by much. And for this? We were kids."

The bars across campus were no longer party rooms. The frat houses and apartments were no longer pregame spots. To a great many in Stillwater, students or otherwise, the places they ran to that night became their support and their comfort. As bandleader and the one on the microphone, Cody Canada was about to become the voice of support to the Wormy Dog, and the Wormy Dog was about to become the image of comfort to him.

• • •

"Stoney says you have my hat"

The 2000–2001 school year was my senior year at OSU. I was the sports editor of the *O'Collegian*, the campus paper, and I had a part-time job in the sports department at *The Daily Oklahoman*, the newspaper in Oklahoma City, 60 miles south of Stillwater.

In the fall of 2000, I had two goals for my time as sports editor: I wanted to take a trip with a varsity team, and I wanted to visit Colorado.

My chance to take a trip with the varsity arose in September of that year. It was a tradition for members of the athletic department to invite a member of the campus paper to ride with the team to an away football game. My invitation came for a late September football game in Austin, where the Texas Longhorns eventually ended up dominating the Cowboys, 42-7.

But when I got the invitation, two weeks before the game, I was in.

On the Tuesday before the game, I stumbled up to the Wormy Dog Saloon for an acoustic show by Cody Canada. I had never met him, although I had spent most of the summer working Ragweed lyrics into my sports columns at the *O'Colly* (it was summer, whatever).

I had, however, met Stoney LaRue. Stoney lived in Stillwater and had spent the summer noticing the same shoutouts in my columns. I was new to Red Dirt, and when I saw I could get a reaction from him by name-dropping him or his musical friends, I started doing it more and more.

So when Canada came to the Wormy Dog for this acoustic gig, Stoney made a point to introduce me. He pulled me over to Canada and started hyping me up like I wrote for *Pitchfork* or something: "He's the *sports editor,* and he's writing about us, like, every day."

Canada was cordial but also immediately had an idea: "Well, if you want to write about us, we're playing in Austin on Saturday night after the OSU-Texas game at Lucy's. Me, Boland, Stoney. Come on down—you can have all access."

The football team's invite never stood a chance. I bailed on the trip and bailed on covering the game.

Instead, I drove to Austin, interviewed Ragweed and wrote up the concert at Lucy's Retired Surfers Bar. Stoney had opened, wearing a big cowboy hat. Jason Boland & The Stragglers middled with easily a 90-minute set, and Ragweed closed with 90 more before they all jammed an encore. The bartenders at Lucy's made a drink that involved setting the ceiling on fire. I made the right call.

I didn't leave the athletic department in a lurch. I sent my assistant sports editor in my place. On the return trip to Stillwater after the game, he was seated next to OSU play-by-play voice Bill Teegins.

A month later, I had a chance to knock the other must-do off my list. I talked the *O'Colly* managers into ponying up money for a flight and hotel to send me to Colorado to cover the OSU-Colorado football game at the end of October. Ultimately, the Buffalos held off the Cowboys, 31-27.

But when I set up that trip, two weeks before the game, I was in.

And then I went to the Wormy Dog.

Stoney LaRue had an acoustic gig and told me he was putting a band together. "We're playing down in New Braunfels, opening for The Great Divide. Come check us out."

My trip to Colorado never stood a chance. I bailed on the trip and bailed on covering the game.

I drove eight hours to New Braunfels, to a dance hall called Saengerhalle, and watched Stoney's first gig with his very short-lived first band. (He called it Gypsy Steel. The name and band didn't take.) When it was over, he called me backstage and introduced me to Mike McClure, lead singer of The Great Divide.

"You wanna write an article?"

Once again, I had made the right call.

By the end of 2000, I was wildly comfortable in the Red Dirt scene. The ethics of writing about something you wanted to be a part of may not have been high, but the results were.

On New Year's Eve, I talked a friend into riding through a snow-and-ice storm from Stillwater to Stephenville, Texas, where Ragweed headlined the year-end show, and I ended up in the band's hotel room for an after-party. You'll never believe this, but Stoney LaRue showed up to the party.

Stoney was wearing what I thought was a cool hat. Later on, I would learn it was a bowler hat, given to Cody Canada by Mike McClure. But that night, it was just a cool hat. I was wearing a Lucy's bar baseball cap I had bought on that earlier trip to Austin.

At some point, Stoney grabbed my hat, placed the bowler hat on my head and mine on his and went back to whatever he was doing.

The next day, after a drive back to Stillwater and Stragglers show at the Tumbleweed, after which my friend who had driven me on the trip got a very questionable DUI, I made it home.

And, I had Cody's hat.

January became less about my last semester in college and more about Red Dirt exploration. I spent an all-nighter at the Yellow House, where LaRue and Boland had brought Bob Childers and Randy Crouch over to jam—the sun had long risen before the musicians ended the session with Crouch's "Big Shot Rich Man." I made a solo trip to Lucy's for my 22nd birthday, the weekend of January 20, where Ragweed played again.

But the weekend of January 27, I had a different plan in mind: The Cowboys were playing at Colorado in basketball. This was my last chance at a Colorado trip, so I decided to make a play at combining my goals. I also knew full well that Ragweed had two gigs that weekend: Friday night in Tulsa at Steamroller Blues and Saturday in Stillwater. But I decided I could suck it up and miss one weekend of music. I tracked down OSU basketball media relations director Will Hancock and asked if there was any way he could make room for me on the team flight to and from Boulder for the basketball game. Will liked me and told me he'd try and get back to me. This was on Monday, six days before the game.

Wondering where I went and who I saw on Monday night? Yeah, you already know.

I walked into the Wormy Dog, where Stoney always played acoustic on Mondays, wearing the bowler hat from New Year's Eve. I hadn't known what to make of it, so I had taken a piece of masking tape and labeled it "THINKING CAP."

Whatever, it was funny.

As soon as he saw me, Stoney pointed at me like I had carried the Mona Lisa itself into the bar. "That's Cody Canada's hat!"

That was the entire conversation, though. It didn't lead anywhere. Stoney played. I listened. I went home. I threw the hat in the corner.

The next morning, on my way out the door for class, my phone rang, with Cody on the other end.

"Hey, man. Stoney says you have my hat. McClure gave me that hat, so, uh, give it back."

"Oh. Yeah, it's right here. I'll get it to you."

"You comin' to the shows this weekend?"

Remember that January was less about college and more about music? The Red Dirt heir apparent was personally requesting *my* presence? Another Colorado trip never stood a chance. Obviously, I was going to bail on the trip and bail on covering the game.

So I said, "Well, I am supposed to be gone for work, but Ragweed shows are probably more fun. But help me with a reason I won't sound lame."

"We'll put you on the guest list. If you want to review the shows or write us up, go for it."

I told Cody I'd see him Friday, and I ran into Will Hancock at basketball practice that afternoon and told him not to bother trying to bring me along to Colorado.

Like the other two times, I ended that conversation confident I was doing the right thing.

In retrospect, I have no idea if I'd have gotten an official invitation, and I have no idea where I'd have been flying if I did (but the traveling media were on the plane that crashed). In the week following the crash, I definitely gave more interviews with a thankful-to-be-alive tone than I would give now. Hell, today I probably wouldn't have even gone public at all. But at the time, we were young, and as I would learn, many people in my circles did indeed think I was on the plane that had crashed.

No. The night it happened, I was at the Wormy Dog, going through hell with every other Cowboy and Cowgirl in the bar.

The Wormy Dog was maybe 200 yards from the door to the newspaper office. When the news came on TV, I was at the bar. But I nearly immediately ran over to the *O'Colly* office. It was a journalistic reaction—I didn't need time alone, I just wanted to know what happened. Being a Saturday night, we did not have a paper to put out the next day. Our next edition wouldn't be published until Monday.

But, I watched the names roll by and the confirmations come in.

My initial, knee-jerk reaction was straight-up horror for Karen Hancock, the Oklahoma State women's soccer coach. My first paid beat at *The O'Collegian* had been covering her team the season before. She was married to Will Hancock. Their only child, Andie, had been born the previous November, barely two months before.

Then, I thought of Eddie Sutton. The Cowboys' basketball coach was clearly in the twilight of his career and coaching his alma mater had been viewed as the ultimate homecoming story in Stillwater. Now, he would have to be the public face of unspeakable tragedy on campus and throughout college basketball.

Next, I thought about Bill Teegins and the radio team. I had met Daniel Lawson and Nate Fleming plenty of times before. This was all in the span of maybe 90 seconds, sitting alone in the newsroom. The magnitude set in swiftly.

A wave of realization swept over me: This was going to devastate OSU, and as sports editor, I was going to be responsible for our coverage.

It's the same professional responsibility that sweeps over me now. When a disaster strikes, journalists get steely-eyed. They get tunnel vision. They find a way to separate themselves from the story and tell it. The good ones do it compassionately. The good ones know their audience. I learned all that, for once and for good, sitting alone at my desk at the newspaper office, while a campus and city were in shock all around me.

I resolved at the time to be the first one at work on Sunday. I'd come up with a plan, and as a paper, we would be the comfort that campus needed. But back in the moment, I also knew all I wanted to do was get back to the Wormy Dog. So that's where I went.

Not long after I got back, two college newspaper bosses ran frantically into the Dog—my editor in chief and my managing editor. They saw me and dashed through the heads and arms and beers to me. We had a group hug.

"So you weren't on the plane, huh," the managing editor, Josh Bozarth, said.

That was the first time I thought of myself. The exchanges I had about going to the game had been so fleeting that I forgot I had told newspaper colleagues I was trying to go. I had been in the same panic as the rest of campus and not even thinking that there was a group of people who thought I had gone with the team (and, it would be several more hours before I'd get home to a succession of voicemails from my own frantic family).

"No. I wanted to come get drunk and listen to music instead," is what I think I said back.

"OK. Well now that we see you're OK, we're going to go out to a press conference at the airport."

"You want me to come?"

"Nah. We got it. You need to be here tonight."

"OK. But I'm in charge tomorrow. Get to the office when you can, but get some rest too. I'll have a plan."

This exchange took place in front of both Canadas as well as bar owner Eric Wooley. When my coworkers left, three sets of blank stares hit back at me.

All I said was, "I think I would have been on that plane."

What else can you do? We cried.

● ● ●

"We're gonna play"

At 10 p.m., the band's original start time, Cross Canadian Ragweed did not take the stage. Right about that time, the bar televisions carried news coverage of a hastily assembled news conference about the crash. The 10 deaths were confirmed by authorities. There would be another news conference the next day with updates.

Beer glasses did not clink. The news conference, gasps and incredibly vivid, stick-in-your-memories-forever sobs were all anyone heard.

When it was over, Cody Canada walked up to the microphone and said, "Hey. What do you want us to do? We're gonna play, if that's OK."

The Wormy Dog erupted.

For everybody in that bar, that was the second that grief and community met. This was bad, but we were going to get through it together, and it was going to take all of us.

"I've said it a thousand times. Without that city of Stillwater, I wouldn't have anything," Cody said, recalling that night. "Ragweed wouldn't have done what we did. I wouldn't have met Shannon or McClure or known about The Farm. That was where I learned to do it right, to be a man.

"When I looked out in that crowd, I saw everybody struggling. Nothing like that had ever happened there or to them. I felt like, in that moment, we had to do for them what it is that we do.

"We play music."

Back at the Wormy Dog that night, Ragweed ultimately did play. It was not a real set. There would be a stretch of songs followed by longer breaks to turn the television back up. The breaks were for hugs and tears throughout the room. The music was a reset for everyone until the next need for a break hit. At the end of the night, Wooley grabbed the microphone and said, "We're going to get every musician we can back up here as soon as we can. There's going to be a concert, and we're going to give every penny we raise to these families. Is that OK?"

Again, the Wormy Dog erupted.

By the next day, with Wooley promising the venue, Canada had rounded up Boland, LaRue, the Red Dirt Rangers and Steve Rice for a benefit concert that would ultimately fall 10 days later—the same night the basketball team played its first home game after the crash. It became a defining moment both for the grieving crowd at the Wormy Dog and for Canada's career.

"There needed to be somebody leading the charge, and I'm very capable of doing it," Canada said. "There needed to be some organization. I remember Coop [John Cooper of the Red Dirt Rangers], who I look up to, looking at me and asking me, 'What are we gonna do, man?' and it was instant: We're gonna do this right here. We're gonna play music, and we're gonna help heal our community the best we can."

Canada wrote "On a Cloud" the next week.

"You know me and my sports, I'm not a sports guy," he said about that song. "But I'm an OSU guy. Boland and I had just gotten to meet and hang out and have a beer with Teegins, and man, he was a celebrity. The voice of the Cowboys. Hearing him on the radio, he could get me excited.

"That was back in the day when I was just writing songs that fast. And it goes back to my style of writing with guts. And I felt like I owed him. That's what 'On a Cloud' was about."

"On a Cloud" made it onto *Cross Canadian Ragweed (The Purple Album)* as the 10th track.

> *Tell my brothers*
> *That I love 'em*
> *Tell my sisters that I'm free*
> *Tell my children*
> *Oh how I miss 'em*
> *But heaven's waitin' there for me*
> *On a cloud*

— — —

- 11 -

The Wormy Dog
and Red Dirt's Wings

IT MAY HELP one to consider the history of Red Dirt in Stillwater as two separate, distinct landscapes.

The first image you would conjure should be the classic Oklahoma sunset. Hazy, breezy, gold-red-brown-hued natural successor to the Dust Bowl. This was the era, dating back to Steve Ripley's band, Moses, calling its label Red Dirt Records in 1974. These were the days of artistic migration to Payne County, when Bob Childers, Gene Williams, Greg Jacobs, Chuck Dunlap and Tom Skinner settled in and around Stillwater and lived out the life that Woody Guthrie had once demanded of himself. This was the campfire era. This was the era of The Farm. The Red Dirt Rangers and Jimmy LaFave rose in stature. Stillwater burst with live music. Willie's Saloon may have been the center, but The Strip bustled with venues like the Mason Jar, Acme Bar and the Jail Saloon. The era snowballed upon itself, and generations of artists moved to Stillwater for the experience.

The second landscape you should imagine, then, would cover all the years since. Picture a monument this time. Make it elaborate. Inscribe the names of everyone from that first era. You can make it a mecca if it helps—a place modern-day artists come and play as a rite of passage, either in the parking lot of Eskimo Joe's or on the hardwood floors of the defiant Tumbleweed, just west of the city limits. There's not a lot of music made in Stillwater now, but everyone is at peace with it. This is the relic era. This is the era of the nostalgic rebuild of The Farm, in which the Red Dirt Relief Fund is actively reconstructing Childers' old Gypsy Cafe. A tangible monument. A tribute to the landscape from another generation. This era happened when a quick succession of artists used a foothold in Stillwater to move onward and upward, carrying Red Dirt with it. The Great Divide was first, followed by Cross Canadian Ragweed, Jason Boland & The Stragglers, No Justice and Stoney LaRue.

If time were geography, the border between these two landscapes would be 1996 to 2001. The hinterlands of the first landscape met the frontier of the second. Bob Childers' trailer burned down at The Farm. The Divide landed a major record deal, paving the way for Ragweed to rise even higher. That five-year period is appropriately viewed as the door through which Red Dirt walked out of Stillwater and into the world's roots music conscience.

Its gatekeeper? The Wormy Dog Saloon.

The venue did not have the staying power of Willie's, which is still in its original location today. It did not have the regional cache of Eskimo Joe's. It didn't even have liquor. The Dog was low-point beer only, although its sister property on Washington Street—the Wormy Dog Concert Hall—was a full-service bar.

What the Dog had was Red Dirt music.

It had a *lot* of Red Dirt music.

Chuck Thomson and Chip Glennon opened the bar in 1992. Its proximity to a religious building on Washington Avenue required the limitations on alcohol sales, so live music became the immediate appeal of the venue. The Great Divide and Red Dirt Rangers were early regulars. An underaged Cody Canada snagged a standing acoustic gig at the Dog in the mid-1990s and found its tiny stage to be the perfect proving ground for the band he and some friends formed in 1994, Cross Canadian Ragweed.

"It's where we established ourselves as a good local band," Canada said. "We were who to see—if Ragweed was in town or I was playing there, we rarely had a light night. It's where we got better."

It's also where he met and eventually wooed a Wormy Dog bartender named Shannon O'Neal. And when the two dated—they married in 1998—Canada took a day job beerbacking at the bar. From there, they plotted a path forward for Ragweed, with the Dog as the launch pad.

"We were kind of the de facto booking agents for the Wormy Dog," Canada said. "We brought in Pat Green, Todd Snider, anybody we could, as long as we got to open for these people."

Ragweed eventually generated enough buzz from the Dog to command headlining gigs in similarly sized bars in Texas, and Shannon would get recommendations from Ragweed's openers.

"I didn't have any music background at all," Shannon Canada recalls. "But during the day, between classes, I would just look up any of these bars I could find, and I would cold-call them. I said to these bands, 'Well, you're playing at the Wormy Dog, how'd you get that?' and I'd use that to call any place I could find and get Ragweed booked."

With encouragement from Reckless Kelly, Shannon pitched Ragweed to the owners of Lucy's Retired Surfers Bar in Austin.

"The guy who owned Lucy's had a bar manager who was not booking bands to his liking," Shannon said. "He was chewing his ass. His manager said something like, 'There's no good bands out there, blah blah.' And the owner said, 'You have this whole pile of promo pitches here. Just pick one. Call them. Book them.'

"And he reached down and the one he picked up was Ragweed's. He didn't listen to them or anything, just told the manager to do his job or he was out. And that was their first Austin gig."

As the two bands, Ragweed and Reckless, built a friendship, the bars the two bands called home became increasingly important to the other's scene. Ragweed became a regular at Lucy's, eventually commanding such a loyal crowd that they could pull off entire concerts at the Austin staple. By 2001, Stoney LaRue would open with an hour set, Jason Boland & The Stragglers would play a 90-minute second set, Ragweed would close with a two-hour set and all three would jam together for an encore.

Back in Stillwater, Reckless developed a cult following.

"That's a little foggy, but I do remember the first time we played the Wormy Dog," Willy Braun, Reckless front man, said. "We sold it out, which we thought was a big deal at the time. Of course, now, that's 150 people, but whatever. It was big then. I remember Ragweed being there and being all excited that we were in town. And Stoney LaRue was either a bouncer or a sound guy—a young, clean-cut kid."

Stoney LaRue's presence was important. At the time, with everyone in their early 20s, the question on the mind of bands playing the Dog was always the same: Where's the after-party?

Stoney always had the answer: "Come over to the Yellow House."

· · ·

The Yellow House

The Yellow House stood at 57 University Circle, at most 100 yards from the Oklahoma State University's undergrad dorms.

It took its name from its builder, a gentleman named Robert Yellow.

Hmmm. Hang on a second. That part is definitely wrong.

It took its name because it was covered in yellow siding. Just a big, bright, yellow house at the far end of a block-long semicircle road.

There is not really a Yellow House today. It was lifted off its foundation and moved across town during the university's expansion and eminent domain boom of the mid-2000s. There's no charity rebuilding it like at The Farm, but it holds every bit the importance to Red Dirt of The Farm.

From 1996 to 2001, the Yellow House supplanted The Farm as the hub of Red Dirt. Jason Boland moved into it with some high school friends from Harrah, Oklahoma, when he was a college student in '96. He won a poker game and landed the biggest room, where he'd live the next five years, launch his career and build Jason Boland & The Stragglers. Cody Canada lived there before he married Shannon O'Neal. Stoney started out sleeping on the couch and waited his turn for a bedroom to open up.

"It's always on my mind," Stoney LaRue said. "Carl, the squirrel who slept on my chest on more than one occasion. A hot tub full of beer cans. Late night bluegrass and weed. Shag carpet. It meant the world to me."

He was far from the only one to feel that way and far from the only one to start out sleeping on the couch in the living room until there was a proper room for him. If you were a band visiting Stillwater, you wanted an invite to the jam session after your concert. If you were in the Red Dirt scene in Stillwater, you wanted to live at the Yellow House.

But nobody's journey to the house and the impact it had matches up to that of Jim "Red" Wilhelm, who moved to Stillwater, about 25 miles from his hometown of Cushing, for college in the early 1990s. Early on, he was a frat boy who enjoyed the life Oklahoma State frat boys lead, and that entailed a whole lot of drink specials on

The Strip. It led him and his friends to a defunct sports bar, Sluggers, which was a block and a half south of the Wormy Dog on Washington Avenue.

"We all used to go to Sluggers for Monday Night Football," Wilhelm said. "They had some sort of special then. You'd pick a team when you walked in, and then you'd get a free pitcher when that team scored. So one of these nights, we all picked the Cowboys or whoever, and they were winning in a blowout, and we were all drinking pitcher after pitcher of free beer.

"At halftime, one of my friends—a Delt [Delta Tau Delta fraternity member]—says to me, 'Let's go over to that Wormy Dog place, because there is a guy up there singing songs, and he is freaking hilarious.' So we go over there, and it's the first time I ever went in there, and on stage is Mike *and* Cody."

At the time, McClure and Canada sharing acoustic shows was commonplace in Stillwater.

"They had some sort of real cheap beer special there, too," Wilhelm said, "so my buddy and I look at each other, and we just go, 'Screw Sluggers. This is much more fun.'

"There were maybe four or five of us, and we maybe doubled the crowd that night. And then we took a seat at a table kind of at the back of the bar. That was in the fall. By the springtime, we were on the rail, next to the stage, standing up when bands would play there."

Wilhelm became enough of a regular at the Dog for McClure to notice, and Wilhelm also had a friend at OSU who had a house in his hometown of Cushing. That house was used as a party house, miles from anywhere. And on one occasion, the friends threw a party to watch a pay-per-view boxing match at the house.

"The whole point was, one price for kegs, barbecue and pay-per-view fights," Wilhelm said. "I do remember the fight was over in, like, 40 seconds, and everyone was pissed off.

"But in my effort to gain some serious cred, I invited McClure to it. I said, 'Look man, come on out, bring your guitar and if you want, if the mood strikes you, get it out and play some songs. We'll pass a hat around and get tips for you.' And it's really funny to me now, because I remember him being like, 'Free beer and barbecue? I'm there.'

"And it was perfect. We spent the afternoon shooting skeet. Beautiful evening, food was great. And then, because the fight was so short, Mike went ahead and put on a house concert. And it just kicked the living shit out of everybody there. There's nobody who was there who didn't go away different.

"The thing that sticks out to me most is, Mike did this 15-minute rendition of 'God's Own Drunk,' and it took me *years* to research Jimmy Buffett's discography, to find the live version that Mike riffed most of the song from. It was about 60 percent Jimmy Buffett and 40 percent Mac just doing his thing. And it took me years to track down where he had heard it."

(For the record, the version was on a live Buffett album called *You Had to Be There*.)

That led to a lifelong friendship between Wilhelm and McClure. The two eventually lived together at a house in Stillwater and were joined by Canada. Wilhelm had an up-close seat as the two artists, prodded by alcohol and marijuana, stayed up late at night concocting stories of an entire alternate reality in which Elvis Presley had never died but rather had faked his death. In those stories, Elvis had a sidekick—a friend named Red whose antics constantly threatened to blow Elvis's cover. And from those stories, McClure and Canada started calling Jim Wilhelm "Red." The nickname took.

Years passed. The Divide took off. McClure moved away from Stillwater. Wilhelm moved back in with his hometown friends for a time. Then, over the first Christmas break after Boland moved into the Yellow House, Wilhelm found himself and Boland in Stillwater after their friends had gone home for the holiday. He paid a visit, liquor store booty in tow.

"It was just me, Boland and a jar of Georgia moonshine, which is not actually moonshine, it's just homemade rum," Wilhelm said. "But whatever, one billion pirates can't be wrong.

"Everybody else had gone home. This was the last Friday night before Christmas. The Yellow House was just him and me. And we sat there, and we listened to Robert Earl Keen, and then I remember Boland playing 'The Devil Pays in Gold' and 'She Wore Red Dresses.' And when you put those songs in order, they kind of tell a longer story.

"And it just floored me. I don't know how to even describe it. It changed me. And by that point, I'd been changed several times. The first time someone really lays 'Sam Stone' on you and you suck it all in, it changes you. It was like that. It's kind of even hard for me to say, but the truth is, I kind of, after that night, just walked away from the life I was living and started living in the Yellow House.

"I ended up dropping out of school. I was working at the Dog at the time, and I was making good tips. The car that I drove that night, I literally left where it was, and later it was hauled away. I just immersed myself in music, and I became the conduit for all those guys."

What Wilhelm described about the Yellow House was of course familial, but it was also professional. The artists who lived there, especially Boland and Canada, found it to be the first testing ground for their music.

"You have to realize, when these guys wrote a song, they had to impress us in the Yellow House with it," he said. "If we didn't like it, they'd just scrap it. And if we approved, then they would take it over to the Wormy Dog and try it out."

Wilhelm relayed a story of the time Canada and a friend drove from Stillwater to Tennessee to catch a James Brown concert. They ended up lost and broke and in a random bar, never making the show, but they did write the song "Alabama" on the way home. That song went on to become one of the biggest hits and best-known Cross Canadian Ragweed songs. On that trip, Wilhelm said that Canada went straight from the car to the living room of the Yellow House to play it.

"I was not there. I was home in Cushing," Wilhelm said. "So Boland picks up the phone—one of those hard-wired telephones—and he holds it up while Cody plays 'Alabama' in front of other people for the first time. And I heard it, and I was so moved by it that I told Boland, 'Stay there!' and I drove the 25 miles back to Stillwater just so I could make Cody play it again in front of me."

With a home base and a home bar, the last of Stillwater's true Red Dirt generations forged a virtual powderkeg. All they needed was the spark.

* * *

Wooley's Place

Chuck Thomson deserves the lion's share of credit for not only opening the Dog, but recognizing its potential as a live music venue. But Thomson was a true adult in the room, disapproving if an artist played drunk and holding them to standards that everyone agreed were parental in nature.

Then, in 1998, he put the venue up for sale.

The person who happened upon it next was anything but parental. He was, in every sense of the word, one of the guys.

Eric Wooley came to Oklahoma State for school in the mid-'90s and by 1998 was the manager of the Copper Horse Saloon, another bar on The Strip.

"During the afternoons there, we'd get some Realtors who would come in, the professionals would stop by for happy hour," Wooley said. "And one day, I remember this group of people talking about this bar on The Strip coming up for sale. And at that point, we were booking Jason and Cody at the Copper Horse, too. Stoney had just played his first gig ever there. So I perk up and this Realtor says, 'This bar, would you be interested in potentially buying it?' And I'm thinking, *Sure, totally.* 'Which bar are you talking about?'

"She says, 'the Wormy Dog.'

"And I'm like, 'Yes. Mark it as sold. Whatever I can do, we'll get this thing bought and done. Do not put this on the market.'"

The sale went down. Wooley took over the bar and the Wormy Dog brand. The building, which also housed longtime memorabilia shop Causley Productions, remained in the hands of James Causley. But the Dog was Wooley's. It was football season, and that meant the crowds were Wooley's as well.

"It was perfect for us," Wooley said. "By that point, the Wormy Dog was down to live music once or twice a month, using penny beer nights and specials to draw people in. We closed it on September 15 and opened it up on the first football game weekend after that. We had Twelve Pearls and another band opening. That was the start of a new era of live Red Dirt music, every night, at that bar."

Wooley was well-versed in Stillwater's music. He was a fan of The Divide, friends with the Canadas and a contemporary of Boland.

"I was traditional country and Red Dirt all the way," Wooley said. "I knew these guys. I respected their music, and I wanted to showcase more of that music in Stillwater."

Just before Wooley took over the bar, Ragweed recorded *Live & Loud at the Wormy Dog Saloon,* the album that put it on the map across Texas. The live versions of "Boys from Oklahoma" and "Carney" defined Ragweed throughout most, and in some ways all, of its career that followed.

But the album also had the effect—in the very early days of the Internet—of sharing the Wormy Dog beyond just word of mouth, and it, too, became a destination in Texas and Americana circuits. Todd Snider, Robert Earl Keen, Charlie Robison, Bruce Robison, George DeVore and The Roam and Roger Clyne and the Peacemakers (in one of that band's first shows after the breakup of Clyne's previous band, The Refreshments) all played concerts that went down in such lore that they commemorated them with permanent stencils on the concrete wall behind the bar's stage. When the Wormy Dog was sold to become apartments in 2004, the new owners required that those stencils not be removed nor painted over.

The experience of Wormy Dog shows between 1998 and 2002 remains the zenith of Red Dirt experiences. The atmosphere—concrete walls, saddles for barstools and old wooden bars offsetting the stage—contributed. So, too, did the lack of rules. ("You can swing from the rafters in here, I've seen it done," Willy Braun said to the crowd during a Reckless Kelly show in late 2000.) And for Wooley, that is what he views as the bar's biggest contribution to the scene.

"Saint Patrick's Day in 1999, we got Pat Green there to headline," Wooley said. "We had Ragweed up before them. We had Jason Boland on the bill. We had Reckless Kelly playing. We had Stoney. If you look at that lineup now, today, that music alone is unreal.

"When you put it in a bar that held barely 200 people, that's what I am amazed by now: that you could have that level of music and be that intimate with the bands.

"It cannot be done again. It was special, and I'm proud of it, always."

By the time Wooley moved away from Stillwater in 2004, the Wormy Dog's legacy was cemented. The Divide's home. Ragweed's palace. Boland's proving ground. Stoney's stomping ground.

Thomson, with some early investment help from a very successful Ragweed at that point, opened a second incarnation of the Wormy Dog in Oklahoma City's Bricktown district in 2004. That bar, complete with the saddle barstools, took on its own life as the hub of Red Dirt and the first major hub Oklahoma City ever had. A bi-level venue, it could easily accommodate the demands of a band like Ragweed, even at the height of its popularity, as well as Boland and the then-up-and-coming Turnpike Troubadours.

But the sequel was also more formal. There were rules. There were bouncers who would enforce them. Last call meant last call. There was no secret basement to hide in once the doors locked for the night. It was the price of progress.

The artists who graced both bars' stages—the ones who witnessed the passing of the torch across the border from one Red Dirt landscape to another—would not want the story told any other way.

— — —

- 12 -

Boland

....

A PAIR OF theories, like math equations, prove each other: Jason Boland cannot possibly be a country music superstar, because a country music superstar would not carry the torch for a niche scene like Red Dirt. And Jason Boland cannot possibly carry the torch for Red Dirt, because if he did, country music would swoop in, snatch him up and make him a superstar.

Anyway, let's get high and talk about Boland.

Has anybody been more sagely representative of Red Dirt while so rarely viewed as the trendsetter for the scene than him? In 2020, Jason Boland & The Stragglers celebrated the 20-year anniversary of their first album. All told, they have released 12 albums, nine of which were in-studio. They have become adopted sons of The Great Divide, Cross Canadian Ragweed and Shooter Jennings—all of which The Stragglers have beat in longevity (even if the 2018 departure of drummer Brad Rice means that only Boland and bassist Grant Tracy remain from the 1998 incarnation). They have recorded one of the songs on a short list of certifiable Red Dirt anthems—the Boland-penned "Pearl Snaps"—and cofounded the current bellwether music festival in the scene, Medicine Stone.

And more than any other band, The Stragglers gave a platform in the late aughts to a band of Okies looking to spread word of their own music beyond Oklahoma. There are people to this day who swear that the Turnpike Troubadours opening for Jason Boland & The Stragglers circa 2009 were the best shows that have ever been done.

But it's also true that The Stragglers' time as the bar-setting band in Red Dirt was comparatively short. The band's rise came on the heels of Ragweed, who burned down the scene until an abrupt end in 2010. Boland had only a couple of years, albeit a time frame that included the masterpiece 2011 album *Rancho Alto*, before Turnpike forged its way atop every bill and onto every Internet jukebox in Tornado Alley by 2013.

It's not fair to Boland, who brought an Ernest Tubb-style baritone voice from Harrah, Oklahoma, to Oklahoma State in the mid-1990s, lacking motivation and a proper future, and who moved to Texas in 2002 with The Stragglers capable of head-lining any venue in Stillwater. But fair or not, those are the cards life dealt. And in his view, the direction was worth it regardless of what it became.

"I don't think anybody ever looked at playing music for people and that being your life, and writing songs and being part of this world was real," Boland said. "You don't have to wink when you say it, like when they tell you, 'You can be an astronaut!' or 'You can be the president!' This was not in theory. All you had to do was live it. And if you express yourself and you express yourself with all of your being and you really find a way to connect and relate to what any of us were trying to do—just say something!—it was possible."

Boland's story itself is common in Red Dirt—a college kid absent direction made his way to The Farm and the rest is history—but Boland's approach to it belied a contemplative mind that drove him even before he realized what it was driving him toward.

"I started playing piano when I was very young, but I got disillusioned with hav-ing to do recitals and playing in front of people, oddly enough," Boland said. "But I developed an interest in the guitar in early middle school. It looked fun, and I had always wanted to get into some form of music. Honestly, I left the movie *Crossroads*, watching Steve Vai and Ralph Macchio, and I said, 'That looks fun,' and my dad said, 'I have a guitar in the attic.' And that shocked me. I went, 'What do you have a guitar for?'

"He got it down and played a couple of classic blues riffs. And I thought, 'Oh my God, why haven't you shown me this?' Well, it wasn't anything to him, just him play-ing around when he was in college. But I started playing, and I was one of the kids back in the day that they would have put me on so many pills nowadays. Back then, all I needed was an ass-kicking or I needed to be smacked or something. But that worked too! It settled me down, but it taught me to fidget in my mind. I go back and look at me as a kid, and I think, *Man, I had it pretty good.* I could not sit still as a kid, I could not read books—maybe in high school I read two books front to back. Since then, I can sit down with a book and calm myself down, but as a kid, no way. At the time, you don't think that's me.

"But I had a friend who wrote a song. And I thought, *Man. You wrote that?* And the next question was, what's stopping me from it? So I tried to just write a song and played it for some friends. I did that for a while, but there was never any notion of what I was supposed to do with it. Nothing in the alternative world was real at that time."

He was in the business school at Oklahoma State. He was in the Lambda Chi fra-ternity. But a handful of chance encounters led him into Red Dirt. One, in particular, sent Boland into the throes of Red Dirt for good.

"A really good buddy of mine who lives down in South Texas now, Derek Crane, was a Lambda Chi," Cody Canada said. "So after a gig at the Wormy Dog one night, I went across the street to the Lambda Chi house looking for him. I didn't know how frats work. I thought you just walked through the door. I said, 'I'm looking for Derek

Crane,' and they said, 'Go around to the basement door.' And that's what I did.

"So I just jiggled the handle and opened the door. When I did that, this guy just put his hand up and said, 'Hey! You can't just come in here!' It was Boland.

"So I said, 'I'm looking for Derek Crane.' Now, Boland said I was just a cocky, smirky shit. I had this hat that had a Santa Fe skull on it. How he tells it now is, 'You had smoke coming out the side of your mouth and going in your nose, going, I'm looking for Derek Crane. Well, I don't give a shit who you're looking for.'

"He wasn't letting me in is what I'm saying.

"And then I looked in the room and saw a guitar. So I said, 'Oh, you play?' And he kind of stopped cold. 'Yeah I do. You?' And I go, 'Yeah. That's why I'm here.' And he says, 'Aw, come on in, man!'

"So I came in, we got to talking and he says that Derek isn't here. So I say no problem, tell him Canada stopped by, but I also said I played every Tuesday at the Dog and every Thursday at Key West. 'Stop in if you ever want to get up and do a tune or something.'

"And then Boland started dropping a $10 bill in my tip jar every Tuesday. That's a lot of money then. It would buy 10 bean-and-cheese burritos from Taco Mayo. I'm serious, I could eat for a week on $10. He always wanted me to play 'O.D.'d in Denver.'

"Anyway, Boland started showing up, and one night I invited him up at Key West. He was really nervous. He got up and sang 'Man in the Moon'—which he never recorded. And I said, 'That's really cool.' It was instant love."

By early 1998, Boland and Canada were sharing the Tuesday night acoustic gig at the Wormy Dog. By 2000, Canada had moved to Yukon and Boland had the Tuesday gig to himself and shared a Wednesday gig at Eskimo Joe's with Stoney LaRue. All three artists, at various points, lived at the Yellow House on University Circle, just southwest of the OSU campus and heir to The Farm as the Red Dirt songwriters' haven.

"Cody was like Tom Skinner to me," Boland said. "He was so inviting and unthreatened by you. He was a really talented guy. All this stuff gets missed by what happened and who got successful. Cody's a talented-ass dude. He's got a stage charisma. He's got a wonderful voice. He's a great songwriter. He had it, man. He went for it. And for a guy like that, I think he felt, not in a cocky way, so unthreatened, so including to anyone else that was playing. He would be like, 'Yeah, man, come out' and get us up on stage.

"Lots of people when they have something, they don't do that for people. They want to keep it and push people away. For Cody to be so brave and so unthreatened at the same time, he just was able to establish a relationship where I could immediately start writing with him and bounce ideas off him. The main thing with him was how inclusive he was, how encouraging he was. That's really rare, to basically encourage someone who's going to come compete with you for something."

* * *

The Stragglers

Boland formed The Stragglers in 1998 with Rice, Tracy, guitar player Roger Ray and fiddle player Dana Hazzard. Boland had met Ray at The Farm in the mid-1990s after a night out and the two struck up a friendship.

Hazzard left in late 2001, and the fiddle spot in the band had multiple players and occasionally went away, but Ray was a mainstay until 2012 and Rice was until late 2018.

In the first half-decade plus, they cut their learning curve. *Pearl Snaps*, their Lloyd Maines–produced debut album, featuring both the title track and "If I Ever Get Back to Oklahoma"—both of which have intensely stood the test of time in Red Dirt—came out in 2000 and was followed a year later by *Truckstop Diaries* (that one produced by Mike McClure and J.J. Lester of The Great Divide).

Jim "Red" Wilhelm lived with Boland at the Yellow House in Stillwater and was the band's first tour manager. He recalls the motivation for *Pearl Snaps* happening almost by chance on a hungover drive from a show at the Brickhouse in Amarillo to City Limits in Stephenville, Texas, in late 1998. He picks up the story at the band's hotel before the first show.

"The Golden Light, when we played there in Amarillo, would put us up in the old Bronco Motel, an old motor court. And in my hazy, '70s-movie-colored, dusted memories, I loved stepping out of the Bronco into that motor court," Wilhelm said. "Well, we graduated to playing the Brickhouse, and they usually put bands up in a Holiday Inn Express. Well, on this trip, that hotel is booked, so their booker asks me if we have a preference of where to stay, and I said, 'We love the Bronco, man.' So they book us there, but when we get to the motel, we walk into the room, and there on the little circular table is a case of Thunderbird wine. A case. Twenty-four bottles. And warm.

"Well, we all agreed, 'Let's not drink this tonight. Let's save it for our trip to Stephenville tomorrow.'

"Amarillo to Stephenville is six hours. How much Thunderbird do you think you can drink if you're a band in a Suburban for six hours? Well the answer is, about a case!

"Well, Roger [Ray] gets up that morning, and he decides that this six hours in a Suburban, drinking warm Thunderbird wine, would be a great time to talk about where the band is and where the band is going. So for six hours, that's what we do. And we say we need an album.

"We get to Stephenville, and I get it together well enough to get us loaded in, and eventually we have a really good show. And that show gets us on the bill with The Great Divide that summer at their Independence Day Jam [held outdoors at City Limits]. And it's at that show that Jason meets Lloyd Maines, tells him he's looking to do an album and asks if Lloyd would mind producing it. Well, maybe to our surprise as a young band, Maines was in, and we were off.

"Going down to Cedar Creek Studios in Austin and recording that with Lloyd Maines was a seminal moment for The Stragglers. Each member of the band picked up so much from that experience with Lloyd, and I don't mean popularity, I mean artistically, that they skyrocketed. That time in Cedar Creek was one of those behind-the-curtain moments, where you see the business of it. If we're playing grab-ass in the studio, this guy we're paying $150 an hour is still sitting there, so it's costing us money. But more than that, we're supposed to be professionals. And that was one of those first eye-opening times where we saw there's a business side to music."

Pearl Snaps was released in 2000. It had the title track, as well as "Ponies," "If I Ever Get Back to Oklahoma," "Somewhere Down in Texas" and "Big Shot Rich Man," all of which are major parts of The Stragglers' sets to this day. The album is regarded by most veterans of the scene as the best debut album in Red Dirt history.

"There are artistic moments, in the production of *Pearl Snaps*, some that are very significant, others that are very minor, that I believe make or break the album," Wilhelm said. "The times when Roger does some underlying stuff on acoustic guitar, in a way that the song would just be distant without, is one example.

"The idea of the dream sequence at the end of 'Ponies,' where the fiddle plays out and it has that very down-on-the-bridge kind of squeak to it, that was extemporaneous. This is funny now, because everybody went into *Pearl Snaps* not focusing on 'Pearl Snaps.' We knew this because he'd been playing it for three years! 'Ponies' was the song that, I think, everybody would look at to interpret Jason Boland & The Stragglers. That original band is defined by 'Ponies.'

"That song, stripped down, is only a minute and a half long. Well, Lloyd heard that and he goes, 'If it's only that long, then you can't put it on an album.' And it was Lloyd—Lloyd composed the interlude. In the middle of the song, when Roger Ray plays the melody to 'Ghost Riders in the Sky,' that was something that he had only touched on when he played it originally. Lloyd was the one who went, 'No. Pick it all the way out. Put it on a baritone guitar and make it sound like Johnny Cash's version.' And then, at the end, during the fiddle sequence, Lloyd just asked the session player to play a dreamy, waking-up-from-a-long-sleep haze. 'Can you play that out for us for, like, two minutes?' And that's exactly what he did."

Boland's first two albums—*Pearl Snaps* was followed up shortly with *Truckstop Diaries, Vol. 1*, produced by Mike McClure and J.J. Lester of The Great Divide—were unapologetically country, even by Red Dirt standards, playing up the fiddle, steel guitar and Boland's baritone. Crowds ate it up, and within five years of forming, the band was big enough to headline any Texas dance hall.

At the time, they were the party band of Red Dirt. It was impossible for a Stragglers show to get too wild, too risque or too drunken. Their shows could easily exceed three hours regularly, and their after-parties could last well past sunrise. No band in Red Dirt before or since has come as close to living out the debauchery side of their songs like The Stragglers. Even on the heels of Ragweed, known for a decade-plus for fun above all else, Boland and his band stood out for partying.

It culminated in a side-of-the-highway seizure in 2005 after Boland tried to quit alcohol cold turkey, and it led him to rehab in 2006. He has not touched alcohol since. Today, The Stragglers are one of the most thorough bands in the scene. No lyrics are off limits and no harmony, so long as it fits the four-piece, is too tough.

But there is also an understanding that the early years involved shooting themselves in the foot.

"We kind of self-destructed," former drummer Brad Rice said. "Boland ended up going to rehab for alcohol, but we *all* personally had our own demons like that. I personally drank until 2014 and haven't drank a drop since then.

"For record labels, at the time they were looking at us, we were probably too much of a gamble. You never knew what Jason would say on the mic when he was drinking. You never knew what any of us would do on any given night. Impressions like that, I think, made us too much of a risk for major labels."

(Note: I sat down with Brad Rice in September 2018 for an interview for this book. He left The Stragglers a month later [in and around his reasons, he had also opened his own metal art shop in Tulsa]. After listening, given Rice's insight, I decided to keep his perspective on the band's history as a part of this book. Rice remains a Red Dirt icon and is a profound person in his own right. It would be impossible to properly tell the band's story without his views.)

The present-day Stragglers, far from their hell-raising origins, would certainly demand attention from any record label—if labels were still required as proof of success in the business.

Boland, his wife, Mandy, and their dog, Gary Stewart Boland, make their home in the Texas Hill Country. But his music rarely strays far from his Red Dirt influences. He put "Big Shot Rich Man" by Randy Crouch on *Pearl Snaps* and "Mexican Holiday," also from Crouch, on *Truckstop Diaries*. He has twice recorded Bob Childers, putting "Outlaw Band" and "Tennessee Whiskey, Texas Weed" on a pair of albums each. On *Rancho Alto*, he cut Childers' "Woody's Road" and Greg Jacobs' story of eminent domain taking families' lands away to build Lake Eufaula, "Farmer's Luck."

At the same time, he has shown a range in his own songwriting that echoes Childers, LaFave and Skinner. His 2016 album, *Squelch*, was profanity-laced, political and pointed (both "I Guess It's Alright to Be an Asshole" and "Fuck, Fight and Rodeo" particularly tick all those boxes). He followed that with *Hard Times Are Relative* in 2018, an album heavy on storytelling, with the title cut in particular spinning a yarn so well it can pull tears. There's even a very good dog in the final verse. He may have stayed independent for two decades, but that only means his music did the same.

"Everybody when they want to make it look or sound muddy, it's them trying to justify in their minds how far they wanted to bend for money," Boland said. "And all we ever wanted to do was what every band truly wants to do: Play your music for as many people as you can.

"But lots of tickets means lots of money, and lots of money means people start acting weird—both ways. It's just gonna happen if you're successful, unless you play all free shows. Nobody ever sits down and says, 'Let's go get rich.' Maybe they do, but they wouldn't be musicians anyway, they'd be entertainers. Most people that have the heart of a musician just don't even think that way.

"Now. How do we do that? We go down the road. How do we go down the road in a market economy? We buy gas. I don't think it's nefarious on anybody's part when money gets injected, but it's whether or not it's your first and foremost goal.

"For us, it was our mission statement. We wrote it out—play our music for as many people as possible without having to compromise."

In doing so, The Stragglers did the near impossible. More so than Ragweed, The Departed, Reckless Kelly or the dozens of other bands who started out in college bars and made a career out of original music in the Midwest, The Stragglers grew up. They stopped carrying on as a party band, even if their crowd kept on. They became a disciplined outfit, dedicated to songs and the entertaining. The all-nighters went away and stopped defining The Stragglers.

"In one word: weed," Rice said. "We went from being hard drinkers, hard partiers, pill poppers—I'm not ashamed to admit that I had a lot of fun in my career with the band. And unfortunately it took me too long to realize I needed to make some personal changes to grow up. The catalyst was to quit drinking. Ever since then, I've gone through more personal growth than I ever have in my life. Weed was what enabled really all of us to get there."

In the most important sense, the means does not matter. Only a handful of artists have been making this style of music longer than Boland now. He still travels coast to coast, even if his biggest draws are in Tornado Alley. He recognizes he has been fortunate but also that he brought a unique perspective to the scene. That, more than anything else, is what Red Dirt was and is at its essence.

"It's impressive. I am honored you know all those words," Boland said. "I am so glad it went down that way. No matter how much you plan anything, one step the wrong way and you don't wind up where you need to be. And that's where I am at. There are times in our lives that you get the encouragement that you're going to end up where you need to be, because it's not just one moment, really: What if I had not gone to Stillwater? What if I had not gone to the Wormy Dog? But then I think, *Well, I would have gone the next night!*

"The drive was there. I just didn't know it was real until it was, and that was eight years into the band, and I looked around and thought, *Man, I thought we were just gonna do a couple of demos.* But, here I look around and I'm still doing it."

Nothing has ever come closer to describing the Red Dirt dream.

— — —

- 13 -

Stoney

IN THE NONFICTION rule book, there are roughly 25 different ways to begin a chapter about a musician. I could start by placing them in the green room of a crowded theater, minutes before showtime. I could recite a lyric the artist is known for. I could talk about how the artist promised to call for an interview at 4 p.m. but everyone knows he is always late. "Time never meant much to them," I would write. Or I could lead with, "The city of Stillwater radiates out from the campus of Oklahoma State University like spokes on a wheel."

Those 25 options—and there are no more—are usually well and good, but they're a problem when writing a book with 26 chapters.

Besides, this chapter is about Stoney LaRue.

You've read all 25 of those chapters, so you would see one of those introductions to Stoney and you would know where his story was going to take you. You'd be able to guess the ending from the beginning, and the structure would move you along—there's the singer-and-his-influences story, the against-all-odds tale of a broken childhood, the rebel-doing-it-his-way narrative and, finally, the journey through the one song that captures his biography. If the artist bares his soul, you'd surely enjoy it.

Again, the problem here is that this is about Stoney. Hell, he fits all 25 narratives. That familiarity, however, flies in the face of what Stoney has always been about. The part about Red Dirt that makes it both strikingly unique and permanently endearing is its grounded nature. The voices are rough and unpolished. The music, even in studios, lacks the finishing touch of mainstream country or rock. The artists always make you feel like if they weren't making music, they'd be making ends meet in the oilfields or your brother's machine shop. And then, one time, someone turns up, and they have so clearly been blessed with a natural talent so out of step with their contemporaries that you have to exaggerate just to describe their place in the scene. So when you hear Stoney rip his voice through keys like a race car driver moving up and down a gear box, you can't help but notice how *different* he is and how none of those profiles are going to capture him.

For starters, he's getting referenced by his first name in this chapter. His given name isn't even Stoney LaRue. He was born Stoney LaRue Phillips. When you are at a Bo Phillips concert and he gives a shout-out to his brother, he's referring to Stoney. In Red Dirt vernacular, it's common to reference Canada, Boland or McClure for single-name shorthand. But Stoney has always been Stoney, as in, "Boland and Stoney are playing acoustic at the Wormy Dog tonight, you going?" So he's going to be Stoney in this chapter, too.

To properly appreciate Stoney—and especially to appreciate his place in Red Dirt—it's best to back off the narrative, not force a story and simply be amazed.

Or dumbfounded. You can be dumbfounded at Stoney, too.

"In many ways, Stoney is the most talented person to ever get called Red Dirt," Jim Wilhelm, who among other things lived with Stoney at the Yellow House in Stillwater in the late 1990s and early 2000s. "And in many ways he is the least talented. You take all of that with him."

Stoney was born in Taft, Texas, in 1977, but by age 5 it was clear his home was broken. So he was raised by his grandparents in Southeast Oklahoma and moved to Stillwater by the time he was in high school. He never had a plan for college, but what he did have was an eye and an ear for the town's music.

He also wrote about all that, in stunningly graphic detail, in one of the first songs he wrote. "Downtown" tells the story of watching, at age 5, infidelity and abuse in his parents' marriage, and then being picked up and pushed for a decade and a half by his grandfather, Harvey Allen Phillips: "Boy, go on and do your thing downtown. Make me proud, son."

"Downtown is all true," Stoney said. "My granddad gave me a tasting of a work ethic. Just always work hard and help others. He raised animals, a garden, an orchard. We built things from other things we tore down. He taught us to fish like it was our DNA. We got bit, stung and itched more than I can count, but he sure did teach me how to be confident in the world."

After high school, Stoney had a stint in the military, then returned to Stillwater. He had a guitar and a voice and made sure that every house party that would have him knew about both. He was underage at the time, but that mattered little to house parties. Eventually, he ran into Cody Canada at one of them, and the door to Red Dirt opened for another young talent.

"Red Dirt had a different kind of energy about it," LaRue said. "It's really hard to explain in words. It was more of a feeling than anything else. It was cosmic—whatever all those words are that give you that feeling you can't explain, that's what it was."

At the time (circa 1997), he was playing top 40 country songs, but he befriended Canada, who invited Stoney to his home—the Yellow House, where he lived with Boland.

"The Yellow House was where I stumbled on my 21st birthday, after I got out of the military, at Cody's invitation," Stoney said. "I walked in, and it looked like my mecca. Nag champa. Music. Cool lighting. Vibes with people passing things around. It was a place I felt I could be around like-minded travelers and learn what turned out to be many, many things."

Stoney's introduction to Red Dirt came with a test, courtesy of Wilhelm.

"First of all, I was happy to be accepted," LaRue said. "But then, don't get me wrong, I wanted to be the biggest Red Dirt star too. Childers used to call me 'Red Dirt Elvis.' And, then, he said, 'Don't worry about writing no more songs, we got plenty of those.'

"Anyway, the Jim Wilhelm story—my *first* gig at the Wormy Dog. First paid one, at least. There were no more than two, three, four people there. And Jim walks in with Boland and a third guy. So, I was playing a cover song, and Jim is kind of being punchy. He says, 'Play me some Jimmy Buffett!'

"And I say, 'Well, I know 'Margaritaville.'"

"Jim says, '*I* fucking know 'Margaritaville.' Play some Jimmy Buffett.'

"So I go, 'That's all I know.' And then he starts listing all these songwriters—John Prine, Guy Clark—you know, doing the 'If you're gonna be playing on *that* stage, you're still too wet behind the ears' sort of thing with me.

"So I got down at a break and went and sat with him and went, 'Why are you pickin' on me? There's nobody here, nobody to impress.'

"And then he told me *why*.

"So, I said, 'OK. Well, how about you teach me? You show me these songs?' And he said, 'OK. Come over to the Yellow House.'

"So I did. And that's where Jim started teaching me not just about Jimmy Buffett's deep cuts, but about Robert Earl, about Townes Van Zandt. And then, I just wouldn't go away."

Canada left the Yellow House and Stillwater in 1999 and also left a void of standing gigs that Stoney filled. He played Mondays at the Wormy Dog with Boland, Wednesdays at Eskimo Joe's with Boland and Thursday nights at Willie's Saloon with Steve Rice. He also showed up to Boland's Tuesday night solo shows regularly and filled in anytime Boland was out of town for another gig. Along with "Downtown," Stoney worked up covers of "Feet Don't Touch the Ground" by Brandon Jenkins and "Carolina" by Tony Rice, as well as another biographic original, "Shot Full of Holes," about a family member imprisoned for auto theft. Those four songs formed the background of sets that would cover Red Dirt traditionals that Tom Skinner or Bob Childers had written to obscure, B side music from old Brooks & Dunn and Garth Brooks albums.

And during the days when his touring was limited to Stillwater and Tulsa, Stoney became the de facto Yellow House host for bands playing the Wormy Dog. It was commonplace for a set by Texas artists like, say, Reckless Kelly or Dub Miller to be followed by all-night jam sessions at the Yellow House with Stoney leading singalongs, hymns and party tunes until sunrise.

"It meant the world to me to be welcomed after being on my own since I was 15," Stoney said. "The music that was played there, I believe, was what held up that house. I'm glad for the opportunity."

From there, Stoney's story is as complex or simple as the constructed narrative demands. He appeared on The Great Divide's 1999 gospel album, *Dirt and Spirit*, and in 2001 recorded an acoustic album at the now-defunct Red Dirt Cafe in Norman. In between, he got what every Red Dirt artist at the time got—help from his friends. The Great Divide, Cross Canadian Ragweed and Boland regularly had Stoney open their shows across Oklahoma and Texas.

"I questioned Stoney's motives when he showed up," Jim Wilhelm said. "Stoney is an opportunist, and I couldn't tell then if he was just looking at what The Great

Divide was doing and thinking he could ride them to become the George Strait of Red Dirt. Maybe he would have if he could have, but we are *all* blessed that he didn't. We all get Stoney, rather than a George Strait clone, and Red Dirt is grateful for it."

Once word got out, Stoney's presence was too heavy to ignore. Brad James invited Stoney to front his Organic Boogie Band in 2002, and they recorded an album—*Downtown*, naturally—at Tulsa's venerable Cain's Ballroom. By 2005, he was cutting his first true solo record, *The Red Dirt Album*, with Mike McClure producing.

And in 2007, he recorded an album for the Live at Billy Bob's series, even bringing a complete backing choir to the Fort Worth honky tonk for the moment. Even by the standards of the Live at Billy Bob's albums, LaRue's stood out as a work of art.

"I was 100 percent there, in every way possible—spiritually, physically, mentally," LaRue said of the album. "With a band, married, had two kids. I was sitting there putting on makeup before the show saying to myself, 'I cannot fuck this up.'"

LaRue has four children. His oldest daughter, Avery, was born just before Chistmas in 2001, right as LaRue's career took off. He has a son, C.J., who picked up golf as a child and as a teenager is pursuing it aggressively. Being a touring musician also obviously meant that LaRue spent plenty of time on the road while his kids grew up.

"My kids, they're all teenagers now," LaRue said. "Three of them live in Edmond, and one lives in Norman, and here I am in Oklahoma City. But, they're teenagers, they have their teenage lives. And I'm *Dad*. So, I have to let them do their things and see them when I can. That's not something that any parent really gets used to."

What makes Stoney's story one of multitudes is that he holds on to his star-crossed childhood and his formidable music years to this day. Save for the Turnpike Troubadours, no other Red Dirt artist gets as many miles out of early recordings. Stoney still plays "Downtown," "Shot Full of Holes" and "Feet Don't Touch the Ground" with the passion and conviction that he did in 1999, and even with 20 years of sharing notes, collaborating and brushing elbows with some of the best songwriters in Texas and Nashville, he never bumps his old material from his concerts.

"I want it to be known that there are new fans getting interested in this music all the time," LaRue said. "Not only mine, but this *kind* of music. So, for a lot of people, no matter how many times I've played a song, it's the first time they've heard it.

"My mindset is, 'Hey. This is what I started out playing, and I *know* that it got me hooked. If it got me, then it can get them too. All the music I've made since then, it can become convoluted or lost in translation. But those early years, those are what got me, and I'll always come back to that."

He is also fiercely loyal to his Red Dirt influences. He worked Childers into his own lyrics ("Somebody sing something soulful, like an old Bob Childers song") and still plays his cut from *Dirt and Spirit* ("Tie My Boat") regularly. His friendship with the late Brandon Jenkins is part of both artists' legacies, and his cover of Scott Evans' "Steel Heart" is, in my opinion, one of the finest single pieces of music ever made in Oklahoma.

The same past has also haunted Stoney on occasion—not like a demon, more like a spirit that can't be forgotten. In 2015, an arrest for disturbing the peace landed him truly negative publicity for the first time, reminding both Stoney and his fans that he is a person who came perilously close to an entirely different life than music. His reputation is that of a party animal, even though he, like his contemporaries, left his wildest days behind in the early 2000s.

What Stoney has either lost or passed over in his dedication to his roots, he has offset with an inner circle that wouldn't have him any other way.

"Stoney shows up for me now like he showed up for me 20 years ago, and I'll love him forever for it," Canada said.

And that is where Stoney loses another structured storyline. Every other artist has a past, in which they grew up musically and got influenced, and a present, in which they are the influencers. But Stoney prefers to live in both worlds. You can neither build his story to a natural crescendo nor bring it full circle and apply a moral. With Stoney, more than anybody else Red Dirt has ever claimed, it's best to just listen to the song he's playing next.

By the end of 2019, the song he was playing next ended up being a collaboration with one of country music's biggest icons. He released the album *Onward*, produced by Gary Nicholson, in November of that year, and its crescendo is "Meet in the Middle," performed as a duet with Tanya Tucker.

"It's funny, now, because it's already turned into a 'whose idea was it first?' sort of thing," LaRue said. "We knew it should be a duet, and I wanted it to be with someone who could bring that natural, good-tempered feeling of 'We're just talking' to the song. And Gary Nicholson goes, 'What about Tanya Tucker?'

"And I said, 'Do you know her? I'd love that. I've played with her a couple of times, but there's no way she knows who I am.'

"So, he gets on the phone, immediately, with her. And he says, 'I'm sitting here with a Texas songwriter. Maybe you've heard of him.'

"Tanya goes, 'What's his name?'

"Gary goes, 'Stoney LaRue.'

"And she goes, right on speakerphone, 'No? I don't think I have.'

"But, of course, she heard the song, and she liked it, and she came and did it.

"She was perfect about it. But, that aside, think about the childhood novelty. We're talking about being true to our past, think about that.

"That's what I wanted. That's why I did it. Songs are supposed to make you remember something. That was the whole feeling I wanted that song to have: A memory a song can evoke."

That is also where Stoney is: simple and straightforward, easy to appreciate. Watching Stoney play is like watching a quarter horse run a high school cross-country race. Everyone is working really hard at their craft, carefully sound-checked and with setlists meticulously thought-out, and along comes this guy who breezes through his gig, shows up the other acts and barely expends any energy doing it.

It's because that is Stoney is in his element. Music comes naturally to him, and the confidence he gained at the Yellow House exudes when the spotlight turns on.

"I keep at it because there is nothing to prove," he said. "Music is sung mathematics—the fluidity, the something you hang on when you run out of rope or the something you pull when you have a lot of it."

Today, he still headlines across the Midwest, balancing nods to his roots with a continuing churn of new songs like "Hill Country Boogaloo" and "You Oughta Know Me by Now" and ending the night by sharing beers, shots, joints and jokes with the hardest of his hardcore fans. It's old hat, yes, but for Stoney, it's also sincerely who he is.

"Perhaps we are just the suggestion of life and live," he said. "I'm sure that whatever the great 'I am' is, I'm so grateful to be here to share it all. I don't know the answer to life. I know I feel good when I sing and write. It goes to a bigger place than me."

There are other chapters and other artists for profiles. For the most part, the artists bared their souls, and I think you will like them all. They came easily and the narrative flowed naturally from the stories they told. Some of them begin with an anecdote from the green room of a theater. Some of them will tell you how Stillwater, Oklahoma, radiates out from the campus of Oklahoma State University like spokes on a wheel.

With Stoney, though, it's best to simply appreciate the music.

— — —

- 14 -

Hold My Beer:
Wade Bowen and Randy Rogers

STARS! THEY'RE JUST like us!

At least to the extent that anyone who has climbed the alt-country ladder in Texas or Oklahoma gets to be considered a star and to the extent that Randy Rogers and Wade Bowen have spent the better part of their career arcs dabbling near the top of Texas music charts and selling out the largest dance halls in Tornado Alley, stars are just like us. Only funnier. And more introspective. And probably having more fun.

I'm thinking specifically of the night of July 25, 2017, at the House of Blues in Dallas. The two artists shared the stage during their 10th annual Hold My Beer and Watch This acoustic tour—a tour that, by itself, is older than the majority of bands that play the Texas music circuit—when they called a newly minted local hero on stage. Jordan Spieth had won golf's British Open, the most prestigious of its four major tournaments, two days before and had nearly gone straight from a transatlantic flight back to Dallas to the HOB.

Bowen is an avid golfer and had spent the previous weekend pulling for Spieth to land his first Open, so he and Rogers invited Spieth on stage for his hero's welcome. Spieth got it, and in return the two artists got to take a drink from the Claret Jug—the trophy given to the Open winner and one of the most historic pieces of hardware in sports. The entire interaction took maybe 30 seconds, but in that moment, no fans in Texas were having more fun than the House of Blues crowd. And Spieth was having more fun than the crowd. And Rogers and Bowen were having more fun than Spieth.

"Stars" is a relative term, just like the alt-country that permeates Texas and Oklahoma is a relative scene. But on nights like that one, it was hard to see Rogers and Bowen in any light other than the one that hits an artist when—if they haven't caught whatever dream they were chasing when they made a career out of performing, they certainly could reach out and touch it for a moment or two.

Getting there, or to the 2018 Medicine Stone music festival 14 months later in Tahlequah, Oklahoma, where Rogers and Bowen both headlined and sat down separately to talk about their music, entailed a path the two men paved together, giving and receiving plenty of help along the way.

Both men's ties to the original Red Dirt scene—Eric Wooley, the last owner of the Wormy Dog Saloon in Stillwater, accurately described both a young Bowen and a young Rogers as "the next big thing" to crowds when he introduced them on stage in 2002 and 2003—ran deep enough that their careers are inseparable from it, and they both bear heavy responsibility for the scene's ultimate migration across the Lone Star State.

* * *

Bowen

A child of Waco, Texas, where his grandfather had founded Bowen Electric, which his father still runs to this day, Wade Bowen set out to Texas Tech University in the mid-1990s with the same half-formed aspirations of a college degree and business that all his classmates had. But Lubbock—famously the home of Buddy Holly and where Joe Ely launched his own career—pulled him into music instead.

"Robert Earl Keen changed my life," Bowen said. "Robert Earl came through right as I had started my band. And before I started my band, I thought you had to move to Nashville and wait tables, wait your turn and do all those things and then get the record deal.

"We take it for granted now how much original music is accepted. Every bar, every venue. But in the mid-to-late '90s, it was still few and far between as far as who would let you come in and do that. And then I saw Robert Earl play. My dad had always liked him. I had just gotten into him. But I saw him play, and I went, 'That's it! I can do that!'"

Bowen showed up at Texas Tech aiming for a degree in marketing and eventually left with a band, West 84.

"My first gig ever as a band was at Stubb's—the legendary Stubb's," Bowen said. "I called Harold Akin, the owner, and asked him what we had to do to land a gig. And he said, 'Well, we do Sunday night open mic. You can bring your band up and play for us, and if we like you, we'll give you a gig.'

"We literally came up with the band name—West 84—on the way to that Sunday night open mic. Stupidly! That's how much thought went into it. 84 was the highway we took going from Waco to Lubbock. Hell, that's the road we go down, we may as well call it that! Little did we know that everybody in the universe would be using that as the way to name their bands."

The plan worked, and Bowen's first band became regulars in the dives that lined Lubbock's wide streets.

Quick history: Stubb's Bar-B-Q was founded in Lubbock on East Broadway, and the owner was keen on bringing musicians into the restaurant. The original location was demolished and Stubb's moved—concurrently to Austin and to a new Lubbock spot. Eventually, Austin became the sole Stubb's location and, from there, marketed its barbecue across the country. But it was those last days for the spot in Lubbock where Bowen found his first home in music.

"Stubb's Lubbock was legendary," he said. "Stevie Ray played there. Ian Moore played there. All the people who came to their original location were legends. They ended up moving across the highway and that's where we played. But still, to get up on stage and play there, it was special. We played four or five songs, and Akin offered us a gig. That was our first place, back in '98."

Texas Tech students proved both a forgiving and loyal audience, as well as a proving ground for his first forays into songwriting.

"At the very beginning, I was just trying to figure it out. I'd play cover songs, and I was starting to write. I didn't know how to write songs yet, but I thought I did, so we would work them into the show. When you're young, you think everything you write is great.

"It took a while. A lot of people try to play their own songs from the get-go. But for us, I thought it was important to learn covers, learn their arrangements and use those to give me templates for songwriting. That's what we did. We took our time with the originals."

An early album with the band—*Try Not to Listen*—met with fringe success, but the process introduced Bowen to J.R. Rodriguez. Rodriguez engineered *Try Not to Listen* but would go on to be the producer for both *Lost Hotel* and *If We Ever Make It Home*, two albums that cemented Bowen as a player in the state's music scene and that bridged his gap between college bandleader and career performer.

(The early album order for Bowen was *Try Not to Listen* and *The Blue Light Live* with West 84, followed by *Lost Hotel*, *If We Ever Make It Home* and *Live at Billy Bob's*, all three as a solo artist.)

"It was life-changing for me to have Rodriguez as a part of my career early. He was a very smart engineer and producer very early in my career, when I really needed someone like that," Bowen said.

At the same time, Stubb's closed its Lubbock location and the live music scene found a new home—a dive bar with a tiny stage in front called the Blue Light. That stage gave Bowen the home base from which to play catch-up with those of his contemporaries—Pat Green, Cory Morrow and Cross Canadian Ragweed to name a few—whose careers had already accelerated.

"Looking back on it, everybody else was taking off as I was starting," he said. "So I started playing the Blue Light. The first call from the manager to me is, 'I hear you guys draw a decent crowd. I'm trying to open this place. Do y'all want to come here and try to start something for me?' He didn't want us for the music, he wanted us because we had a reputation for decent crowds. So we were really the first band to play there, and that helped them start bringing in that college music at the time.

"The cool thing about it, looking back, is those other bands started coming through too. The Blue Light only held 300, so none of us were big. But they used the Blue Light as a place to learn. Learning to write, learning to share your music. It was huge for me. And it was really cool to be there and watch everybody come through and take off with original music."

Green and Morrow were already established, but it was the Blue Light where Bowen formed alliances with two others who qualified as rising stars, Ragweed and Jason Boland.

"My first goal was to get on stage with these guys. I want to open up for them, get gigs with them," he said. "My goal was just to get in good with them. That was really critical for me. And it built from there."

While that worked out, Bowen still had the matter of songwriting to address. His early albums with West 84 proved entertaining enough to make his name known, but also had not distinguished themselves among the sudden glut of contemporary Texas music artists who were churning out original music in the early 2000s.

Then, in 2005, Bowen released *Lost Hotel*. The album was full of deeply personal songs, intense writing balanced by vivid storytelling. Trial and error, and time, had shown Bowen that introspection was the way to go.

"The big step for me was making *Lost Hotel*," Bowen said. "To make a record that proved me as a songwriter. It was really important to establish that. It felt like all those guys I was playing with were taking off because they wrote their songs. That was kind of the battle cry of everybody. I was never one that did the whole 'Nashville sucks' bullshit, but I do think the big difference was that those guys and I at that time were writing our own songs. It makes a difference. It goes back to what worked for Willie Nelson when he did it—we're gonna do this our way, and we made it."

Bowen made it. He met his wife, Shelby O'Neal, through his music. Shelby is the sister of Shannon (O'Neal) Canada, wife of Cody Canada, and both families now call New Braunfels, Texas, home. Shelby and Wade have a pair of sons. Bruce, born in 2005, has his dad's voice and at least one eye on Broadway. Brock, three years younger, pairs a child's shyness with wicked instincts on drums and a love of basketball.

"People can act like it doesn't change you, but it does," Bowen said of parenting. "Everything changes in your whole life, especially your career. It makes it harder to leave, when I go on the road, but it makes it more fun to go home. At least that's how I work it out in my head.

"But it changes the way you look at the world. As a songwriter, that's the biggest difference it's brought me. It's not always a good thing, but it changes the way you view the world as a parent, and that, in turn, affects your songwriting. That's what we do as songwriters, we analyze the world—why is this person doing this thing? It immediately affected my songwriting."

Bowen stepped into gospel circles in 2016 to release an album dedicated to his mother, Glenda Bowen. He called it *Then Sings My Soul: Songs for My Mother*. While it is decidedly traditional gospel, Bowen mixed heavy hymns like "Softly and Tenderly" and "How Great Thou Art" with raise-your-voice sing-alongs like "I'll Fly Away" and "Saved." A year later, he was back in the studio recording *Solid Ground*—his most versatile album yet, which led with the single "Acuna," a throwback to the days artists would routinely play in the border town at the Corona Club, before drug wars and border tensions scared away the tourists.

Solid Ground was released in February 2018, but the momentum of the release almost immediately gave way to one of the worst personal stretches of Bowen's career. In quick succession, mounting voice problems caused him to cancel nearly two full months' worth of shows, as well as a planned European tour. They were serious enough to threaten his career and required surgery to repair. Shortly after that, his nephew and member of his road crew, Chase Cavender, took his own life, leaving behind a wife and newborn child. The toll piled on Bowen and his family. In early June 2018, he attended his own festival—Bowen MusicFest in Waco—unable to sing, so his kids and fellow musicians filled in for him. By mid-June, nearly three months since he started canceling shows, Bowen returned to the stage. He has to do voice exercises before shows now, but they do their job. Getting back out on the road eased Bowen's mind immediately.

"I swear to you, this is not just some bullshit cliche. I've been through the worst part of my career with this. But all that goes away when I get on stage. It's the most powerful thing I do."

. . .

Rogers

Not long after Bowen set his music in motion, several hundred miles away in San Marcos—the center of Texas Hill Country and home to Southwest Texas State (now Texas State)—Randy Rogers saw his own path forward.

"Eighteen years ago, October 3, man. In the year 2000," Rogers said, singing the last sentence in reference to the old Conan O'Brien talk show bit. "That was our first-ever gig. That was in San Marcos, when I was attending Southwest Texas State.

"About a year into it, Pat Green, Ragweed, Jack Ingram and a few others had kind of popped and were having success, at least drawing crowds. I was fortunate enough to get in with them and that scene. It wasn't strictly Red Dirt at that time. Robert Earl Keen, Pat Green and Charlie [Robison] didn't classify as Red Dirt. But I started opening shows for them, and I started opening shows for Ragweed, and I built fans from both."

Rogers' musical home was Cheatham Street Warehouse—which he partly owns now but at the time was run by the late Kent Finlay. Finlay's joint, literally a creaky warehouse next to some railroad tracks, welcomed aspiring songwriters with open arms and has gone down in Texas music lore the way the Wormy Dog did in Stillwater lore.

"I was just working on my own songs," Rogers said. "I was attending open mic every Wednesday at Cheatham Street and playing my songs out live. And the band would play there every Tuesday—and the band was also playing, like, Lynyrd Skynyrd and Charlie Robison songs, playing Merle Haggard songs and Buddy Holly songs. We were playing songs that we related to. We were developing a sound, I guess. Finding an identity, and all that went into it.

"That weekly gig was key. We could change the set. If things didn't work, we could see it really quick. If new songs weren't necessarily good, we knew it right off the bat. That all led to an album called *Like It Used to Be*, and then that band broke up, and I then found the guys who are on this bus with me now."

That last part is both true and important to Rogers. The proper reference to his band is the Randy Rogers Band, and it consists of Geoffrey Hill, Jon Richardson, Brady Black, Les Lawless and Todd Stewart. A pair of albums in 2004 and 2005—*Rollercoaster* and *Live at Billy Bob's*—led to record deals with Nashville's Mercury and MCA labels, and by 2010, when Cross Canadian Ragweed broke up, the Randy Rogers Band was selling out the largest venues in Texas and theaters and concert halls from coast to coast.

"The success of *Rollercoaster* really put me on the map in this scene," Rogers said. "That album was great and is great, and not just because of the songs but because of the band. We had been playing those songs together live for a year and a half before we recorded them. The greatness of that album was we knew those songs so well that we went into the studio and only needed four days to make that record. And now people always say that's our essential album.

"The truth is, I don't think we can ever beat that record because it was just so different then."

At that time, Rogers found plenty of friends on the Red Dirt side of the musical border. He wrote a pair of songs with Cody Canada—"Again" and "This Time Around"—that made it onto albums by both the Randy Rogers Band and Cross Canadian Ragweed. He fell in with Shannon Canada's management company, 36D Management, where he was largely managed by Robin Devin (now Robin Devin Schoepf). In 2016, the two launched their own management company, Big Blind Management, which handled some of Rogers' day-to-day operations but more importantly was instrumental in launching the career of Parker McCollum into the stratosphere.

Back in the wake of *Rollercoaster*, Rogers found Red Dirt as much of a proving ground as Texas. The night before recording 2005's *Live at Billy Bob's*, the band used a gig at Oklahoma City's Wormy Dog Saloon as a dress rehearsal for the *Billy Bob's* recording.

"We were riding the coattails back then," Rogers said. "I don't think it was us, I think it was the scene, man. I recall this show where Cody was on Pat Green's shoulders playing his guitar backward or something, and I just remember thinking, *I'm fucking lucky to be here to be associated with these guys.*

"I'll never forget those validating moments. Whether it be, like, a Family Jam in Oklahoma City, a Woodlands Pavilion show with Pat or a Starplex show in Dallas with Willie and Pat, where I really felt like part of the scene...like I had arrived. I owe a lot to those guys."

Rogers also credits the relationships that were being built among his contemporary artists with helping tear down the musical borders around Texas and Oklahoma, and regional sounds from Lubbock, the Hill Country and Oklahoma all started blending together.

"It was a relationship thing," he said. "I wrote songs with Cody at that time. I wrote songs with Wade—although Wade wasn't somebody I looked up to. He was my peer, he was my buddy. But he was embedded in the West Texas scene and I was embedded in the San Marcos scene, and we started collaborating, and I think that's something that wasn't recorded enough when those collaborations happened on stage. I remember all those silly verses to "Boys From Oklahoma" and getting up and singing with Pat, Willie and Robert Earl on stage.

"Walks of life merged. Time merged. Age didn't matter. We were just all part of this growing, budding, barrier-breaking kind of scene. And suddenly there was just this moment where everything had changed."

When it did, it was as sudden as the decades leading up to it had been creeping along.

"When Ragweed died, you mean?" Rogers said.

Yes, actually.

After Ragweed, Rogers became the torch-bearer for all those scenes. If you were even a casual fan of country music in Oklahoma, Texas or anywhere in the Midwest, you also knew who Randy Rogers was. Today, only the Turnpike Troubadours have found a greater reach than Rogers out of the new Red Dirt and Texas markets, and even then, it's most accurate to say that Turnpike and Rogers share the torch-bearing responsibilities for the scene equally. Actually, the artists found success and all started looking out for one another.

"I'm not always comfortable in the role of being the elder," Rogers said. "I've cursed many times the day that Ragweed died, because headlining all these events, watching people leave because they've been here for 10 hours and it's hot halfway through my set. Shit that I never had to put up with, now I do. So the best advice I can have for younger artists is to enjoy it, man. It's a slow build and it's a slow burn, and it's more enjoyable when you're bringing it up and working for it."

Rogers and his wife, Chelsea, carved out a home life for themselves as well. They had four children, all girls, although the third child, Rumer Rain, died as an infant in 2015. A career and life ostensibly filled with blessings came with the worst kind of pain too, but he had built his music and professional relationships into a veritable network—"a community without a Facebook page," as he put it, that made coping easier. And one guy in particular stands out even in that group.

• • •

Randy and Wade

So about this partnership—the one that flourished to the point that it was Spieth's homecoming choice after winning the Claret Jug. Where did it begin? Alphabetically, "Randy" comes before "Wade," so he gets to go first:

Rogers: "I went to see Wade play a show in San Marcos at a bar called Nephew's. I was having a keg party. And I had just finished *Like It Used to Be* [his 2002 debut album]. I invited him and the guys over to play music and stay up all night. And Wade and I hit it off and became friends. He listened to my entire album from start to finish that night sitting in my living room. And we decided then to take the show on the road."

Bowen: "Man, it sounds stupid and cliche, but we just hit it off from the moment we met. He came out to my show at Nephew's in San Marcos. He had just started his band, and he was living in a place called the White House. That's what he called it: the White House. It was just a big house that was obnoxiously white. He came out to my show and went, 'You guys wanna come back and party?' Sure. So we go back over there, and there's all this college kid chaos going on, because that's what we were. He had just finished *Like It Used to Be*. It wasn't even out yet. And he had a desktop computer with speakers and asked if I'd listen to it. I ended up sitting there listening to almost the entire thing. And 20 or 30 minutes go by and he goes, 'You still fucking listening to my record?' And I have to say, 'Yeah man, it's good!' He was blown away that I actually cared more about that than partying. But it was really cool! I liked it a lot. So then he starts passing around a guitar and making people shut the hell up. He started kicking people out if they talked or laughed too loud. And I just went, 'I like this guy,' because it was the living room, and it was just a feeling like—yes, finally somebody gets it and gets the songs like I do."

Shortly after that, the two went on an acoustic run.

"It was me and him on that acoustic run," Bowen said. "Me, him and Django [Walker], and we drove everywhere. So we had a lot of hang time. It wasn't like it is now where everyone's on a stupid bus and we never see each other until showtime. We spent a lot of time driving around the whole state together, and we got really close. So we decided to start playing a lot of shows, and that led to 'Let's do an acoustic show too' and really we just got along, man. And it's been that way ever since. Real friendship.

"That's what's been with me and Randy all along. We go do shows with other artists, but there's something about the yin-yang part of our friendship that just works."

What the artists found in that partnership was what had been a staple of Red Dirt for 30 years: someone else doing the same thing you're doing who is invested in your success too. In the beginning of that friendship, the Texas side of the scene was competitive, but Rogers and Bowen shunned competition in favor of an approach that had both artists and their bands lifting each other when they could.

"It was two bands and 20 drunk people doing shows together," Rogers said. "Those shows weren't sellouts. They weren't huge shows. But we learned how to tour. Our tour managers learned how to be on the road, how to handle promoters. There was so much we learned together—things you can't learn unless you're actually physically there doing it."

Learning eventually brought a trio of albums for the two: *Hold My Beer, Vol. 1* was a 2015 duet album that included the defiant song, "Standards," and landed as high as No. 4 on the U.S. country charts. They followed that with a live acoustic song-swap album, *Watch This*, which captured the duo's annual tour in all its essence.

The third, a second duet album—*Hold My Beer, Vol. 2*—was released in May 2020 amid the global coronavirus pandemic that shut down concert tours and just about every other avenue artists have to ply their trade. But the record was loaded with upbeat and flat-out funny tracks such as the opening single, "Rodeo Clown" ("You'd get throttled / if they knew that Ronald McDonald was doin' her now," to sample a lyric), and "Ode to Ben Dorcy (Lovey's Song)," which crafted in an old Waylon Jennings demo.

"Now, more than ever, people need music," Bowen said of the album's timing. "And this is a fun album, it's a feel-good album. People are sitting at home, they're bored. So we decided, let's give them something."

Their friendship also laid the groundwork for the path to success now for artists who are a part of the blurred Red Dirt and Texas scenes: Today, you have to look out for other artists, and they have to do the same for you.

"I've started a management company, and it's important for me to take care of those younger guys," Rogers said. "Radney Foster mentored me. Cody Canada mentored me. I was taught by people who cared about me. And I feel like it's almost a duty to give back—to make sure nobody falls down a rathole they can't get out of.

"It's a brotherhood. I'm on a text thread with 11 other lead singers. Those lead singers range from the countriest of country like Cody Johnson to me, and we talk about everything: beer deals, what fans brought weird cookies to the bus, what we need, charity, hurricane relief, who screwed you out of money or bounced a check. There is a community, there is a brotherhood that we all know we're a part of."

At the center of it, for both, is personal. The two artists both credit their time together with providing a baseline now, after they have ascended the musical ladders, for how to interact with the rest of the scene.

"There's not a switch we flip," Bowen said. "Randy and I don't say, 'We're gonna go do this thing.' Literally what we do is, we hang out on stage, and our friendship carries it. That's the case with a lot of these friendships. It was the case with Cody and Boland. It was the case with Pat and Cory and part of why they got so big.

"We don't have to become artists on stage. We're just ourselves."

- 15 -

The Braun Brothers' Ragged Road Through Red Dirt

WILLY BRAUN ALWAYS has a choice when he introduces the final verse of "Crazy Eddie's Last Hurrah."

He could introduce his band, and he occasionally does. He could request that the crowd sing along, and he occasionally does. He could ask them for a shot, break to tune instruments, switch it up and play a verse of "Oklahoma Hills" or maybe "Sin City." He's done all those things.

But more often than not, the front man and guitar player for Reckless Kelly sets up the crescendo of his set closer the way he did at New York City's City Winery in summer 2018, in front of 300 fans in the intimate venue who already knew he was getting to the part of the song where the narrator shoots the person who broke his heart:

"Everybody remembers the great band, Cross Canadian Ragweed, right?" Braun asks, to a callback of cheers. "That's a good answer, too.

"Those guys recorded this song quite a while ago. And then, right after they did, we played it at our shows, and suddenly everybody knew the words. We loved it. So we're gonna do the Ragweed version right now and y'all are gonna sing along, OK?"

From there, it was a matter of keeping the beat so the willing crowd could shout back at him: "Well I gathered up all of my guns / and a pipe bomb just for fun. And I drove to her house and parked out on the lawn / she's right, I always was a crazy one" and so on, right up to the part where everybody screams "I shot him full of holes from his nose to his knees" and all the other parts of that final verse that are absolute macabre in 2018.

"Anything that was fun, then, I was gonna do it," Ragweed front man Cody Canada said, referring to a late 2001 recording, *Live and Loud at Billy Bob's Texas*, the band was putting together. "I got ahold of somebody that had a cell phone, backstage, right before the show. I called Willy and I said, 'We're about to do our *Live at Billy Bob's* record. Can we cut 'Crazy Eddie'? We know it really well,' and he said, 'Fuckin' A, man!'

"And I'll never forget this part. I said, 'Songwriters are you and Micky [Braun], right?' and he goes, 'He fuckin' wishes.'"

Nearly two decades later, Willy's preferred introduction to the final verse of that song is that story.

Why does he choose that route? "Crazy Eddie" was a B-side cut on *The Day*, a 2000 album all but forgotten in Reckless Kelly's extensive discography. Reckless Kelly itself is only one part of a family tale that started in Idaho, extended back generations, found a spark in Austin and, when kerosene hit the spark, sprang across the country like a mechanical timepiece that came unglued, beyond any natural border Red Dirt or Texas music had ever drawn, and today is kept alive and well by four brothers spanning two bands and, officially, 18 albums.

Neither Willy nor his brother, Cody, also in Reckless Kelly, gain anything from the Ragweed name-drop. For that matter, neither do the two younger Braun brothers, Micky and Gary, who together make up the core of Micky and the Motorcars—themselves established far beyond where conventional wisdom says Red Dirt and Texas should fade into the horizon.

Yet here they were, dropping away, forgoing the other 16 options and positively owning the capacity crowd at City Winery.

Why?

The answer spins a yarn of family, music, unabashed fun and what it means to be an artist without borders.

● ● ●

From Idaho to Austin

Stanley is the town you imagine when somebody says "Idaho"—a forgotten trading post town of maybe a hundred if we're being generous, bisected by the Salmon River and surrounded on all sides by the Sawtooth Mountains. It's the town where people share the land with moose, bears and buffalo and don't think much of it. Winter is measured in words like *feet* and *below zero* and summer is quantified with *stunning* and *heavenly*.

Go another 20 to 25 miles outside of Stanley and the utilities don't quite make it. If you want to warm your home in winter, then you'd better find something to burn.

It was against this backdrop that Muzzie and JoAnn Braun raised four boys in the '70s and '80s—Cody, Willy, Gary and Micky. They raised their kids on Idaho and on music. Muzzie and his brothers, Gary and Billy, played Idaho as the Braun Brothers—themselves sons of the late keyboard player Eustaceus "Mustie" Braun.

"My family's always been musical," Willy Braun said. "My dad was a musician. My uncle was a musician. My grandpa was. That's always been the family business. We grew up with instruments laying around, and we were allowed to play anything we wanted to—drums to guitars to mandolins or accordions. You name it, we had it.

"That happened pretty naturally, man. Dad had a band, and I started getting up and singing with him when I was, like, 5, and Cody started getting up and playing fiddle with him. And before we knew it, we were all kind of in the band. That ended up being something we did for nine or ten years."

In 1989, Muzzie and the Little Braun Boys—decked out in matching shirts and Stetson hats—played *The Tonight Show* with Johnny Carson. It went so well that Carson had them back for a second performance a few months later.

"For us, it was just getting up and doing it," Cody Braun said. "It wasn't really ever taught. We didn't have lessons about how to do it—mostly we had trial and error. Get up there and try not to look dumb, try not to fall over.

"The adults would give us pointers, though. Try to look at people, look around the crowd. Put your hand in your pocket instead of standing there like a zombie—little stuff like that."

There is a fundamental difference between those Braun brothers and nearly every other artist covered in these pages. For most artists—hell, for most people in general—there is a calling, a point of no return when it's clear you are going to make music for a living. The Brauns were born already on the other side of that point.

"Once we started listening to our own style of music—it started out being a lot of Dad's stuff, guys like Guy Clark, Robert Earl Keen, Rodney Crowell and Steve Earle—we wanted to move a little more into our own. We really loved country rock," Willy said. "The Eagles, Gram Parsons, that kind of stuff.

"Cody and I, when I was 17, we moved to Bend, Oregon, and we started our own band. And that's when the family thing kind of went its own way. We never really had a grand plan or anything, it just kind of evolved for us."

This represented the first substantial difference for this generation of Braun boys from the one before it. Muzzie was and still is an Idaho musician. Moving to Bend—still in the Pacific Northwest—did not take them far from home, but it did cut them off from the supply line of immediate support, not just from family but from the Idaho fans they had cultivated.

"It was tough. The family band had been together for nine years, so there was a pretty heavy fan base of people who had grown up along with us," Cody said. "There were a lot of people that were sad that it was coming to a close."

The original trip to Bend called for Cody and Willy to join a country band called the Prairie Mutts.

"We did about nine months in Bend, just really rehearsing," Cody said. "It was our first time to get out and play rock and roll and not be under any parental supervision. So we were not great. That first nine months was pretty wild."

That one didn't work out for the brothers. Nor did it work out for guitarist Casey Pollock or bassist Chris Schelske. Working out their anger at an open mic night in 1995, they found Jay Nazziola ("Nazz" on subsequent references)—himself bored and having just moved to Bend—on a whim, from New England. Nazz, like the Brauns, hails from a family of musicians. His roots lie in Simsbury, Connecticut.

"My dad was a musician," Nazz said. "Back in the '50s and '60s, he was playing music and had a band, had a family and always kept music as his side job. My brother wound up playing drums with him as a teenager, until he went to music college. When he went to college, I was able to take his place. So at 13 years old, I was playing in bars, playing weddings. We'd be playing '50s and '60s style of music—shuffle, straight ahead rock, four on the floor—so I got great roots of basic drumming, and I learned the value of making money at a young age, making music. But my dad would tell me, 'No matter what happens playing music, always keep it as a hobby.' For him, he was able to do that, and it brought in extra income."

By the end of his teen years, Nazz considered shelving the hobby. He went to college at the University of Rhode Island and did not bother sharing his history on the risers.

"When I got to college, I was kind of burned out from playing drums," he said. "So I kind of always brought my drums with me wherever I went, but I rarely played. My college buddies were shocked to learn that I even played drums.

"I wasn't about to graduate with my friends. I had taken a semester off. So we decided, before everybody went their separate ways, to head out to Bend, Oregon. Just really to see snow-covered mountains in the summertime. It was something I couldn't even imagine. So when I got out there, we went to an open mic night one night—we had just gone to a bar, but it happened to be an open mic night. The band—the Prairie Mutts—had just walked in, so I asked if I could jam with them for a couple of songs.

"Afterward, Chris, our original bass player, said, 'Listen, our drummer quit yesterday,' and the other guitar player asked if I'd fill in until they find someone else. And that's basically how it started."

Almost instantly, they became a five-piece band. Reckless Kelly was the name they picked, after the protagonist in an obscure Yahoo Serious movie. To this day, the two Brauns and Jay Nazz remain in Reckless Kelly.

"I was doing this and had no plan to stick around," Nazz said. "But early on, a relationship with Willy and Cody was built on the similarities between our dads. Their ethic, the whole thing of being young and going through those years where Dad says, 'You're dragging the beat. I'll show you dragging the beat!' Where you're immature but you also learn how to be an entertainer."

Nazz played with the band that summer. It was 1996. By August, it became obvious Bend was not going to be the long-term home of the band.

"We lived in Bend for about a year, and there was not a lot going on there at that point in time. There were a few bars that had music, but it was the tail end of the grunge scene, and nobody wanted to listen to our happy-go-lucky shit," Willy said.

It sounds bizarre in hindsight, but Austin was not an automatic choice for the move.

"My dad actually recommended it," Cody said. "We were thinking of going to New York or L.A. or maybe Music City. But he knew we had been fans of a lot of Texas music growing up. Austin has tons of places to play and a college scene. Texas in general just seemed to have tons of places to play music. What we really wanted to do was get out and play in front of people. We'd been just rehearsing for months and months, and there weren't many options for us to play in the Northwest. We just wanted to go somewhere we could play every night."

So they settled on Austin—armed with little more than the knowledge they could find a market in the Texas capital.

"We had always loved the idea of Austin," Willy said. "We had never been there, but most of our favorite bands at that point were coming out of there.

"We knew there was a music scene down there, and we wanted to check it out. So we just decided to go and see what it was all about. And we got there and just immediately fell in love with the place. We started playing six or seven nights a week, and it was the perfect place to get our sound together. So, yeah, we just stayed."

When they did, they had a bandmate in tow that was not part of the original plan in Bend.

"I had driven one of my vehicles out to Oregon, but my friends and I actually took two cars," Nazz said, referring to the summer he joined Reckless. "At this point, I had a couple more gigs to go, and my friends had left already. I was gonna meet up with them in Reno on our way back to the East Coast. And Cody and Willy sat down and said, 'We're going to Texas.'

"This is really one of my favorite parts about being in this band. We had a meeting. They said, 'We're going down to Texas. There's an opportunity for us to play every single night of the week and get better.' Not 'take over.' Just, here is an opportunity for us to go where we can play as much as we can. And they said, 'We want you to be a full-time member of the band.'

"I had really fallen in love with the music and our relationship. Even though they're a few years younger than me, their maturity and professionalism struck me. These guys party like crazy, but then they show up and they do their job."

They quickly fell in with the Sixth Street crowd and quickly built a following. Most notably, they started headlining Monday nights at Lucy's Retired Surfers Bar on Sixth Street.

"Everything we knew about Austin was either through music that we already knew or the few people we knew who had been there. We didn't have any expectations. We just went down there for the music, and that part was as advertised," Willy said.

At the same time, several hundred miles to the north in Stillwater, Shannon O'Neal was booking bands at the Wormy Dog Saloon—in its heyday a dive that looked like it had been lifted right off Sixth Street. At the time, Shannon was dating her future husband, Cody Canada. And one night, Shannon demanded they road-trip to Dallas for a Texas Uprising Festival. On the bill was Reckless Kelly.

"Shannon took me and [Jason] Boland and Ted [Roberson] to Dallas for the Texas Uprising one year to see Steve Earle, because I'd never seen Steve Earle," Cody Canada said. "She said, 'You're gonna go see Steve Earle,' and of course I went, 'Uh, can my friends come?'

"We went down there and we saw Reckless, and I just said, 'Holy shit, who are these guys?' Then they said, 'Last night was one of our first gigs. We played at a grocery store in Austin.' And I remember Boland and I just looking at each other and going, 'Holy shit.' So we booked them at the Wormy Dog."

In the 1998 to 2000 time frame, Reckless Kelly played only a handful of gigs at the Wormy Dog, but they became the most anticipated shows in Stillwater. Aside from the heavy hitters of the day—Robert Earl Keen, Pat Green, Charlie Robison—there were three bands that would play that dive and cause either students to miss class to stand in line or find someone to stand in line for them: George DeVore and the Roam, Roger Clyne and the Peacemakers and Reckless Kelly.

"But one of the things I remember the most about the Wormy Dog is we were loading in, up those huge, god-awful stairs, and these two guys were hauling up new glass for the window in the bar," Willy said. "So I asked him, 'Oh? New windows? Kind of a rowdy night last night? You guys broke a couple of windows?' and the guy goes, 'No, these are for tonight.'

"And it did get crazy. I remember people literally swinging from the rafters in there. I remember one guy swinging from them and, like, punching the air conditioning duct to the beat. Back in those days, I remember it being one of the craziest, wildest shows we ever played. The crowd just was so fucking into it."

Reckless Kelly returned the favor, helping Ragweed find an in with Lucy's in Austin, which became a regular tour stop for them—at one time, Ragweed rarely went more than five to six weeks without a Lucy's gig.

Those early relationships kicked off a nearly parallel rise between the two bands. In the early 2000s, contemporary Texas music was highly competitive, and it was nothing for artists to use the stage or the press to cut down other bands they viewed as a threat. But Reckless and Ragweed brought a community spirit to Texas, and around 2002, both bands smashed the state's musical ceiling.

"Man, we were just playing really similar styles of music, and they were great guys," Willy said. "We did a lot of shows together. In the early days, they'd open for us, but all of a sudden those guys caught fire. They blew up so fast, it was crazy, and all of a sudden, we were opening for them. But they treated us really well and started inviting us on tours, and we really just had a kind of mutual admiration society with them."

In late 2001, Ragweed cut "Crazy Eddie's Last Hurrah" on their *Live at Billy Bob's* album—their second live album and final release before they were signed to Universal South records. A half-decade later, Cody and Shannon Canada had their second child, a boy. They named the kid Willy.

"I've said a thousand times that Reckless Kelly is the best band in this scene," Cody Canada said. "They are tight. Their work ethic is unmatched. And they are funny bastards, too. That helps.

"Before we got them up at the Dog, we drove down to see them in Dallas at the Gypsy Tea Room for Shannon's 29th birthday. And I was determined—I'm gonna be friends with these guys. I walked straight backstage and hung out. We were drinking and smoking weed, and I remember jumping in a circle with a harmonica while they were playing a song and the look on their faces. I'm sure after we left they were like, 'Who are these jerkoffs?'...That's one of their favorite words. But it was almost an immediate friendship."

Both bands went on to wield influences that by Red Dirt and Texas standards were outsized, and musically they kept enough differences—Ragweed always a bit more electric and Reckless always more deft with fiddle and mandolin—that they never stepped on each other's toes. When Reckless put a near-bluegrass cover of "You Shook Me All Night Long" on their 1999 release, *Live at Stubb's*, Ragweed turned around their own version—same pace but wildly different style. Both covers became encore staples for both bands for half a decade.

Today, Reckless is Cody, Willy and Jay from the original band, plus Joe Miller—the latest in a line of bass players that started with Schelske and continued with the late Jimmy "Jam" McFeeley before Miller.

Pollock joined the band in Austin, from Bend, and was wildly popular, especially for his guitar playing on the Stubb's album. But by 2000, he left.

His replacement for the next 19 years was David Abeyta, a student of music who had spent his formative years in Bartlesville, Oklahoma, and who had played guitar with Austin mainstays Jimmy LaFave and George DeVore. And he had fronted his own band.

"I was born in Seattle and lived in Portland for a while," Abeyta said. "In Portland, there was a guy in my neighborhood who had a ukulele band—like I happened to land in this one neighborhood with this ukulele band. Kids could learn to read single-note music. I got a ukulele from my grandmother when I was 4. When I was 5 or so, I was playing in this band and learning to read music with them. Then, when I could hold a baritone ukulele, I got a baritone. When I could hold a guitar, I got a guitar. So it kind of chose me."

His family moved to Bartlesville when he was in first grade, and his youth and teen years were spent playing, usually around town, buffered from Tulsa and the Tulsa Sound, 45 miles to the south of Bartlesville. It was enough to ingrain music in Abeyta's blood but not enough to make a career out of music.

That awakening came in college, at Boston's Berklee College of Music.

"I called my mom and I'm like, 'How do people even do this?' and, bless her heart, she just said, 'You keep doing good work, and one day you'll wake up and you'll just be doing it.' And it's so true. It was one of the wisest things she ever said to me. There were lots of times of floundering around and working day jobs and struggling, but I was always super ambitious about music, whether it was in a jazz quartet or more like this kind of stuff with singer-songwriters. I was super obsessive. I think the word perfectionist has been thrown around too."

Abeyta moved to Austin after college. Jimmy LaFave's influence on him is covered in the LaFave chapter, but what Abeyta really did in Austin was immerse himself in every genre the city offered, far beyond just Americana.

"Berklee was huge for me," Abeyta said. "There were people from all over the world. I was super lucky to get to go, and it was just, like, into the deep end of jazz studies for me. I made leaps and bounds, but it also turned me into a jazz snob. So when I got out, I thought, *This is what I'm doing.* So when I got to Austin, I was kind of caught in between. Some of the first people I saw were LaFave at La Zona Rosa, Rusty Wier at the Saxon Pub. I remember seeing David Halley [another Oklahoma transplant] at La Zona. I stumbled into the Joe Ely Band at Liberty Lunch, just blowing me away.

"I was always a big fan of, like, Robben Ford and people who take jazz ideas and impose them over blues forms or rock and roll. David Grissom was doing that with Ely at the time too. So I had an inkling that I could do this, but I basically still wanted to have a John Scofield quartet. So I did that. I struggled with it and worked a day job, but I also played with other people.

"My drummer friend—John Chipman, also from Oklahoma, plays with The Resentments now, played with Jon Dee Graham—he introduced me to DeVore. His guitar player had left, so I got with him. That was a really important two years for me, because we didn't do anything much in the way of touring, but what we did do was a really great residency at the Saxon Pub every Tuesday night. And I stood in that same spot, and I learned to work with the room and a weird sound system and have energetic crowds and things that I hadn't had much of. That was huge, and I don't know if I've ever told George, but I really value that time. And I don't know that I would have ended up with these guys without DeVore. We were all buddies, all hanging—talk about epic hangs."

Those epic hangs eventually combined with Reckless's vacancy. Pollock happened to leave the band right when DeVore and Reckless overlapped with each other regularly, if not at shows, certainly after hours in Austin.

"He joined the band right when we were making *The Day* album. He didn't play guitar on it, Jon Dee Graham did, but right around the time we were finishing that, he joined up, our original guitar player bailed out," Willy Braun said. "David was playing with George DeVore. And we always thought he was just the cat's ass. We'd watch George play and go, 'Holy shit, who's that guitar player?'"

The time with DeVore was the perfect bridge into Reckless. The crowds were similar, if not overlapping. DeVore, like Reckless, draws from a wide variety of styles.

"I don't remember it being a stretch, because I was pretty in that vein with DeVore," Abeyta said. "We were doing a lot of shows. We would do shows together. I remember that well, DeVore would open and Reckless would close, and they were great nights. So when the time came, when Casey left, they had a couple of guys who didn't last long. They were looking for somebody, and I thought, *I think we've done all that we can do.* But I'm a super-loyal dog. I've been in this band 19 years, almost. So when I called George to tell him I think I'm gonna join Reckless, I was super emotional. I caught myself by surprise. That was a tough phone call. But there was really no doubt in my mind.

"So we were playing an Antone's show, and DeVore was opening. It was my last night with DeVore and my first night with Reckless. I played the opener, stayed right where I was and came up and played my first set with Reckless."

Ultimately, Abeyta left Reckless in 2019, after an 18-year run in the prime of his and the band's career. Reckless has pushed ahead, with Idaho artist Jeff Crosby and Turnpike Troubadours guitarist Ryan Engleman both taking turns as the band's lead player since.

The fifth of the five-piece is Miller. Like the others, his becoming the fifth piece of the five-piece can be chalked up to fate.

"Joe joined the band pretty much because his old band, Back Porch Mary, was breaking up," Willy Braun said. "The lead singer, Mike Krug, and I took a trip with a couple other guys to see two or three Red Sox games, the Baseball Hall of Fame and a Springsteen show. While on the trip, Mike told me that if we needed a bass player—which we did—Joe was our guy. I called him when I got home and he's been with us since then."

That trip—"Willy and Mike went on a bromantic weekend" is how Miller put it—came in 2012. Back Porch Mary had been a band for 19 years, and Miller had been its bass player since 2001. For Miller, a rural Kansan by birth and, like Reckless, Austinite by choice, Reckless was an easy trigger to pull.

Like the rest of the band, he is a lifelong musician.

"I'm doing what I'm doing today because I saw *Hee Haw* on TV when I was about 5. I grew up in Burdett, Kansas, or rather 10 miles outside of Burdett, on a farm," Miller said. "And I caught the whole 'Class of '86' thing—Dwight Yoakam, Steve Earle, Foster & Lloyd. They'd play it on country radio and I could hear that stuff while I was driving a tractor. And I always knew there was some kind of alternative country music. Some stuff was hip and some stuff was just cheesy."

Miller got a guitar around age 10 and started playing drums in his school band around fifth grade. He followed that up by learning bass guitar at age 13, largely because his school had a Fender P bass and the electric instrument appealed to him. But his teen years were spent playing drums in a quintessential 1980s country bar band. "That was New Year's Eve of 1987, my first paying gig. I made $17 at the VFP in St. John, Kansas, and got free beer. And I was hooked. So I did that my junior and senior year in high school."

After graduation, he ended up at Kansas State University in Manhattan, with a goal of joining a rock band as a bass player. "I picked the bass because everybody needed a bass player. Simple as that," Miller said. It paid off with a bass gig in a country band called Rio, from 1992 to 1995. It was a four-piece band—starched Wranglers,

George Strait covers and early 1990s country, and weeklong gigs at hotel bars and dance halls—made up of ag majors and country boys, all of whom graduated high school in 1989.

A chance meeting with Randy Taylor (cowriter of "Much Too Young to Feel This Damn Old" with Garth Brooks) near the end of his time in Rio turned Miller's head to a music scene one state due south of Manhattan: Red Dirt.

"I worked in radio at K-State, for a little station in the cooperative extension service," Miller said. "There was a guy in the ag engineering department who I talked to on the radio about soil compaction by the name of Randy Taylor.

"Randy and I then got to jam a couple of times. And he told me, 'Man, you need to go check out this band in Stillwater called The Great Divide.' So I knew there was something going on in Stillwater."

Miller visited Stillwater after he graduated in 1995, but it was in the summer and nothing was going on in town other than the chance to grab a beer at the Wormy Dog. But the knowledge that the alternative scene he had a hunch about actually existed was enough to spur him to investigate. Thus, circa 1997, Rio broke up and reformed in Austin as Big Iron. Miller played with them from 1998 to 2001.

"I'd heard about something in Stillwater and never followed up much about it. But I did hear enough compilation albums out of Austin and I went, 'Man, this is cool.' Whether it was retro, progressive or whatever, it was just hip."

During his Big Iron stint, Miller and another band member also dabbled in Back Porch Mary, a band best described as cowpunk. They played the Americana circuit, but with a heavy punk edge to the songs. Miller joined Back Porch Mary full-time in 2001.

In between arriving in Austin and joining Back Porch Mary, Miller also learned about Reckless Kelly.

"In March of '98, I went to Liberty Lunch to see Reckless Kelly," he said. "And I was blown away. I'm just like, how in the hell? I was jealous. They were kids then. I was 27. I worked my ass off. I worked my ass off at a day job too, and I don't have half their talent. And they're kids. They're children. I don't know nothing about Muzzie and the Little Braun Boys. I just see a bunch of young punks who were so good. And what was really frustrating to me and my drummer at the time was—and I knew it could happen—how do you take country and rock without it being Nashville cheese? We had been Chris LeDoux fans, and he had done it. But here in front of us was Reckless Kelly. It was such a big deal that the next day, I went to Waterloo Records and got a copy of Millican. I listened to it every day, got over the last girl who screwed me over with it. Every song was personal. And I'm like, 'This is a young kid that wrote this.' And from there on out, I always bought their albums. I was always impressed by the musicianship and the songwriting. And that became my favorite Austin, Texas, band."

By the time Back Porch Mary ran its course, Reckless Kelly had an opening for a bass player. That's how Willy Braun's trip with Krug ended up landing Miller the closest thing to his dream job that he was going to get.

"They're a killer bunch of guys," Miller said. "Willy Braun is as cool as you think he is. I love those Brauns. They're a great family. They're great people.

"It's definitely been worth it. I remember having a conversation with my stepdad in the middle of a long tour when I was pretty road-worn and weary. He brought up a million valid points, and one of them was, 'How much is the art worth to you?' And

I'm like, yeah. The art is the whole deal. It's absolutely worth it. I'm a bass player, it's what I do. I had good predecessors here too."

Reckless Kelly managed to be both wildly fun and wildly professional for 20-plus years. Along the way, a record deal with Sugar Hill and Yep Roc produced four albums. Today, the band is back to independent releases, but they remain one of the bellwether bands in Texas. Their 2016 album, *Sunset Motel*, reached No. 12 on the U.S. country charts. Over Memorial Day weekend 2020, Reckless released a double album, *American Jackpot* and *American Girls*, in digital-only format at the time due to the coronavirus pandemic (a CD and vinyl release came in the summer). The combo debuted at No. 6 on the iTunes albums download chart for all genres.

"It's funny because we've been together for so long, sometimes I think the thing that keeps us together is the time we put into it. We have a lot invested as far as the miles we put in together," Willy said. "If we had just started this band two weeks ago, and the way every now and then somebody's pissed off at someone, maybe they'd go, 'Alright, fuck this.' But it's such an investment in it, that helps. And we surround ourselves with great players and guys that you can just hang out with.

"A guy can be the best guitar player in the world, but if you can't stand him, the band's not gonna last. That's the main reason we're still together—we all still like each other. Everybody's gonna have days on the road where you're sick of everybody. But at the end of the day, we always say you gotta have thick skin and a short memory."

Nazz asserts that creativity and drive play the biggest role in Reckless Kelly pushing forward.

"I still get that feeling. It's an awesome feeling when we're firing on all cylinders," Nazz said. "Some people ask me if I get tired of playing the same song over and over again. But every single time I play a song, I have an opportunity to play it the best I've ever played it. And that hasn't happened, and it'll never happen. But that's what keeps me going.

"We're an old married couple at this point. We know each other in and out, but we still have this hunger for creation and doing it together. But any year that comes up, I've never felt like it was a guarantee, because the nature of a band isn't a guarantee. I don't take it for granted."

While all of the above was going down, another set of Braun Brothers had eyes for Texas and was destined to wade in Red Dirt.

· · ·

Micky and the Motorcars

The Braun family band did not exactly disband when Cody and Willy bolted for Bend. The two younger brothers, Gary and Micky, hung around Stanley and found their own sound.

"I started getting up on stage, just following my brothers up on stage when I was 5," Micky Braun said (at the time, Cody, the oldest, was 10). "Cody was playing fiddle with my dad on a couple of songs. Willy was getting up and doing some singing. Anyway, eventually all of us were on stage, so Dad just worked up a couple of kid-type songs for us—kind of novelty sets when he was playing outdoor venues or fairs. And eventually that just kind of turned into him buying us instruments or giving us instruments that he had lying around the house for Christmas, and we just started playing."

The family band lasted nine years, breaking up when Micky was 14. Gary and

Micky stayed home—they were home-schooled in the Idaho mountains. Around that time, Micky developed a passion for songwriting.

"I started playing acoustic guitar when I was 13. That's when I got into writing," Micky said. "Mainly it was just—I can write a song, and I know these three chords, I can make up my own words to it. Now, none of them were good, but they were mine. My dad helped a lot there. That was probably the most teaching he did with my musical side was getting me going on songwriting. How to rhyme, how verses go together and choruses.

"That was my favorite part about my dad teaching me that. He said that there really are no rules in writing. He said people will try to put rules on it, where you have to rhyme every other sentence, but you know, you don't have to. If you don't want to, you don't have to. If it's working for you, you can do whatever you want.

"That's the beauty of writing. You get to be free in how you want to do it."

The Northwest landscape is dotted with towns like Stanley. They all have something like a general store or a local barbecue joint. These places all have little wooden stages, and they book bands all weekend, all summer—Friday night, Saturday night, Sunday afternoon. The tourists who come looking for scenery or moose also need to be fed and entertained. That's where Micky honed his own musical chops as a teenager.

"I loved to perform," Micky said. "I always did. That was my favorite deal. I was actually trying look into a school I could get into, where I could get into acting. But I already knew how to play, and that was a style of performing, so I was kind of getting what I wanted out of playing music anyway. So I went and played bass with my dad after the brothers broke up for one summer. And then the next summer, I had enough songs on the acoustic that I could play. So I got a buddy of mine, and I got my own shows. I had, like, three of my own shows in a week, and I kept playing with my dad, and I was building houses—well, moving sheetrock at least—while all that's happening."

While his brothers found their way in Austin, Micky forged his own following in and around Stanley and across Idaho. Eventually, he had enough connections to put together a band.

"There was a short little stop we had," Micky said. "My buddy Mark McCoy—he was my best friend and was living down the street from me. I was living in town. I taught him how to play bass guitar. My other buddy, Travis [Hardy], was playing drums, so I needed a bass player, so I taught Mark bass. We moved down to Arizona for the wintertime, and we rented a little double-wide trailer on a little ranch. I had my dad's old PA that he gave me, and we set it up in the living room, and all we did was jam."

Meanwhile, Gary had taken a detour out of music.

"I took a few years off and just worked on a ranch. Kind of cowboyed and did that kind of stuff," Gary Braun said. "Then, Cody and Willy had started Reckless Kelly, and seeing those guys come back and playing again and starting to draw a crowd was just like—well, I can do that too. I got that itch again and decided to get back into it with Micky full force. And we just dove in, quit our jobs and basically played music full-time since 2001."

The fledgling band spent the winter—the town was Cave Creek, a suburb on the northern fringes of Phoenix—working side jobs, practicing and generally saving enough money to get them through the next summer in Idaho. That summer, 2001, the Motorcars formed.

"We formed the band in June," Micky said. "We played our first gig: It was a wedding. We were driving to the gig, and we didn't have a name for the band. We were in two pickup trucks. So we threw all the names we had in a hat and said, 'When we get there, have your decision.'

"When we got there, it was pretty solid. Everyone said, 'OK, we're Micky and the Motorcars' and we have been ever since."

The brothers drew well in Idaho, drawing on a mix of Micky's songs and Americana covers of artists like Robert Earl Keen, Gram Parsons and Rodney Crowell—bucking the bar band trend of contemporary country covers.

"Up there, they were kind of thinking that was our stuff, in a way," Micky said. "So that's why we stayed there that year through January—to get enough of our own material, because we knew when we went to Texas, we were not gonna be able to pull off playing Robert Earl Keen songs all night, every night."

Eventually, it happened. The Motorcars moved to Austin in 2002—first rooming with Willy and quickly finding a place to rent as a band. Reckless Kelly had already established itself as one of the top draws on Sixth Street. The family ties helped the Motorcars cut some early corners.

"They opened a lot of doors. We got to jump on with their booking agent, which helped out a lot because he tossed us onto a lot of shows in the bigger venues as opening acts," Micky said. "We got into a lot of cool rooms right out of the gate, and that also spread our name really fast, which helped out a lot. And then we just picked up local, one-night-a-week gigs when we weren't touring.

"All we wanted to do was play. We were hungry. So any gig that came down the line, we would play. And when we weren't playing, we were playing. We'd sit around and jam and invite friends over."

Gary described the early attitude of the band as willful ignorance of the larger concept of the music business, with a focus on singing songs and having fun instead.

"I just wanted to make a good living, play music and party and not have to do the old nine-to-fiver," Gary said. "And I thought that would just kind of develop into a huge success, because I was a little more naive when I was younger. I think we all were."

A pair of early independent albums helped spread the Motorcars' music, and rather quickly, a familiar partnership extended a hand as well.

"I would say some of the people who opened the doors for us a lot were Cross Canadian Ragweed," Micky said. "They were probably one of our biggest helping hands. Shannon Canada took us in and managed us for eight years. She took us on really early, and she got us into a booking agency that was a bit more broad. And Ragweed put us on a ton of tours. They took us everywhere—West coast, East coast, up in the Chicago area. They were huge at the time in Oklahoma and Texas, and they really put us in front of the masses and at least got our name in front of everyone. You can't put a price on that."

In 2007, the band released *Careless*, on Smith Music Group, and followed that with one of the longest, purest recordings that the *Live At Billy Bob's* series has produced. For all the bands that have cut a live album there, few capture the essence of the band's show as well as the Motorcars' concert did.

"We had never done a live record anywhere," Micky said. "I wanted to do one. They were trying to get us to do one about two years before that. But I just wasn't there. Gary didn't feel it was good at the time. I wanted to get one more studio album out and get those songs out there to feel comfortable doing an hour and a half where a good portion would be our songs. We had just gotten a new guitar player. So we were in a little bit of limbo—it wasn't just a good time to go represent ourselves.

"We wanted to tighten up the ship. We did. I loved doing that record. I got a lot of control over that record that a lot of people didn't with them. I wanted to bring in our own engineer, we wanted to mix it ourselves, and they signed off on those things. I didn't want them to just do a 'Get it out there so we can get our money back' thing. I wanted it to represent our live show. We did get lucky. Everybody kept their noses clean and just played awesome that night."

The Motorcars have undergone more changes than their older brothers' counterparts, but they have always been a steady force in Texas, Oklahoma and the states' corresponding scenes.

Today, the band is Micky, Gary, Joe Fladger (bass), Pablo Trujillo (guitar) and Bobby Paugh (drums). They carry a sound that's more steel than Reckless, although the raspy vocals of both Willy and Micky would fit either band.

In June 2018, Micky and his girlfriend, Ali Jenkins, welcomed a daughter, Hattie, and moved to suburban Boston. Her family is from there, and Micky has family nearby as well, making the area an ideal fit to raise Hattie—who by 2020 was a backstage showstopper at Motorcars' gigs, dancing right along with her dad.

"Ali has a pretty decent-sized family here, and they're all close," Micky said. "They all love each other. They all live in Ashland, right outside of town here, and they hang out all the time.

"It reminded me a lot of my family. And my mom is from Massachusetts as well, so I'm not a stranger to this neck of the woods either. I was in Austin for 16 years, so it's a nice change of pace to move to a different city. I'm getting some different ideas, songwriting-wise. It's a four-hour flight there, it's three-and-a-half hours back. People ask me if it gets old, and I'm like, 'Man, it's a four-hour drive from Austin to Dallas. And you can't drink or sleep. This is no big deal.'"

In fall 2019, the Motorcars released *Long Time Comin'*—a Keith Gattis–produced album of intense, personal music—arguably more so than any other in the band's catalog—that nodded often to the Brauns' Idaho roots.

"It was a combination of wanting to work with Keith and wanting to do something outside the norm for us, and it made sense," Micky Braun said. "Number one, we hadn't put out a record in three years, and you have to do that to stay on the road. But I wanted to wait until we had the right package together instead of just jumping in the studio. I wanted this one to shine and show off some more versatile stuff than we'd done in the past."

The journey through the album—with different emotions evoked on just about every track—builds to a crescendo. There's love ("Road to You" and "Thank My Mother's God"), heartache ("Stranger Tonight" and "Break My Heart") and existentialism ("Lions of Kandahar").

But the high water mark is "Hold This Town Together," an ode to rural Idaho—and the potent Salmon River Quiver weed strain—that Micky wrote with Idaho artist Jeff Crosby. The song is both very specific—most of it paints a picture of Sandpoint, Idaho—and very generic—most of it can be about your town, where you grew up, too.

"It's Idaho, but it's also anywhere," Micky said. "We'd just grown up in it and lived it. We did a lot of name-dropping in the song. He was using his people. I was using mine. We were both thinking of bars that we knew. And that ended up being the point. We both had a similar vibe going with Idaho and we ran with it."

* * *

A Lasting Influence

Both sets of Braun brothers were welcomed in Texas. But equally important is the fact they also welcomed Texas. They moved to Austin and played the same Idaho hick rock they had played with Muzzie. The fans came to them in droves, and they respected the history of Texas music as their contemporaries, but they did not bother trying to fit in. They just played the way they knew how.

"We were so young, playing that style of music up to that point were mostly older players—Billy Joe Shaver and the guys doing the outlaw country thing," Cody Braun said. "When we came in, we connected with the younger crowd, the college crowd. And Robert Earl Keen at that point was the *in* thing with that crowd, so there was this huge audience that was looking for someone to latch on to. I think they found that in what we were doing, what Ragweed was doing—that younger generation of artists that were playing rock-and-roll country. It was a different take on the outlaw scene."

This is vitally important to understanding the migration of Red Dirt. There was always going to be a market in Texas for Texas artists. When Reckless Kelly made inroads and discovered they could relate, they paved the road that Ragweed and Jason Boland soon followed. They all played the same bars. The outsiders generally passed on Texas-centric songwriting, and Reckless was the band that made doing that OK. They showed younger Texas audiences that they could adopt musicians from other states and showed the musicians they could embrace Texas, and neither side had to feel like they were betraying their roots.

If Reckless Kelly does not do this first, in all likelihood this book either is not written at all or is a past-tense retrospective of a music scene that once existed in Stillwater and then died off—rather than a living, breathing dynamic that fanned out like a prairie wind and never really stopped.

Robert Earl Keen made college kids fall in love with roots rock. Pat Green, Cory Morrow, Jack Ingram and Bruce and Charlie Robison gave the same audiences a generation of artists they could relate to as their own. Reckless showed how outsiders could crash the scene, and along with Ragweed they showed how far it could be pushed. Everything after that point revised the history of two scenes that, until that point, were distinct and separate.

Jay Nazz crystallized Reckless's approach and rooted it in a touch of perfectionism that each member shares.

"Originally, it was about camaraderie. It was about that feeling I got after we played something well together," Nazz said. "I remember early on, we had meetings with a lot of record companies. We hadn't even been in Austin a year, but we'd do South by Southwest acoustic, and these record label people would walk by and see the crowd. So we'd be going out to lunch with them, and we—probably to a fault—were a five-headed monster that was so cautious about anybody tainting the water. So as that all took its course, I'm so grateful that we've had a career.

"I tell any young player, the two things I'm most grateful for are I bought a house playing drums and I have health insurance. And if you align your goals with the things that are gonna serve you, then you'll make the right decisions."

The Braun brothers join Muzzie every summer (minus the 2020 incarnation that was moved online due to the global pandemic) in Challis, Idaho, for their flagship festival. The Braun Brothers Reunion has become one of the most in-demand festivals in Red Dirt or Texas music, and it happens several hundred miles from the base. Both the Motorcars and Reckless headline, and the entire family jams out a set together in the shadows of the Sawtooths. There are other festivals that carry major cache in the scene—Medicine Stone, for one, or Larry Joe Taylor's for a longer-running one—but Braun Brothers is the climax of festival season.

"It's just music that we really like," Cody Braun said of the reunion. "People that we have either discovered or become friends with out on the road. Guys that are writing good songs, performing, touring and doing it for the right reasons."

"Our fan base is really broad up there, with the age difference. It's teenagers to people in their 70s. So we try to keep some of the traditions that my mom and dad started. We want older artists up there. We want to introduce new ones. But a lot of them are just friends that we want to come back and play with every year."

Getting to that point, for both Reckless and the Motorcars, has been a tale of give-and-take, mostly willingly (although the Reckless-Ragweed prank wars caught a few bystanders in the crossfire). And both bands have given back to those who lifted them up.

In 2010, Reckless released *Somewhere in Time*, an album exclusively featuring songs written by Pinto Bennett, an Idaho songwriter and longtime family friend.

"Their band—the Famous Motel Cowboys—they were like the cat's ass when we were kids," Willy said. "They were the best band on the block, and Pinto has always been one of my songwriting heroes. And that came from my dad, he was always saying, listen to this guy. And when I started songwriting, Pinto was the guy I'd draw from. So we've already been enormous fans.

"It actually took us longer to put out than we wanted. But you know, we can't do that for our second album. We had to establish ourselves before we could make the Pinto tribute record. We finally got to the point where we had one record left with Sugar Hill, and we said, 'We're doing the Pinto tribute record,' and they were like, 'Well...' and we were like, 'No, we're doing the Pinto tribute record. So if you want a record, you can have this one. Otherwise, bye.'

"We wanted to do it while he was still alive. Here it's almost 10 years later and he's still around, but we didn't know that at the time. We wanted him to be involved in the making of it. We wanted to really make sure we paid tribute to the Motel Cowboys and Pinto's songs. We were gonna make it happen. Pinto's just one of those guys to me who should be playing stadiums, if there was any justice in the world. Those guys were great, and we just had to make that album."

That same give-and-take paid off for the Motorcars as well. The younger of the two bands, Micky and Gary's outfit shaved time off the early dues-paying days not only by having Reckless as a model, but also from finding others in the scene willing to help out and help build a fan base.

"We were fortunate enough to have guys like Cody Canada, really all of Cross Canadian Ragweed and very much Shannon [Canada, an early longtime manager of the Motorcars] on our team right away," Gary Braun said. "When we moved to Texas, they already knew who we were. They kind of took us under their wing. They gave us an opportunity to open up for their fans—the same with Robert Earl Keen, Reckless. Shit, we've been out with Asleep at the Wheel. The bands that were already established when we came to town were very good to us, and that probably saved us."

The Brauns' compassionate streak does not extend solely to their influences. David Abeyta spent late 2017 caring for and supporting his sister after she underwent treatment for a tumor—including time away from Reckless. One of the songs he found personal comfort in was Slaid Cleaves' "One Good Year" ("Give me one good year / to get my feet back on the ground. I've been chasing grace / but grace ain't so easily found"). When word got back to the Brauns about this song, they asked Abeyta to perform it during Reckless shows. Abeyta set it up with a powerful story of caring for his sister and delivered it with raw emotion that is not always expected during the band's sets.

"It's not us, really. We have a style that's more strong, silent type. That's a Willy and Cody thing," Abeyta said. "It's their band and that's the way it is. But I've been with them so long that if Willy asks me to play that song, he's comfortable with it. He knows what it means to me, and he knows that I'm gonna say a little something before it. To me, it's all cathartic. I just turned 51, and from about 40 on, I never really let the lid off much, and I ended up really struggling because of that with anxiety and depression. And I learned that talking through stuff is very important and not something to be ashamed of. And I learned that even if it's not their style, there's someone in the room who it's going to speak to.

"My sister had seven brain surgeries last year. And she survived, and she is physically good, but it's still a major challenge that we deal with every day. And it means a lot to play that song."

For the Brauns, though, the most poignant modern-day moment came via an old friend, Canada, and his 2015 song "All Nighter"—a song he started writing about the Brauns and that featured Canada, the four Braun brothers and Muzzie, all singing verses, complete with a video shot at John T. Floore's Country Store in Helotes, Texas, that captured the family atmosphere Canada was after when he wrote it.

The song, unfortunately, was borne of pure tragedy. The kind that wrought a living hell, particularly for the Motorcars.

Mark McCoy—everyone called him Gus—was a founding member of the Motorcars and Micky Braun's best friend when the band started. He left the band in 2011. In late April 2012, Gus and a friend, Steven Herrett, took a raft into the Salmon River, the same one that cuts near Stanley, to go fishing. The raft struck a log. Both men fell in the river. Herrett made it out. McCoy drowned. His body was found six miles away near the mouth of the Yankee Fork River.

McCoy had friendships throughout the music scene. He had lived with Chris McCoy (no relation), former Cross Canadian Ragweed and current Randy Rogers Band sound engineer, in Austin. He had a polarizing relationship with Cody Canada that was contentious for a time but ultimately found both men hugging and sharing a gut laugh one night after a show.

"It wasn't too long after that night that it happened," Canada said, referring to McCoy's accident. "I'd been talking to Muzzie for a couple of years about how awesome his relationship is with his kids, and I asked him, 'How do you do it?' And he said, 'I just suggest you keep 'em close by your side. You have to be their dad, and a lot of people say don't be their friend, but I say do it. Be their friend. My boys are my best friends, and they'll say the same.'

"We were at the Reckless Softball Jam when we all got the news. We knew he was missing, and you can all have hope, but it was pretty bleak. And I saw Micky up against the wall, and I knew that he'd just heard the news and he was in bad shape. Nobody had to say anything, but people still said things—they found him. It was a bad day.

"I had been kicking that tune around, and I had the first and only New Year's Eve I've ever had off. And Mattson Rainer, Kim Rainer, Shannon and I were gonna go to a sushi place here in New Braunfels and have a night. Not a hammered night, just a fun night. And I was thinking I'd tried to get Micky to write it. And he said, 'Man, I can't,' and I understood that. So I had pushed it toward Jason Eady, and Eady said, 'I think this one's all you, man.'

"So Kim and Shannon weren't ready yet that night, and that's when I did it. I said, 'This is gonna be my last song of this year.' And I called it 'All Nighter,' because we pulled all-nighters with those guys.

"We played out in Idaho again with someone else, not the Braun Brothers. And I told Muzzie, 'I got a song I want you to hear. I started it about Gus, but it's really about all you awesome Idahoans in this family.'

"I played it for him, and he goes, 'That's a really sweet song. I guess you got that from the stove, huh?' And I said, 'What do you mean?' And he said, 'You kidding me?'

"So he takes us over to their wood-burning stove. And the front of that stove, in stamped steel or iron is a little cabin, with smoke coming from it. And the name next to it is *THE ALL NIGHTER.*

"I said, 'I had no idea,' and he goes, 'You're bullshitting me.'

"So I asked if he'd do the honor of singing on this song. And he said, 'You just say when.'

"I got 'em all in there, and what happened with that song was exactly what I had planned to happen. I wanted Micky to sing about the Gus part. I wanted Willy to sing about the posers—because he and I have the same outlook on posers. And I wanted Muzz to sing about his part. And the coincidence of it was it ran in order, from youngest to oldest."

The song took on a larger meaning than simply McCoy or the Brauns—Canada sang it at Tom Skinner's memorial in August 2015. But the brothers were also OK with that.

"I'm not sure what the initial contact was, but I do remember them saying that Cody had written a song about Gus, and it was kind of loosely written around the stove at my dad's house," Willy Braun said. "To me, that already brings back memories. That stove is still at Mom and Dad's house. So the title alone is just a trip down memory lane type of thing. And then he said he wanted us to sing on it—hell yeah. So I don't recall the initial contact, but we were all in."

Micky also caught both the spirit and intent of the song when he heard it.

"Cody called me, I wanna say, six months or so after Gus passed away," Micky said. "And he told me he was working on a song about Gus and the whole deal, and he asked me if I wanted to come write it with him. And I just wasn't in a good mindset for it, and I just went, 'Man, I don't know what I'm gonna contribute to it at this point. If it's fresh on your mind, run with it.'

"I'm glad that he just moved forward with it, because it's a killer tune.

"That's how I heard about the song. Fast-forward, later on, he calls and goes, 'I finished the song, I'm gonna put it on the next album, and I want you and your brothers to come in and all do a verse.' And I said, 'That's awesome, let's do it.' We went in and cut it. Drank some beers and a little bit of wine and whiskey and had a good time recording it.

"They really got behind us, as they always do. They've always been so supportive no matter what they do. On the night of the funeral, all the guys who couldn't make it wore ties at their shows, because that was Gus's deal, he always wore ties. So that was also a really cool tribute."

If, by now, this has not explained to you why Willy Braun still brings up the time Ragweed covered "Crazy Eddie's Last Hurrah," I'm not sure I can help you.

The footnote to this story, though, happened a few years earlier, when Shannon and Cody Canada were expecting their second child.

"If it was a girl, it was gonna be Lee Ann or Codi, with an I. Shannon wanted that. I wasn't hip to it," Cody said. "But I said, if it's a boy, it's Willy. And she said, 'I love it.' And Willy came.

"Willy Braun has really taken my Willy under his wing. My Willy plays drums now, and that was Willy Braun's first instrument. And when he found that out, I'm pretty sure that Willy Canada knew that, and that's why he did it. But Willy Braun just took him in, started buying him records that he learned drums on. You couldn't ask for a better group of friends.

"Better group of assholes, though."

— — —

- 16 -

How The Dirt Was Spread

THE ANSWER IS surely evident by now.

How did Red Dirt go from being a niche scene in central Oklahoma to an abstract concept, a label that could be applied as easily as Americana, roots rock, alt-country or indie folk to any artist who sang country music but raspy?

The most consistent answer, from Oklahoma artists and those who have never spent more than the night after a show in the state, has been resounding: When Cody Canada and Jason Boland moved from Yukon and Stillwater, respectively, to the Texas Hill Country in 2002, they carried the Red Dirt creed of artists helping one another with them and never wavered.

Before we get to that—wherein "that" means "Texas"—there are a couple of other stories to tell first. One is a story about a sound guy and technology. The other is about the rise of a sports bar a thousand miles northeast of Oklahoma. Together, they illustrate the curiosity and power Red Dirt amassed between 2000 and 2010.

Some context: In the late 1990s, Oklahoma artists were welcome to play in Texas. But the state was possessive of its music.

"You don't *try* Texas music, you *are* Texas music," was how one emcee regularly introduced bands at Stephenville City Limits, in one phrase making clear how (rightfully) proud the Lone Star State was of its sound and how outsiders should not expect to walk in and lay claim to it.

I caught this up close and personal in summer 2001, at the original Lucy's Retired Surfers Bar in Austin. I was there with Ragweed, and I was asked to introduce the band before its set. And on that night, the band—still very much touring Oklahoma and Texas in a van built to hold eight but often holding 10 or 12—was preparing for a show a week later at the Philadelphia International Music Festival. Lucy's was sold out that night. Ragweed was not yet based in Texas, but they had won over the state's fans and at the very least were honorary Texas artists. So I tried to incorporate both of those facts into my 20-second band introduction. It went something like this:

Me: "Ladies and gentlemen, it's time to welcome back a band that Lucy's loves and that loves Lucy's right back..."

Crowd: [raucous cheering]

Me: "And show them some love because, next week, they're taking this music all the way up to the Philadelphia International Music Festival..."

Crowd: [booing exponentially more raucous than the cheering had been]

That's just my example. Most everyone has one. That same summer, multiple artists sang in concerts about how Texas "oughta put up a wall." I know, I know. But this wall was supposed to be meant to keep Oklahoma musicians out of the state.

I have a second example, also from the summer of 2001, this time in Houston. Ragweed played in a fancy downtown club opening for a popular mainstream band at the time. You'd for sure know the name. Anyway, as Ragweed tore through an opening set, the headliners gathered backstage in the green room and proceeded to trash Ragweed.

"They're not very good, are they?"

"I think I learned these three chords when I was in kindergarten."

"They need to hurry it up and get off our stage."

I remember all this because they said it all as I stood two feet away. I guess I did not give off the "I'm with them" vibe or they didn't care. That was something I'd never experienced in Stillwater—artists bagging on other artists. I had only ever seen it in jest or at least in private if it was serious.

Regardless, for a lot of Red Dirt musicians, that was a reality. This is how it changed.

* * *

The Sound Guy Story

The subject of this is Chris McCoy, who now runs sound for the Randy Rogers Band but who first ran it for the entirety of Cross Canadian Ragweed's time as a band. I could never make time with McCoy for this book, but the artist who hired him and the first guy he hired to join him as one of Ragweed's crew members made plenty of it.

This story takes place circa 1999.

What essentially happened was, McCoy ran sound at the Wormy Dog Saloon. He was properly obsessed with his job, and one of the ways this manifested itself was through soundboard recordings. He would record both full band and acoustic shows at the Wormy Dog—sometimes to listen to and sometimes to share around town. Bootlegging, pre-YouTube, was a musical drug, and it was no different in Red Dirt circles. If you wanted some unfiltered Cody Canada or Mike McClure songs and lived in Stillwater, McCoy was your dealer.

Here's what set McCoy's bootlegging apart: This took place in the heyday of Napster—the original file-sharing site. This is the one that spawned all of the "don't steal music" backlash from record labels and eventually led to enough lawsuits that the site shut down, only to be immediately replaced by a bunch of other sites that did the same thing.

McCoy uploaded upward of 50 bootlegs to Napster. Inadvertently he led Stillwater's Red Dirt artists hard in the other direction, taking a "steal it if you must, just spread it around" approach.

Suddenly, the musical drug of Canada singing "The Road Goes on Forever," "Paint it Black," "My Hometown" and "Sunset Boulevard" no longer required a connection to Stillwater or McCoy that could get a CD or mini disc in your hands. All it took was the proper Napster search.

"A lot of our word spread with McCoy and the Napster thing," Canada said. "He helped my career more than I think he'll ever know. That happened for about a year before we put out *Highway 377*, and by the time we put out *377*, people were ready for us."

The crowning moment of McCoy's bootlegs was a start-to-finish bootleg of a Jason Boland acoustic show during the Wormy Dog's seventh anniversary week celebration in 1999. Now, skip on over to the roundtable chapter for Boland's take on one specific song—the "Nymphomaniac" song—that became one of the early banes of his existence after it spread on Napster and fans requested the sexually explicit number at nearly every show he played afterward. But there were also upward of 40 other songs on the bootleg. Boland played covers of "The Road Goes on Forever," "Pancho and Lefty," "L.A. Freeway" and "Don't It Make You Wanna Dance" as well as early originals like "Pearl Snaps," "Truckstop Diaries" and "The Drinkin' Song."

At the time, Boland had not released a song, much less an album. Less than a year later, with The Stragglers, he put out *Pearl Snaps*. The album has reached legendary status in Red Dirt circles for debut records, and Boland's popularity soared.

In essentially reverse-engineering the concept of online piracy, McCoy helped send Red Dirt over, around or through the barriers that had previously either slowed or stopped Oklahoma artists from reaching out, especially into Texas.

"I really think that you and I wouldn't be sitting here if it weren't for McCoy doing that stuff," said former Ragweed front of house engineer and current Departed tour manager Brian Kinzie. "He really propelled that whole genre of music.

"The way he was doing his recordings was awesome. He had an old soundboard, a European soundboard that shouldn't have even worked. McCoy was using that and recording to a VHS tape, and then compressing that to MP3 format before any of us knew what MP3 even was, and then putting that on Napster."

The songs went viral before there was even such a thing as going viral. The original Texas music message board was a site called Galleywinter, and it was just the old BBS format, where you'd post a message and someone would reply, and threads never ended unless they got locked or fizzled out. For most of 2000 and 2001, there was at least one and oftentimes multiple active threads taking place on Galleywinter specifically about McCoy's bootlegs.

"Maybe he was just trying to figure this stuff out," Kinzie said, "but he's the one that explained how MP3 and Napster work, and then we all saw it play out."

• • •

The MusicFest Story

John Dickson went to college in the mid-1980s at Southwest Texas State.

The San Marcos university is just called Texas State now, and Dickson is one of the biggest names in Texas (and by proxy, Red Dirt) music who never plays a chord or sings a word. His company, Dickson Productions, puts on festivals and music cruises across Texas—Rio Frio Fest and Fest Out West are Dickson's, as were the series of cruises headlined by Cross Canadian Ragweed in the mid-2000s. But it is Dickson's flagship production that is most responsible for Red Dirt music going national.

The MusicFest at Steamboat celebrated its 35th year in the ski resorts of Steamboat Springs, Colorado, in January 2020. The festival descends on the mountain town each January and fills hotel ballrooms, bars and the Big Tent—MusicFest's massive main stage—to capacity with a mix of veteran artists and first-time performers. Cross Canadian Ragweed was such a mainstay headliner from the time the band landed its Universal South deal in 2002 until its end in 2010 that front man Cody Canada was chosen as the festival's annual tribute artist in 2020.

Its origins had little to do with music and everything to do with Dickson pocketing some free ski trips back at Southwest Texas State.

"I was a poor college student down in San Marcos, and I picked up an ad in the paper that said if you sell 15 ski trips, you get one free," Dickson said. "So I answered the ad. I was working for the university at the time, and they said, 'You know, you have to sell these trips through the university.' And I went, 'I'll do it.'

"I sold 600 trips that first year, and the university was used to selling 30 or 40 on annual trips. With the extra trips that I got, I wasn't trying to make money. I was a poor student. I was looking to travel. So I gave those extra trips to my musician friends. Back then, we all had garage bands, where you go play in your garage and pass around a cup for donations for the keg of beer, and that's who my friends were."

The trips became annual practice, and Dickson, who acted as an event producer in college and helped bring Merle Haggard and Chris LeDoux to shows in town and who worked with Robert Earl Keen in the early 1990s, got the idea to incorporate music into the trips and treat them as festivals. Once that started, travelers from across the country who had only come to Steamboat to ski were exposed to the music Dickson was bringing in.

"Nobody could make any money coming from Oklahoma or Texas up to Colorado to play music," Dickson said. "But what we found out was that they were getting exposure all over the country by playing MusicFest. That, to me, was the most rewarding thing personally, to know that I was helping those guys out.

"From there, it just morphed and grew on itself, and the demographics became completely music-oriented. And what struck me was that the artists would get up there, and they would just share the stage with each other. Pat Green would bring Cory Morrow on stage, or Cross Canadian Ragweed would bring up Randy Rogers or Wade Bowen to play. It struck me then, and it does now, how these guys help out one another.

"For me, that's just what I wanted to be a part of."

* * *

The Chicago Sports Bar Story

Joe's on Weed St. has already been name-checked.

Among other things, it hosted the final Ragweed show in October 2010. It has given Red Dirt, Texas and Americana acts a permanent home in Chicago, just west of the North and Clybourn Red Line stop. Today, Joe's has expanded to include a massive entertainment complex in the Chicago suburb of Rosemont, including a state-of-the-art entertainment venue, Joe's Live, that hosts both mainstream country acts and top-of-the-line artists from Oklahoma and Texas. It has taken over Chicago honky-tonk mainstay Carol's Pub. And Joe's is the brand behind the Windy City Smokeout, a three-day music festival just outside the Chicago Loop every summer that features a heavy rotation of Red Dirt musicians in and around those from Nashville. Joe's is mainstream enough to have won Nightclub of the Year from the Academy of Country Music and Red Dirt enough to command sellout crowds any night of the week for artists throughout the scene.

Getting to this point, for Joe's, followed a familiar path: Ragweed came in, blew the place away and told management about dozens of other bands they needed to book.

"We started doing country music at Joe's right after 9/11," cofounder and owner Ed Warm said. "We'd been doing some rock bands, some '80s stuff. The Outfield, the Eddie Moneys of the world. That was all well and good.

"But I started figuring out that there was a reason we were getting the rock bands we were getting: The big boys didn't want them. So I finally said, 'OK. I'm gonna do the music that I like, then.'

"At that time, I was gravitating toward Texas country and Red Dirt. When I got out of college, 10 years prior, one of the things that really opened my eyes was when someone took me to see Jerry Jeff Walker. That just opened my eyes to everything, to Robert Earl, a little bit to Lyle Lovett.

"Well, everyone gets disconnected out of college, and suddenly here I was with this music venue, and I just decided to start doing what I liked and what I was passionate about."

Suddenly, Chicago had a country music venue. A midsized venue that could fill to near 1,000 but could still look and feel intimate and special with only a hundred or so fans in attendance. Nashville agents began pushing up-and-comers on Warm, but he rarely took them up on the bands.

But one time circa 2003, an industry colleague Warm trusts got a very specific up-and-comer on his radar.

"All of a sudden, somebody said, 'Hey, you gotta put this guy on. He's about to put music on. He's good and he's the future,'" Warm said.

"It was Dierks Bentley.

"It was just before he hit, and when he hit, he hit *big*. Dierks was managed by Scott Kernahan, who was from down there, and connected to a lot of people, and he opened a lot of doors in the Red Dirt scene. He's Wade [Bowen]'s manager today. He's one of the smarter guys that I know. So I trusted him, and I met Dierks, and we loved him."

Bentley, in turn, recommended that Warm get Ragweed booked to play the Joe's stage.

"Dierks goes, 'You gotta get these guys out of Oklahoma called Cross Canadian Ragweed.'

"Ragweed came in, and not only did they just turn my head upside down with their music and their passion and the way they played and the camaraderie that they had, they legitimized *us* as a venue more than anyone. They were the band that every other band wanted to be. They could play, man.

"I have a debt to those guys. I will always have so much gratitude for them. And they were great people—great and cool and knew who they were. And from them opening the door, it was just like, wow, *we* can do all this right here."

Bentley and Ragweed toured twice together through Joe's on a pair of High Times and Hangovers Tours, selling out the venue both times. Soon after, Ragweed was big enough to sell out the place by themselves, and they went out of their way to bring any artist they could to open and push any artist they enjoyed on Warm and his bar.

"That opened the door down there for Randy [Rogers], Wade and Stoney LaRue, wherever he was living at the time," Warm said. "All those guys came through, and it was such a great scene.

"Those guys all brought somebody along with them. They all helped somebody along the way. And I think we missed a generation for about five years after them who wouldn't do that for each other. I really believe that.

"You could see this in Dierks and Ragweed too. Their tours together were epic. We had some amazing nights with them—including post parties. Legendary stuff. And they always either brought somebody up or told me who the next person was.

"It fed on itself, and we really created our own small scene with it in Chicago.

"Thankfully, I'm seeing the resurgence of headliners and artists who are bringing others up with them. Koe Wetzel and Parker McCollum are turning fans on to great new acts—and there's a lot of them. I'm energized by what I'm seeing and hearing."

Ragweed was not the only alt-mainstream act to carry a torch for Joe's. Warm brags to this day that Pat Green sold out 21 shows in a row at the bar—himself opening doors to other artists he thought deserved a shot in Chicago. Boland, Bowen and Rogers also made homes out of Joe's, as did Reckless Kelly, Roger Clyne and the Peacemakers, Robert Earl Keen and Charlie Robison.

The result was that a seemingly random location became an incredibly important venue.

If you were a Red Dirt or a Texas artist in the mid-2000s, could you really say you had made it if you weren't getting booked at Joe's? Probably not.

"Ragweed took us under their wing and brought us up here to Chicago 15 years ago," said Gary Braun, of Micky and the Motorcars. "The bands that were up and running when we came to town were very generous to us."

The fans' turning out made Joe's a win-win, but the bands credit the hospitality of Warm and his staff for elevating Joe's above most other Midwest tour stops. Even to this day, with multiple venues running, Warm makes it to most shows he hosts and sees that artists are personally welcomed and attended to.

He can recall only one time when he passed on a show, and it taught him a lesson.

"Cody Canada called me," Warm said. "I don't remember the year, and he said, 'I got a friend coming through town. Can you give him an acoustic gig or something?' And I just kind of sighed, 'Ah, Cody. It's a Sunday night. I'm happy to give him the gig, but I'm just afraid nobody's gonna be there, and I feel bad for the guy.'

"Cody said, 'It's OK, just put him in your front room, let him do acoustic. He'll be appreciative.' So that Sunday comes. I'm tired and I'm hungover. It's snowing and cold, and I just go, 'I can't stick around for this one'—and I stick around for every band to make sure they feel welcome. But I can't this time, so I tell my manager, 'Look out for this guy.'

"So I left an envelope for $150 for Ryan Bingham and I never got to see him play in my bar."

Shortly after that in 2010, Bingham won an Oscar for a song in the film *Crazy Heart*.

That's why Warm rarely misses a show at Joe's now.

• • •

The Kaitlin Butts Story

There is nobody in all of Red Dirt whose tale better illustrates all of the traits that spread Red Dirt: acceptance, sharing and love—and illustrates them more quickly—than Kaitlin Butts.

She grew up in the Tulsa suburb of Broken Arrow, learning to sing by age 5 and play guitar by age 15, and had an interest in theater buoyed by supportive parents. By 20, she was getting an associate's degree in vocal performance at the University of Central Oklahoma's Academy of Contemporary Music. And then, as a student in April 2020, she was hit with a twist of fate that is staggering even by Red Dirt's "everybody has their holy-shit moment" standards: An instructor at the school booked a few gigs for students and, by happenstance, booked her at the 2012 Bob Childers Gypsy Cafe event, at The Farm.

"I grew up listening to country radio and what was put in my face," Butts said. "I never knew that there was even a Stillwater scene at all. I thought that you were either nobody or you were at Miranda Lambert's status. It never crossed my mind that you could just make money and make a life out of playing shows and making music on a smaller level. Life was pretty closed off for me, until I was old enough to go into bars.

"So, I was announced on the lineup, and this guy—Rick Reiley—reached out to me on Facebook, and he ended up giving me a history lesson on all the other people who were going to be there at The Farm. He is, like, the sweetest man alive. There are some people who look at new artists like, 'Who's that?' but that community isn't anything like that.

"And then, I showed up, and I didn't know faces or names. I wasn't even 21 at this point. They did not know that. So I drove up to The Farm, and I only knew what Rick had told me about it. The night before Gypsy Cafe, all the musicians gather at The Farm and sit around in a circle, playing songs like they did when it was The Farm. And I was just hanging in the background.

"I was the one person there who no one really knew. And then, Randy Crouch leans over, right in center of the circle, and goes, 'Who are you? Where are you from?' And I felt like I was back in a school room, up in front of the class telling people who I am.

"And he goes, 'Why don't you play us a song?'

"I said, 'Really? I'm, uh, enjoying listening to y'all. So why don't I just do that?'

"He goes, 'This is what the circle is for. You're supposed to play us a song. So play us one of your songs.'

"So I played them a song I had just written called 'Wild Rose.' And just immediately, they embraced me right there and welcomed me into their circle."

Butts met not only Crouch but the Red Dirt Rangers, Gene Collier, Jacob Tovar and Mike McClure, who happened to be inviting artists to trek to his Boohatch Studio in Ada and record with him as the producer.

"I met so many people just in that one night, without even realizing what a huge turning point it was for me," she said. "I just felt like I was in on this secret. I wasn't supposed to be there, I wasn't worthy of it. I just happened upon it.

"Then, come to know, it's been there for years."

Within days of the Gypsy Cafe event, Butts had landed time at the Boohatch with

McClure. She also had 10 songs she had already written. Still in school, she would make the drive from Edmond to Ada after class, record from 7 p.m. until 3 a.m., and then make the drive back and repeat the process again and again until she had an album recorded.

Several months later, Butts had recorded *Same Hell, Different Devil*. She released the album in 2015 on her own. Not knowing how to release or promote an album, she sent copies to radio stations. A copy found its way to the offices of Fort Worth's 95.9-FM, The Ranch, one of the stalwarts of Texas music radio, and the album made it onto their airwaves.

"The first time I ever played a show in Texas, people already knew the words," Butts said. "In Oklahoma, there's not much of a local radio scene, and in Texas, there's an entire scene, and I knew nothing about it until I was submerged into it. So for this first show, my mom had come with me. We drove down to Denton, Texas, to the North Texas Fair and Rodeo. And my grandma had jumped in the car with us too. They're sitting in the audience, and I start playing 'Wild Rose,' and I'm wondering if there's an echo or something wrong with my voice. But it was people singing along to it.

"It was so cool, and I cried after the show."

She shared the bill with Courtney Patton and Erick Willis, two artists she had never met. Today, Butts and Patton play regularly together and along with Jamie Lin Wilson are mainstays at Red Dirt festivals around the country. But the goodwill from The Ranch playing her songs also led her to one more chance encounter, when Cleto Cordero was looking for a voice to sing on a track for an upcoming album his band—Flatland Cavalry—was recording. To say that song, "A Life Where We Work Out," sparked a relationship between the two is underselling it. Butts and Cordero are engaged now (where "now" is the publication of this book, of course).

"Cleto, who is now my fiancé, heard my music on 95.9 The Ranch and he wanted me to sing on his project," Butts said. "Now, we're getting married."

"If I hadn't met Mike McClure and produced that record with him, if I hadn't written these songs, and especially if I hadn't have gone to Gypsy Cafe, I wouldn't be where I am. My life, my career, my future husband, I wouldn't have any of it. All because of that one night.

"I feel like my entire career has been rooted in a scene that I didn't even know about until I was completely immersed in it."

* * * *

The Texas Red Dirt Quandary

"Texas Red Dirt" is not a thing.

The phrase that has been parroted for marketing slogans and radio jingles and festival titles does not exist. Pretending it does shortchanges everybody on both sides of the Red River, and reduces them to a cliché in the same way that mainstream country reduces meaningful, profound thoughts and situations to clichés.

To Texas music, it's wildly disrespectful because Texas music was flourishing long before Red Dirt. Once Willie Nelson put down roots in Austin, once Jerry Jeff Walker discovered the Broken Spoke and once Townes Van Zandt and Red Dirt's own Jimmy LaFave learned Austin was weird, Texas music's fate was sealed.

Pat Green and Cory Morrow proudly waved the Lone Star flag from their first gigs, and the notion that they needed help from anyone in Oklahoma is asinine. Charlie Robison was always going to stop any crowd, of any size, with "My Hometown," and the road was always going to go on forever for Robert Earl Keen, no matter the colleagues he made along the way (Lyle Lovett notwithstanding, but the College Station partnership only furthers the point that a substantial subset of Texas musicians do not need Red Dirt to boost their image).

To Red Dirt, it's wildly disrespectful because it implies the artists needed to ride Texas coattails when the major inroads Red Dirt made into Texas were of the scene's own making—a product of young, ambitious artists with enough savvy to either defer to Texas pride or learn the right ways to avoid conflict with it.

When Ragweed hit it big, not long after Canada moved from Oklahoma to Texas, he had a pair of go-to phrases on stage: The first was "It's just a river," referring to the Red River separating the two states. If that did not quell hisses directed at the northern neighbors, he would fall back on "We're not from Texas, but we got here as fast as we could." And that one always worked.

Even today, the notion that Casey Donahew is Red Dirt or that Turnpike Troubadours are Texas is absurd, but the barriers are long since down, and either band can sell out Cain's in Tulsa or Billy Bob's in Fort Worth without breaking a sweat.

Here is what actually happened, and it is decidedly not "Red Dirt and Texas became the same thing."

First, Ragweed and Reckless Kelly mutually rose in esteem at the same time, and they both openly pushed and rooted for the other, with Reckless making Ragweed look cool in far-flung Texas bars and Ragweed making Stillwater treat Reckless like family when they'd play the Wormy Dog.

Second, Ragweed moved to Texas at the first height of their appeal—in the wake of the *Purple Album* and fresh off their Universal South record deal. There was rarely a venue large enough to hold them, and those that could often ran out of beer, parking spaces or both (see: Billy Bob's, and Lone Star Park in Grand Prairie). They were too big to shun, and they were mentors to a substantial generation of artists only a year or two behind them, from both states: Boland, LaRue, Bowen and Rogers for a few name-drops.

Along with that, Ragweed and Reckless cornered the market on cool.

Other bands could match or even exceed their popularity, but the coolest cats in the Lone Star State for the first decade of the 2000s were transplants from Idaho and Oklahoma. Being cool meant they called their own shots, and the shot they called most often became, "Red Dirt? Texas? Americana? We're just gonna call it *music* now, and y'all are gonna be OK with it."

Third, both bands brought a ton of like-minded, compassionate people in tow. Reckless opened the door for Micky and the Motorcars, and the Brauns comprised the musical family every artist envied.

Ragweed brought Shannon Canada, who at various points managed Boland, the Motorcars, Bowen, Rogers, Robison, McClure and Shinyribs. Shannon brought along her close friend Robin Devin, who worked in Amarillo for the American Quarter Horse Association until Shannon convinced her to move to New Braunfels and help her manage musicians. Today, Devin is Rogers' manager and partner in the duo's Big Blind Management, which has helped Parker McCullom launch his career, and Devin is married to Joel Schoepf, famously a former engineer for Ragweed and tour manager for The Departed. Bowen and the Canadas are in-laws courtesy of his marriage to Shannon's younger sister, Shelby. Today, Red Dirt and Texas music are too intertwined to be pulled back apart.

That is a wholly different concept than the mixing of scenes. Red Dirt artists and Texas artists stand separate in their music. The platform is distinctly Texas, but the idea of a music family, which seems so obvious today, is distinctly Red Dirt. The assistance LaFave offered Childers 30 years ago is the assistance artists in both states offer instinctively today—alive, well and borderline awe-inspiring in the life of Kaitlin Butts.

The "Texas" artists featured in this book—Randy Rogers, Wade Bowen, the Brauns, Jamie Lin Wilson and their wide circles of friends and fellow musicians—stayed as true to their roots as any Red Dirt artist. They are invaluable because they were as happy to carry the torch for Red Dirt as Ragweed, Boland and LaRue were to carry it for Texas.

They are the reason the Dirt spread.

"Nobody's gonna hand it to you, no matter how much help you have," Gary Braun said. "At the end of the day, it's kind of up to you to keep the faith and keep after it. But anytime you can get somebody to give you a hand, just try to remember that down the road."

That is why two separate scenes are viewed as one now. It's two genres that accept each other. It was jump-started with some savvy foresight by Chris McCoy in 1999. It was exemplified thousands of miles away by artists from both states in the rise to prominence of Joe's on Weed in Chicago, and it is explained via a series of life decisions made by a handful of artists who, 15 years later, continue to exert their influence over the music they and their peers make.

That is the legacy of Red Dirt.

There are not many artists left in Stillwater today, but its legacy has long since exceeded the sum of its parts. Red Dirt did the unthinkable: It won over Texas.

"What everybody does now, that's just how we lived," said John Cooper, of the Red Dirt Rangers. "We would talk about—you want to play this club. Don't talk to that promoter, he's a shithead. It's *that* stuff. It's the insights, the family stuff. We were never jealous. I mean that. I tell people that, and they don't believe it. We were never jealous of anybody's success. When one boat goes up, they all go up. That's how I look at it.

"Red Dirt was a scene that came out of love. And they couldn't fight the love, man."

— — —

- 17 -

You're Gonna Be My Friend: Jamie Lin Wilson

JAMIE LIN WILSON is particularly important to Red Dirt, because she is a thread that ties together the narrative (thus far)—of either Oklahoma artists infiltrating Texas or Texas artists accepting Oklahomans.

Wilson picked up a guitar for the first time as a sophomore at Texas A&M in the early 2000s and within two years had joined The Gougers. Seven years in that band and a solo EP later, Wilson joined The Trishas in 2009.

The Trishas—Wilson, Liz Foster, Kelley Mickwee and Savannah Welch—put out a mini album (2010's *They Call Us The Trishas*) and a full-length project (2013's *High, Wide & Handsome*) before the artists settled for solo careers. The Trishas blazed trails throughout Texas and Oklahoma. Wilson went back as a solo artist and made herself at home in hallowed Red Dirt grounds like The Blue Door. She had a way with words that trickled into cowrites with mainstays of the scene such as Evan Felker, and her harmonic vocals landed on tracks with Wade Bowen, Cody Canada and a list that becomes exhaustive quickly.

In 2015, Wilson released her debut full-length album, *Holidays & Wedding Rings*, followed by 2018's *Jumping Over Rocks*, which boasts a cowrite with Felker, "Oklahoma Stars," that the Turnpike Troubadours recorded on their 2017 album *A Long Way From Your Heart*. Wilson drew inspiration from her home life on her little ranch home in D'Hanis, Texas, which she shares with her college sweetheart turned husband, Roy, and their four children, Joanie, Maggie, Thomas Roy and Griffin.

Anyway, that was supposed to be part of the Jamie Lin Wilson profile here. It was to be weaved in and out of a series of anecdotes, adjectives and transitions. There may have even been mini-headlines to break it all up.

Then, Wilson picked up the phone for the interview that was meant to unlock it all, and things went south.

Wilson spoke with such conviction, charisma and authority—over her music, friends, family and history—that writing wasn't about to do her story justice. Much better to shut up, let Wilson talk and write it all down.

What follows is, edited only for clarity and with questions noted when necessary, Wilson's version of her story.

What are your musical roots and earliest influences?

Wilson: I didn't get a guitar until college. I was 19, and I got one for Christmas. I kind of fell into the scene that was at A&M shortly thereafter—a little songwriter scene that centered around these open mic nights. I fell in love with some friends who taught me how to write songs and the fact that writing songs was even a thing.

Right after that, I joined The Sidehill Gougers. We mainly played College Station that first year or so, and then we started venturing out, and eventually that became The Gougers.

And right before that, where were you musically, and how does it translate with the other artists you interact with to this day?

I was studying mechanical engineering at Texas A&M, man. I didn't know how to play the piano. I never sang. I was in the band in junior high for a couple of years, but music wasn't something I did.

I knew that I could sing, and I knew that I loved it. When I was little, I would think to myself, *If I could do anything in the whole world, I would be a singer*. But singers wear ballgowns and go on TV, you know? That was Reba McEntire and Lorrie Morgan. That wasn't something that was really feasible to a small-town kid from Southeast Texas.

Actually, the reason I got a guitar was because I went and saw the Dixie Chicks at a show. I saw Natalie Maines sing "Cold Day in July" by herself, with just a guitar. No band. No nothing. And I was like, "Hey! I could do that. I could sing a song holding a guitar. Cool!" So I got one.

I learned how to play onstage.

Then, The Gougers started touring, we made some records, and in 2006 we made what ended up being our last record, but it was probably the quintessential record. It was the one, and we started being able to tour farther around Texas and Oklahoma, and that's when we got into this scene.

But, we were kind of on the fringe of this scene. Every once in a while, we'd get on a Reckless Kelly show, or Randy Rogers was our friend so he'd put us on his show. But we didn't quite fit in, because we were a bit more...I don't know what we were, but college kids didn't really like us. So we weren't the party scene band, which seemed to be what a lot of the Texas-Oklahoma scene was based on. I hadn't gotten to really know or listen yet.

And then, The Gougers split up. I guess that was 2008 or 2009. That's when The Trishas started.

I started getting to know more folks in the scene while playing with The Trishas and kind of just went, "Oh, these people are really nice." I didn't get to know them before, but now that I was able to make my own discernments and decisions, I realized how awesome they were, and I wanted to make friends.

In Steamboat at the MusicFest one year, I had a solo show. I saw Wade [Bowen], but I didn't know Wade. Then I saw him at an after-party and he goes, "How was your show? We played at the same time." I told him I thought it went pretty well, and he said, "Of course it did. Everything you do is good."

I just remember how surprised I was, for no good reason really. It was just a moment of realization that all these folks are really nice and maybe I should make more of an effort. So I messaged Wade on Twitter a couple of months later and said, "Hey, I know that we're not really friends, but will you write a song with me? You're gonna be my friend, cool?"

Shortly thereafter, we wrote "Just Some Things" together.

Right about then, you were making some friends in Oklahoma...

During The Gougers time, we were touring up to Oklahoma and we were hanging out with the Mike McClure Band and Travis Linville. We used to stay at Travis's studio, the Dirty Bird studio.

I helped Travis's dad install the flooring at that studio. We were up there one weekend just staying at Travis's house, and he was like, "We're gonna work on the studio today." His dad came over, and we put laminate flooring in.

Then another time, in between bands, I took the train up to Oklahoma City and Tom Skinner picked me up, and we went and played The Blue Door, and The Grape Ranch in Okemah.

I think that's when I realized the difference between Oklahoma and Texas songwriters. Even though Bob Childers songs are different from Tom Skinner songs and those are different from Mike McClure songs and those are different from Jason Boland and Cody Canada and Stoney LaRue and Evan Felker songs...and then you go to Parker Millsap and John Moreland and Bryon White...they're all different, but there's something spiritual about Oklahoma music.

If you're from Oklahoma, you know Oklahoma has a dark history. From the way the Native Americans were treated to the Dust Bowl to the Great Depression...there is an understanding of something that is dark within all of them. And sometimes, when they have the talent to show it, it comes out in a really haunting way.

They've got Woody Guthrie to look to. The way they string words together up in Oklahoma is just so good. And they'll tell you: There's nothing else to do but drugs or write a song. And occasionally you do both.

Texas songwriters have a history of being proud storytellers. Texas has a rich history, but our history isn't as dark and lonely as Oklahoma's. Texas music can be sad and lonely, but it just doesn't have the darkness that Oklahoma music has. Oklahoma folks have that within them, and sometimes they have the ability to pull it out and make something beautiful out of it.

And what did The Trishas add to your career?

When The Trishas happened, that was a conglomeration of all of our styles. One of us is bluesy, one's more rock, one's more folk, and one's more country. There was so much there with the four of us that our sound became a completely different monster.

Within the band, I was pretty much the rhythm. Before and after we had a drummer, I played kick drum and acoustic guitar. I learned a lot from that. Harmony was a big factor, and we learned how to do that. The whole thing was a learning process.

I learned how to travel on the road with women. I had never done that before. I had always been in a boys' club, but so had all the other girls. So we went in there kind of acting like we were traveling with dudes.

But then we realized that women have more compassion. If you're with boys, you'll say, "I'm hungry. I want to eat there," and they go, "No. I'm going to Arby's," and that was the end of it. Women will say, "I want to eat there, is that OK with you?"

Another thing those girls did for me was help me raise my first two babies. When we started, I told them I was ready to start a family and they never batted an eye. It was seamless. Girls, shows, guitars, writing, babies, road nannies, diaper stops, nursing and pumping, all of it. If I didn't have them at the beginning of this, I don't know that I would have had the confidence to travel with kids. And look at me now! Acting like a pro.

That spanned four or five years, and it was like what I had been doing before, but with girls...and babies. That's when I got a lot more into the scene. We didn't infiltrate everything as we were still Americana-leaning, just not as far. Even to this day, I'm in the scene regionally, but college kids still don't like me.

So then after we wrapped up The Trishas, I just sort of kept going.

Everyone started doing their own thing, and I just never stopped doing what I was doing. It made my first solo album really weird, because the press was all, "Jamie Lin Wilson's first record," and I'm going, "I've made seven of those!"

And now you're a part of a pretty strong network of independent musicians who support one another.

I think it's just because this scene really rallies around everybody, and that's the thing that stands out here: We're not in competition with one another. We are all a family that realizes that if one of us does well, we all do well. It helps the scene, and there's no reason to try to sabotage.

I started as just a little girl on stage. I didn't know anybody, and these artists all reached out to me at one point or another and welcomed me into their circle. They gave me confidence in being worthy of their scene.

And from there, it was quickly "Hey, you know we're here if you ever need anything, right?"

One time, I got a flat in New Braunfels. The first people I texted were Cody and Shannon Canada. I said, "Uh, I'm on the highway in New Braunfels and I got a flat." And I was pregnant!

And Cody goes, "I'm on my way."

Somehow our relationship has gone from being acquaintances to being friends to being family. My husband has an aunt in New Braunfels, but I automatically thought of Cody and Shannon first. I just knew they'd help me. The family we've morphed into is bonded by a common drive. We all enjoy doing the same things, and we love doing them together.

Tell me a bit about your album *Jumping Over Rocks*.

I went into the studio with the need to record *live*.

I think whenever you do that, whenever you hear those old records that used to be made when everyone was in the same studio, you can feel it breathe. You can feel the musicians playing off each other, and I think that adds a whole different feel to the song. I wanted to do that. That was the main objective, and we pulled it off. We let everyone play what they wanted to play and it ended up perfect.

There's a song, "Oklahoma Stars," that you cowrote with Evan Felker on there.

Yes! I love that song. That song was actually born at Medicine Stone, the festival that Turnpike and Boland were throwing up in Tahlequah. Some friends and I were walking around in the middle of the night—Cody was there, you were there!—and there are all these little campsites going. Everyone is walking around making friends, playing songs—it's very cool. At some point, I stopped and looked up and noticed there was a meteor shower. We lay down in the grass and looked up and just watched. The next day on the way home, I started to put the pieces together. The folks at the festival last night were like these shooting stars. They burn so bright—making connections and having a blast—then they disappear and go home. A little dramatic, I know. But we turned it into a provocative little lost love song. I sent what I thought was a finished song to Evan and he wrote back and told me he'd have another verse for me within the hour. And when one of the best songwriters of our generation says he'll tie your song up in a nice little bow, you don't tell him you thought it was finished!

I love that it made it on both albums—"Oklahoma Stars" is on Turnpike's *Long Way From Your Heart* as well. That is really cool to me because their version is the opposite of mine, in all ways. The feel is different, and I love both versions and I love that my band did it one way and his did it the other.

I want to ask about the song "Death and Life" on this album.

That's my favorite. I'd sit and work on that song and then go, "Nope, that's not it," and I'd have to put it away. That's a song I couldn't force out because I knew it had to be really, really good because the subject matter is personal to me. You can't write about something that's true and let it be just OK. You've gotta get it how it's supposed to be.

The first verse is about a widow. It's actually my husband Roy's aunt. She lives across the street. I had a talk with her one day. My kids had gone to the graveyard one day and they wanted to look at everyone's tombstones, because you know, that's normal. We do that, I guess! They wanted to walk around and find everybody, and they went to find Uncle Joe's plot, but he didn't have a stone yet.

So I told her that. I said, "I noticed there's not a stone yet."

And she goes, "Well, I wanted to get it perfect, and I'm looking for this and this and this..." and she's telling me all this and I suddenly say, "And also, it's kind of not permanent until you see it in stone."

And she goes, "Yeah...that. I just can't do it yet."

I had that conversation in my head for a long time. I thought that maybe that was a song all to itself. And then I also wanted to write a song about the situation with my husband Roy and the situation with his dad. He had six months to live, and he asked Roy if he'd build him a coffin. Of course Roy said yes, and then he didn't do it, because how can you build a coffin for your dad?

When he died—which didn't end up being from cancer, it ended up being from a fall, which is almost a blessing and was almost six months to the day—we went home, and Roy went to the lumber store. All the women went to the house and did the casserole and enchilada thing, and all the men went to the garage and watched Roy build his dad's coffin.

Yeah... it was pretty heavy stuff.

But it wasn't until later that I really analyzed it and realized that his dad knew that that's how Roy deals with stress: by working. That was kind of like his dad's last gift to him. It helped him grieve. My father-in-law was a good man.

Then three years later, we had a son—an accidental boy named Thomas Roy. He was born on Roy's dad's birthday, and all that stuff is too coincidental to be a coincidence.

And one more thing: What about the question that everyone always asks you about being an artist with kids and how it changes...You can finish the question for me, right?

One thing that changes drastically is the gigs that you take. A few years ago I finally said, "You know what? I don't want to play that gig" if I didn't want to play a gig, because time became more precious.

It made me go, "I'm not going to take for granted all these people who are helping me."

It makes you go into business mode and less into playing-200-dates-a-year mode.

It makes me say, "The shows I play are gonna have to have two out of three things: fun, exposure or money." So if it's a lot of fun and a lot of exposure, cool. If it's a lot of fun and exposure but not a lot of money, cool.

Having kids made me set a standard in my decision-making about shows.

It also taught me the power of saying no. If you don't take every show, your value goes up. If I don't play every single gig in Dallas, the really good spots will book me.

It makes you take it seriously, and as a result, other people take you seriously.

- 18 -

A Hard Question: Where Are the Women of Red Dirt?

RED DIRT HAS a gender gap.

There is no talking around it. Without getting into a single feeling or reaction, regardless of whether you think this is a travesty, a reflection of a sexist culture greater than music, a true measure of relative talent or a scene that's exactly the way you like it, let's say that part really loud. Men dominate Red Dirt.

Texas Country Music Chart compiled a list of the top 200 songs in the genre in 2019 based on reported radio airplay. Cody Johnson's "On My Way to You" was No. 1, with 39,555 total spins in the year.

The highest-charting female was Sarah Hobbs, whose "Like I Love You" came in at No. 13, with 18,077 spins.

The next women on the list were No. 20 (Kylie Frey), No. 26 (Bri Bagwell) and No. 47 (Natalie Rose).

By that metric, four of the top 50 songs in Texas in 2019 were by women.

You can pick any other metric you wish. Pick festival headliners. Pick concert gross. Pick dance hall bookings. The gap will be the same.

Personally, I am not wild about being someone questioning whether a music scene overlooks women. Enough has been mansplained since 2018 to fill the collective lifetimes of anyone who will read this. But "it's hard and I feel awkward" are awfully piss poor reasons not to get into it. So I asked around.

The answers are, naturally, complicated. A theme that emerged is straightforward: Guys generally get into music in some fashion to impress girls, especially in Red Dirt. Women generally have myriad reasons for doing it, and rarely, if ever, is the answer "to get guys to notice me." But that's oversimplifying.

I asked the same open-ended questions—what are challenges you see or have experienced in this industry that might be unique to female artists?—to some female artists profiled in this book. Jamie Lin Wilson and Kaitlin Butts, two of the hottest acts in Oklahoma and Texas music (and who, alongside Bri Bagwell, Courtney Patton and Sunny Sweeney, rank among the most popular female independent artists in those two two states), were two. Shawna Russell, who has spent more than 20 years performing live in clubs large and small across the country and whose career dabbled in Nashville but remained independent, was another. And Camille Harp, a longtime mainstay of the Norman-Oklahoma City independent music scene since 2000, was another. The answers they gave shed light on both the challenges and the reasons. With minimal interruption from me and lightly edited for clarity, here are their thoughts.

●   ●   ●

Jamie Lin Wilson: There's obviously something. There are fewer women doing what we do here, and even fewer that are deemed "successful." I think there are several reasons for it, and they run the gamut.

One is that I believe our level of "success" down here is so wide. Sell out 100-seat venue at $30? Success. Sell out a 500-seat venue at $10? Also, success. Not to mention the 1,000-plus capacity venues that we have down here. Those are filled by the beer drinkers, and that's not really an audience that I've cultivated over the years. But to believe that if you can't fill those large venues then you're not successful or worthy of prime festival spots is a joke.

Two, there are a lot of women who start off here and leave for Nashville. If they stayed, we'd probably have more heavy hitters! I don't blame them one bit for moving—I may have done the same thing if life had gone a different way. But, most of the leading Top 40 women are from Texas and Oklahoma!

Three, music is subjective and you can't force somebody to like something that they don't like. But I hear all time "I don't like girl singers, but I like you." It's something that every woman singer hears at some point. I always just say, "well, if you like me then that's not true. You just haven't found the ones you do like," then I give them some names. But the truth is, it's a given that you won't like something that you're not exposed to. And that's where festivals come in.

I definitely would love to see more women fill the bills of festivals. Women are assets to your festival! We're fun, we love to collaborate, and we work our asses off and deserve it. But complaining and whining won't change it. We can try harder, make friends, be nice, don't quit, hope that people dig what you're doing, and eventually they'll take notice.

What did Steve Martin say? "Be so good they can't ignore you."

Yeah, that too.

●   ●   ●

Kaitlin Butts: I feel like, as a girl, we always kind of assume our positions already. We kind of step back and let people step in front of us. I feel like that's just women's nature, but in music it's just more apparent because we're in the spotlight.

I think it's really important to also know that I got started because I saw other women, like Miranda Lambert and the Dixie Chicks and Taylor Swift, being such superstars and doing such a great job that it made me want to do it.

That makes me want to encourage other women to do it too and show that it's possible.

At the same time, it's really cool that I get to call Jamie Lin and Courtney and these other women my friends. I have a blast doing it, and it would be hard to not have fun playing with those girls on stage.

● ● ●

Shawna Russell: Well, you know, you kind of have to go into it sometimes knowing that's just part of the deal.

But when I was growing up, it seemed at the time like there were as many female artists on the radio as there were male. It seemed like gradually, over time, that kind of dwindled some.

And then I didn't really see this until I was trying to pitch my music. And then you kind of look at the lineup of songs that are charting and you go, "My gosh, there are only, like, five females out of the top 50." And you look at these festival lineups, and there might be one female out of 20, and you just go, "I don't understand."

But I think in certain genres—the Red Dirt, the Texas genre—I've been trying to wrap my head around *why?* Why is that? And you kind of don't know. It kind of is what it is.

Luckily, over time, women have broken barriers and it's getting easier. But there are just certain genres where a sense of raw production, instrumentation and vocals, lends itself more to a male-dominated sound.

But it definitely makes it more difficult when you know going in that there are only this many slots that females hold, on charts or festival lineups or for bookings. So you just kind of have to be authentic at the end of the day. You don't want to change yourself to fit into that.

You just hope that what you're doing will stand out in its own way. Of course you want to be in that club, you want to be liked. But at the end of the day, you have to be true to yourself, too.

Hopefully, that's what sets apart the people that *are* breaking through.

● ● ●

Camille Harp: I can only speak for myself. I always just tried to be one of the guys, you know.

Maybe that was me being naive. Maybe that was detrimental to me instead of trying to be the strong female. But I just realized recently that I wanted to be my dad when I grew up. I didn't necessarily see that I was this female that was set apart from my counterpart.

I have been told before that I've shared the stage with a bunch of men, and this guy said, "If you were a guy, you'd be more successful than anyone up there." And that was a huge compliment.

Honestly, I think lately I've made the realization that I am. I am a homemaker. I've always wanted a home. And I had a hard time giving up that home life, even when I was single, to live in a van on the road.

— — —

- 19 -

Oklahoma's Roots Landscape

THE IRONY OF "Used to Be" is that the song held up as the classic Red Dirt anthem has nothing to do with Stillwater.

Bob Wiles and Tom Skinner wrote it. The Red Dirt Rangers cut it first. Later, The Great Divide—joined by Jimmy LaFave—cut it for Atlantic Records. In the era of the Wormy Dog and the Yellow House, it's likely no song was performed more in Red Dirt venues. The song has a simple principle: Wiles and Skinner simply riffed on the landmarks along the classic Route 66, the Mother Road that cuts across Oklahoma. The highway dates back to the 1920s, and in its heyday, it was the major route linking Chicago and Los Angeles.

To Oklahomans, Route 66 and the Dust Bowl are intertwined. Route 66 was the highway taken by the Okies leaving the ruined prairie to take another crack at life in California. It was the highway that made Woody Guthrie famous and that Woody Guthrie made famous. Guthrie was born in Okemah, Oklahoma, in 1912 and moved to the Texas Panhandle when he was 14. Five years later, he was married. He spent most of the 1930s as a husband and father, but in 1937, he left his family behind and joined the Okies on the Mother Road to California. That experience led to Guthrie's *Dust Bowl Ballads*, his first album and one that would go on to influence the music of Pete Seeger, Bruce Springsteen, Bob Dylan and generations of artists who followed.

Route 66 had long since faded by the time Wiles and Skinner wrote their song about it in the early 1990s. The interstate highway system rendered it pointless as a commerce route, but it still cut through the center of some historic towns in the state—not just the big cities of Tulsa and Oklahoma City but classic towns from Miami to Sayre. One of those towns, Bristow, was home to a saloon and dance hall called the Log Cabin Club. It was an old "gun-and-knife" establishment outside of town that was so sketchy, it was eventually burned down by the town's law enforcement. Skinner and Wiles imagined its patrons dancing all night on its sawdust floors after working all day at the local cotton gin. They turned it all into "Used to Be." After they cut the song, Mike McClure and Jim "Red" Wilhelm went on a scavenger hunt and retrieved the sign that marked the entrance to the Log Cabin. They brought the sign back to The Farm, and it spent a decade on land owned by the Red Dirt Rangers in Lone Chimney and has now been restored and sits at the Salty Bronc, a Stillwater bar now owned by The Divide's Scotte Lester and Kelley Green.

Bristow is well south and east of Stillwater in Creek County. If you can drive between the two in under an hour, it means you sped the entire way.

Since Red Dirt can take its anthem from elsewhere, there is clearly more to Oklahoma's roots music than Stillwater.

The dance halls are mostly gone, although surprisingly recently. The Great Divide used to regularly headline Tulsa City Limits, and Cross Canadian Ragweed played to sold-out crowds off Interstates 40 and 35 at Weatherford's J.C. Cowboy's and Davis's Arbuckle Ballroom before both shut down. But the local scenes and small venues that boosted Red Dirt long before it broke out of Payne County have powered ahead.

* * *

Oklahoma City

At last, the hill I will die on: Oklahoma City is more important to Red Dirt music than Tulsa is. No place meant more to its growth and migration away from Stillwater than Oklahoma City, and no place, Stillwater included, is better now to connect to its history.

If Red Dirt's forefathers, especially Bob Childers and Jimmy LaFave, did not view themselves as next-generation Woody Guthrie, they certainly carried themselves as Guthrie did. They wrote and sang about the land and people who tied their lives to the land in a near-spiritual manner. Their music was meant to lift up an audience less fortunate.

In need of a forum—an open-minded venue with the activist vibe of Austin but closer to home—they got it when Greg Johnson showed up in Oklahoma City in 1993. A native Oklahoman, Johnson had spent a decade living in Austin as a music journalist. He also entrenched himself in Austin's scene by organizing and promoting a regular series of Woody Guthrie tribute concerts. When he returned to Oklahoma, jaded to the music business, a chance conversation with a family friend led to a suggestion that Johnson try putting on some shows at a "funky place" on McKinley Avenue in the shadows of Oklahoma City University. Michael Fracasso played the first show, followed quickly by Childers, Ray Wylie Hubbard and the Red Dirt Rangers. The building—a wooden hall with no chairs, no bar and liquor license (to this day, The Blue Door is BYOB)—had something special going for it: The acoustics inside were as pure as live music allows. With minimal setup and a bare-bones sound system, artists could capture the intimate, around-the-campfire setting that only Austin's Cactus Cafe or Nashville's Bluebird Cafe matched. Johnson moved into the building soon after starting the concerts and named it after its oversized blue front door.

More than any other place, including Tulsa's revered Cain's Ballroom, The Blue Door grew into *the* standard for Red Dirt artists. During the crucial (for the scene) decade of 1993–2003, Red Dirt had two tiers of artists: those who had been invited to play The Blue Door and those who had not. Childers was its patron saint, performing with the same White Buffalo Road Show that Garth Brooks recalled in Stillwater a decade earlier. His crowning moment was his 2003 album with Terry "Buffalo" Ware, *Two Buffaloes Walking—Live at The Blue Door*, and his official memorial was held at the venue after his death in 2006. After Childers, The Blue Door had a list of regulars that any city would be proud to claim: the Rangers, Tom Skinner, Travis Linville and Terri Hendrix. Even Jack Ingram brought his Acoustic Motel Tour to Johnson's wooden listening room multiple times. The Great Divide released *Dirt and Spirit*, its 1999 gospel album featuring a series of scene legends, with a full-on revival on The Blue Door's tiny wooden stage.

"The Red Dirt movement was from Stillwater to Oklahoma City and had little to do with Tulsa other than Brandon Jenkins and Susan Herndon," Johnson wrote in an email. (Side note: I never spoke to Johnson for an interview for this book, although we both tried to get in touch. I am the first to admit that The Blue Door meant more to Oklahoma music than the sub-chapter it is getting, but honestly, that is what second editions, podcasts and follow-up stories can be for.) "If not for The Blue Door's 25-year history and my 30 years of doing Woody Guthrie tributes, this scene would be so different."

Oklahoma City has (and had) other landmarks that matter, too. The tiny, funky VZD's Restaurant and Bar was first a proving ground for the Rangers, Ragweed, Travis Linville and just about every other late-'90s band. Wakeland, another band with a passing mention in this chapter but a major significance on Stillwater music in the early 1990s, reunited 20 years later and made VZD's its de facto home.

The Will Rogers Theater was the home of the Red Dirt Rangers' annual post-Thanksgiving festival around the turn of the century, and it was where The Great Divide retreated to record *Afterglow*, its first album after losing their Atlantic Records deal.

Classics on Western Avenue, north of downtown, was the city's Red Dirt dive bar. It didn't even have a stage, just space in one corner of the concrete floor where artists like Ragweed, Linville and Stoney LaRue would play when their crowds hovered around 150. And you already know that the Wormy Dog Saloon had a second incarnation in Oklahoma City's Bricktown district from 2004 until its closing in 2017.

Ragweed's signature festival, the Family Jam, ran for six years at the Oklahoma City Zoo Amphitheater, peppering acts like the Toadies, Buckcherry and Lee Ann Womack in and around Ragweed's Oklahoma and Texas contemporaries.

An influx of youth, money, gentrification and a growing arts scene post-2010 led to the refurbishing and reopening of the Tower Theater, which dates to 1937. American Aquarium, Cody Canada & The Departed, Roger Clyne and the Peacemakers and Reckless Kelly have performed there to sold-out audiences.

And back on McKinley Avenue, The Blue Door has held steady, to the betterment of all of Red Dirt.

• • •

Norman

The home of the University of Oklahoma is difficult to pin down musically. Only one bar—the Red Dirt Cafe, during its 2000–2005 lifespan—has ever hitched itself to the scene. But The Deli, an eclectic, Austin-style funk bar that was around before and after the Red Dirt Cafe, has been enough of an outlet to keep the scene alive. And a handful of artists who either claim the scene or influenced the scene call the town home today and continue to churn out music. Let's start with Travis Linville.

From the time he was born, Linville was surrounded by music. His grandparents on his dad's side had a family band in Chickasha, about 30 miles west of Norman, which his father and uncles joined. They had a music room in their house and a weekly live performance on local radio.

"I grew up with my dad's guitar in my closet, and there was always a curiosity about it," Linville said. "I sensed that it was a part of my heritage in some way, and it got me in the door early. I was into music from an early age. We were rural, and it was fishing, flat-bottomed boats and music."

He picked up jazz guitar and had a job playing with a bar band by age 17. Every weekend night, Linville had a gig, whether it was in a garage, a dive bar or a dance hall. By 2000, he was living in Norman. Chance encounter after chance encounter brought him into Red Dirt circles, and he fell in. Linville had the musical acumen of LaFave and the soft vocals of Childers. He was a natural fit.

"I was coming from a place where I was playing 1990s country cover music in honky-tonks, and I was only slightly aware of Red Dirt," he said. "When I started writing my own songs, I just became aware of it. I learned about Jason Boland because he'd pass through Norman and play. Back then, it was just nice to have somebody passing through town who you meet, who is a nice person and maybe has some level of commonality with you—it's not glamorous, but it's how you get started.

"One of the first times Boland came to play at the Red Dirt Cafe, they put me on the show to open, and then the band all stayed at my house afterward. Just found a place to sleep on the floor. Stoney LaRue was at that show, too, and it wasn't too long after that the calls from Boland would come in: 'Hey, Stoney's out of town on Wednesday. Do you want to come up to Stillwater and play Eskimo Joe's with me?' 'Of course I do.'"

The next time Boland was in town, he was playing acoustically with Canada, and Boland invited Linville on stage to sing. By the summer of 2001, Linville was touring with Ragweed, opening in places like the Aardvark in Fort Worth and Saengerhalle in New Braunfels. He played guitar with Stoney semi-regularly, and he also formed his own band. Travis Linville and the Burtschi Brothers toured hard around Norman and Stillwater, but what eventually became Linville's calling in Red Dirt was his sheer grasp of music.

He taught guitar to 9-year-old Parker Millsap. He opened a studio at his house outside Norman—the Dirty Bird (named for nearby Lake Thunderbird)—that began as a joint effort with Mike McClure and eventually just became his. From there, he produced John Fullbright's debut album. Hayes Carll was impressed enough by Linville to invite him to join his band when Carll was truly an up-and-comer, and Linville has run with Carll since.

"Diversity has always been the key to me, to have a lot of things going on," Linville said. "There are a lot of ways to make money in the music business and survive, as long as you have flexibility. And if you do a little bit of recording and a little bit of teaching, write your own songs and play a little music for another person, all those things make a career.

"For me, Hayes Carll was my step out of it all. I had planned to move to Austin in 1999, and I didn't. Some people decided to bail, and I didn't know anybody, so I stayed in Norman. I already had a band there and a record, so I stayed there. I can't say this enough: Everything good that happened to me happened because I was active in Norman. One night, Hayes played The Blue Door, and then he came over to a show I was playing. It was another couple of years before we started playing music together, but later on—and I have played with him now for more than a decade—I look back on it, and there's no gig that I would want more now than Hayes Carll in Austin, and if I hadn't have hung around Norman and met him that night, I'm not doing it now."

Now, Linville lives in Tulsa with a mobile recording studio and easy outlets for his own music. He plays with Carll and tours solo coast to coast.

"In 2017, I released a record that squarely put me back in doing my own thing," he said, referring to his *Up Ahead* record. "I really feel like I'm back to being the artist, Travis Linville, first. The record did pretty well nationally, and I'm kind of back in control of my own destiny as a singer-songwriter and bandleader."

Linville's tale illustrates the range and flexibility of Red Dirt, and the power of happenstance meetings with like-minded artists. The story of Camille Harp illustrates the effect it has.

Born into a musical family in Blanchard, Harp moved to Norman in 2000 just as the Red Dirt Cafe opened, and she nearly immediately took up a regular gig at the long, narrow Campus Corner bar.

"I almost immediately met the guys who would become Mama Sweet," she said. "They were a new little fresh baby band when I moved here, and I started opening for them. I just met them at an after-party singing my guts out at 2 a.m. somewhere, and things worked out.

"I made some big connections, especially with Stoney and Jason Boland. Then the Red Dirt Rangers had me open for them and it took off."

Harp was in her 20s but not in college, and initially she didn't realize she even had fans.

"In the college era, I don't feel like they connected with me," she said. "I wasn't even in college at the time.

"I didn't have enough confidence to realize that there were people following me. I thought the people who came to my shows were more friends than fans. It took me years and years, into my 30s, to realize people came to my shows because they liked my music and not because they liked me."

She toured regionally for roughly a decade, but the idea of a home life and family appealed to Harp much more than the road. Her married name is Camille Harp-Young. Her spouse is a fellow Norman musician, Tom Young, and the two have a pair of kids, Phoenix and Scout. She still performs, but almost always locally in or near Norman, and always on her terms.

"Really, I am two people—pre-kids Camille and post-kids Camille," she said. "I don't necessarily know what happened, but there was a *huge* change in me after I had kids. There's just a little bit of peace now. Why stress yourself out over this career that may or may not pan out?

"As far as playing for people now, I just want to make music, and I just want to have fun. I go once a month to play for the folks at the VA. That's not something I gather any fame or monetary gain from. It's just what I do.

"At first, I had pressure I put on myself to *be* someone. But now, I just play to have a good time. That's my purpose now. If I can bring anyone joy through my music, that's where I am now."

Another Norman mainstay, the self-deprecating Mike Hosty, as musically studied as Linville and as introverted as Harp, has cornered the market on under-the-radar blues-rock in the college town, as well as Oklahoma City, for nearly 30 years, often playing as a one-man band with drums at his feet, a guitar in his hands and a micro-phone and sometimes a kazoo at singing level.

"From the start, I just played original music, and that is what made me different in my area," Hosty said. "I saw bands doing it, like Chainsaw Kittens and Wakeland, and they had a following, so I did it too. I played in Stillwater, but I never really ran in those circles. I was always older than, like Cody and Jason, and the others like Skin-ner and Childers weren't really playing around Norman. And anyway, my style was rock and roll, and I kept doing it.

"The real Oklahoma way, for me, was one person at a time. I got the opportunity to meet and build a relationship with the people I played for, and that's how I did it. I got to know damn near all my fans. For me, I like that I'm not playing to a nameless group."

Because he played his own songs, he cultivated a set of devout fans and made it a point to play to the same fans repeatedly—several times in a month or even a week—to cement his support. Over his career, he has performed solo, as a trio and most famously with drummer Mike "Tic Tac" Byers as the Mike Hosty Duo.

"I just draw a big circle, about 12 hours from Norman, and that's where I'll play," Hosty said. "I'll go to Texas, Colorado, Arkansas and everywhere between here and there, but that's where I can make a living. It really doesn't make any sense for me to go play in Chattanooga or Rhode Island if I'm only going to go there one time, and I can't pay for it. I'd love to go, sure, but I've never been."

Even if Hosty's style and tour philosophy do not fit into Red Dirt, he still left a mark on the scene that will carry on regardless of where his next gig is. Stoney LaRue took Hosty's swamp-rock "Oklahoma Breakdown," added a country-bent lead guitar and made it his own. The song is a high point of LaRue's 2007 *Live at Billy Bob's* album and one he still performs—often shouting out Hosty by name—at his shows today. Hosty views Red Dirt as part of a larger folk movement that encompasses all of Oklahoma's roots scenes.

"What happened in Tulsa in the 1970s, with Eric Clapton and those guys, is hap-pening again," Hosty said. "Only now the big thing, the local bands are folk music, like John Moreland, Parker Millsap, Fullbright, Samantha Crane and Travis Linville. There's a Central Oklahoma folk scene that's a big thing, with backgrounds in all kinds of music. And now folks really blew up, and it has helped them all out."

Currently, Norman's pipeline to the scene rivals any Oklahoma city, Stillwater in-cluded. Bryon White, with or without his band The Damn Quails, is an essential player in Red Dirt, willing to perform solo, as a front man or as a bandmate in every setting. White, who we get into in the "Loose Ends" chapter, left an unforgettable mark at Tom Skinner's memorial when he performed a drop-everything-and-listen rendition of "Nickel's Worth of Difference," but he is better-known for his Skinner style of humor and turning of a phrase. Kierston White is also a regular across Red Dirt's touring cir-cuit, both as a solo artist and with a quasi-supergroup called the Tequila Songbirds, which also features Harp and has included Kaitlin Butts, among others.

• • •

Okemah

At a glance, there is nothing about Okemah to separate it from the hundreds of other small towns that make up the backbone of Oklahoma. On former Osage and Quapaw Indian land, the town was plotted shortly before the 1907 statehood and today sits just off Interstate 40, its surrounding landscape coated in farms and ranches.

Like most towns in the state, Okemah is big on conservatism and religion and small on the idea of hippies and folk music. This made the town's best-known musical export a point of contention for half a century. Woody Guthrie, the patron saint of hippies singing folk music, was born in Okemah in 1912 and lived there until 1926.

It took the town until 1998 to accept, approve and promote a festival honoring him. It seems strange now, given that the Woody Guthrie Folk Festival is on the short list of most important and influential folk music festivals in the world. It takes place in the town's blistering July heat, with a mix of indoor venues at the bars in Okemah's downtown like the Rocky Road Tavern, Crystal Theater and Brick Street Cafe and an outdoor main stage, and it's the most important annual event for the city's economy. Considering that Guthrie spent his musical peak in New York City and wrote a column, "Woody Sez," for the Communist newspaper *The People's World*, one could be forgiven for any shock that Okemah ever became the hub for honoring him.

"There was a local group of citizens that had the idea to start the festival, which was met with quite a bit of resistance here in Okemah," said Gary Hart, former manager at the Rocky Road Tavern and member of the Woody Guthrie Coalition that puts on the festival. "Through sheer perseverance and getting the support of other people throughout the state, especially Red Dirt musicians like Jimmy LaFave, Bob Childers, Tom Skinner and people of that genre who were heavily influenced by Woody, it finally took off.

"The town became more acceptable when people realized that Woody Guthrie was nothing to be scared of, and I'm sure the economic boost helped, too."

Since accepting WoodyFest, Okemah has become rather unique among its small-town peers. It is a thriving, if small, base for playing and performing original music, especially with a roots or Americana bend. Evan Felker has family in Okemah and lived in the town himself during the height of the Turnpike Troubadours fame, routinely dedicating "Pay No Rent" to the town and the Rocky Road Tavern during Turnpike concerts. John Fullbright is the town's current favorite son, having grown up in and around Okemah before briefly joining up with Felker and Turnpike and then launching his Grammy-nominated solo career. Shawna Russell and Melissa Hembree, both longtime citizens of the town, launched and sustained decades-long musical careers without ever leaving the town. And the Rocky Road Tavern, boosted by Turnpike and Fullbright, gained notoriety as a local year-round Americana venue.

The full name of the venue is Lou's Rocky Road Tavern, named after its original owner, Lula Johnson—aunt to Evan Felker—who operated it from 1998 until her death in 2016.

"The one reason the Rocky Road became iconic is the Woody Guthrie Festival," Hart said. "It ties it together. Lou, before she passed, used to say, 'Without the festival, my bar would not be what it is.' The festival has its listening rooms and its campgrounds, but this is the hangout spot. This is the axis of the festival, where you come to visit with friends, drink some cold beers and then go on to the next venue."

Hart and Hembree started a regular Tuesday night songwriter's night at the tavern in 2016 and kept it going for four years. They held it on an outdoor stage behind the bar, evocative of The Farm and other Red Dirt campfire settings.

"This is the Rocky Road, but this is Lou's bar and it always will be," Hembree said. "She has always been a supporter of live music. She's also part of Evan's family, and so Evan has always been a big part of this bar. John Fullbright has always been a big part of this bar. And they have brought the bar to many musicians. I think that's what sets this bar apart is the musicians who have embraced it. They make us feel so important here."

Felker and Fullbright paid tribute to Lou, writing "Pay No Rent" together just before her funeral and debuting the touching ballad at the service. The story goes, Lou had asked Felker to play Willie Nelson's "Blue Eyes Crying in the Rain" for her, but when the time came, he learned she—in the true spirit of an Okemah dive bar owner—had made the request of several others as well.

Hembree's Tuesday night event was created and upheld in the same spirit.

"I wanted to embrace the spirit of WoodyFest all year here, and the only way to do that in a palace that is an hour from everywhere is to have your musicians committed," she said. "I found it easy to get them to come down here for me on a Tuesday night and do a show, because they love this bar."

Hembree recorded in Nashville when she was young—as early as age 9. She started writing her own music as a teenager.

"Being able to speak your truth was so different for me," she said. "Writing my own music gave me a platform and an outlet to speak my mind, and it lets you be creative in your own way. You can always look for an artist in your wheelhouse, and that's who influences you, but I love writing for myself."

She was drawn to what she called outlaw music, especially the females who were a part of it.

"I loved Jessi Colter," Hembree said. "It was such an amazing time. Women were so very select in that particular genre, because there were a slew of men. And I remember thinking, 'Man, these women are tough, and they're strong, and they're rolling with these men that are tough,' and back in the 1970s and '80s, it was an amazing platform that they had.

"Those people told real stories, like movies that you could follow in their songs in your head. I loved it."

Hembree was born near Dallas but raised by an adopted family in Oklahoma that realized her talent early on in her life, and they were responsible for her early move to Nashville. She has been making music for more than 40 years since.

"I moved to Okemah because I was seeing someone here, got married and started a family," she said. "And then I got a divorce, and I stayed here anyway. I got to see a major transformation in Okemah. Folk music, especially Woody Guthrie, was not very well-received when I got here. It's been a beautiful opening and acceptance, and the town has come around more and more every year. Once people came out and saw that it was a great embracing of music, they embraced it too."

Hembree points to Fullbright as the example of the town's musical awakening. Fullbright is unabashedly an Okemah native, and he is quick to remind audiences from New York to Los Angeles of that. Hembree says it is no exaggeration to say the love between artist and hometown is mutual.

"Everyone loves him," she said. "He comes here and hangs out, and they love him. And he can come here and hang out and be left alone. The people that hang out at the Rocky Road Tavern leave him alone.

"He's just like us when he comes here. So are the boys in Turnpike. They can come here, hang out, shoot pool and go home. And we make *sure* that they are able to do that."

When I drove to Okemah to meet with Hembree in summer 2019 at the Rocky

Road Tavern, I saw a for-sale sign out front as I was leaving, so I want to be very careful to hedge the talk of the bar with that. But its place in Okemah music history is secure, and its value to Red Dirt will last as long as the scene does, partly because of the festival but equally because of its ties to Fullbright.

"The community at large embraces Fullbright and has a lot of pride in what he has done," said Tim Russell, who has lived in or around Okemah for most of his life and has been playing, producing or deejaying country or folk music for 50 years. "There is a part of the community that really cares, and it really embraces him."

Tim and his brother, Keith, have been musicians throughout their lives, brushing both mainstream and Red Dirt circles for as long as the scene has existed. Their biggest push for regional acceptance, though, came backing up another family member.

Since elementary school, Shawna Russell has pursued music from any angle she could find. Shawna, along with her father, Keith, and Tim have played together in some form, from family band to touring band, since 1992 when Shawna was 13. Shawna fronted Tim's band, Way Out West, in the late 1990s as they toured dance halls, hotel bars and classic honky-tonks like Tulsa City Limits and the Grizzly Rose in Denver. The two also played in fellow Oklahoman Ty England's band in the early 2000s, before touring for another 12 years in support of Shawna. Tim also wrote for England, and the two topped the Texas Music Chart in 2005 with England's single, "Texans Hold 'Em," at the time setting a record for the longest time atop that chart.

Meanwhile, Shawna Russell—managed by Tim—released two solo albums and an EP during the span. It culminated with a yearlong stint hosting *Our Land: The Music Highway*, a performance-and-interview show on The Country Network. But all that came about from Okemah. There was never a serious push at moving to Nashville or Los Angeles to pursue a mainstream career.

"It's easy to wonder, now, if Shawna had taken an invitation when she was 21 years old to pack up her things and move to Nashville," Tim said. "Well, that exit has its own set of rewards and pitfalls. So, now, she lives on a beautiful ranch, with a husband she's had more than 20 years, with relationships with her family that are extremely close. Seems like a fair swap."

Shawna, now raising bison with her husband, Brandon Burnett, at the White Lightning Ranch outside of Okemah, has been around music since she could talk.

"I started singing at about 7, living in Broken Bow [Oklahoma] at the time," Shawna said. "My aunt, Pam Condict, was a member of the baptist church. She put on a play and couldn't find enough people to fill out the singing parts, and she asked me if I would sing in it. Now, I was totally a shy kid, hated talking to people and being in front of people, but it came really easy to me. I learned my part immediately and learned everybody else's part, and then I got up on stage, and I had a great time! My dad was watching, and he didn't even know that I had any sort of talent at all. He was completely surprised and told my mom, 'I can't believe she's doing this. She's...really good.'

"It was literally the next night that he and I were in the kitchen learning 'Daddy's Hands' by Holly Dunn."

Over the course of her career, she opened for The Great Divide, Reckless Kelly, Stoney LaRue and more mainstream artists, and she eventually built enough of a following that she headlined the annual Oil Patch Festival, a July 4 celebration in Drumright, Oklahoma, that drew 9,500 fans in 2011. Her self-titled album released the same year was produced by Russ Kunkel, noted session musician, drummer and producer who has worked with Linda Rondstadt, James Taylor, Bob Dylan and Stevie Nicks, among hundreds of other artists you'd know by name.

Without ever having a major-label deal, Shawna managed to build and sustain a fan base that let her play music for a living—a Red Dirt hallmark, but Shawna built it on the house band circuit in the early 2000s. She would play classic dance halls like Billy Bob's, the Grizzly Rose, Tulsa City Limits and Fred's Code West in Oklahoma City, playing an array of cover songs over four-hour sets, opening for whatever headliner happened to be booked and finding ways to mix in her own originals when she could. The gigs were steady and paid her well.

"I tried to play all the best songs that I could at the time, and I tried to show off my musical capabilities, just hoping that would kind of shine," Shawna said. "And we traveled so much, we'd build a fan base. Everywhere we'd go, it was like playing for family. It's sad, but that entire scene has kind of collapsed now, because we had so much fun doing it."

In the early and mid-2010s, the casino boom in Oklahoma gave Shawna, along with classic Red Dirt bands like the Red Dirt Rangers, new outlets: weekend gigs headlining lounges overlooking slot machines. That was enough to keep the bills paid at the White Lightning Ranch, which was all Shawna was after. According to Shawna and Tim, she was offered multiple opportunities to sign with labels in both Los Angeles and Nashville but they always came with catches or compromises Shawna was uncomfortable with.

"You get to a point where you get on that roller-coaster for a long time and decide, if I stay independent, I can write my own songs, decide what singles go out, decide who I want to manage me and generally have a lot more control," Shawna said. "Well, probably not. It's like a David and Goliath type thing. But at the end of the day, if I had gone into the music business to be famous, I'd have taken a different path. I felt better doing what I love as long as I could, especially if I felt that the end product that I was giving people was one hundred percent from me."

* * *

Tulsa

What makes it a chore to quantify Tulsa's relationship to Red Dirt is that the city has its own scene, full of history, stories and even its own identity crisis.

The Tulsa Sound—the swampy, keyboard-heavy rock associated with J.J. Cale, Leon Russell and Eric Clapton—not only predates Red Dirt but gained widespread acceptance as a genre decades before its Stillwater cousin. But Cale, who died in 2013, often disputed its significance late in life, telling reporters, among other things, "There is no more a Tulsa Sound than there is a Cincinnati sound. Every town has some good musicians that have done pretty good, but I think that was a marketing tool."

The real issue is that the Tulsa Sound pulled from rock, blues, jazz, gospel and folk all at once. One could argue that Red Dirt did the same, but the combination of Stillwater's size—much smaller than Tulsa and constantly forcing the same artists to overlap at the same venues—and communal sites like The Farm and Yellow House in Stillwater helped Red Dirt build a tightly knit base of artists that more easily blended musical tastes and sounds with each other. It may still be hard to exactly articulate Red Dirt, but at least the same general half phrases apply across the board: *It's spir-*

itual. *It's about the land. It's the descendant of what Woody Guthrie sang.* The Tulsa Sound, conversely, never got the benefit of that effort. History has tied it more to its instruments than its songwriting, and even veterans of Tulsa often fall back on "You know it when you hear it" when really pressed to define the Tulsa Sound.

Only Steve Ripley, credited with helping name Red Dirt when he slapped the moniker on his record label in the mid-1970s, has ever truly been claimed as part of both Red Dirt and the Tulsa Sound. He melded both when he took over Cale's Church Studio near downtown Tulsa for a decade starting in the late 1980s.

Regardless of any of the above, where the Tulsa Sound fits in history is for another book. Here is what's not up for debate:

• Cain's Ballroom, the dance hall first famous as the home of Bob Wills and the Texas Playboys, in downtown Tulsa has been a major host for Red Dirt artists for 25 years. Jason Boland's Leftover Turkey Festival and Cody Canada's Hangover Ball are two annual holiday festivals the venue holds. Ragweed's final live album was recorded at Cain's. The Turnpike Troubadours cemented the ballroom's place in Red Dirt when they recorded "Easton and Main" about it. But like a lot of Tulsa, Cain's is bigger than Red Dirt, and the scene represents only a fraction of the music it hosts even today.

The history of Cain's, in and out of Red Dirt, is fascinating and deep and balances eras of complete failure and booming success. John Wooley, a longtime Tulsa-area journalist and the closest to a dual expert in Tulsa and Red Dirt music histories in existence, captured the history eloquently in the book he cowrote with Brett Bingham and released in 2020, *Twentieth-Century Honky-Tonk: The Amazing Unauthorized Story of the Cain's Ballroom's First 75 Years.*

• The Woody Guthrie Center, a public exhibit, tribute, archive and music experience, is in downtown Tulsa. The center is adjacent to a park, the Guthrie Green, and less than a mile north of where old Route 66 passed through the city.

• Like Linville, Fullbright is now based in Tulsa. He was a regular contributor to Tom Skinner's Wednesday Night Science Project at The Colony, a British pub. The Science Project became such a success that the bar hosts live music every night a week as a result, even five years after Skinner's death. And Fullbright has carried Skinner's legacy with him beyond the Science Project—it's possible that no other artist besides Mike McClure continues to play as much Skinner music and tell as many Skinner stories as Fullbright.

• Past and present bars like The Colony, The Mercury, The Venue Shrine, The Blue Rose and Steamroller Blues were integral to the spread of Red Dirt. They welcomed the Rangers, Ragweed and The Stragglers. The Mercury helped launch Turnpike, which turned around and wrote and recorded "The Mercury" about the bar.

In the big picture, while the relationship itself requires pretty substantial untangling, there is no arguing Tulsa always has a place for Red Dirt, is home to one of the must-play venues in the scene and has been welcoming to its artists throughout the genre's history.

There are other landmarks to Red Dirt's first half-century. Gary P. Nunn was born in Okmulgee and started pursuing music when living on his family ranch in Hanna.

Although Nunn moved to Austin and was largely claimed by Texans as one of their own a generation before Red Dirt gained traction outside Stillwater, Nunn's endorsements and support contributed to the rise of The Divide, Ragweed and Jason Boland & The Stragglers.

Vian and Tahlequah, in the hills of East Oklahoma, were Red Dirt pipelines long before it was the de facto home of both the Turnpike Troubadours and their Medicine Stone festival. Roxy's Roost, a bygone rural bar along the Illinois River, was an early stomping ground for Boland and Travis Linville. Vian is home to Roger Ray and Grant Tracy, founding members of The Stragglers and two of the best musicians in the scene's history.

Greg Jacobs immortalized the towns covered up by Lake Eufaula and the eminent domain laws needed to take the land to build it in "Farmer's Luck." Then the lake turned right around and played backdrop to Music and Mayhem, an annual festival headlined by Ragweed until the end of the band and a precursor to Medicine Stone as Red Dirt's rural heat, mud and humidity party.

Some places were more important to Red Dirt than the others, but they all played their parts. Without them, at a minimum, the trajectory of the scene would have played out differently and may well not have played out at all.

- 20 -

Turnpike

"**I'M GOING TO** make music. At the end of the day, that's what I feel I was put on Earth to do."

Evan Felker had just spent a year off every grid imaginable. Yet in early August 2020, he handled the obvious "What's next?" with the same charisma that commands attention from every eye in sold-out amphitheaters when he's on stage.

"And I'll tell you another thing. It's really hard to get *good* at something!" Felker said, breaking into a full-throttle laugh. "Look, I've tried over the past year! And I learned: May as well stick to your day job."

For two years, a dull roar—ranging from nonsense and rumors to speculation to an urgency to anoint bands as "the next Turnpike" permeated Red Dirt and Texas circles, making it really easy to overlook that same charisma and humor that made Felker and the Turnpike Troubadours the brightest stars the modern scene has known. Neither chance nor accident landed the artist and band at that summit. They got there with a dedication to their music, to each other and to ceaseless work. At all times, they wore sincerity on their sleeves like a hallmark.

So when the Turnpike frontman and cofounder was thrown the most baseline question about how life is going right now, his voice and his tone made it clear he was sincere: "I'm *good*, man!"

Felker's confidence in his own music had always been the bedrock of Turnpike—four (official) albums since 2010, built overwhelmingly on Felker's songwriting, and an absurdly high number of songs to which fans know every word and chord—but it was hard not to hear those words from him and react with anything other than, *Oh, he means it. The dude's happy. You can hear it in his voice.*

• • •

In October 2018, Felker sat casually on an old leather lounge chair on the first floor of Irving Plaza in New York City.

One floor above, the Turnpike Troubadours' equipment sat covered, pushed to the back of the stage in the two-story ballroom that dates to the 1940s, once carried the Fillmore brand and has played host to Paul McCartney, the B-52s and Pope John Paul II before he was a pope.

Over the chords and swampy vocals of opener Charley Crockett running through sound check, and in and around a laugh with R.C. Edwards—bassist, vocalist and co-founder—at the notion that the 1,200-seat venue might be sold out that night, Felker did not mince words.

"This is all we want. I'd rather be driven by creativity than success. I want to make great art and to play with my pals.

"The best art I can make."

That same confidence surfaced.

"Sometimes, the places we play are too big to connect with the audience. I catch myself thinking, back in our Mercury Lounge or Red Barn days, everybody in those places was having the same amount of fun. Now it seems like the people farthest away from you are the ones that are having the blast. You don't get the energy feeding back and forth."

And then, Felker followed Edwards upstairs and led Turnpike through a two-plus-hour set in the sold-out, two-tiered concert hall.

The fans in the balcony seats, as far from the stage as possible in the room, did indeed have a blast.

• • •

Jim "Red" Wilhelm describes the rise of Red Dirt since the mid-'90s as a series of peaks.

"There were really three, we'll call them mushroom clouds, of Red Dirt exploding," Wilhelm said. "Each one of them was bigger than the last one. The first was The Great Divide. Then came Ragweed and finally Turnpike. Turnpike was the one where there was no limit. The first two bands had to break down the door, and Turnpike walked right through."

Equally impressive, they did it without leaving Oklahoma.

The Troubadours reached an orbit never before touched by Red Dirt. Founded in 2005 and remaining independent throughout the entire arc of the band while officially releasing only four albums (not including their debut *Bossier City*, which was released nearly immediately after the band formed as a form of spreading the word and is now out of print), Turnpike is the first truly national Red Dirt band that pulled it off entirely while living in Oklahoma.

The Great Divide and Stoney LaRue both became regional sensations despite living most of their lives in the state, but to this day they focus their touring heavily on the dance halls and listening rooms in Tornado Alley.

Cross Canadian Ragweed and Jason Boland & The Stragglers absolutely commanded (past tense in the case of Ragweed) or command (ongoing in the case of Boland) a crowd in every venue, coast to coast, but the peaks for both came after early-2000s moves to the Texas Hill Country, where access to venues and business partners came a lot easier.

Turnpike saw the door and put six cowboy boots through it all at once.

"We never left," Edwards said of the Sooner State. "The other bands we talk about, most of them kind of moved down to Texas, and that was the smart move for them. But we're still there with those people, and we still live the same lives, basically, that we always did."

In the straightforward story, Felker plays guitar and harmonica and writes most of the songs. Edwards plays bass, contributes vocals occasionally and is also a frequent songwriter. They are joined by Kyle Nix on fiddle, Ryan Engleman on guitar, Hank Early on steel guitar and Gabe Pearson on drums. Oklahoma permeates the band. The state flag is a permanent part of the band's stage setup.

Felker and Edwards named the band after the state's Indian Nation Turnpike, which connects Tulsa to all points south and east in the state and to Texas beyond that—the same turnpike the two drove back and forth to bar gigs in the mid-2000s, back at the point those early connections with crowds were driven home for both.

"When I started actually thinking that I could possibly do this, it was simply because of bands like Ragweed and Boland," Felker said. "I would have never gone down this path without those guys, because they made it possible. Music to me seemed like you had to be either Garth Brooks or Nirvana. There was no in-between. But there's actually this vast in-between, and there's so much that can be done just being a bar band."

It was the bar band experience of Edwards, who hails from Tahlequah and cut his teeth, musically, in Tulsa, that showed Felker the way. Before Turnpike was Turnpike, Felker would open for Edwards.

"I always dreamed of music. I asked for a guitar for Christmas for as long as I can remember, until I finally got one when I was a teenager," Edwards said. "My buddies and I all had a punk rock grunge thing like Nirvana or Rancid—I think everyone in our band at some point had either a punk or heavy metal band or something in between. Then you kind of grow up and you turn into country bands.

"But the other thing is, The Great Divide, Ragweed and Boland made it cool to play country music when you were young. When you're a teenager, there's a whole thing where country music isn't cool sometimes, and they made it cool. So you started learning their music and their influences. That's how I learned about Robert Earl Keen, Todd Snider, Townes Van Zandt, Guy Clark and John Prine. They send you down that rabbit hole, and that's what happened."

Felker, who worked in a welding shop before becoming a musician, met Edwards through a mutual friend when Edwards played with the Awesome Possum Band.

"We have a mutual acquaintance who got us together and let us open up for his band. We opened up, song-swapping, and got to be buddies. So R.C. had a band and I just started opening up for them," Felker said.

Turnpike churned through a handful of members early on, including John Fullbright, but it is the current lineup that rolled from venue to venue with fast-paced fiddle-and-steel-laced rock and country.

"I grew up hearing and playing music at family reunions and stuff like that," Pearson said. "I went to school at a branch of A&M, but I quit so I could join a band around '07. There's a guy out of Texas, Rodney Parker, who I met and played with. That's where I met Hank. It was in Denton."

Nix made a name for himself in Stillwater in the early 2000s before joining Turnpike and also has a family history in music.

"My grandpa made fiddles, and I grew up a block away from another fellow who played fiddle and was just a little bit older than me," Nix said. "It was something I always wanted to do, so I started taking lessons from his teacher, out in Enid, and I started playing bluegrass. I played festivals early on and got the bug to start trying to play in my own bands.

"I ended up having my own band, and then I jumped in and started playing with Scott Evans, and I learned how to improv and play an acoustic act. Then I met Bo Phillips, and we did acoustic things and had a band for a while. Finally I ended up meeting Evan and R.C. playing with Bo. They were playing with us one night, and it seemed like a good fit after we jammed."

Engleman, similarly, is a lifelong lover of music.

"I started playing guitar at about 11," Engleman said. "I played piano as a kid until I hated it and didn't want to play anymore. But I picked up the guitar and just loved the escape of it, how you can kind of get lost in it and not have to think about problems.

"So I fell in love with it, played here and there, and once I got a little older, I got into girls, and a little older than that, I could drink, and off we go. And then I ran into these guys. I was playing with a lady named Camille Harp for probably a year and a half. We opened up a show for these guys, there were four or five bands. Anyway, their guitar player at the time, Casey Sliger, went out to Tennessee for a couple of months and couldn't play. So Evan got ahold of me on MySpace and asked me if I could fill in the dates. So I drove up to Tahlequah and met up with these guys, and it was just different from most of the bands I'd been around and played with, because they had a better hold on playing certain markets. Everybody I knew would just play The Deli twice a month. But these guys would play Stillwater every two months, Tulsa once a month. It was already laid out that they weren't going to play a market too much. So I joined up with them and that was 10 years ago.

"And then in 2015, I broke my wrist and, well, enter the dragon."

The dragon he was referring to is Early.

Early filled in for Engleman and simply never left.

"I started playing when I was a kid," Early said. "My uncle was a bluegrass musician. Still is. My family is pretty musical. I played music in church growing up and ended up studying it in school. And then I started teaching it. Mostly guitar and piano.

"It was after that, around 2007, that I started playing the steel, and I started playing with Rodney Parker, too. So I freelanced for about 10 years—not quite 10 years but close—before they picked me up in the DFW area. I was doing guitar and bass and steel guitar, really doing whatever. I was in a bluegrass band based out of Denton called the Bluegrass Bandits. Doing this and that and a lot of pickup gigs and studio work. Then they called me when Ryan had a busted arm. Gabe threw my name in the hat, and I've since fallen into a utility role."

That's the straightforward Turnpike: a group that came together at an older age than most Red Dirt bands—post-college—and made a go of it.

· · · ·

During its early—or at least formative—years, Turnpike toured heavily with Jason Boland & The Stragglers, and Red Dirt fandom is filled with stories of the two bands riffing off each other as they toured in 2011 after the release of Turnpike's first album.

If they played a venue that seated 500, there are 5,000 fans today who swear they caught the show.

The Stragglers and Turnpike went on to create Medicine Stone in 2013, and even though Turnpike also hosted the Harvest Maroon Fest with Randy Rogers in Texas and was a regular at just about every Americana festival, Medicine Stone was the one that turned into the premier event in all of Red Dirt.

How Turnpike got as big as it did is a testament to both talent and timing.

The best-known bands in the generation that preceded Turnpike had careers and songs that resembled the rise of an elevator. As they grew and developed, their ceilings went up, but the floor did the same. Songs they played when they were 20 got jettisoned when they turned 25. Songs that used to be staples of their live shows either became unthinkable (see Ragweed's "The President Song," for example) or backburnered to make room for new music (see Ragweed's "Look at Me"). But for Turnpike, it never happened that way.

The band kept a tight catalog, and nearly every song from 2010's *Diamonds & Gasoline* is still in play at live shows. "Every Girl" and the title track are rarely left out.

Neither is the final track, long written in as their set closer.

Turnpike's performing John Hartford's "Long, Hot Summer Day" is practically an out-of-body experience regardless of venue or location—it's hard to know what the limit is for crowd insanity during a concert staple, but judging from Turnpike fans stomping and screaming during this one, it's way the hell up there—and they proudly drop Hartford's name every time.

Songwriting is an art, but so is choosing your covers, and Turnpike turning Hartford's original falsetto-yodel into a full-band jam would be in the Louvre if music were a painting.

With Turnpike, there was never a raising of that elevator floor as the ceiling went up. Rather, they just went and threw a party on the roof. Nearly every song they have cut since 2010 is still fair game in set lists every night. This lays bare fans' expectations before they take the stage, and the willingness to draw upon so many songs that have been around for a decade keeps an edge to the band's sound.

"It's a nice situation to be in, when your crowd has an expectation that they're gonna have a really good time, because it actually takes a lot of the pressure off," Early said. "As long as we get out there and we have a good time, they're gonna be happy. It's when it's a mixed crowd, when it's a half listening room, half party crowd, that the pressure is up. Being able to put on a high-energy show as well as a tight, well put-together show is really important to being able to meet the expectations of both of those crowds."

Age also worked in Turnpike's favor. Or better put, Turnpike worked in *its* favor. The group never needed to perform as a true college band. They, collectively at least, never had to transition into playing as a post-college, mature band, and that has afforded them a limitless range in both songwriting and arrangement. But their appeal has backfilled into college campuses across the Midwest anyway.

"A lot of it is word of mouth," Engleman said. "Someone will come out who doesn't know much about us and will really enjoy themselves or whatever, and that spreads to their friends. Especially with college kids, because they have more time to sit around and do shit like go find music."

The band also views Felker's songwriting as a responsibility. If his words are the painting, it's their job to create the canvas.

"The content of what Evan writes is pretty serious," Pearson said. "But at the same time, we don't want it to get stuffy. We try to have a good time on stage. When we play our best shows, we're all joking around on stage, even in the middle of songs. Keeping the energy up and people seeing us having fun, maybe it juxtaposes the two things, but it's huge.

"People can see us and say, 'Oh my god, I saw this songwriter band, but it wasn't boring!'

"Not that songwriters are boring...except they kind of are." (Pearson delivered that line with a laugh, to be clear.)

Felker, for his part, rejected the notion that his bandmates are anything other than full partners in his songs.

"Well, it's not them and us," Felker said, with "us" meaning him and Edwards and "them" meaning the other four members. "And that comes into play a lot—the them-and-us thing—and I think it's horseshit.

"We're a band, and a really good one."

The band—which it should be said also assembled a crew that is revered even among other bands' crews in the scene—viewed their success as a benchmark rather than a goal or an end of a journey.

"It helps to keep trying to put out good records and good music, too," Nix said. "Every time you put out something new, there's a buzz that helps get your name out there as well, and if your name's going to be mentioned, it better be good."

To bring the story full circle, keeping those mentions good is not just a challenge for the band, but it is also an artistic standard to uphold, especially for Felker and Edwards. One of the outlets for both is a subset of their songs that feature recurring storylines, characters and themes.

The fictional "Lorrie" is the subject of unrequited love in "Good Lord, Lorrie," off 2012's *Goodbye Normal Street*. Five years later, "Lorrie" returned as the quick-thinking, stable rock of a wife and mother in "The Housefire," the first track on 2017's *A Long Way From Your Heart*. A Browning shotgun was also saved in "The Housefire"— quite possibly the same Browning shotgun the narrator used in "The Bird Hunters," the lead track to the band's 2015 self-titled album. Both Edwards and Felker acknowledge the undertones.

"I'd like to say it's all Hemingway short stories," Felker said. "And it is, but part of it is, Stephen King's got this thing where everything is one giant universe and everything's canon. Maybe it was sitting around drinking beer that made me think that all those characters could be cool."

Hemingway's *The Nick Adams Stories* can be viewed, at least vaguely, as inspiration.

"Evan is the one who pulled it off, but we definitely had conversations about how cool it was when writers did stuff like that," Edwards said. "Stephen King, Hemingway and J.D. Salinger created their own universes and their own families and characters that interact. And Ev's been able to work that into multiple albums in a really neat way.

"I've seen elaborate fan theories on some of the lyrics. You're always getting questions about them. The classic one is, 'Who is Lorrie?' and my favorite answer is, 'Keep listening.'"

Those who keep listening notice another common thread binding Turnpike lyrics: the state itself.

The songwriting of both Felker and Edwards—sometimes explicitly and sometimes quite subtly—is dripping with Oklahoma imagery. "The Bird Hunters" comes right out and says that it's set in Cherokee County, in the East Oklahoma backwoods and pastures outside Tahlequah. It's impossible to listen to "The Housefire" and not imagine the home is on the outskirts of Okemah. Even the band's musical or business forays into Louisiana—their record label is Bossier Records and a pair of songs, "Shreveport" and "Bossier City," wax poetic about the northern part of that state—feel much more like the result of constant road trips from Southeast Oklahoma and less like native views.

"It's the only place I know and the only place I've ever lived," Felker said. "That's it. Oklahoma is my only frame of reference."

Felker's connection to small-town Oklahoma is a lifelong one. He has family in Okemah, and the town's Rocky Road Tavern caught a ton of his onstage shout-outs, but Felker said it is by design. He can find refuge and comfort surrounded by a small circle of friends.

"We live in fairly small towns and have a pretty normal life," Felker said. "People probably cut us a little bit of slack because we do good music, but pretty much other than that, life can be the same as it's always been."

Turnpike's roots undoubtedly lie in the Sooner State. And Felker undoubtedly found a heavy influence from Bob Childers and Tom Skinner during the stretch of his life he lived in Stillwater. And they have unabashedly taken the music from coast to coast, playing and selling out progressively larger venues with each trip across the country.

But rarely has a band had such an opportunity to go bigger and chose to stay independent. Nashville called Turnpike and the band let the phone ring on the floor.

"It always just seems like you're gonna get screwed, and it doesn't feel good," Felker said. "If we wake up one morning and say, 'Let's go block off 30 days and go make a record,' we can just do that. And we can put it out ourselves, and it'll be really good.

"We have a really great life. I don't know why we would want to add any more people to it."

．．．

2018 happened.

Since then, pandemic aside, Turnpike has been *the* question hanging over Red Dirt music. The band has been surrounded by both a consistent mix of genuine concern and tabloid-ish enthusiasm for scandal, throughout the entire time frame this book came together.

It cannot overshadow the legacy of Turnpike, but it also cannot go unchecked.

The tabloids came first. Felker, who it needs saying again is a private person by nature, suddenly found himself under a microscope far beyond just message boards and Instagram comments. He split from his wife, Staci, and was linked in tabloids with Miranda Lambert, and the resulting saga was as public and as ugly as any celebrity, certainly from Red Dirt circles, has ever endured. It was compounded when you consider the band's dedication to independence.

It also brought about a gut check on music fandom and how it can spiral out of control in a social media age.

"Stay out of the tabloids. Stay off the Internet," Edwards said back in that 2018 sitdown. "Your real friends that know you, they know you don't want to talk about that stuff, and they don't bother you about it. And you go do your own thing."

The tabloids were bad, but Turnpike had such credibility built up that its music and shows never suffered. Then, suddenly, they did. The band left a summer 2018 tour with Lambert and Little Big Town before it completed and took a monthlong break. Then, that fall, a week after that Irving Plaza concert and interview, another monthlong break. Both breaks resulted from Felker missing concerts. In a "normal" job and life, if you need to get your head right, you take time off and heal your mind. In music, if you do that, shows get canceled by the bushel.

2019 happened.

Another cancellation cut differently. That one happened the day of a sold-out Chicago show with Jonathan Tyler & The Northern Lights, and shortly before a headlining spot at Mile 0 Fest in Key West in January.

It was only the second-ever Mile 0 Fest. The event is a wildly popular, island-wide party. Mile 0, which debuted in 2018, is the brainchild of Okies and run by Okies. Kyle Carter, a native of Yukon, was talented enough to perform for a living but opted for a more conventional business life until Mile 0 presented an opportunity on which he could not pass. He started the festival with the support of the Red Dirt Rangers. It's as Okie of a festival as one could conjure.

Thus, Turnpike missing out on Mile 0 felt particularly heavy.

At the festival, on the night Turnpike had been slated to headline, Cody Canada spoke up about Felker from the main stage, directly and intensely: "It's a common misconception that as musicians, we're bulletproof, and we're not. Life catches up to us from time to time. And you, as fans, should let us chill the fuck out for a minute and let us catch our breath. Sometimes, on the roller-coaster of success, we have to step off. We need to work on ourselves for a minute. And then we'll come back, as long as you're here. We're musicians. We're a little brittle. We're not gladiators."

Turnpike regrouped and set off on a four-month run that was, purely technically speaking, as successful and intense as any ever played, culminating in a headlining gig in March at the Houston Livestock Show and Rodeo at NRG Park for a crowd of 70,000.

Obviously, that is wonderful for fans, but it takes humanity out of the whole equation and essentially makes robots out of the people making music. Felker was still reeling from 2018, unhappy and had no outlet to get right by himself.

It bubbled back to the surface in early May, during a benefit in Guthrie, Oklahoma, for local fiddle player Byron Berline, who had lost his fiddle shop in a fire weeks before. Berline is especially close to Nix. During the show, which also featured Oklahoma icon and Berline pal Vince Gill, Felker was visibly off, missing entire lines and choruses in a painful set that ended with an abrupt and awkward exit from the stage. Another social media frenzy followed.

Less than three weeks later, the band announced an indefinite hiatus in a heavy note on Instagram. The Turnpike Troubadours, to borrow a Broadway term, went dark.

Fans, though, did not turn on Turnpike, especially after the hiatus—when their absence was truly felt. But, that cut two ways, as Red Dirt social media spent the better part of two years dominated by questions about the band: What's next? Are they breaking up? Is Evan alright? That incessant churn alone can overwhelm artists even in the best of times, and these times were anything but.

The band members found solace, usually in Oklahoma. Edwards pressed forward with R.C. and the Ambers. Engleman jumped on board with Reckless Kelly, replacing David Abeyta on lead guitar. Kyle Nix wrote and recorded his first solo album. Turnpike's crew, regarded even among its contemporaries as one of the best in live music, found places with other bands one by one.

Felker, though, took the path he needed to take, and it was a much longer one.

● ● ●

For more than a year, he kept a profile so low it seemed impossible. He surfaced once, in the spring, in a couple of pictures on social media of working on a ranch in Southeast Texas.

Nearly two years to the day after I had done the first interview for this book—a phoner with Willy Braun as he stood outside the Tractor Tavern in Seattle and I ducked into a *New York Times* conference room—I was two or three hours away from sending it to the press.

I had set August 1, 2020, as the deadline for edits. I had written a full chapter about Turnpike. But it was open-ended, and it weaved the story of the band back and forth with the suddenness and abruptness with which everything turned. Was I extolling Turnpike? Was I eulogizing Turnpike? I had no idea, so in a way I tried to do both. The original ending to this chapter was: *The last word on the Turnpike Troubadours is still out there, yet to be snagged out of the Eastern Oklahoma air.*

In the months leading up to that deadline, I sent out tons of advance copies. Mostly they went out in hopes of creating a buzz, but some also went out to artists in a "this is what I am writing about you" spirit. I shipped out five extra copies—with Felker's name on them—basically into the ether. Most went to artists who I knew to be his friends in hopes they would get one to him. One, though, went to that ranch I mentioned earlier—talking real wing-and-prayer here—and fell into the hands of the grandfather of a friend of Felker's. From there, it found its rightful owner.

A couple of hours before I intended to ship this book to the printer, my phone rang, and I kicked it straight to voicemail. A few minutes later, I gave it a listen:

"Hi, Josh. This is Staci Felker. We have not met, but I just heard about your book and that you might be sending it the printer soon. I just need to say that a *lot* has happened since 2019, and I'm hoping you get this in time to talk. Give me a call back."

That's why you're reading this. At that ranch, they saw the book in the mail and tipped off Staci to it, and Evan said he was up for a chat (to answer the question this begs: Yes, Staci and Evan are happy, and they are together). I had no plan other than to listen and not interrupt. I sent him an electronic copy, and the next morning my phone rang, with him on the other end. He was ready for the "How are you?" that followed.

"The past year, nearly, has been some of the best moments and best parts of my life," Felker said.

"First and foremost, I found sobriety and recovery. And I stepped away from the road and got a clearer view of the world. I got back to just being *me*.

"I could not have ever done that while we were touring like we were.

"I had initially blamed everything on being on the road. But it's only when you take the road out of the equation that you see you've still got problems. I was able to start fixing those."

It is important to point out that the band launched itself from the same "any time, any place" spirit that permeates Red Dirt. So, after finding success, Turnpike kept up a relentless tour schedule even when they would have been justified in cutting back to a few weekends a month of concerts.

The only way Felker was ever finding peace, personally and professionally, was by getting away from all of that. In a bit of fortunate timing, he has reached that point. Now, finally, he can be clear-headed about music again.

"I've been thinking so much about music lately," Felker said, "how maybe I want to tour again. I'm trying to write songs again. I've taken a full, almost a year away from that.

"Music was the only thing I thought about for most of my adult life—or some version of it, whether it's actually creating or touring or having a relationship with the band or who I was perceived to be versus who I actually *was*. All of these things, I needed to sort out.

"I didn't think that it could function without all of us being comfortable and in a good spot. And I was a lot worse off than any of the other guys. I didn't realize it at the time. It was really important to me, but it's really important to anyone who's going to be in public. You can't be on the edge of falling apart all the time. You can paper over it for a long time, but eventually, it just doesn't work.

"We pushed for a very, very long time—way longer than should have ever been considered. But you know, our heroes are that way...look at the Stones! All these icons are complicated people in their lives.

"We really didn't take a real break until we just hung everything up for a while. And that's been our whole career as a band: ten years of that. It's a strange kind of grind, just always being in motion like that. You can lose perspective."

Knowing this part in particular will be parsed and analyzed, the step-back take-away should simply be that Felker is doing just fine now. But right behind that, maybe there still needs to be a reckoning with expectations of artists on a grand scale, especially when getting as far away from it as one possibly can for a year is such a path to clarity. Felker did not so much need to see the sunrise over Oklahoma to find his—he needed to *be* the sunrise over Oklahoma for a while to pull it off.

"I always go back to the Stephen King quote," he said. "Life isn't a support system for art. It's the other way around."

• • •

When Turnpike hit the pause button, it did not surprise anyone that Nix was the first one to cut a full record on his own. He released the 17-track album *Lightning on the Mountain & Other Short Stories* in June 2020.

"'Hope you like it some' is a line from one of my songs on the record," Nix said. "And I do hope you like it some, but I also hope you get something out of it. Whatever that may be is up to the listener. That's one of the beautiful things about music: the listener's experience! It's definitely one of my favorite things. It's like opening a present when you hear a record for the first time. Some presents you hold on to, others you discard. Hopefully, I have something you can hold on to."

Nix's backing musicians may be best cast as a who's who of roots music in 2020.

Pearson, Engleman, Early and Edwards all played on it. So did Ian Moore, Haystack Foster (Jason Eady, Sunny Sweeney), Dan Walker (Ann Wilson, Heart, John Fullbright), Grant Tracy (Jason Boland & The Stragglers), Kullen Fox (Charley Crockett), Chris Jones and Isaac Stalling (Chris Jones and the Flycatchers), Chanda Graham, Myra Beasley and Ken Pomeroy—an up-and-comer from Norman.

Byron Berline played on the album, too.

"All-stars, every last one," Nix said, not bothering to hide a smile. "Some folks are blessed, and I count myself as one of them. I could get into Byron being a hero of mine and Ian being one of my favorite musicians ever, but that would fill tape, paper and a whole lot of time."

Throughout the time Nix spent talking about his album, he never spoke of Turnpike in the past tense. He simply talked of his current project with the same joy and optimism any artist would of their debut.

But being the first, was he prepared to test the waters his predecessors—from those first two Red Dirt mushroom clouds—had to navigate? To put it another way, what if, out of every five questions someone asked about Kyle Nix, four were about Turnpike?

"All I can say is thank you," he said. "Who wouldn't want to be asked about it?"

"I snagged some world class players for this record, including my fellow Turnpike Troubadours. They all volunteered their time. I probably wouldn't have set out on the maiden voyage without them. My boys!"

• • •

The bow on Turnpike, at least for now, can still be whatever bow that people want to tie in their minds. Jim Wilhelm's Red Dirt mushroom clouds are real, and Turnpike's is still towering—and would be no matter what the future holds.

With live music shut down as of this writing, it's fine to kick the idea of an end to the band's hiatus even further down the line anyway. You are still invited to read all of this and simply appreciate the story of a band that made Oklahoma stompin' roots really, really cool for the rest of the world.

And, as I look around the room, I see everybody is ignoring that and tying a different bow.

To that point, this is the bottom line: Turnpike will be back. The timing and the form of that return, however, will be on their terms, and that applies to the entirety of the band and not just Felker.

With that said, it's hard to listen to him now and not at least acknowledge that music is on his mind, in the best way possible. When he talks about Turnpike, there's reflection, of course, but there's also a nod to the pull of the stage, the song and the music. Artists do not stop being artists when they get away from their art, and book chapters can always be rewritten.

"What we did is pretty much exactly what I wanted from the start," Felker said. "To be able to get out there, play all over the U.S., improve as musicians and writers, and then keep on chasing after it."

— — —

- 21 -

In the Thick of It: Medicine Stone 2018

Editor's note: *I don't really know how to tell you this, but just about everything in this chapter is dated. The Turnpike Troubadours went on hiatus in May 2019. In December of the same year, Turnpike and Jason Boland split with their management team, Cory McDaniel Entertainment (CME), with the breakup including a lawsuit pitting the bands and Medicine Stone LLC.—which they own—against CME, which aside from managing the bands was also hired by the bands to produce the Medicine Stone music festival. Medicine Stone was, obviously, caught in the middle. Throw the coronavirus pandemic on top, and nobody knows when or if there will ever be another Medicine Stone. I am making the choice to leave this chapter, mostly untouched unless noted, as I wrote it in September 2018. Consider it my own tribute to the experience of one of the most quintessential Red Dirt festivals ever put on.*

● ● ●

THE FIRST THING you notice about Medicine Stone is its commitment.

From noon until 2 a.m., for three days every September, you are surrounded by music and offered the chance to float the Illinois River—Oklahoma's Illinois River runs a few feet deep as it cuts through the northeast quadrant of the state and is the closest thing Oklahoma has to a rafting mecca. Man-made lakes and their beaches, swimming and skiing dot the state map like freckles, but floating the Illinois is understood from Ozarks to Panhandle as the holy grail of Oklahoma watersports.

Medicine Stone exists to put the music in your face, and the festival site was chosen to put the river in your face. The Gravel Bar, a few steps off Highway 10 northeast of Tahlequah, with its Stillwater Strip vibe and small stage with music to match, serves as the entry point to the Diamondhead Resort. Stroll past rows and rows of tents, trailers, RVs, keg stands and charcoal grills and you get to the main grounds. A flat, Oklahoma expanse lined with street food stands on one side and vendors selling Red Dirt trinkets and B-12 injections on the other gives way to the main stage: a concrete slab with a pre-fab roof that, in September, faces directly into Oklahoma's setting sun until 8 p.m.

Walk another 30 yards past that stage, and you'll hit the last covey of pup tents. Walk another one yard past that, and you'll step in the Illinois River.

There's one other area, just left of the main stage: a tented, picnic table–lined area fronted by a stage that's clearly bigger than the Gravel Bar's but dwarfed by the main slab. This one is called Mary Ellen's Greenhouse.

About that name: It's a reference to the Jason Boland & The Stragglers song of the same name, from the *Rancho Alto* album, and the refrain line "There's a lot of love in Mary Ellen's Greenhouse."

Every landmark, stage, road or area at Medicine Stone that doesn't have a year-round name thanks to Diamondhead is either a reference to the Stragglers or the Turnpike Troubadours, the current bellwethers of Red Dirt who have cohosted this festival since 2013. Signs reading "Normal Street" and "Easton and Main" serve as landmarks across the hilly, tree-lined campground as it gives way to the concert yard.

My wife, Andrea, and I had flown into Dallas Thursday morning, tossed our belongings in a Tahlequah hotel and made it to the grounds by 3 p.m., a few hours before the main stage music was set to start but well after the Gravel Bar stage was up and running.

* * *

Day One

It was hot. It was humid.

Pro analysis: You're at an outdoor music festival in the middle of the Oklahoma sticks next to a river, and it's summer. Heat and humidity are what you sign up for.

But this year, the forecast called for a wild change the next two days, with the potential for flooding-level rains, so most of the backstage angst Cory McDaniel, manager (in 2018) of both Turnpike and the Stragglers, and his wife, Marci, the project manager for CME, revolved around contingency planning.

Meanwhile, an evening of music on the main stage began with Read Southall and Koe Wetzel, a pair of Texas-based acts who had taken that state by storm the preceding year, served as a warm-up to co-headliners Wade Bowen and Randy Rogers.

By the time Rogers' set ended at midnight, giving way to a set of roots rock from Micky and the Motorcars at Mary Ellen's Greenhouse and overlapping country set from the Vandoliers at the Gravel Bar, organizers could have been forgiven for thinking the first day alone gave the fans their three days' worth of money.

Bowen, who spent most of April and May of the year canceling shows, undergoing vocal rest and ultimately having vocal cord surgery, now spends his final pre-set minutes doing a series of voice exercises he may have to do the rest of his career.

"Man, I'm scratchy tonight."

Once he hit the stage, though, anxiety gave way to energy, and Bowen put on a high-energy show. He played 15 songs, opening with "You Had Me at My Best" and ending with "Saturday Night."

Rogers got in a full 90-minute set, starting with "This Time Around" and ending with "Kiss Me in the Dark," before stepping back out for "Trouble Knows My Name" for an encore.

The best compliment I could pay both of these sets is that my wife and I danced during both.

Thursday night is the only night of the three not headlined by either of the co-hosts, Boland or Turnpike, and both Bowen and Rogers embraced their roles. The front-of-stage grounds were full for Bowen and remained so for Rogers, and both artists looked willing to play another hour had schedules allowed.

Thursday was my first-ever Medicine Stone experience, and I spent the bulk of it holed up with Bowen and raiding his bus's liquor cabinet. The only clear mistake I made was a Solo cup of Fireball whiskey in between the Rogers set on the main stage and the Motorcars at Mary Ellen's Greenhouse a few minutes after midnight.

However, one mistake was enough, and I tapped out of the festival before the final sets ended.

The ride back to the hotel was in a shuttle van that looks like one you'd take to an airport. It seated around 15, counting the driver, and at 1 a.m. the first night, 14 of those were happy drunks. A woman in the passenger seat commandeered the driver's iPhone and deejayed the 15-minute ride with an assortment of Turnpike Troubadours songs that most of the shuttle sang along to as loudly as they would have at a concert itself.

• • •

Day Two

In the grand context of omens, Friday was off to an acceptable start. The forecast for more than a week had been for an Old Testament–level of rain on this day. A cold front was sucking a leftover tropical depression from the Pacific across Oklahoma. Eighteen straight hours of rain was in just about every forecast. So when I rolled out of the rack at the Tahlequah Econo Lodge at 9 a.m., the mere act of pulling back the window curtain was dramatic.

But I looked outside and saw dry ground.

Dry ground is good.

First of all, it's dry, and it is easier to have an all-day outdoor music festival when it's dry. And second of all, it would be much more difficult for the Illinois River to lay claim to Medicine Stone the longer it were to remain dry. This was the ideal beginning. The Departed's bus had stopped for a bit in the parking lot, so we hitched a ride. When my wife and I boarded at 10 a.m., armed with a change of clothes, ponchos and shoes we were willing to sacrifice, it was still dry.

Twenty minutes later, when we pulled into Medicine Stone, a steady rain started.

It's important to describe the rain accurately here: This wasn't a typical Oklahoma storm, where the sky turns the color of a glass of water used to clean off a black watercolor brush and you have to have one eye on shelter at all times. This was the type of rain that, had it simply stopped at any time, would have been history in an hour. You could go outside in it for, say, a quick walk across a parking lot and not get soaked.

But it just never stopped. The late comedian Mitch Hedberg had a throwaway joke about a turtleneck feeling like being choked to death by a really weak man, and that's an apt analogy for Friday's rain.

The original plan for the day was for a damn-near historic run of music: The greenhouse stage, the one under a tent just off the main stage, was to open at 1:30 with an acoustic song swap from Mike McClure, Cody Canada and Jason Boland, giving way immediately to a John Fullbright set before the main stage opened. Its itinerary was Jamie Lin Wilson (and an assembled band of Medicine Stone all-stars), Reckless Kelly, The Departed, The Toadies, and building to a Turnpike Troubadours crescendo. Finally, at 12:15 a.m., Charley Crockett was slated back in the tent. This is all to say nothing of the Gravel Bar schedule back by the entrance, which featured Dave Kay, Brandon Aguilar and the Dirty River Boys.

By 11 a.m., after an hour of rain, all that was in jeopardy.

"I sure hope we didn't drive all this way just to pick up a check," Canada lamented at one point. "I called Marci [McDaniel] last night and she said they were gonna try their best."

I had a full day of interviews scheduled for this book, so I spent most of the midday hours planning to make the most of that. The same, steady rain kept falling too. By the end of the day, two inches of rain had fallen on Tahlequah. We were lucky. Some nearby places passed six inches easily.

Around noon, Cory McDaniel showed up on The Departed's bus with the verdict: "We're moving everything to the tent. We'll move Turnpike's set to tomorrow before Boland. We'll let The Toadies decide what they want to do, but otherwise, all the set times are good."

Canada and Cody Braun from Reckless Kelly both proposed ending the night with a jam session if The Toadies canceled, but within an hour, they responded that they were playing. We had a plan.

At 1:30, the acoustic trio walked past the waterlogged main stage, where water would eventually make it around and through the prefab roof and cover the surface and into the tent. That stage was maybe 10 feet deep and 20 feet wide and gave way directly to the grassy crowd area with no buffer. Eventually, all the available tents on the grounds were set up next to the big tent to offer as much shelter as could be had.

Boland took his place at the stage left mic, McClure in the middle and Canada on the right. Under the tent were about 500 of the hardest-core Red Dirt fans you'll ever see. Most of them would still be in their same spots 12 hours later when Charley Crockett finished.

"You do the best you can in the moment," Boland declared, assessing both the absurdity and resiliency of the situation. Then, he kicked off "Pearl Snaps."

The hourlong set flew by, highlighted by a group of children in the front row making requests in between nearly every song. Boland paid tribute before playing Bob Childers' "Tennessee Whiskey": "One of our biggest mentors was Bob Childers, and it went from Bob to Mike to us, and we like to keep his music going."

McClure played "Used to Be," adding in a tag that referenced cowriter Tom Skinner directly, ending with a painfully beautiful refrain of "Don't you know I miss you."

By the final song, Canada's, the nagging chorus from the crowd demanded "Carney Man."

"Look. We're gonna play 'Carney Man' tonight. If we play that song twice today, everybody's gonna have to go home, and the Turnpike boys can't play tomorrow, because we'll have broken Medicine Stone.

"Alright, we'll play it twice."

The tent blasted an approval cheer back at him.

• • •

Trio set list: *"Pearl Snaps" (Boland), "Yesterday Road" (McClure), "Lonely Girl" (Canada), "Mary Ellen's Greenhouse" (Boland), "Fightin' For" (McClure), "Brooklyn Kid" (Canada), "Tennessee Whiskey" (Boland), "Used to Be" (McClure), "250,000 Things" (Canada), "Gallo del Cielo" (Boland), "Saints in the Twilight" (McClure), "In Oklahoma" (Canada), "If I Ever Get Back to Oklahoma" (Boland), "Never Could" (McClure), "Carney Man" (Canada).*

• • •

The reason artists have managers is because they're artists, and left to their own devices they cannot be wrangled. Nervous about this, I immediately escorted the trio to The Departed's bus, where we held a roundtable that will appear in the next chapter. McClure ended it by informing us all that Bryon White, currently in his band, plays "Carney Man" in past tense with minor chords, and I cannot stop thinking about it.

Back in the tent, John Fullbright was in his element. He's a headliner in his own right, but he absolutely knows how to work a cobbled-together crowd under a tent with a driving rain outside. Fullbright played 90 minutes while the crowd stomped and shuffled through the layer of grass, uncovering an increasingly prevalent layer of mud instead.

Jamie Lin Wilson was up next, the first of the main stage shows moved to the tent. Backed by a band that included Cody Braun (Reckless Kelly) and Eric Hansen (The Departed) and with a guest appearance from Canada, the first female artist on either concert stage in two days earned one of its loudest ovations.

"Cody Braun started setting up his fiddle with my band before we even talked about him playing with me," Wilson said. "He just said, 'Oh, Jamie's playing, I gotta go set up,' and I went, 'Are you playing with me?' And he goes, 'Yeah, is that cool?'

"Uh, *yeah!* That's cool."

Between sets, I caught Willy Braun in his back lounge for an interview where we talked about one of his mentors, Pinto Bennett, and I was offered a drink that I can only describe as "it was a Willy Braun drink." A Solo cup full of Crown with a dash of Coke on top, I guess for depth. This is the biggest reason I did not get a comprehensive set list down from Jamie Lin's show.

"Today is a perfect example for this whole scene, here in Tahlequah," Willy Braun said. "Because it's pouring rain. We're all moved over to the cheeseburger tent—that's what we're calling it, by the way, the cheeseburger tent. There's no cheeseburgers, but whatever.

"But Cody's gonna get up and jam with us for the last part of our set. And if anybody needs to use our gear, they're more than welcome. I know if we need to use somebody else's gear, they'd probably let us. Our crew's gonna help their crew out. Everybody will be just kind of making sure that the show goes on. There's nobody here who's not gonna go play. Nobody's gonna go, 'No, we're a main stage act.' We're all here to make sure that the show goes on, and that's not something that I know happens in every scene, but it definitely does in this scene."

When Reckless hit the tent stage at 6 p.m., Medicine Stone was Oklahoma Woodstock. The grass was gone, and the mud was deep enough that your feet would slide with every step and the footprints left behind would fill with water. The stage stayed dry, though, and that was all Reckless needed. A 70-minute set covered most of their crowd-pleasers, interrupted only by Canada delivering a round of tequilas to the stage.

Willy Braun demanded Canada stick around, and he regaled the tent with the story of Cross Canadian Ragweed making "Crazy Eddie's Last Hurrah" famous and demanding "We're gonna do the Ragweed version up here, OK?" before having Canada lead it.

"Crazy Eddie" is my favorite song to shout like a maniac at the top of my lungs, so that's what I did. There's just something so…liberating…about "And I shot him full of holes from his nose to his knees, then I polished off my little sweet pea," even if it's more sinister in 2018 when you think about it too long.

Canada stayed on stage for a pair of Tom Petty covers before Reckless ended by itself with "Purple Rain," and the mud-covered tent patrons sang it right back to him.

. . .

Reckless Kelly set list: *"Everybody Went Low" (John Hiatt cover), "How Can You Love Him," "Radio," "Good Luck & True Love," "Nobody's Girl," "Vancouver," "1952 Vincent Black Lightning," "Seven Nights in Eire," "Ragged as the Road," "Moment in the Sun," "Crazy Eddie's Last Hurrah" (with Cody Canada), "Saving Grace" (Tom Petty cover with Cody Canada), "Listen to Her Heart" (Tom Petty cover with Cody Canada), "Purple Rain" (Prince cover).*

. . .

Backstage, Canada gathered his band for a prayer circle that also included Jamie Lin Wilson and her infant son, born 33 days prior, who got a special mention for being in his first such circle—one of the more poignant moments of the entire weekend. Just before taking the stage, Canada swapped out a soaking wet shirt for a Jamie Lin Wilson shirt.

The Departed is a bar band all the way, and as such, the tent was the ideal setting for its 75-minute set. Canada opened with "Mexican Sky," an old Medicine Show cover and one of most underrated songs of the entire Ragweed era.

With Canada backed by Hansen and Jeremy Plato, the set was very tight and very direct. Having finally found the right mix of old Ragweed songs and new Departed music, Canada cut a commanding figure. A good way to tell where he is, personally, is his stage presence, and at Medicine Stone, he stood out even among the Red Dirt giants that powered the weekend.

Canada ripped through "Alabama," earning the day's loudest single moment when he demanded a "Sweet Home Alabama" callback in the final verse, before yielding the floor to Plato, who in turn brought up Jamie Lin Wilson for a duet cover of the old Johnny Paycheck song "It Won't Be Long." Canada also invited Cody Braun back on stage for fiddle accompaniment on a pair of songs, then Jason Boland up to lead a rendition of "Proud Souls," before picking up his harmonica. It was the "Boys From Oklahoma" signal the crowd wanted, and they sloshed and kicked their way through yet another saga of improper joint-rolling.

Backstage, we all had to vacate so The Toadies could load in, costing us views of half of the set. We did notice, however, that the mud had gotten so bad that event staff had taken to shaking out hay bales over the ground to give the crews half a chance to get in and out.

We all made it back, though, for The Departed's final song, and a "by applause" offer from Canada:

"You have a choice with your last song. It's either Neil Young or Pearl Jam."

They ended by tearing through the latter's "Not for You."

• • •

Departed set list: *"Mexican Sky" (Medicine Show cover), "Hammer Down," "Lipstick," "Dimebag," "Satellites and Meteors" (with Jamie Lin Wilson), "It Won't Be Long" (Johnny Paycheck cover with Jamie Lin Wilson), "Constantly," "Alabama," "11 Months and 29 Days" (Johnny Paycheck cover), "Proud Souls" (Jason Boland & The Stragglers cover with Jason Boland), "Boys From Oklahoma" (Gene Collier cover), "Number," "Not for You" (Pearl Jam cover).*

• • •

The Toadies put on an incredible show. I was in and out, but mostly in. What I remember most was that Cody Braun, Willy Braun and Cody Canada all set up shop beside the stage and cheered and howled for every song.

Charley Crockett's set was a blur. I mostly remember that the mud had soaked through the hay that was supposed to protect everyone from the mud, and it felt like walking through a swamp backstage. I do recall that most of the tent stayed around for that final set, too, which was a tribute to Crockett's music on this day. The shuttle ride back was less "fun drunk" like the previous night and more "angry drunk" as the rain-soaked passengers just wanted to dry out.

But blur or not, Crockett can flat-out sing and flat-out perform. He plays with the charisma one would have if he were raised a descendent of Davy Crockett, found his footing in music and in life by playing the New York City subways and roaming the streets of Paris alone before settling back in Texas mixing blues range with Americana twang. In other words, the same hard-core fans who showed up at noon ready to brave the weather were still there right up to the end of Crockett's show.

Around 2 a.m., the rain stopped.

• • •

Day Three

I stepped off the shuttle on day three just as Randy Crouch was finishing his set at the Gravel Bar, the roadside dive atop the hill leading into the campgrounds. My earliest memory of Randy is of him pulling an all-nighter during a jam session at the Yellow House and refusing to rest or go home, instead leading a finale of "Big Shot Rich Man" several hours after the sun came up. That was January 2001, and he's been an icon in my mind since.

So missing his set was a bummer, but it warmed my heart to see the crowd around him wanting autographs. Randy has trouble walking these days, but not making music.

The other heartwarming part of Saturday was how it was not raining and how it was impossible to notice just now much it was not raining. You went outside? Not raining. You walked from point A to point B? Not raining.

In fact, it was not raining so much, the entire last day of the festival was moved to the main stage. The tent grounds had been so wrecked the day before that shows there were impossible anyway, and a side effect of keeping fans away from the main stage during the rain meant there was not a ton of mud on festival grounds.

A combination of the rain wrecking the schedule, my own laziness and/or desire to see shows and artists being needed elsewhere had backlogged my book-writing plans, so I spent most of the last day running between interviews and shows. I caught Mike McClure, Brad Rice of The Stragglers, Jason Boland himself, John Cooper of the Red Dirt Rangers and most of the Turnpike Troubadours for interviews.

In and around it, I caught an absolutely delightful last day of shows, starting with the Mike McClure Band at 1:30. I leaned into the previous night's hangover and started drinking when he started playing. This led to me trying to shout "break in the wind!!" at him when he played "Break in the Storm." It's funny. Don't @ me.

McClure often kind of glides through his shows in a haze, and today was no different, but in a good way. He took his hour seriously and for the second day in a row honored Tom Skinner with a beautiful tag onto the end of "Used to Be." The early-arriving crowd filled in well, better than Thursday's early arrivers at least. By the end of his set he had several hundred fans taking in another Skinner song, "Blind Man," as Cooper sat in.

Concurrently, word spread that Fullbright had returned for a second day and played guitar with Austin Meade up at the Gravel Bar. I ran up and caught the absolute last song of that set, and it was worth the hungover sprint.

The third day was also the biggest day of the festival for "Free Jonny Burke" shirts, which were ever-present all weekend. Burke is an incredible artist, from New Braunfels but a favorite in Tahlequah, but he missed this particular year's event doing time in a Texas prison. At a glance around the festival, he needed to make plans to return on the other side.

I did catch up with Cory McDaniel, [at the time] manager of both Turnpike and Boland, and, as noted earlier, one of the producers of Medicine Stone, along with his wife, Marci. Originally, my plan was to ask him how this event gets pulled off every year. I did, and he answered cordially:

"This is how it goes down: Turnpike gives us their wish list, and Boland gives us their wish list, of who they want to bring here. We go after all of them. Obviously sometimes your wish list is a one-hand-and-the-other thing, but that's the main thing is getting the lineup done.

"On some level, this is year-round. Allie [Sisoian] is my right hand, and my wife, Marci, same deal. Allie works on Medicine Stone, at some point, every day of the year. Marci handles a lot of the artist stuff after we've gotten it situated. And then all the girls are in there putting it together, running it by me, and we're all in it.

[Present-day note: Allie, now married to Todd Laningham of Wade Bowen's band, is an event-management specialist in New Braunfels, running Hey Function.]

"Marci and I will take time off. After this, we'll take a few months where we don't even mention Medicine Stone, probably until about November. And then I'll sit down with the guys and they'll tell me what they saw and we'll put together the next wish list.

"A lot of the artists have their own festivals too, like the Brauns, and it's not a must-play sometimes. I talk to Cody [Braun] and he says, 'Man, we know. We're running Braun Brothers. It's impossible to have all the same acts every single year. We don't expect to play Medicine Stone every year.' That's how it goes. We're talking with Robert Earl [Keen], getting him here, and we're close. The event is established now and getting better reception from the agents and managers."

That was a good, all-encompassing overview, and interesting as hell given the demands on their time. But the events of the day before meant I had to ask Cory about how he handled it. So I did so, straightforwardly: *What did you have in your head as the worst-case scenario, given the rainy forecast for this week?*

"A flood."

OK, fair enough. But when it became obvious that yesterday was going to be a washout, what happened?

"Yesterday morning, I was hoping that it would be a day where we're on the river and everyone's dirty and funky anyway. I was hoping we'd have some heavy showers but then the sun would come out and dry it up. We had something similar to that the second year, where it rained quite heavily, but then it stopped. And I was kind of hoping for that.

"Aaron Lain, our production manager, who's also Turnpike's tour manager, has 30 guys out there who take a lot of time to put this together. So at about noon, we sat down and said, 'This is what it's gonna be all day long.' It just wouldn't have been fun and frankly it didn't leave us much choice. So, screw it, we'll move everything to Mary Ellen's and see what happens.

"Everybody was great, as far as the artists go. Not one person was even bummed."

There you have it. You want to know how the weirdest day in Medicine Stone history went down, you got it.

I missed enough of the Red Dirt Rangers' set for interviews with Rice and McClure to feel bad, but not enough that I didn't see half a dozen songs played with Randy Crouch sitting in on fiddle. Randy got around with a walker on Saturday, but his stage presence was not hampered.

Two more sets got completely missed for interviews. The highlight was getting the musical histories from individual members of Turnpike.

I absolutely did not, however, miss the last two sets on the main stage. Turnpike Troubadours first, Jason Boland second.

Saturday was September 22 and would be Turnpike's first show since a string of cancellations that started on August 17, ultimately involving both medical emergencies and tabloids chasing lead singer Evan Felker around. Felker pulled up in his pickup about two hours before his set and certainly looked—from a distance—to be in good spirits.

It's weird to me that anyone from this scene has been able to dabble in mainstream while also dodging tabloids, and it's a testament to how fun Turnpike is as a band that they had broken through to that level.

Turnpike is a stompin' jam band, with every beat of the kick drum requiring a clap or other acknowledgement, but Felker's lyrics are often very personal—not always in a bad way, quite often in a fun-as-hell way, but it makes it easy for fans to connect with him.

My entire theory about their ascent in Red Dirt revolves around that principle: Turnpike makes great music, no doubt, but they make *relatable* music even moreso.

Back to the show itself. Turnpike drew the largest crowd of any single set the entire weekend. Honestly they just looked happy to be playing again after a month off. I'm sure as an artist you notice your music more after a long break anyway. They opened with "The Housefire," and it was four songs in before Felker acknowledged the upside-down festival schedule with, "Thanks to Jason Boland for letting us open up for him."

Normally, Turnpike would headline on Friday and Boland on Saturday, or vice versa. This marked the first time in event history that both hosts shared a night.

A few songs later, in between "7 & 7" and "Gin, Smoke, Lies," Felker flashed some self-deprecating humor at the crowd, too.

"After that rainstorm yesterday, I was starting to think we would never play another show."

Snapping into present-day to say that statement is a lot less funny now. At the time, I laughed. The set closed with three songs that are as good as any three songs in live music: Bass player R.C. Edwards led "Drunk, High and Loud" before Felker picked up his harmonica and said, "Oh I forgot about this song" and launched into "Long, Hot Summer Day"—for my money the best set-closer in all the land.

Turnpike came back up for a two-song encore. Felker hugged his bandmates as he left the stage for the last time.

Yes, there were indeed fans who had only come to the festival for them, but almost the entire crowd waited out an extra-long changeover before Jason Boland & The Stragglers closed out the main stage.

● ● ●

Turnpike Troubadours set list: *"The Housefire," "A Tornado Warning," "Winding Stair Mountain Blues," "Every Girl," "7 & 7," "Gin, Smoke, Lies," "Morgan Street," "Shreveport," "Pay No Rent," "Whole Damn Town," "Kansas City Southern," "Before the Devil Knows We're Dead," "Bossier City," "Diamonds & Gasoline," "Drunk, High and Loud," "Long Hot Summer Days" (John Hartford cover). Encore: "Good Lord Lorrie," "The Bird Hunters."*

● ● ●

Between sets, I caught up one last time with what few friends were left backstage, and the drag of the festival—really, it was the drag of constantly being switched "on" to write this book while wanting to be switched "off" and gawking at music makers—hit me.

I was spent all day, and by the end of Turnpike's set, my plan of drinking whiskey and Coke to stay awake was absolutely backfiring, so it was only through sheer force of will that I made it through Boland's show—the longest of any of the festival, clocking in at nearly two hours long.

Jason Boland & The Stragglers are one of the bands I've seen the most in my life, and they know two things: how to have fun and how to keep a crowd moving. Kicking off just before 10:30, Boland set the tone right from the get-go with an absolutely rocking version of "Down Here in the Hole," off of his *Rancho Alto* album, that snapped me back into a concert trance.

Founding member of the Stragglers Roger Ray sat in on steel guitar for the entire show, and I'm sure his presence helped, but either way, their performance was an instant classic. They only played one song off of their 2018 album, *Hard Times Are Relative*, and it was the two-stepping "I Don't Deserve You."

Hell, most of the set was two-stepping or waltzing. I finally propped up my wife long enough for a few swing dances near the end. Boland closed his set with the wink-wink political jab "Fuck, Fight and Rodeo" and the hauntingly relatable tornado story, "Blowing Through the Hills."

And then, he came back.

They all came back. The Stragglers and at least one of the Troubadours, Kyle Nix, with his fiddle. The encore lasted five songs, with Boland introducing "Tulsa Time" eloquently: "This is the part where we see how many people are just standing around out there. Let's go to Cain's right now, what do you say?"

"Tulsa Time" gave way to "Boys From Oklahoma," the second time in two days the festival got that one, and the crowd once again went through the trouble of the improv hand motions.

Finally, at 12:06 a.m., Boland announced, "We're gonna leave you with some Randy Crouch" and the bass guitar kicked off "Big Shot Rich Man." "Big Shot" is a call-response number and the perfect tune on which to end a three-day festival.

• • •

The Stragglers set list: *"Down Here in the Hole," "When I'm Stoned," "I Don't Deserve You," "Comal County Blue," "Dark and Dirty Mile," "Fat and Merry," "Pushing Luck," "I Guess It's Alright to Be an Asshole," "Truckstop Diaries," "Proud Souls," "Mexico or Crazy," "Mary Ellen's Greenhouse," "Electric Bill," "Shot Full of Holes," "Tennessee Whiskey" (Bob Childers cover), "Telephone Romeo," "Lucky I Guess," "Gallo del Cielo" (Tom Russell cover), "Fuck, Fight and Rodeo," "Blowing Through the Hills." Encore: "Somewhere Down in Texas," "Pearl Snaps," "Tulsa Time" (Danny Flowers cover), "Boys From Oklahoma" (Gene Collier cover), "Big Shot Rich Man" (Randy Crouch cover).*

• • •

The stage gave way to the Greenhouse tent and Gravel Bar, but we beelined for the hotel shuttle.

This time, nobody in the van talked at all.

— — —

- 22 -

Red Dirt Roundtable: McClure, Canada, Boland

THERE WILL BE no wind-up, long-story introduction or quirky anecdote here. What you need to know is that on the middle day of Medicine Stone 2018—the day it rained so much it washed out the main stage shows and forced them to a tented side stage, very much a Red Dirt Woodstock event—Mike McClure, Cody Canada and Jason Boland opened the day with a song swap under the tent. Afterward, they sat for a roundtable discussion of Red Dirt history, their paths into the scene and what it's like to carry the torch for Red Dirt.

What follows is that session in question-and-answer format, as it happened, edited only for clarity and only when absolutely necessary.

Mike McClure, Cody Canada and Jason Boland, let's do this.

What was your introduction to Red Dirt?

McClure: Mine was probably about 1993. We bought a PA from Daddy O's Music, and we were practicing at Kelley [Green, Great Divide member]'s house over on Stanley Street by the hospital. We didn't know how to hook any of it up, so Brad James came over and hooked it up. When he was checking it out, he played "Used to Be" by Tom Skinner and "Restless Spirits" by Bob Childers. And I'd never heard any of those songs, and I asked him, "Whose songs are those?" and he replied, "That's Red Dirt."

That's really the first time I had heard it called that. That put it on my radar, and then I wanted to find out more. Brad said, "Ah, you need to go out to The Farm." And I'd never been there at that time. Then one day, I came home—Kelley and I lived together—and Bob Childers was sitting on my porch. Bob had long hair and I didn't know him, and I was going, "Who is this guy?" and Bob said, "I'm a songwriter," and he invited me out to The Farm. So I went out and just kind of started hanging out over there. I met Scott Evans and the different people who hung out there. The Red Dirt Rangers were usually around if they didn't live there.

The Farm was the place—the hub for musicians. I'd never been around a place like that, where there was so much sharing. I played kind of butt rock in the '80s years, where everyone was just an asshole to each other, trying to step over people to get somewhere. That was kind of the way, so seeing these guys helping each other stuck with me. That was my introduction to it.

Canada: My introduction to it was Mike. I was 15 or 16, living in Yukon, and I opened up for Toby Keith. And I met Dave Dodson, who I saw last week, by the way. He's still kicking ass. He gave me the "What are you doing?" and I said, "Man, I don't know what I'm doing." He said he could introduce me to a band, and he introduced me to Mike and the guys. Really, that's where it started for me.

I came up there and auditioned for The Great Divide, and I played with them for a couple of months. But it didn't work out with me.

McClure: I voted yes, by the way.

Canada: Yes, you did. I was working at a western store in Oklahoma City called Tener's when I got the call from Mike: "I voted you in, but the other guys voted you out." So I said, "Well, I'm gonna start a band then." So we started Ragweed. Mike was there for the first gig, and then I started going up and hanging out in Stillwater.

I don't remember where we were, but we were just hanging out somewhere behind The Strip. Tom Skinner was there and he sang "Rosalie." Daddy O [Mike Shannon] sang "Long Way to Nowhere" and Scott Evans sang "Steel Heart." And I thought, *Shit. What did I get myself into?*

McClure: That's the thing with The Farm. I remember playing my first songs there and just going, "Wow, these are really shitty." It was kind of the first place you had to go measure your stuff up.

Boland: I had several of the same experiences. One of them was hearing "Used to Be" on the radio—a local station—and wondering who that was singing with [The Great Divide], and it was Jimmy LaFave.

The first time I remember seeing Red Dirt was on the cover of the Red Dirt Rangers' album, *Red Dirt* [1993 release]. I remember thinking that they call it this, and everyone's just trying to put a label on any little, closed-off thing that wasn't mainstream back then. People called it alt-country and no depression music. I think everybody saw themselves as being something alternative at that time.

And a road trip to see The Great Divide was a big first for me. I think it was Incahoots. It was right when they really started to slay it, and I thought, *Who are these guys? How big could somebody be from Oklahoma that ain't on TV? I ain't heard of 'em, and most of these people are probably just here dancing anyway.*

The lights went down, and the dance floor was a big track. The whole track just stopped, and everybody just turned and faced the stage. They came out and played "Copperhead Road" or something like that, and it was just one of those moments.

Country music had taken such a dive, and it's gotten so bad like the frog in boiling water. And, we were already noticing that country was throwing out the baby with the bathwater. It was "OK, the jokes are funny and dirt roads are funny and shit, but this is folk music." "Rainbow Stew" is a protest song. They don't all have to be heavy, it's just that it became so uninteresting.

So I had heard Mike, and then I heard Cody over at the Wormy Dog. He and I started hanging out and picking tunes together. He had already been busted under-age and sent down to the Underdog [the Wormy Dog's 18-and-over venue]. I started playing with him, and then I got invited out there to The Farm one night.

And that was always everybody's pivotal moment—whenever they saw not just the place, but the people. You walk out there, and I was used to walking up to camp-fires where bros would go "sup?" or something and it's awkward. So I walked up and I could see silhouettes of people around the campfire, and one of the guys on the lease stepped away from the fire, and he said, "Welcome!"

And then you sit down, and someone plays "Restless Spirits," and I go, "Did you write that?" and they go, "No, he did," and he'd point to Bob Childers sitting next to him. "I wrote this song, this is 'Steel Heart.'"

Canada: That was what always blew my mind, that they would sing each other's songs to each other.

Boland: Yeah. And you would think, *Wow, cool version!* You always wanted Scott Evans to do your songs.

Canada: I remember the first time I saw Tom sing "Restless Spirits" to Bob. That's one of my first memories. It was just really cool. For somebody to sit through it, that took a lot.

And all of you have ties to the Wormy Dog.
Boland: The way I heard it was, Chuck Thomson [Wormy Dog founder] and his friend weren't invited back to some of their old hangouts. So they just thought, *OK, we'll open our own place where we can throw beer bottles on the floor then.*

McClure: That place was pretty important to I think all of us. I was in there all the time, especially on Monday nights when no one was in there. So I asked Chuck, "Let me play acoustic" and started building up a Monday night crowd. That's the first time I had done that.

Eventually Cody came and played with me, and he got Tuesday nights.

Canada: Yeah, I got busted. I went up there and hung out with my buddy Jim Bob Carson. We were drinking in his front yard and I got busted. It was my 20th birthday, and I said, "Man, don't bust me on my birthday," and they didn't then, but the next Monday night, bam! Busted.

It was the old MIP. They took me to jail and took my mug shot, and it was $75 to get out. And Shannon [O'Neal, now Canada's wife] was the bartender, and we weren't even talking yet. And she came down and bailed me out, and I remember going right back and playing. There were five people left, but I played.

OK, I want to ask about a couple of people whose names come up again and again. They're icons now, but there's more nuance to them. Let's start with Bob Childers. What is his legacy?
McClure: For me, Bob is very similar to Tom. They said, "I'm a songwriter," and then they built their life around that instead of saying, "Well, I'll try this and see if

it works." It's just who they were. Those were the first real songwriters that I met. So for me, just seeing them, I wanted to do that. It was my first up-close brush with someone who wrote songs. I had written a few, but I never thought of it as an occupation. They opened my eyes.

Canada: I was so dumb. I thought that you either wrote songs or sang them. I was pretty young, but I thought that you wrote a song, and then you sold it to somebody. Mike, Bob and Tom were the first three that I really met up there who did both.

Bob was like the overseer. He was the godfather. He was the one who was like, "This guy's OK, let him through the door, he's fine."

I remember his stack of songs, too. It was so impressive. I could count my songs on one hand, and he had, like, a Red Dirt bible.

Boland: Bob's big thing to me was just—you're dealing with insecurities and fear when you're writing songs. I ended up there going to school, and I was getting out of that because I was so disillusioned with what I was doing there. I was sick of it, and then there's Bob, who's saying "Woka Hey." It was "don't be afraid, just do what you feel like doing."

Bob was cool enough to really let people in and really take the time to encourage and inspire you. He was so good at including people.

McClure: I remember rolling up, I was riding my bicycle up to The Farm one day. And I saw smoke billowing up. Bob lived in a little travel trailer out behind the Gypsy Cafe [a converted garage where songwriters gathered], and it had caught on fire. It just burned all his shit to the ground. He was there raking the ashes.

I rolled up and went, "Bob, what happened?" and he goes, "Oh, God said it's time to move."

That was pretty Zen-ish.

He and Skinner are thought of as the pillars here.
Boland: The other pillar for me was [Randy] Crouch. There was Bob, Tom and Crouch. They all just had that gravity.

Tom had that inspiring inclusivity. Tom was the first person to get me on stage other than Cody.

McClure: Tom was more "put other people before yourself" than anybody, almost to a fault sometimes.

Boland: Whatever, we do a lot of things to financial fault in this scene. People just look at it like the Okies fix-it-with-duct-tape-rather-than-buy-a-new-one mentality.

McClure: I saw Tom make an entire road case out of cardboard and duct tape.

Boland: I have a funny story about Crouch. We were up at Winfield [Kansas], and I popped out a bridge pin. And Crouch said, "You can make one out of pecan." And I thought, *God, hippie. You're not gonna stick a pecan in there.* Because I know things. I'm a kid.

And later on, I bump into him, and he says, "I found you a piece!" and it was this perfect piece of pecan wood, like a twig. And he had whittled it down to the tip. And he stuck it in there, and that was my bridge pin until I got home from Winfield.

McClure: That's just them, you know? Take what you got and do something with it. That's just an Okie thing.

Canada: It was just the first community of people where I felt accepted. I remember going to a party in Yukon and playing my guitar and the hottest girl at the party going, "Will you stop playing that fucking guitar?" and that was that. So I got to Stillwater, and people were interested in me playing and what I had to say. I didn't know shit about writing songs, but that didn't matter.

So how important was collaboration? I'm thinking specifically of *The Red Dirt Sampler* and *Dirt and Spirit*, but really I am asking it broadly.

McClure: A guy named Bob Cline put together the *Red Dirt Sampler*, and we recorded it over at Jeff Parker's house. Bob had a cut on there. Tom did too, Red Dirt Rangers, Monica Taylor, a lot of people, and I was asked to contribute, so I put "Wildflower" on there. Mitch Cason put "Song for L" on there.

The harmony parts of that album are just legendary. That was just one of the first groupings of the music around there that everyone was a part of.

Then, for *Dirt and Spirit*, I got a loan. I had asked Skinner where he recorded some acoustic stuff. He said there was a guy named Walt Bowers in Broken Arrow—a great keyboard player.

[Side note] I remember when he lost his Leslie [a Hammond keyboard] out of the back of a trailer, leaving one of our gigs. He had one of those pickup trucks where they take the bed and make it into a shitty trailer. He was pulling that, and it flew out on the highway and splintered it!

Boland: Red Dirt! Red Dirt! When someone asks, "What's Red Dirt?" it's that story.

Because it's a Hammond. What's a Hammond even doing here? It's kind of jazzy, kind of bluesy. I don't know, man, it was a gig. "What did you haul it in?" An old truck bed trailer. "What happened?" Uh, it kind of flew out!

McClure: Yeah it splintered, and he found all the pieces and glued it back together.

Boland: And there's your Red Dirt ending: *And it's glued back together, and it still plays to this day. Some say it's haunted by the spirits of the highway.*

Canada: One of my favorites was when Boland, Stoney [LaRue] and I were loitering at The Farm. Coop [John Cooper of the Red Dirt Rangers] was always on our side.

He was talking to Bob about us and he said, "The kids are alright."

And that was the first time I felt like, *OK, we're here now.*

McClure: Tom used to make these cassettes on those old four-tracks at his house. And he recorded one of my songs called "Dresser Drawer" one time. I didn't know he did it, but I heard it on one of those tapes, and that was a high-water mark.

Canada: Tom called me up to play a Steve Earle song at The Farm. I swear I've never been that nervous. I remember being kind of that nervous at the Bluebird, but never close to that.

Boland: In front of Robert Earl Keen, that was one for me. Tom got me up and I did "Devil Pays in Gold," and I don't even know if I got through it.

Connections back then were real because they just happened. You couldn't invent them or go viral.

There's a picture, and I still see it. There's a little video on YouTube, and it's a collage of a bunch of pictures of Bob, with Jimmy LaFave doing "Restless Spirits." There's a picture of him in his trailer.

John Cooper had seen in the *Oklahoma Gazette* an ad that said, "Guitar player, bassist and front guy looking for a drummer. Influences include Robert Earl Keen, Todd Snider and Bob Childers," and he had blown it up and given it to Bob to put on the wall.

And later on in life, we're hanging out with him and we looked up and said, "That's our ad!" You could still see it in that video.

I look at it and think, *Those connections were real.* They weren't anything forced or faked.

And the shitholes we thought we were playing turned out to be places you could not have known how lucky you were. You go back to the Wormy Dog, The Golden Light, George's, Adiar's, all those dumps—that was where there was all the crazy energy. That was where it was really happening.

But it was bizarre because you'd still look at watching things like grunge or post-punk and think, *Boy, that's awesome. If only we could do something like that!*

Canada: And not knowing that we were in it.

Boland: Meanwhile, there's people hanging upside-down in front of you from rafters, chugging beer in the middle of your set or slam-dancing onto your stage.

I want to end on your present-day take on Red Dirt. We're here at Medicine Stone. It's the highlight of the calendar [editor's note: this was 2018]. It has moved around and now it's one of the biggest events in two states. What are the responsibilities the artists here and in this scene now have to the legacy?

McClure: Our band got into a position where we could help another band, be it Ragweed or Jason. So we could have them come play and open up. We all did that for each other and spread the word about each other.

Canada: It's the old pay-it-forward thing.

Boland: You let me on stage way before it would have ever been expected, man. I remember a couple of times you'd call me up and I was like, "Holy shit, you don't even know me."

One of the funniest things you learned in life, those people when you were a little kid and someone would say, "I used to know this guy who could hear a song three times and play it." And now you think back on it and go, "Was he real slow? What was his problem?"

It was the way we learned to play. It's magic. It's high magic, until you learn a few things. But the way we did it was just getting thrown into it.

You'd go "I do not know this song," and someone would just say, "Well, you know, try not to hit bad notes. Play all the good ones you know and lay back on the ones you don't."

Canada: That's how I learned to play lead.

When I moved down to New Braunfels, we were picking up steam. Boland was picking up steam. So was Stoney. There was nobody left in Stillwater. So we moved down to New Braunfels. And I get there, and it's Ryan Bingham, Doug Moreland and Dub Miller. They were all living in trailers behind River Road Ice House. But it was exactly the same thing as The Farm. It was all these people sitting around singing each other's songs to each other. And I went, "Holy shit, this is exactly what I just left."

Boland: It's weird how there were all these places that it springs from. Look at Still-water now. There's not all these bands playing here this week that claim just Stillwa-ter as their heritage, sure. But Turnpike Troubadours claim a connection to it, as does Read Southall.

It has a lineage, and that will always continue.

But on the other hand, these are just lines that someone drew in the sand. We always toured from Nebraska to Corpus and Louisiana and Arkansas. It was Tornado Alley.

Canada: I still remember McClure coming back from Put-in-Bay.

Boland: Ohio! With "Nymphomaniac" and "Asshole"!

Canada (to McClure): "Nymphomaniac" was your fault, by the way. You brought back "Nymphomaniac."

Boland: Yeah. And everybody learned it, and everybody did it. But Chris McCoy was trying out his recording gear one night, and he recorded me doing it. And he gave it to some friends, and they went and put it on Napster.

Canada: And now you break everybody's heart every night by not doing it.

Boland: Every night. We never did anything with it. Pat Daley wrote it! I don't think people get it, though. They just go, "I don't know what you're doing with this Pat Daley thing. I don't know what this is, but I do know you need to do that song that's in my five-CD changer."

I stopped doing that in '04 or '05. It's now been more than double the time that I played it and I still get it.

McClure: I do think we all kind of do that now, though. We're artists.

Boland: Yeah, but there's a line you can draw. I'm a lot less uptight now.

Canada: Me too. My feeling on it now is, if you ask for it 10 times and you're drunk as shit, then you're not gonna hear it. But my thing is, if it makes them happy, it's just four minutes. It might be dumb as shit to me. I think "Carney Man" is the dumbest thing ever...

McClure ("Carney Man" cowriter): Hey!

Canada: Sorry, man, I didn't mean to Red Dirt do you like that.

But if "Carney Man" makes people happy, I'll do it now.

— — —

- 23 -

The Loose Ends

A THOROUGH STORY is not an exhaustive one.

The reasons vary. Sometimes, I made contact and couldn't set up an interview. Sometimes, I reached out and never heard back. Sometimes, an artist just flat-out was not interested in this project. And sometimes, I did not reach out at all. Regardless, there are hundreds, minimum, of artists whose own lives add depth, perspective and context to the history and the future of Red Dirt. These are people with stories to tell, too.

I want to highlight a few now who were on my original list of must-have artists for this book and never got the time with me or the space in these pages I thought they deserved. If there is ever a sequel, they are first up.

Gene Collier: There are Red Dirt staples, and then there is "Boys From Oklahoma."

No single song has gone farther from its Red Dirt campfire roots than Collier's simple two-four ode to marijuana. Even before Cross Canadian Ragweed cut the song for *Live and Loud at the Wormy Dog Saloon,* the song was in demand across Stillwater. The Great Divide, Tom Skinner, the Red Dirt Rangers, Jason Boland & The Stragglers and Stoney LaRue played it and dropped Collier's name at every turn.

"Just don't tell my mom I wrote it" was Collier's response to the song going mainstream, according to Cody Canada.

Collier was a part of the Stillwater scene when Bob Childers and Gene Williams were regulars, and today, he can still be found sitting in often with the Red Dirt Rangers, happy to play his scene-bending anthem and anything else that crosses his mind.

Randy Crouch: "I have known Randy for 30 years, and Randy has been playing with us off and on for 20 years," said John Cooper of the Red Dirt Rangers. "There's no one like Randy."

Since Crouch was a child and his grandfather, Daddy Mack, taught him how to fiddle, Crouch has been making music. Accomplished at the fiddle, piano, ukulele and guitar, Crouch is the most bluegrass of anyone in Red Dirt.

Old enough to have been an original at The Farm, Crouch played heavily with Childers when the two lived in Stillwater during the 1980s, and the two maintained a partnership that lasted until Childers' death in 2008.

Crouch's songwriting also made an impression on the generations of artists that came after him. Jason Boland & The Stragglers cut two Crouch songs, "Big Shot Rich Man" and "Mexican Holiday," while Stoney LaRue recorded "Hope You Make It to the Mountain."

Crouch refers to his music as "Oklahoma protest music" and maintains a heavy presence in Red Dirt, even as he lives in his self-constructed geodesic dome in Eastern Oklahoma. He played fiddle with the Stragglers in the mid-2000s, and it is nothing to see him sit in with John Fullbright or vice versa today.

"Randy Crouch doesn't play music. Randy Crouch *is* music," Cooper said. "It exudes from every pore in his skin. He eats, drinks and sleeps music. It's who he is more than anybody I have ever met."

Chuck Dunlap: Dunlap is another forefather who was no stranger to The Farm and who played with Childers, Jacobs, Skinner and their contemporaries.

Dunlap recorded and released a protest song about the Iraq War called "Patriot's Plea," imploring audiences to question the authority and motives of the government in the years following September 11, 2001, and to chase the money as it made its way through governments and halls of power.

He overhauled the song into "The People's Plea" for the launch of the Red Dirt Relief Fund in 2014, motivated by the lack of health care for independent musicians. Dunlap coordinated more than 50 Oklahoma artists to join as a backing choir for a video accompanying the song, and the Red Dirt Relief Fund went on to become a major charity supporting the state's musicians after disasters and tragedies and during the 2020 coronavirus pandemic.

John Moreland: By all rights, Moreland should be lauded, esteemed and held up as an Oklahoma music torchbearer. He should be on the cover of this book, his name and dedication to the state lending credence and sellability to anyone who spots it.

Moreland is based in Tulsa, is decidedly roots music and wears the state on his sleeve. Two of his albums, *Endless Oklahoma Sky* and *High on Tulsa Heat,* reference Oklahoma directly, and one of his best-known songs is "Hang Me in the Tulsa County Stars."

The hitch is, Red Dirt claiming John Moreland because his music extolls Eastern Oklahoma would be like Tulsa claiming Orion because it happens to be in the sky. Moreland may be closer to Woody Guthrie than any Red Dirt contemporary—his music is for everybody and his reach and influences extend so far beyond Red Dirt that it is unfair to the artist and the scene to label him as such.

Monica Taylor: "The Emmylou Harris of Red Dirt" is how Cody Canada describes Monica Taylor, and the comparison is spot-on.

For every event, landmark or watershed moment in Red Dirt history, there's a story of Taylor playing a part. She was a regular at The Farm, even living there in a tent for seven months in 1996. She has surely played The Blue Door enough to qualify for a bulk rate. And whenever Red Dirt needs harmony, it turns to Taylor. At Tom Skinner's memorial service, Taylor's rendition of Gram Parsons' "She" was as haunting as it was moving.

There are other artists left out of these pages, and the best that I can say in response is that this book is not a one-off chance. I do not plan on going anywhere, and I hope to keep telling Red Dirt's stories as long as I am physically capable.

• • •

Two More Legacies

Time having done its things and all, there are two more artists no longer a part of this mortal world whose stories are as rich and important to Red Dirt as anybody. The first man died just as this book was taking shape. As for the second, I learned of his passing as I was scouring social media hoping to reach out to him to secure an interview. Their legacies have, thankfully, been widely shared and will continue to be, but they need a few words here, too.

Steve Ripley: Ripley needed a chapter. Maybe he needed a whole book.

He was the first person to make use of "Red Dirt" to describe music when he called his independent record label "Red Dirt Records" in 1974.

While he didn't run in the same circles as the forefathers of Red Dirt, they viewed him as their pioneer. Ripley's band, Moses, is referred to by veterans of the scene as the first Red Dirt band.

His is a familiar story: Born in Idaho, raised in Glencoe, Oklahoma, went to school at Oklahoma State and eventually settled in Tulsa. Along the way, he fronted the Tractors, which saw mainstream country music success and an Arista Records deal in the early 1990s. He worked with Bob Dylan, Eric Clapton and J.J. Cale. He invented the Ripley Studio Guitar, famously used by Eddie Van Halen on "Top Jimmy."

Ripley also saved the Church Studio from ruin. In 1987, Ripley bought the former studio of Leon Russell, and landmark of boogie-rock scene the Tulsa Sound, and used it both as a home and as the creative hub of the Tractors. He sold it in 2006 to owners who brought it back to a full-time studio, and it landed on the National Register of Historic Places in 2017.

Ripley liked to describe himself as "too country for rock and too rock for country" throughout his career. It's also fitting to describe him as "too Tulsa for Red Dirt and too Red Dirt for the Tulsa Sound."

"Without a doubt, Steve Ripley is the most important person in the history of Red Dirt music," Cooper said. "And here is why: When I got here in 1976, he was already gone. But the people who were here—Childers, LaFave, Greg Jacobs, Chuck Dunlap—always talked about how great his band was. And then, we all watched his career as he went on to be Leon Russell's engineer for eight years, and then went on the road with Bob Dylan, and then started making guitars with Eddie Van Halen, and then had a band that sold four million records.

"For me, he was this mythological figure. He was the guy who *my* heroes would talk about in hushed tones."

Ripley died of cancer in January 2019.

"To me, his legacy is that we have the ability to do anything," said Cooper, whose Red Dirt Rangers recorded three albums with Ripley, including two at Church Studio. "Just because you're from Stillwater, Oklahoma, you have the ability to do anything, and the world is your palette."

Brandon Jenkins: There was no confusing or mincing descriptions of Brandon Jenkins.

He wore the nickname "Red Dirt legend" like a badge of honor, flaunting it to anyone who listened.

Jenkins, nephew of Grammy-winning bass player Gordon Shryock, was Red Dirt from his first note to his last. Born in Tulsa in 1969, he wrote and sang about being from Oklahoma and never apologized. "Refinery Blues," one of his best-known songs, is from his youth along the Arkansas River in Sand Springs, Oklahoma, where oil refineries dot the landscape.

He made a career out of traveling from Tulsa to Austin and from Austin to Nashville and ultimately lived in each of the latter two.

"I remember Brandon back when he was in Stillwater, starting to play at Willie's," Cooper said. "You could tell there was a lot of heart and soul to his songwriting, and that's what he was at heart: a songwriter. Brandon was our brother on the road, always between Tulsa and Nashville and Austin. He was a true road warrior. He lived his life on the road."

His time in college, naturally at Oklahoma State, came in the late 1980s, but his biggest Red Dirt influence came a decade later when Stoney LaRue gave him a listen.

"He had a level of writing that was very thoughtful and thought-provoking," LaRue said. "Brandon had a voice that was thunder and an electric sprint. He was a magical man."

One of LaRue's first concert staples, dating to his days playing acoustic at the Wormy Dog Saloon in Stillwater, was Jenkins' love ballad "Feet Don't Touch the Ground"—a song about love powerful enough to overcome a flighty heart and the constant need to move from place to place. Its refrain, "With you by / my side / I can do without the city lights," can be delivered only with sincerity, and LaRue's raspy voice is perfect for the job.

The two collaborated together to write "Down in Flames," which both artists cut in 2005 and LaRue regularly performs in concert to this day. They combined as a duet for "High Time," which Jenkins released on his 2018 album, *Tail Lights in a Boomtown*.

That album came out shortly before Jenkins died unexpectedly in Nashville, succumbing to complications from heart surgery.

"He was my music brother," LaRue said. "He was a very deep soul and introduced me to masonry and being a good man.

"I smoked some of his ashes when he passed, per his request."

●　●　●

Bryon White: Red Dirt's Friend to All

In "Woody's Road," Bob Childers wrote of Woody Guthrie, "He was a ramblin' friend of man / reachin' out his hand / maybe that's why I went walkin' Woody's road." Aim Red Dirt through a modern prism, and Childers could just as easily have been talking about Bryon White.

White, a native of Shawnee and regular entertainer for the past 15 years at The Deli, the rock dive in Norman on Oklahoma University's Campus Corner, has also become Red Dirt's favorite sidekick. He's a ramblin' friend of anyone playing original music, any time, any place.

"Playing music is the thing that has always motivated me," White said. "I love spontaneity, I love being thrown in with somebody I've never played with, getting thrown in on a new song that I've never heard before. Those are the moments that are truly magical."

White grew up in the 1990s as a teen punk musician in Shawnee, and he played the same venues as John Moreland, developing an appreciation for free thinking and original music in the process. Then, he got into folk music in college and discovered The Blue Door in Oklahoma City.

"The Blue Door is really the nexus of the universe for me," he said. "It's one of my favorite places to play, or to see somebody play. It's where I met Skinner and started hanging out with Tom."

White forged a tight friendship with Skinner over roughly the last decade of Tom's life—and while it culminated in his serenade of "Nickel's Worth of Difference" at Skinner's memorial in 2015, it is far from his only mark on Red Dirt. White and Gabe Marshall formed The Damn Quails and released their first album in 2011 with Mike McClure producing. The debut album, *Down the Hatch,* made the same type of instant impact on Red Dirt that Jason Boland's *Pearl Snaps* had done 11 years earlier. The Quails were, in the scene's terms, overnight successes. That work with McClure is what bonded White with Skinner.

"We put that album out, and started going out on the road with McClure and Tom," White said. "That's where we kind of buddied up. Tom showed me that you'd never go hungry if you could find a hotel nearby that had a good breakfast—then, you just walk in like you own the place, and boom, you have breakfast.

"He was real funny and clever and witty, and he had a lot of jokes. So I really liked him as a human being. But, then you start hearing him play, and the voice that came out of him was just gorgeous."

The Quails packed a roller coaster of a career into the years since 2011, becoming crowd favorites at Billy Bob's in Fort Worth among others, while constantly stepping on rakes of their own dropping. There was a band member-on-band member stabbing once. White did jail time and went to rehab, publicly. They had their tour manager disappear in Houston and resurface in Colorado with little details. But they also never had a problem putting on a three-hour show and sticking around for a half-hour encore, and it endeared them to fans, and White became a modern icon in Skinner's image. He has shared the stage with the Turnpike Troubadours and regularly backs Jamie Lin Wilson whenever she wants to play with a band.

"The first time I sat in with Jamie, it was like a lightning bolt," White said. "You get that electric feeling. It's the best drug there is when you play with someone like that, and believe me, I've done them all!"

Like Moreland, and like a lot of artists who hail from Norman, White's stylings extend beyond Red Dirt, and by the summer of 2020 he was polishing off an album, produced by Tulsa songwriter John Calvin Abney, that explored his musical past.

"I'm really happy with it," he said of the record, which was being held up by the 2020 pandemic, with White not wanting to release an album he could not tour on.

"It's going to knock people off-kilter. It's not necessarily a Red Dirt record, or an Americana record, or anything. It's just a 'me' record, and I'm super proud of it."

● ● ●

Austin Meade's Story

In 2013, Cody Canada recorded a live acoustic album—*Some Old, Some New, Maybe a Cover or Two*—at the Third Coast Theater in Port Aransas, Texas. The show itself was a vintage Canada set, featuring original songs from The Departed and Ragweed as well as some unreleased material interspersed with Todd Snider, Neil Young and George Strait covers. Long enough to make it a double album and long enough to need a break mid-set.

During that break, Canada handed over his guitar to a blond kid from Texas A&M. Just like Mike McClure and Tom Skinner had done for him, Canada admonished the crowd to pay attention during his introduction: "Y'all listen to this dude, you won't regret it. Give it up for Austin Meade."

Meade played two songs, and Canada insisted on a third before he got back on stage, and Meade had won over a new set of fans.

"My dad and I drove down to that show, and after two or three beers, I worked up the courage to go talk to Cody during his break and shake his hand," Meade said. "I just said, 'Thanks for being a big influence on me,' and I pulled out this really sweaty paper cover around a burned CD of something I'd recorded in my room, and I handed it to him.

"He came back up after intermission and said, 'Where's that Austin kid?' I was already in the front row, but it didn't register that he was talking about me. So he picked up that CD and went, 'Where is Austin Meade?' and I went, 'Oh. He *is* talking about me!' I think about that night a lot."

By 2015, Meade had a band and traveled the country opening for The Departed. Five years later, he had a proper album, *Waves*, a closing gig on the first night of the 2019 Medicine Stone Music festival and a heart-wringing single he put out on Valentine's Day 2020, "Happier Alone."

Meade's music is a unique sound—closer to Jimmy LaFave's blues-rock than anything else. He draws on a background of gospel, jazz and blues, and sports long hair and a mustache that could more easily place him in a New York jazz club circa 1970 than most Texas stages. His willingness to push a unique sound won over his contemporaries and earned him a long list of artists willing to share the stage with him.

"We have gotten really lucky in the friendships we have right now," Meade said. "There's a lot of musicians out there who are just regurgitating shit that's already been done, and I think a lot of artists are pretty refreshed to hear an opener that sounds different than they do."

● ● ●

Back to Joe's

It is very fitting to close a notes chapter with one more trek to Joe's on Weed St. in Chicago.

This one came on July 15, 2019, when Garth Brooks chose the bar to kick off a mini-tour of honky-tonks and nightclubs around the country in support of a new song—a duet with Blake Shelton called "Dive Bar."

Joe's was never a dive bar in the classic "dirty floors, swinging doors, coin jukebox and century of history" sense. But musically, it absolutely is. Its music room is a stage surrounded by bars serving up pitchers of Shiner Bock. Bands pull up out front and load in and out down a single alley. If you show up enough, its bar staff declares you extended family. And most importantly, the center of the stage is no more than 100 feet from the back of the room. If you're at Joe's and the place is sold out, it's a packed, intimate setting. Loud, but intimate.

It is tailor-made for Brooks.

And Brooks, who cut his teeth on Stillwater's loud but intimate venues like Willie's Saloon, is tailor-made for Joe's.

I grew up on Brooks, and, more than anybody else, he was the first to set me on a path toward Stillwater and Red Dirt. But for the last 15 years or so my relationship with his music became very casual. He is an icon, and I feel like I belong with the misfits—anti-icons, if you will. So, ever since I lined up for tickets to one of his sold-out shows at Tulsa's Drillers Stadium in 1997 and stood through it all—the fire from the stage, Brooks rising through the floor—I didn't attend another show of his until December in 2015 in Wichita. That 1997 show, which can be accurately cast as a major production, was my primary frame of reference.

As a result, I am not afraid to admit this now: I was nervous for Brooks before the Joe's gig. I knew what connected with the Joe's crowd, and it wasn't a production. And knowing that this entire concert was connected to promoting a single, I struggled to see Brooks paring down his overwhelming stage presence to fit Joe's.

I was far from alone. I was joined by a friend and regular at Joe's, Alison Lundy, herself a veteran of the Texas music scene. We both spent the two-hour wait in a single-file line to enter the concert tempering our expectations by saying things like "Well, it'll be interesting, that's for sure" and other benign bits of anti-hype. We knew the crowd would be appreciative. It was a once-in-a-lifetime show, but would *Joe's* be appreciative? Could Brooks match the energy of Roger Clyne and the Peacemakers' 2010 set at the bar? Could he match the intensity of Ragweed's final concert ever, which also happened at the bar? If you want to go down into lore of Joe's, you can't be an icon, you have to be the *bar*.

Before Brooks took the stage, a representative from *Jimmy Kimmel Live!* came out to inform us that the first few songs would be recorded for the show, including a live performance of "Dive Bar" that may require several takes to get right and asking if we mind showing some real energy. Again, we were happy to oblige but skeptical it would translate into a magical evening.

At Joe's, the stage is connected via a small staircase at stage right to the green room.

Damned if Brooks didn't walk down those stairs and show everyone a magical evening.

He stepped onstage as if he knew everyone was skeptical and got right to the point before he played a word. "Look, we're doing this for Kimmel, and it's important to us, so we need you loud. Louder than normal.

"This town doesn't do *anything* normal, so I think 'apeshit' might be a bit more like it!"

He delivered it with such conviction that I was hooked immediately. Brooks had told me a few months earlier that he does not approach any of his shows now any differently than he did when he was playing Willie's, and he put it on full display for the crowd at Joe's.

After opening with "Two of a Kind, Workin' on a Full House," followed by two takes of "Dive Bar" for Jimmy Kimmel, Brooks went all-request for the night.

No set list.

No pre-made speeches.

Just music.

A lot of music.

If he heard someone call out for a song, he played it. Sometimes, he'd stand in the middle of the stage and play acoustic, and sometimes, he'd digress into a full-band jam session.

Being all-request, "Friends in Low Places" was the first song played after the Kimmel filming stopped. He played "The Red Strokes" sans piano and "All-American Kid" despite fearing that he'd mess up the words. He threw in a sample of his "Blame It All on My Roots" concerts from his Wynn Las Vegas residency, playing pieces of his own musical history like Merle Haggard, George Jones, George Strait, Ricky Skaggs and Randy Travis.

By the time he got around to "The Dance" and I found myself FaceTiming the entire song back to my mom in Oklahoma—she says it's her favorite song of all time—I had accepted that my preconceived notions had been misplaced. Garth Brooks did not need to prepare for Joe's, because he *is* Joe's. He is personal, direct and more invested in the fans' experience than what's happening on the stage.

He left the stage just shy of two hours after he first came down the stairs.

He returned by himself, guitar slung over his shoulder, for an encore.

"Well, what do you want to hear?" he boomed.

The first reply was "The River," and with just himself and a room full of fans, he closed his first Joe's gig with one of his standards—a ballad about chasing dreams no matter how absurd.

• • •

Garth Brooks set list: *"Two of a Kind, Workin' on a Full House," "Dive Bar" (twice), "Friends in Low Places," "The Red Strokes," "That Summer," "All-American Kid," "Much Too Young (to Feel This Damn Old)," "Two Pina Coladas," "The Dance," "Callin' Baton Rouge," "The Beaches of Cheyenne," "Mama Tried" (partial, Merle Haggard cover), "The Race Is On" (partial, George Jones cover), "Amarillo by Morning" (George Strait cover), Ricky Skaggs tribute, "I Told You So" (partial, Randy Travis cover), "Don't Close Your Eyes" (partial, Keith Whitley cover), "Fishin' in the Dark" (Nitty Gritty Dirt Band cover), "Rodeo," "Ain't Goin' Down (Til the Sun Comes Up)," "The Thunder Rolls," "Shameless" (Billy Joel cover), "Standing Outside the Fire." Encore: "The River."*

— — —

- 24 -

Back to the Roots:
Mike McClure

THE STRUGGLE WITH this book is condensing the stories into chapters. Just about every artist has a background rich enough and stories wild enough to fill a book on their own. And it has been difficult to leave out so many anecdotes from the road, stories behind songs and before-they-were-worth-a-damn histories.

But the purpose of this book is to explain what Red Dirt is—how it grew out of Oklahoma and fanned out across the land. And the method with which I've done it has been to keep a heavy focus on the artists: their stories and their thoughts. There is a part of me, writing this book, that hopes that some of the deeper stories get told one day, whether that's by me or someone else in another book or some long-form article on some website out in the wild.

I thought about that with Mike McClure more than I did anybody else.

He is both the contemporary and the forefather, and he could easily be the thread that binds all these chapters. He was a regular at The Farm. He got early help from Garth Brooks. (And later Brooks put McClure's song, "Rather Have Nothin'," on a pair of albums. Brooks produced Ty England's *Highways and Dance Halls* album in 2000 and included the cut, then in 2005 Brooks cut it on his own *Lost Sessions*.)

McClure saw musical heights with The Great Divide that few in Red Dirt have experienced. He carried the torch for Red Dirt when he fronted its hottest act—he appeared on the *Red Dirt Sampler* and headed up the *Dirt and Spirit* gospel album, both major compilation records, during his time as Divide lead singer. He produced most of Cross Canadian Ragweed's albums, and the 2018 release, *3*, from Cody Canada & The Departed. He produced albums from Jason Boland and Stoney LaRue. He's a friend to Jamie Lin Wilson. He has toured with Travis Linville. He has written with Evan Felker ("The Funeral" made it onto McClure's album *Onion* and the Turnpike

Troubadours album *Diamonds & Gasoline*—which McClure produced).

He's a relentless songwriter. The Divide put out five albums featuring his music. He has put out 10 solo records and countless duet and compilation albums.

He's a parent. McClure has two daughters, Marleigh and Mayme. McClure wrote songs for both of them ("Marleigh's Song" on the *Twelve Pieces* album and "Little Sister Sunshine" on *Did7*). Marleigh joined McClure and Cody Canada for a few songs on their 2015 live album, *Chip and Ray: Together Again for the First Time*, recorded at Third Coast Studios in Port Aransas, Texas.

Today, McClure still plays for anyone who will listen and pay up. He produces out of his home in Ada, Oklahoma, at his Boohatch Studios. He has even begun hosting songwriter workshops out of his house—the first featured Susan Gibson, a successful songwriter and wonderful musician in her own right and friend of McClure.

His bio is wildly long, so take away this about McClure: He's well-traveled. He's made enough music to fill this book alone. He was influenced by Guy Clark, Lloyd Maines and every Red Dirt forefather. He influenced Cody Canada, Jason Boland and Stoney LaRue, and he never shied away from having any of them open for or share the stage with The Great Divide. This statement applies to many in this book, but nobody with the range of application that McClure has: Without him, there is no Red Dirt.

You can understand why I can't escape the notion that there's a ton more to be said about McClure than what these pages can hold. So we're going to try to make you want to seek out his other stories, too, especially as McClure discussed his life and career on two separate occasions for this book.

The first time came in fall 2018, sitting across from me on a pair of damp hay bales behind the stage at the Medicine Stone festival in Tahlequah. At the time, McClure was newly single after two decades of marriage, and he was happy to join me for drinks during the interview. (In retrospect, a *lot* of drinks.)

Then, in summer 2020, with the world at a standstill in the coronavirus pandemic, McClure reached out again—eager to talk about starting fresh in life and in music. As a new relationship, with Chrislyn Lawrence, a photographer and musician in her own right, had taken root, McClure decided to get sober, too. Against that backdrop, McClure reflected on his music and his career a second time, all while putting the finishing touches on his first studio album in five years, *Looking Up*, at the time hoping to release it in September 2020.

His drummer of 12 years, Eric Hansen, offered up a brief perspective on McClure, too. It's all here—sometimes sarcastic, sometimes contrite, and maybe it'll be obvious which lines came from 2018 and which were from 2020, but it's vintage McClure.

On his early songwriting influences

My dad had a guitar. And I saw Willie Nelson in *Honeysuckle Rose* when I was 10. That was 1981. And my aunt got me that double live record, and I just fell in love with it. We didn't have a whole ton of records—there was some Johnny Horton, some Willie Nelson *Sings Kristofferson*. That's when I first got into wanting to know the words. I'd play the record, and I'd write them down. And just looking at that form, Kris Kristofferson's a master at it. So from doing that, I learned the form of a song, at like 10 or 11.

Merle Haggard had *Big City* and *The Fightin' Side of Me*. And I did the same thing.

On growing up rural in Pottawatomie County, Oklahoma

We had a party line. That's how rural it was.

I don't know how many people will get that.

We lived outside of town on five acres, pre-Internet. We had a TG&Y. Remember those places? Toys, Games and Yo-yos, I was always told. I would walk from my folks' house, which was five miles from TG&Y, to buy 45 records. I can remember buying "Pancho and Lefty" on a 45 and seeing "T. Van Zandt" on there. And it stuck in my head.

On when he decided to make a career out of music

Once Great Divide started going, my parents were helping me go to college in Stillwater. I called my dad and said, "Hey, I'm in a band, and we're thinking about going all in on this thing and just trying it."

My dad told me, "Well, now's the time to do that. Go do it and you'll never regret it." Which was great, because he sunk I don't know how many thousands of dollars into helping me go to college for something that, although I enjoyed it, I was more into music. [McClure went to OSU to major in psychology and minor in English.]

On the rapid rise of The Divide in the early 1990s

I heard Steve Earle, and I liked his lyrics, and it felt like country was blended with rock. That's what I wanted to do, and that's what it was. And the timing was right. We played on our own record, which was different—you'd sign a label deal and they'd bring out all these musicians, and they'd tell you, "This is going straight to number one!" which I didn't give a shit about. So we played on all of our own records. It was original. That was the band that was playin' it. It was pretty rare at the time.

On the notion of artists helping artists

The Divide had Lloyd Maines teaching us how to make an album. And I was older than some of the other artists, so I'd take what I'd learned and share it. That's a common theme in Red Dirt: You share. One for all and all for one.

On The Great Divide's heyday

Those guys [J.J. Lester, Scotte Lester, Kelley Green] believed in my songs. They were older than me, but we just had a good time hanging out. What I wanted out of it was to have an outlet for my songs.

That's what happened. We printed our own CDs and tapes, and people listened.

The other day, I was at one of my shows, and a kid came up to me and said, "My grandma had your tapes."

My. Grandma. Had. Your. Tapes.

I probably wouldn't have done it on my own, but those guys had more of a work ethic than I did. They'd tell me that we're going to divide up work—'Great Divide and conquer,' it rolls off the tongue. One of us would work on the van or the bus when it broke down. Another on promotions. We took things on ourselves. That helped a ton.

On "Pour Me a Vacation," The Divide's top 40 hit and the requests to play it that followed

I wrote that with Randy Taylor, the same guy who cowrote "Much Too Young (To Feel This Damn Old)." People liked it. And it's one of those things, when you do something that a lot of people like, as an artist, you start to question it. Jack Kerouac said that once a scene gets a name, it's as good as done. And Guy Clark said to be careful what you write because you're going to have to sing it forever.

As an artist, you don't want to be known for lighthearted stuff. But it is a thing that can come along, and if it makes people smile, you can get back to realizing: *That's why I got in The Great Divide. It makes people happy.*

Now, do I want to sit and play it at a songwriter showcase?

On The Divide's helping Cross Canadian Ragweed and Jason Boland & The Stragglers rise to prominence

I felt like I was given a platform. I didn't want to stand out there alone. I'd rather be with my friends. That's who I am: Take what you've got and give a little to somebody who deserves that spot, too. Ragweed took that spot and ran with it.

On moving on from The Divide and releasing solo records

That's my favorite part. When I did my second solo record [and first after The Divide's 2003 breakup], *Everything Upside Down*, it had 19 songs on it. I was writing all the time. I'd have 50 songs, and then every two years, The Great Divide would make a record. Supply greatly outnumbered the demand. But all I wanted to do was get it out. That's the art. That's the fun part to me.

On producing

When I was young, we did our first records in the early '90s with Lloyd Maines. I looked up to him. And he was gracious and he taught me a lot, and I thought, *That's a cool job.* Some of it is just sitting and reading a group, being able to feel people, understand what they're trying to do and help them do it. I like doing it.

On Tom Skinner, in one sentence

I miss him the most.

Eric Hansen, on McClure and expanding his musical reach, post-Divide

When Mike finally left The Divide, he called me and said, "You wanna do this?" and I was too far along in my life, and I said, "No, man, I'm too far off. I don't want to do it." Well, a couple of months go by, and I absolutely changed my mind. So I dropped out of grad school—I think that's the fifth school I dropped out of to play music—and I moved up to Oklahoma and dragged my shit up there, and we started the Mike McClure Band in 2003.

When we'd go play some country bar, two years into the Mike McClure Band, and some sumbitch yelled out "Play me some Buffett!" Mike would want to burn the bar down. It was kind of torture for him.

So you're starting over. It's heartbreaking. It's heartbreaking for Mike.

It started out pushing and going pretty hard, but it slowly faded. He started finding other things he could do—financial panic set in and he realized he's good at engineering and producing. So he does whatever he can to make it and keep himself afloat. He gets good at it, and here he is.

Back to McClure, on having Hansen as his drummer for 12 years

He predates me. I remember seeing him with Skinner, and Tom getting me up and playing, and I remember looking back there, and just—I could feel him. That's not super easy for me to do with drummers. Guitar players, you can ease into each other, but drummers, you need to be super-synced up, kind of telepathically, and we could do that. He played with Tom a lot, just loved Tom, and we kind of bonded over love of Tom, really.

He's my Charlie Watts. We played so many nights together, and I know what he's thinking. He knows what I'm thinking. Sometimes we pushed each other, sometimes we screwed around.

On him and Cody Canada both having an "asshole phase" after breakups with The Divide and Ragweed

I did it. He did the same thing. It's a humbling process. You need it, because you rock along there, and everybody kisses your ass, and you start believing the hype—and you should believe a little bit of it, for self-esteem. But not all of it.

And then what happens is, you get mad at the people in the band of that music that you make it with. And you take it out on *everybody*. You don't realize it. It took me a long time to realize it.

It just got so ugly with us. It did with Ragweed too. And that phase is when people are yelling "Play 'Pour Me a Vacation'!" or with Cody "Play 'Carney Man'!" And then you just think, *I'm pissed at those guys, and now you're asking for that song.* I went through that. I understand.

You're mad at the wrong people. You take it out on everybody, instead of just coming to some sort of acceptance of it.

On Cody Canada and growing up as artists and people

We're just buddies. I always liked him. We come from the same place. He comes from his heart, and I do too. He didn't back down from a major label, and he brought me along as his producer when most would go with the system. I'm thankful for that.

Red Dirt, when you get down to it, is just someone coming from their heart, no matter what the parameters are or their influences. If they're coming from their heart, you can feel it, and I always felt that with him.

I was a few years older, and I knew a few of the ropes, so I showed him the ropes the way other people showed me the ropes.

We're grown up now. It's always been fun, but that gets out of perspective when business starts coming in or you get a record deal or you're in a bus now. It's easy to lose that. It's fun again.

On life in summer 2020 and working Looking Up, his first album since a metric ton of life changes

I haven't made a record in five years. The last one I did was with my friend/partner/mentor Joe Hardy. We've worked together since Tony Brown introduced us over the Cross Canadian Ragweed album *Garage* in 2005.

Joe passed away last year…and a couple years before that, Tom Skinner passed, and so did Steve Ripley. They were my go-to group of older musicians that I loved, respected and looked up to. Some of that ache is in this album.

It's also filled with love and hope. Having recently gone through a divorce, I met a new love, I sobered up and started looking within for answers. Love has changed me for the better, and it is all over this record.

— — —

- 25 -

The Departed

THERE IS NOTHING left for me to write about Cody Canada or Ragweed or The Departed.

Well, I guess I could tell you how the Canadas opened a School of Rock franchise in New Braunfels in 2018 and grew it into the regional hub of rock-music education for children in the Hill Country.

I could tell you about Cody's father, Ronnie, a Vietnam vet and subject of Ragweed's "Long Way Home," a gruff Okie who is wrapped around the fingers of Dierks and Willy Canada and his son and who still shows up at Cody's shows and tries to outparty the band, crew and anybody who may have just happened to walk down the same street on a given night.

I could tell you about Oklahoma State University's football homecoming celebration, the largest such event in major college sports. And I could tell you about Canada being the standing headliner at Eskimo Joe's Tailgate, annually held in the bar's parking lot the night before.

I could probably gin up a memory from the Lincoln Theater in Raleigh, where the last Ragged and Reckless tour with Ragweed and Reckless Kelly stopped in early 2010. And I could tell you how I got so high off a volcano vape that I made myself sick and missed the after-party that Canada and Willy Braun held—they called it "The Twelve-String Jam," and it was a song swap with the stipulation that every song must have been played on a 12-string guitar.

I could mention the band's ascent, throughout 2019 and continuing until the coronavirus pandemic brought about a pause. The Departed has never been more popular nor consistently drawn more fans to its shows than the present day. And I could probably get away with saying something like, "In embracing his past, Canada has finally charted his future."

I could even come up with a new way to introduce a chapter that isn't telling you about some other way I could be introducing the chapter.

Look, though. I need to level with you: I'm *spent*.

Long before this book, I was the unofficial biographer for both bands. No other writer, big or small, has written about Ragweed or The Departed to the depth, degree and volume that I have since 2000. I've done my time. I've shared my stories, and right now, I'm exhausted. Yes, their story isn't over. Yes, there will be another chapter for Canada and his band, and I'll be there in the front row to tell it, but that's all between Future Josh and Future You.

To close out this book, I am going to do something I've done several times already: get the hell out of the way.

What appears next is unedited, uncensored and unfettered, straight from the mouths of Cody Canada, Jeremy Plato and Eric Hansen, along with a few people in their innermost of circles. The topics? Whatever the hell they want, man.

On the band's relationship, morale and mood on the bus:

Hansen: There is no morale. It's baseline, with not a single negative thing about it. It doesn't even cross your mind. No one steps on anyone. You don't even think of it as a thing.

Plato: Everybody wants to kick each other in the fucking party bone all the time.

Canada: This band was a revolving door for a long time. And now, we have cut it down to the three Okies who were there the whole time, from the start, and it's all down to the basics. That's really what it is now. It's drinking some beers and taking a couple of shots on stage, doing a two-and-a-half-hour show, and then going back to the bus and smoking some weed, listening to music and playing some songs. And then we go to bed, and we wake up, and everyone's happy. I haven't had a stressful moment in four years now.

On singing Merle Haggard's "Footlights" with Robert Earl Keen on the album 3:

Canada: I texted Robert, which is the best way to get ahold of him. And I said, "What is your absolute favorite Haggard song?" And he texted back, and scrolling on an iPhone through a text, it was 10 scrolls. It was so long.

He said, "'Pancho and Lefty' is black and white, until Merle starts singing. And it's exactly like *The Wizard of Oz*, when it all turns into Technicolor. That's how I always hear it." And for a moment I'm thinking, "OK. 'Pancho and Lefty' with Robert Earl. That's gonna be pretty cool." And then I keep scrolling, and he brings up another Haggard song. And on and on, I keep scrolling and scrolling. And I get all the way to the end, and he writes, "And the winner is, 'Footlights.' When I turned 41, I realized it was too late to get out. If I wanted to get out of this business, it was too late. I'm in it for life." And then he said, "But I'm glad I did. But that also means that, every night, whether you're in a good mood or a bad mood, you gotta get out there and do it." And my response was, "Awesome. Will you cut that song with me?" And he said, "Absolutely."

On recording in a studio with Canada:

Hansen: I try to add absolutely nothing above and beyond the most simple, straight-ahead interpretation of what I hear, because usually that stays the hell out of the way. We're a three-piece band. I've been in way more chaotic situations than this, and I've been way more expressive and experimental, and in the end, that's just a racket that distracts from the melody and words, and that's what needs to come across clearly.

Plato: It's business as usual for me. The way it goes is, I'm wanting to get a good rhythm track, and I want to focus on drums. I want to play with Eric, but I don't want to mess him up. Because as long as we get a good drum track, I can come up and clean up the bass.

On Jamie Lin Wilson contributing harmonies on *In Retrospect* and *3*:

Canada: We had Jamie for one day when we recorded her on "Satellites and Meteors," and I had already gone in and done all the high-string stuff on it. I think that sounds so Oklahoma—the high-string melodies. And to get Jamie Lin to sing harmony, I went on for 20 minutes saying, "There was this girl in Oklahoma, and she was like the Red Dirt Emmylou. She would sing on everyone's records, and it was so awesome to hear every time." And on and on and on. And Jamie Lin cut me off, finally, and went, "Cody, all you had to do was ask me to be your Texas Monica Taylor."

And she nailed those parts. I think that song needed Jamie Lin's touch just to sound like that era—that 1994 Red Dirt time of Childers and Skinner, with Monica backing them, is exactly what I wanted out of it.

On watching Mike McClure and Cody Canada both leave bands (The Great Divide and Ragweed) and start new ones (the Mike McClure Band and The Departed):

Hansen: Everyone who is in a successful band, even at the local circuit level, has no idea of how much they have to lose. They think in their mind, *I wrote all these songs. I'm a singer. Nobody necessarily knows my name, but it doesn't matter. They're gonna figure it out. Maybe I'm going to lose 10, 15 percent of my crowd, because I am 100 percent of the product that they love.* They don't realize that most of that crowd is the social gathering behind the small percentage that actually receives and understands the artist. So if they think they're going to drop a quarter of their crowd, it's actually 90 percent. Just down to those people who really knew what they were about. And it's heartbreaking. It was heartbreaking for Mike, and Cody went through the exact same thing. They're damn near starting over.

On what Eric Hansen brought to the band when he joined in 2016:

Brian Kinzie (tour manager, sound engineer): Lightness. He doesn't hold anything back, and he doesn't let anything get him down. He's a damn good drummer, but his simplicity is what we need. We're a simple band.

On the transition from Ragweed to The Departed, as their manager:

Shannon Canada: What I wanted to do as a manager wasn't possible because I was also the wife. So the managerial advice that I gave Cody was not heard. It was more, "You're my wife. You should support me in whatever I decide to do. So if I don't want to play these songs, don't make me." And my answer was, "If you want to stay on top of the hill, you've gotta play the game." But he didn't want to do that, and in the long run, I had to support him in that, because that is really who I am: Cody's wife.

On starting a School of Rock franchise in New Braunfels, which meant dropping most artists she represented at 36D Management:

Shannon Canada: I was in a really great place with 36D Management. I was working with Cody and Shinyribs—Kevin Russell is one of the most fun artists I've ever managed, because he is such a positive energy, and you have to love him. Even if you're the biggest asshole on the planet, you're still happy around him.

But Dierks started to want to play, so we needed to find instructors for him. We did—we found awesome instructors. Charlie [Robison]'s longtime guitar player, Mark Tokach, was teaching him, and he was learning well, but he was by himself. So with Cody's background being picked on at school, kind of isolated and the odd man out because he was playing guitar, I didn't want that to repeat with Dierks. So we began just a search of "Where can he play music with his peers, with people his age who enjoy classic rock and classic metal?" And in that search, we found the School of Rock. The closest location to us is an hour away. But as I started to research it, I fell in love with the idea of the school.

I was also watching my kids grow up without Cody home all the time. Being in that situation as a family where your breadwinner is an artist—What if he can't sing? Where do you go from there? It's not like there are a million skill sets that we have. That kind of all came together, and we realized this is a perfect fit for us. It's a franchise. We're pretty rooted in our community. People know we're good people, and we want the best for our kids and other people's kids.

And then I had an epiphany. Over 20 years, I've been working to help build other people's careers. And then they go off and have their career, and I'm still here waiting to help another one.

I just realized it's time for me to have *my* career now, and it's time for my family to take priority. The artists were super understanding about it. Kevin said, "This is your passion, your family. Go do it."

But of course, that brought me full circle. I want to manage Cody. I want to manage my family, people who are in my heart forever.

On Cody's influence and his reasons for pursuing music:

Dierks Canada: My dad got me into music really young. He and my mom have supported me ever since. I find it a lot of fun to express feelings in music and bring happiness to other people.

On why he said there's nothing wrong with making everyone happy every night:

Hansen: An old high school friend of mine, his name was Todd Beer. And in the 1990s, Todd got a job at the Causley T-shirt shop. And he came to me one day, while I was completely disconnected and didn't know Cody or any of those guys, with this song "Carney Man," and he was just laughing so hard about it, repeating these lines to me, because he's just heard it. And I was like, *Holy shit.*

That was my first realization that in this semiserious pursuit of being a musician and making art and songs that can relate to your peer artists and relate to the public, there's also room for mother-fucking humor. And that's so much bigger than I ever knew it was.

They wrote that song as a joke, and then this person who has no connection to them hears it and brings it to me. And that turned my focus all around.

On why he has stayed with Cody, now as The Departed's tour manager, nearly two decades after joining Ragweed in 2002:

Kinzie: Probably after I met the woman that I knew I was going to marry and the way they treated her.

I met Melanie the first time at Cowboy's in San Antonio. Our first real date was to River Road Ice House, after we had all moved to New Braunfels. And then I introduced her to the guys. And the first time I really brought her around was to an Amarillo show. I had asked if she could ride the bus and everyone went, "Yes, sure." She rode the bus to Amarillo, and she was going to ride back here after, but then Shannon talked her into riding up to Steamboat. There was a lot that happened—she had a wedding she was supposed to be in!—but everything turned into Steamboat time. The way that Cody and Shannon treated not only me but people I knew were going to be my family and the way they treated my family. My family is in Kansas. They come out to a lot of shows, and when I saw how welcoming the Canadas were to them, too, I knew: This might be where I just need to stay.

On processing 30 years of writing songs, leading a band that reached as high as any Red Dirt band ever has, seeing it fall apart and building it all back up again:

Canada: This has been a few homecomings ago. Maybe the first time I did the Joe's Tailgate thing. Shannon and I went to Stillwater, and we stayed there with another Red Dirt lifer, Ragan Parkerson. And he told me then, "You know? You're still the same."

And I immediately just went, "Well, that's a good thing!"

Ragan goes, "No, what I mean is, there's just other folks that I've seen—not all from this music scene, but some—that it changes. The busier you get, the more popular you get."

I remember my stepmom telling me when I started out, "I know why you're doing this. It's to be famous." And I was like, "Bullshit."

The last thing I want to do is be *seen*. It really is. I have friends in Texas that will want to do that, and I just can't. You've killed the groove when you say you want to be seen.

I don't want to do that.

I want to be heard, man.

— — —

- 26 -

Home

THE INDIAN NATION Turnpike stretches from the Red River, marking the border of Oklahoma and Texas just south of Durant, to Interstate 40 at Henryetta, where the highway continues on as US-75, 40 miles north to Tulsa. The Indian Nation Turnpike stands at 105.3 miles from end to end and takes a week and a half to traverse in a car, no matter how fast you drive. You never see as much as a town. You see exit signs, including one that promises an Army ammunition dump, and you see farms and ranches. During half the year, the hue of green tells you whether the field is made of wheat, soybeans, corn or cattle grass. During the other half, the hue of brown tells you the same.

This is the piece of highway Evan Felker drove when he decided to call his band "The Turnpike Troubadours."

Of relevance, this is also the only sensible way to drive from Dallas to Northeast Oklahoma. It's a main trucking line from North Texas to Tulsa and beyond to Kansas City, St. Louis, Chicago, wherever the long haul requires. You make this trip and you're thankful you're not driving up Interstate 35—100 or so miles west—because at least the Indian Nation Turnpike has hills. Every now and then, the patches of fields are broken up by lines of trees. These are the river bottoms. Every river is two feet deep and half a mile wide. The entire landscape has a creepy beauty to it. A setting sun can hit a cloud just right and light up in red and purple in 100 miles in every direction, and if you're at the top of one of those hills, you can make it all out. But it also looks like the place where tens of thousands of age-yellowed newspaper stories all end with "and they were never heard from again."

This is a place you come to get lost. This is the part of the country where Belle Starr hid out as the Queen of the American Outlaw and where she had her last dance with Frank "Pistol Pete" Eaton the night she was killed at age 40. This is the part of the country where Jesse James would disappear after a train robbery and resurface two states away. I've been told my entire life that Starr and James are on my family tree, and I never feel like I relate more to them than when I drive the Indian Nation Turnpike.

Fifteen miles past the north terminus of the turnpike is Okmulgee, where my family lives. If you hang a right at the second stoplight in Okmulgee, you can drive another 60 miles on US-62 and be in Tahlequah. This is a college town, home of Northeastern State University, in the foothills of the Ozark Plateau. The farmland gives way to dense woods, lakes, anti-abortion billboards, Native American casinos and, like, an absolute metric ton of meth.

After four and a half days of driving at 85 miles per hour, I made it from the southern end of the Indian Nation Turnpike to the Diamondhead Resort on the outskirts of Tahlequah. Five thousand people had gathered for the 2018 Medicine Stone music festival, where there is nothing else to do for 100 miles besides wonder where you would hide out if you lived in outlaw times.

History's first recognized rock and roll concert took place in Cleveland, Ohio, in 1952. The Moondog Coronation Ball was held at the Cleveland Arena, which held 10,000 people. It was meant to be a dance. One of the bands scheduled to perform was famous for wearing Scottish kilts. They sold between 20,000 and 25,000 tickets, and within an hour of starting up, law enforcement shut it back down. The arena was demolished in 1977 and is now home to a Red Cross office. One block away, though, is the Agora Ballroom, one of Bruce Springsteen's most famous haunts. A mile away from *that* is the House of Blues. That was where Cross Canadian Ragweed played a sold-out show before pulling a late-nighter at a bowling alley across the street and before their bus got ransacked by the Ohio State Highway Patrol, which was eventually codified into "51 Pieces" by Cody Canada and Micky Braun.

* * *

Key West, Florida, has a year-round population of 25,000. That's just about as many people as had tickets to the Moondog Coronation Ball. It has 10,000 more residents than Tahlequah, Oklahoma, has, and somehow, five million more bars.

Key West is where Kyle Carter was drawn in the summer of 2017 when he got the idea to start a music festival. Carter is native of the same city of Yukon where Cody Canada spent his youth. Carter once famously—at least in Red Dirt lore—beat Canada in a regional talent contest in the early 1990s. He also happened to graduate from Yukon High School in 1992, ten years after the school's most famous alum, Garth Brooks, did the same. That year, Carter's high school band got to serenade Brooks at a ceremony in town.

"They were renaming Highway 92 in the middle of Yukon as Garth Brooks Boulevard," Carter said. "One of those neat, small-town things, and our high school band was asked to play at the event. We had a band then called West of City—that's how the old Yellow Pages phone books would list your address if you lived outside town in Yukon—and we played for him and got to hang out with him in the green room of the auditorium. He couldn't have been more giving of his time or more truly interested in what we were doing."

Carter went to college at Northeastern State University in Tahlequah, almost 20 years before the Turnpike Troubadours and Jason Boland got the idea to host Medicine Stone in the town. He went on to live a life you could call normal. He didn't pursue music as a career, but he never lost touch with it either. He stayed in touch with Canada as Ragweed's career took off, and he was not a stranger to the Red Dirt festivals of the early 2000s. But by the 2010s, he decided he had outgrown festival nature—camping out for days, enduring hundred-degree heat and covering yourself in grime and sweat does not appeal to everyone. Carter enjoyed The MusicFest at Steamboat, but it was also in Colorado in January. Eventually, he had enough and decided to create a festival that fit him, on the logic that there must be thousands more music fans with his mindset. He wanted someplace chill, laid-back and warm but not sweltering. He set out on a nationwide search but canceled it after his first stop: Key West.

"I waited long enough, and I got old enough, and I started looking at places," Carter said. "I always wanted to come to Key West anyway. One of my musician friends back in school rebuilt a boat, and we listened to *Boats, Beaches, Bars and Ballads* by Jimmy Buffett for a year straight, and it made me always want to come here.

"We had the good fortune of coming to Key West right at the point that town leaders wanted to become known as a music city. They're clearly known for their bars, but they wanted it to be a destination. They were building an amphitheater on the Truman Waterfront. It took them 12 or 13 years to get it built. The first time I had come, they only had the Key West Songwriters Festival, which I'm now a part of. But I got to see how the community set up and worked with that festival, how their hospitality worked, how their emergency services worked, and it was just fitting for a party. You can bring in five, ten thousand people here every day, and they're made for it."

Mile 0 Fest launched the following January and within three years had commanded enough respect in Americana circles that Jason Isbell could be persuaded to join a cast of Red Dirt and Texas icons like Robert Earl Keen, Randy Rogers, American Aquarium, Wade Bowen, Jamie Lin Wilson, Reckless Kelly, The Departed and Stoney LaRue as headliners on the festival's main stage.

"There was enough interest when I started reaching out to industry professionals," Carter said, "that there were enough like-minded people like me who really were interested in growing the market and felt like Red Dirt and Americana was ripe for more festivals. We got it started, and we learned pretty quickly that we were right."

• • •

Ragan Parkerson drove the entire way from Stillwater to Key West and back for the 2020 festival. Round trip, those miles would get you all the way across the country with room to spare. He didn't leave immediately after the five-day event, either. He stuck around to tailgate Super Bowl LIV at Rick's Cabaret, watching the Chiefs rally past the 49ers and opting to start the drive home on a weeklong hangover the next day.

Ragan is not the only one to do something dumb to get to and from Mile 0. A year earlier, I bought a round-trip ticket from New York on a dare from Cody Canada, 36 hours before the festival. The flights and hotels cost more than my first truck did by a considerable distance. The flight home was at 7 a.m. after staying up until 3 a.m. at the after-party to the after-party. It was delayed because the pilot forgot to show up and fly the plane.

Sense and music have never been compatible. The little voice inside everyone's head that tells them right from wrong shuts off when it's time to drink, fuck or stand in front of the loudspeaker.

For 50 years, Red Dirt music has played out in all those shadows—in the towns off of the Indian Nation Turnpike, in the town at the end of the United States, in Colorado ski resorts. The only real requirement is that a bus can make the drive. Ride on one out of Challis, Idaho, with the driver hugging the edge of the cliff that is hugging the edge of the mountain on a road that has no guardrail, and then realize, *Lewis and Clark did all this with some oxen and no onboard Wi-Fi.*

If you cut corners like I do and fly over the five or six hues that make up the roots music landscape, you still have to *get* to the venue, and that venue can be anything.

The LimeLight Eventplex in Peoria, Illinois, is in a sheet metal building that at one time used to be a giant adult film set. Hill Country Barbecue in Manhattan looks like it was sawed out of the town square in Lockhart, Texas, and transported to the Flatiron District. Cabooze in Minneapolis rises up from one of the most diverse neighborhoods in the country. The Tractor Tavern in Seattle has a barroom dog that will follow you around through load-in and all of sound check. The Shed in Maryville, Tennessee, is an enclave of a suburban Harley-Davidson dealership. Songbirds in Chattanooga is in the middle of a guitar museum with some exhibits so rare, they are protected by steel doors and laser fields. If a musician leaves their bag at Mercury Lounge on New York's Lower East Side, someone will pick it up first thing the next morning and overnight it to their next gig. Bryan Zannotti, Wade Bowen's drummer, did that once, and I did the shipping. Find a flight deal into Fort Lauderdale on short notice needing to get to Key West for Mile 0 Fest over Super Bowl weekend 2020, and Jimmy "Taco" Flex will simply show up with his wife, Kari, and both of the Kinzies and upgrade their rental car to fit you in for the ride.

This is all why I am not, as I write this, sweating the future of Red Dirt when the world gets to the other side of the coronavirus pandemic. Red Dirt plays out in the world's in-between spaces. Even in Dallas, Houston or Kansas City, Red Dirt is happening in a bar that, one way or another, involves a dark alley. If one doesn't lead to the front door, it leads out the back. And its fans, conditioned to seek it out in dim corners away from the mainstream, know where to find it.

Mattson Rainer of KNBT in New Braunfels agrees.

"The path forward for Red Dirt and Texas has to be as strong as any genre," Rainer said. "Because these guys connect with their fans.

"The ones who thrive after this, meaning they don't have to go sell insurance or whatever, will thrive because of one thing: Their fans are dying to see them just as much as they're dying to see their fans. For these musicians in this genre, it'll bounce right back."

That is how Red Dirt happened.

It put down roots in Stillwater and sprang up like a field of dandelions in the Oklahoma prairie. When those dandelions outgrew Payne County, the wind picked up the whole thing and blew it to the Texas Hill Country. From there, the process repeated. This time, the dandelions made it up into the jet stream, from where they can now fall anyplace in the world. The best Red Dirt venue in Cologne, Germany, is the Blue Shell. Check it out when you are over there.

Time has blown Red Dirt far from its origins, often to the far edges of itself. Sometimes—for example, when a tried-and-true Texan like Randy Rogers, with a fanbase that spans the globe, reminds you that two of his best-known songs are Cody Canada co-writes—you'll need a flow chart that traces it back to rural Payne County.

But there are other times those same winds blow Red Dirt back where it came from. Sit through a Stoney LaRue concert when he hits you over the head his interpretations of Brandon Jenkins and Bob Childers, and makes sure you leave the bar that night knowing both of their names, and it's easy to imagine yourself across a campfire at The Farm from those forefathers.

"I still don't think they got their shot," LaRue said.

"I still don't think they had their day. I don't think this whole *scene* has had its day yet. I think it's on it's way to it though, and I'll be here when it does."

● ● ●

I do not know if those two people in my head from Chapter 4—the one who is professional and has a job and a family and a New York apartment and a dry erase calendar with to-do lists on it, and the one who stands over that person shouting "MUSIC!!" at unfathomable decibels at all times—will ever bump into each other and say hello. But I do know that I no longer care if they do. They coexist now in ways they did not for the first 40 years of my life. I love to show up unannounced at Joe's on Weed St. in Chicago, four hours after making a newspaper deadline in Manhattan, because Micky and the Motorcars are playing a short-notice concert there. I love to walk out of Rose Music Hall in Columbia, Missouri, after a Cody Canada show has turned a 3:30 a.m. dive into the bus's music library, with a flight taking off at 7 a.m. to get me back to the office in time to plan the next day's paper.

To quote Reckless Kelly: *White picket fences look a lot like iron bars, and a pink house with shutters reminds me of old gray walls.* Chasing Red Dirt music around the world does not. It feels normal and natural, almost as if it is where I am supposed to be and what I should be doing.

And I know that I will perpetually live somewhere between those two people and that Red Dirt is the bridge between them. I understand that the road goes on forever and the party never ends. And I know that, no matter what I am doing, I'll always find a way to make it to another one, even if I have to walk every mile on my knees.

I have seen how big the world is, and I know that Red Dirt plays out in its negative space, in its soft spots and cursed backroads trailing out into pastureland and river bottoms, and I also know that space is where I belong, with every other misfit, hippie and free spirit who found this scene and experienced what they mean by the words "music family."

I understand that just because the scene circled the globe does not mean it will ever be mainstream. I hope you understand that too. I hope you know that the classic notion of a music industry will always be unfair to Red Dirt and that it will never see a triumphant coronation or universal validation, and I hope you do not care.

I hope you get to play in this Dirt, and I hope it kicks up into your eyes and waters them when you do.

I hope it sends you *home*.

— — —

Bob Childers, center right, and Tom Skinner, center left, join The Great Divide—with Mike McClure in the center—on stage at Cain's Ballroom in Tulsa during the Red Dirt Christmas, an annual festival put on by the Red Dirt Rangers, in 2000. **COURTESY ERIC WOOLEY**

Top: Tom Skinner. Bottom: Bob Childers, Jason Boland, Eric Wooley and Stoney LaRue pose together in December 2000. **COURTESY ERIC WOOLEY**

Left: The song order for Tom Skinner's memorial outside Kellyville, Okla., in August 2015. Right: Mike McClure, Jake Akins, and Cody Canada perform at Skinner's memorial.

Below left: Stairs leading to the door of the original Wormy Dog Saloon in Stillwater. Below right: Wormy Dog signage overlooking The Strip. Bottom: Gene Collier sits in with the Red Dirt Rangers during a Yellow House Alumniati tailgate before the 2018 Oklahoma State Homecoming football game. **WORMY DOG PHOTOS COURTESY ERIC WOOLEY**

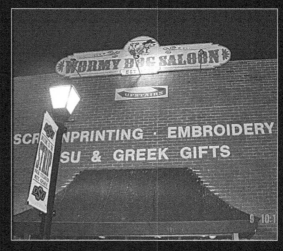

The Daily O'Collegian

'We'll miss every single one of them'

A void has been created in our lives that will never be filled.

of the OSU family.

We may not have known them all, but we know how much they will be missed.

As Oklahomans, we will endure this void and wrestle with the pain and suffering of this tragedy as we have others — together.

The Daily O'Collegian Staff

FOR RELATED COVERAGE, SEE INSIDE

WE REMEMBER

1. Daniel Lawson
2. Nate Fleming
3. Bill Teegins
4. Will Hancock
5. Pat Noyes
6. Brian Luinstra
7. Kendall Durfey
8. Jared Weiberg
9. Bjorn Fahlstrom
10. Denver Mills

Cross Canadian Ragweed plays a headlining set at The MusicFest at Steamboat in 2008 after the release of their Mission California album. COURTESY TODD PURIFOY

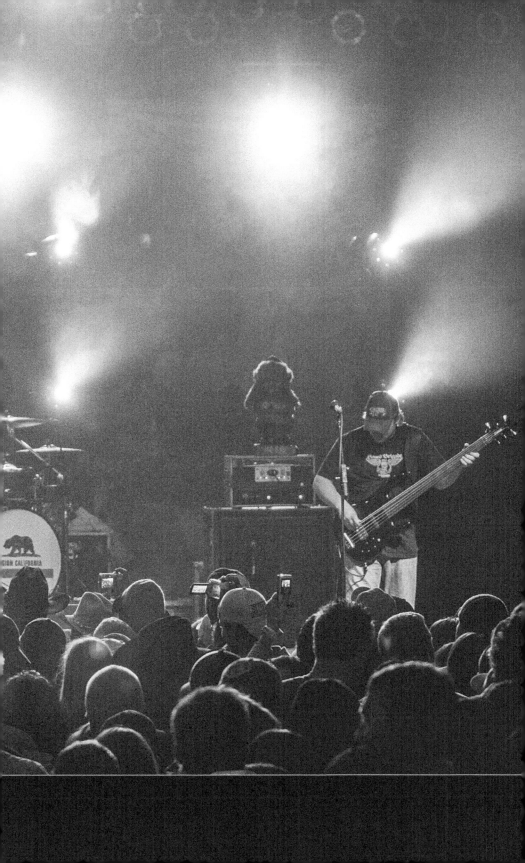

Left: A jam session at The Gypsy Cafe, the centerpiece of The Farm, during the 2016 Bob Childers Gypsy Cafe festival. Top: The Gypsy Cafe in 2016. Above: The Gypsy Cafe after restoration efforts provided by the Red Dirt Relief Fund in 2020.
COURTESY RAGAN PARKERSON

The Turnpike Troubadours play to a sold-out Irving Plaza in New York City in October 2018.

Above: Jason Boland & The Stragglers celebrate 20 years since their 2000 album, Pearl Snaps, in 2020 at Hill Country Barbecue in Manhattan. Below: Randy Rogers waves to the crowd at New York's Gramercy Theater in 2018.

Jamie Lin Wilson at New York's Bowery Electric in 2019.

Above: Reckless Kelly, with Willy Braun front and center, performs to the Mile 0 Fest crowd at the Truman Waterfront Amphitheater in Key West in 2020. Below left: Roger Clyne, Cody Canada and Muzzie Braun watch Steve Earle perform at the 2019 Braun Brothers Reunion. Below right: Willy Braun, Micky Braun, Wade Bowen and Cody Canada on stage at Braun Brothers in 2019.

The mountains surrounding Challis, Idaho, provided the backdrop for the Braun Brothers Reunion in 2019, hosted by Reckless Kelly and Micky and the Motorcars.

Above: Wade Bowen at the House of Blues in Houston in November 2018. Below left: Dierks Canada and Jamie Lin Wilson rehearse before the 2020 MusicFest tribute to Cody Canada. Below right: Cody Canada is joined by his son Willy on stage at the tribute show.

Cody Canada. **COURTESY TODD PURIFOY**

The crowd at Joe's on Weed St. in Chicago for a Departed concert in August 2017.

Index

- About The Author -

JOSH CRUTCHMER IS the print planning editor at *The New York Times*. Mr. Crutchmer is responsible for the organization of the daily newspaper as well as the look of the final edition of *The Times'* Sunday front page—and he gets the occasional byline. Prior to joining the *Times*, he was the assistant managing editor of *The Plain Dealer* in Cleveland. Previously, he has worked at the *Chicago Tribune, The Buffalo News,* the Minneapolis *Star Tribune*, the *Omaha World-Herald, The Arizona Republic* and *The Oklahoman*.

He has a long history in music journalism, with a heavy slant toward Red Dirt. He was tapped to write obituaries for Merle Haggard and George Jones for *The Plain Dealer* and Nashville *City Paper*, respectively. He covered the rise to prominence of Cross Canadian Ragweed for *The Oklahoman* and the band's final show in 2010 for an entertainment arm of the *Chicago Tribune*.

Mr. Crutchmer has had an award-winning journalism career that dates to 2000. He was the graphics and planning editor for "At Day Care and in Deadly Peril," a 2013 Pulitzer Prize-winning series at the Minneapolis *Star Tribune*. He was also the planning editor for nationally-recognized news projects at both *The Buffalo News* and *The Plain Dealer*. His work in Red Dirt has been previously honored by the Oklahoma Society of Professional Journalists, and his work on the Rock & Roll Hall of Fame inductions was routinely given top editing and design honors in the Society for News Design's annual worldwide competition.

At *The New York Times*, he plays a key role in organizing and planning the *Times'* daily and enterprise content, working with writers and editors across the organization to ensure subscribers have a robust newspaper in their hands every day. He was the designer of the paper's 2017 obituary of Tom Petty and a major organizer and producer of the paper's coverage of the 2018 Winter Olympics, World Cup and U.S. midterm elections. He directed the print planning for the paper of the impeachment of President Donald Trump, the 2020 coronavirus pandemic, and the protests for racial equality that gripped the U.S. that same year.

A native Oklahoman and graduate of Oklahoma State University, Mr. Crutchmer has had a close involvement in the state's Red Dirt music scene since 2000. He has cultivated relationships with the modern standard-bearers of the scene as well as its forefathers. His intimate knowledge of Red Dirt extends not just to the artists but to the crew members, sound engineers, bar owners and tour managers behind the scenes whose efforts define what it means to live and work with a love of music.

— — —

- External Sourcing -

Chapter 3

https://www.tulsaworld.com/archives/band-members-survive-crash/article_8e0be-6ac-e01e-54bb-895c-6213600e2597.html

Chapter 4

https://newsok.com/article/2789892/bands-kicking-up-red-dirt-music-scene-cross-canadian-ragweed-great-divide-play-to-full-houses

Chapter 7

O'Meilia, Mark. Garth Brooks: The Road Out of Santa Fe. University of Oklahoma Press, 1997

https://en.wikipedia.org/wiki/List_of_highest-grossing_concert_tours

Chapter 8

http://lonestarmusicmagazine.com/bridging-the-great-divide/

Chapter 15

http://www.itunescharts.net/us/charts/albums/2020/05/22

Chapter 18

https://www.texascountrymusicchart.com/top-200-of-2019

Chapter 19

https://www.npr.org/2020/01/21/798160492/in-deep-red-oklahoma-the-blue-door-is-a-lighthouse-for-progressive-protest-music

http://www.bluedoorokc.com/blue-door-history/

http://swampland.com/articles/view/title:jj_cale

Chapter 21

https://www.oscn.net/dockets/GetCaseInformation.aspx?db=tulsa&number=CJ-2019-5016&cmid=3320539

- Suggested Reading -

Postgraduate thesis

Playing in the Dirt: Stillwater and the Emergence of Red Dirt Music, by Aaron E. Moore
https://shareok.org/bitstream/handle/11244/9080/Moore_okstate_0664M_10984.pdf

Book

Twentieth-Century Honky-Tonk: The Amazing Unauthorized Story of the Cain's Ballroom's First 75 Years, by Brett Bingham and John Wooley

Book

Dirt and Spirit: A History of Red Dirt Music, by Tonya Little (upcoming)

Made in the USA
Coppell, TX
22 October 2020